PENGUIN BOOKS

Mallee Sky

Kerry McGinnis was born in Adelaide and at the age of twelve took up a life of droving with her father and four siblings. The family travelled extensively across the Northern Territory and Queensland before settling on a station in the Gulf Country. Kerry has worked as a shepherd, droving hand, gardener and stock-camp and station cook on the family property, Bowthorn, north-west of Mt Isa. She is the author of two volumes of memoir, *Pieces of Blue* and *Heart Country*, and the bestselling novels *The Waddi Tree*, *Wildhorse Creek*, *Mallee Sky* and *Tracking North*. Kerry now lives in Bundaberg.

T0363048

PENGUIN BOOKS

UK | USA | Canada | Ireland | Australia
India | New Zealand | South Africa | China

Penguin Books is part of the Penguin Random House group of companies
whose addresses can be found at global.penguinrandomhouse.com.

First published by Penguin Group (Australia), 2013
This edition published by Penguin Group (Australia), 2015

Cover design by Grace West © Penguin Group (Australia)
Text design by John Canty © Penguin Group (Australia)
Cover images: House by mollypix/iStock, Horizon by Anne Morley,
Sky by zroakez/Shutterstock.com
Typeset in Sabon
Colour separation by Splitting Image Colour Studio, Clayton, Victoria
Printed and bound in Australia by Griffin Press, an accredited ISO AS/NZS 14001
Environmental Management Systems printer.

National Library of Australia Cataloguing-in-Publication data:

McGinnis, Kerry, 1945- author.
Mallee sky / Kerry McGinnis.
9780143572091 (paperback)
Divorced women–South Australia–Fiction / Farm life–South Australia–Fiction.
Mallee (Vic.)–Fiction / Australian fiction.

A823.4

penguin.com.au

KERRY McGINNIS

Mallee Sky

PENGUIN BOOKS

To the memory of Don Kube,
farmer, padre, friend
And to Judith

I

Kate dreamed of home.

She was a pigtailed child again in the sunlit stubble of the wheat paddock, with the wind in her face and the sound of laughter drowning the song of the ground larks. Megan squatted beside her, plucking the scarlet poppies and plaiting them into a chain. In the dream her adult self remembered how hard it was to actually split the slender stems. Instead they wound them together, producing scarlet coronets with which they crowned each other. 'It's too red,' she said, giggling to see the results when set on Megan's ginger curls.

'Don't care.' Megan wound another strand around her pale freckled wrist. She had lovely creamy skin that burned red and peeled; she was supposed to stay covered from the sun, but her hat was off now and her face already turning pink. They had been looking for the fox's den in the next paddock when the blaze of poppies amid the silvering stubble caught their eye. Tomorrow the sheep would be turned into the paddock, as they always were after harvest. So it was now or never, and with one accord they'd abandoned their quest in favour of gathering the fragile blossoms growing wild in the wheat.

'They won't last.' Kate's voice was sad. And as if her words had conjured it, a cloud covered the sun, cooling the air and hiding their hunched shadows.

'So what? There'll be more,' Megan said, but Kate turned her head and looked away down the slight slope to where her family's farmstead lay in the hollowed shell of mallee scrub that had been left as shelter against the hot north-easterly winds. The farmhouse with its red roof and stone chimneys lay under the cloud but the iron roofs of the sheds, some patched with rust, glinted in sunlight. Sheets flapped on the washing line and smoke rose from the kitchen chimney.

'There's Dad.' Kate pointed at the distant figure but Megan was silent. Kate looked back then, but in the way of dreams her friend had vanished and the stubble and poppies with her, leaving a formless grey emptiness. Her heartbeat quickened. She shivered in sudden cold and woke to find a fine mist of rain blowing in through the open bedroom window.

Lying in the unfamiliar bed, Kate blinked, wondering where she was, then memory returned and she sat up, reaching for the digital clock beside the bed. The bright figures showed it to be past seven. Kate rose and shut the window, then stood studying the day, or what she could see of it over the motel courtyard with its parked cars and line of dripping bushes thrashing in the wind. The sky was a uniform grey and the window ran with light rivulets of rain. She hated driving in the wet. The driver's window leaked slightly and the wipers needed new rubbers – just another thing that Guy had let slip, along with his job, the rent payments, and his marriage. Perhaps she should have flown after all, she thought, but then she'd still have needed public transport to finish her journey – and country bus schedules were a pain. No, she decided, heading for the shower, Guy's lack of wheels was his problem. Or rather Luci's; she was his latest conquest. No doubt he preferred her smart new Hyundai to the battered old Commodore anyway.

By the time Kate had breakfasted the drizzle had stopped.

'Thanks, love,' the woman behind the desk said as she accepted her room key. 'Going far? Not the best day for it.'

'No. But perhaps it'll clear.' Dodging the first question, Kate gave her a meaningless smile. The glass door mirrored her slim form in its cotton top and jeans, the bounce of her heavy fair hair, as she stepped through the doorway and out into the forecourt, where large puddles lay on the asphalt, their surfaces shivered by the wind. A dumpy maid pushing a trolley of cleaning gear wished her good morning and her lips moved mechanically in reply as she nodded, hand fumbling in her shoulder bag for the keys. Unlocking the boot of the red Commodore, she fitted her bag in, then paused to tip her chin upwards when a bird sped past with a raucous cry. Cuckoo – the identification was automatic. A large, strong bird, but for all that not so much flying as blown by the thrusting force of the wind. *Makes two of us, mate.* The words were a faint echo in her head. How often had her father murmured them while his hands smoothed a piece of timber, or sharpened a chisel blade? The difference being that as a child she had never understood the quiet resignation behind them.

Kate's mouth twisted, thinning her lips so that she seemed momentarily older than her twenty-eight years. Sadness shadowed her eyes but there was nothing to be gained by dwelling on the past. *Done and dusted*; her father's words too. Best to remember them now that she was finally going back. The seat was damp as she slid in and belted up. Three times she turned the key (the last with her fingers crossed nervously) before the engine fired. When it did she drove out of the forecourt and made a right-hand turn into the traffic, wriggling about and pressing her shoulders back into the seat, getting comfortable for another long day's drive south.

2

Kate Gilmore arrived in the rural town of Laradale, South Australia, just after nine on a Wednesday morning in early October. A world away across oceans, the operation known as Desert Storm raged in the Middle East, but here in the sleepy rural town in the heart of wheat and sheep country, the skies were clear and hot and dry, the peace punctuated only by the whoop of train whistles passing the grain siding, and the rattle of farm vehicles along its quiet thoroughfares. Kate drove slowly down the main street, the weight of her right foot tentative on the pedal below it, grey eyes searching for remembered shopfronts. She could easily have made it the previous day but despite having made the decision to return, her reluctance to do so had increased as the distance to her destination diminished.

The town hasn't changed much in nine years – that was her first thought. The familiar shape of the grain silos dominated the skyline, and there was the same sprawl of tractors and headers behind the dealers' chain-link fence. She wondered if the Quicklys still owned it. Their name had stayed on the car dealership, and the park where the cenotaph stood. The family had been pioneers in the Mallee, as had Kate's own ancestors, but, unlike the Quicklys, the Stones had not diversified. They had started with the farm block and after one hundred and three years the land, substantially increased in size, remained in the family, but that was it. Apart from the farm gate the only other place you'd find the Stone name was engraved on the list of war dead, or more recently, in the town cemetery.

There was a new service station, she saw. A small Woolworths now occupied the space where the old library had been. The ten-pin bowling alley had become a furniture warehouse, the cinema had closed, and the park beside the school, where the pine trees towered even taller than she remembered, now boasted a concrete and steel skate bowl. There had been a sandpit in that space once, and a pair of swings – torn out, she supposed, to make way for modern entertainment.

An empty school bus came towards her, the driver signalling a turn into Bevel Street where the depot had always been. Behind her a horn bipped and Kate started. Flushing, she fumbled with the gears, realising that she'd come to a halt in the middle of the road. Be just her luck to find Doug behind her. She pulled aside to let the vehicle pass, keeping her head lowered, but a quick sideways glance showed only the panting, friendly face of a red kelpie poking from the window space beside a heavy-set older man she couldn't place. Farming communities didn't change much but it had been almost a decade since she left, and she hadn't been back since. The main thing was that he wasn't her brother. Still, it *had* been nine years – he was a married man now, the parent of two boys, so perhaps he'd changed?

There was an angled car park close by. Kate pulled into it, switched off the engine and wondered if it was possible. Was she allowing old grudges to prejudice her? She'd been a quarrelsome, headstrong girl (with a legitimate reason to hate him the last time they'd met) but perhaps she should wait and see. He might have reformed – the responsibilities of marriage and keeping the farm viable might have altered his thinking. And pigs might fly.

She slapped a hand against her seatbelt release, then sat tapping a nail on the steering wheel. The problem was that she hadn't really thought this through. She'd wanted to get away from the place that was no longer home so she'd run all the way back to a place that once was. The trouble being she'd made no plans about what was to happen once she got here. Except for the notion – well, more than that, the need – to find work. She was a teacher – *had been*, she amended silently, until the accident that had led to her contract being terminated. But, unless things had changed, Laradale had only the one school, which would already be staffed. She would have to find something else. And she might as well begin now. Drawing a breath she flipped her fair hair back from her brow, picked up her shoulder bag and stepped out of the car.

The café would be as good a place as any to start. And if Bert and Doreen Pringle still ran it, to get herself up to speed on local news. Back in high school days they'd called Doreen the Town Registrar. And Bert, she suddenly remembered, the Addendum. There wasn't much got past the pair of them – births, deaths, marriages and the inevitable scandals. The Pringles heard and retold them all, and never forgot a one, to the mortification of their gentle daughter Janice. A silent, terminally embarrassed teenager, she'd gone through high school head down and ears shut, as if in compensation for her parents' greedy interest in the town's affairs. But right now that could be useful.

Passing the newsagent and the clothing store they'd always known as the men's shop, Kate stepped through the open door of the Chocolate Teaspoon. The same old counter and tables met her glance although the décor was different. New coverings, new paint, vertical blinds in place of curtains. But the Mickey Mouse clock still hung above the cash register, while a large tub of ferns in the corner had replaced the cut-down school desk that had held Laradale's weekly paper and six months' worth of old magazines. Browsing material for waiting customers – nowadays, Kate presumed, they just waited. She smiled at the woman watching her from behind the counter: a little plumper, a little greyer, but substantially the same.

'Hello, Mrs Pringle.'

'Mornin', love.' Shrewd brown eyes regarded the slim young woman, then she nodded slowly, looking gratified. 'I know you, don't I? You're Edna's girl, Cathy – no, Kate! Kate Doolin. Well, this is a surprise! Went off overseas with that young fella of yours straight after the weddin'. And this is your first time back.'

'That's right,' Kate said. 'So how's Bert, Mrs P? And the family? Did Janice marry?'

'Oh Lord, yes. Three kids now – the eldest is five, just started school. She wed the youngest Hobson boy; he's a machinery contractor, works the Brathway holdings mostly but contracts out to other farms as well. You been home yet?'

'I just got here,' Kate said. 'Thought I'd have a cuppa.' Her eye ran over the menu on the wall-mounted blackboard. 'And maybe some pancakes? I haven't eaten yet this morning.'

'And you farm bred.' Mrs Pringle shook her head reprovingly. 'You travelling alone? What, all the way from Queensland? Where's your husband, then?'

'Byron Bay,' Kate corrected. 'Not quite Queensland. But you didn't tell me about Bert. How —'

'Oh yeah, Bert.' The woman stuck her head through the doorway and repeated the name with a bellow, adding, 'You'll never guess who's just come in.'

An indeterminate noise indicated Bert's answer. His wife yelled back, 'Plate of pancakes, pot o' tea. He'll be out shortly. You can ask him yourself,' she said, dismissing the subject. 'How long you back for? Just a visit? Overdue, any road. Your mum wasn't real good a few months back. Coulda done with a visit. She got that flu that's been going round, but I expect that's stale news.'

An interrogative rise to the sentence invited but didn't receive an answer. 'And you're missing out on seeing Dougie's family grow,' she scolded as an afterthought. 'You don't get them years back, you know – the crawling, the toddling, the hugs. It's school before you know it and next thing they're teenagers. Got kids of your own, Kate?'

'No.' The pancakes arrived then, along with Bert and the dozen fresh questions on his lips. Kate, settling herself at the nearest table, avoided the most personal by asking her own and tucking immediately in to the food. 'It's very good.' She spooned apricot jam liberally. 'Your making, isn't it, Mrs P? So – you told me about Janice – what's the rest of the old crowd doing? Bobby Halford, and the Kelly twins – and the Quicklys? I see their names are still up on the machinery yard. Still doing all right, are they?'

Bert hurrumphed. 'Well, *they're* not gonna fold in the first drought happens along. Mind, there's some —'

'They'll outlast the town, that lot,' Mrs Pringle took firm hold of the conversation again. 'There's more Quickly cousins, nevvies, and grand-nevvies round than grain in a wheat paddock. And more birthed and schooling every year. Mary Kelly married Joe Quickly, and darned if her first don't turn out twins, though that's more like to skip a generation, I believe. At least, it did with Heather Swain – as was – that is – she —'

'Mrs Wantage was a twin?' Kate lowered her laden fork. 'She never told me that.' Megan's mother had always treated Kate as an extra daughter. 'I suppose I was a bit young for confidences,' she conceded. 'Do they still have the farm? How is she these days?'

'Not much change there.' The woman shook her head with heavy significance. 'Still waiting, poor soul. They'll be selling the place eventually – no point hanging on. It's not as if their boy'll be back. Ken'd be long gone, I reckon, only he can't shift Heather.'

There seemed nothing to say to that and Kate didn't try. 'So what's he doing – Martin? He went off to uni, I remember. He must have graduated by the time I was married.'

'Trained for an engineer,' Bert nodded.

'Mmn, so he'd need to leave to work.' Kate seized the opportunity as it presented. 'How's the job situation generally? Much doing in town?'

'Not a lot.' Mrs Pringle raised a hand like a cop stopping traffic, and Bert's mouth, which had opened, closed again. The café was an unofficial job centre – mainly because the Pringles always knew everybody's business. 'The hotel wants bar help. Gleeson's Autos are looking for a mechanic – one as can actually fix something, old Jack said, and there's a bit of casual stuff – a few hours of cleaning or waitressing down at the Chef's Place. Not much for the kids. There's one or two gets an apprenticeship but the rest have the choice of McDonald's or trolley boy at the supermarket. 'Course they're put off soon as they can't pay junior wages no more. And there's not too many of 'em needed. So – you still at the teaching, Kate?'

'Long service leave just now,' she said economically. 'But yes – little towns . . . I expect they're all the same.' Kate set her knife and fork together with a click. 'That was wonderful.' She handed Bert a note from her purse. 'You haven't lost your touch. It's good to be home again but I'd better be getting on.'

'They'll be watching out for you down Mooky Lane, sure enough,' his wife agreed. '*And* more'n likely wonderin' what's held you up. Tell your mum hello from us. And Doug and Clove too, of course. I hear she's breeding again. Haven't seen her since Show weekend. Tell her I hope she's keeping well and mind you come see us again. Well, I never thought when I got up this morning —'

'Yes, thank you – and yes, of course I will. Bye, then.' The only escape was to keep moving, Kate knew. She raised a hand, mouthed 'bye' again and trod swiftly across the pavement, knowing that she was leaving a storm of speculation in her wake. She had given away as little as possible, but with the Pringles it took but an ear of wheat to fill a silo, as her father would have said. By the close of business half the town would know she was back sans husband, and that she had stopped in at the café for a feed when a mere six kilometres more would have taken her to the kitchen table at Stones Place.

Standing touching the sun-warmed handle of the car door, Kate sighed, wondering why she had come. To simply put distance between herself and the place where both her marriage and career had failed – or because there was nowhere else? The Railway Arms stood square on the corner two blocks down. She could take a room there, she supposed. Or try the smaller Melbourne Hotel, which might be cheaper. There was also the caravan park on the riverbank at the edge of town. They'd probably have cabins.

'Decisions, decisions,' Kate muttered, as if this would help her reach one. She slid behind the wheel and pulled the seatbelt around her. 'Okay, the Melbourne it is.' She reversed the car, causing a four-wheel drive to beep as it swerved wide around her, then she was at the roundabout heading for the bridge, but when the corner came up she didn't take it. Instead she continued on past the school and the feed merchant's, where a kelpie waited on a truck bed while his owner carried something out on his shoulder. Then she drove round the edge of the park – whose ornamental gates she had once believed were there to keep the huge trees inside – until the bitumen surface changed to fine gravel and town lots gave way to fenced Forestry pines. The pine lot was five kilometres through. And beyond it, still marked by the wooden fingerpost of her childhood, ran Mooky Lane.

The lane was a service road for the half-dozen farms along its length, of which her family's was the first. Kate's lips thinned but her glance still ached over familiar bends and gullies. Just . . . *there* was where she'd taken the header off the bike, gravel-rashing both palms and knees raw; *there* by the farm gate was where the school bus had pulled in, Monday to Friday, to collect its youthful cargo; and over *there* was the gully where Gypsy Pete's horse had broken its leg and where, later, drawn to return by the momentous nature of the event, she'd found the baby galah and taken it home.

Traffic along the lane was audible from the farm, but the belt of protective mallee hid it from sight. The Commodore, trailing its plume of pale dust, ran past and a hundred metres on reached the track leading into The Narrows, also known as Wantages' Farm. Either Ken or his father (now deceased) had, in a whimsical moment, named the land for its chisel-like shape.

Getting out to open the gate, Kate paused with lifted head to take in the familiar sounds and scents of her homecoming. The smell of dust settling behind her, the drill of cicada song and the dry rustle of summer grain heavy on the stalk. A magpie carolled in the distance and she heard the faint popping noise of a motorbike fading behind the farmstead, where a dog had begun to bark. The gate creaked as she let it go and the rattle of the chain as she shut it took her right back to childhood. Not that she and Megan had bothered much with roads and gates. Straight across the paddock had been the shortest way for them both.

At the end of the gravel track the old stone farmhouse stood square to the road with its unfenced garden spilling around it, the trees and lawn a cool haven in the warming day. The Narrows' garden had always been the pride of the district and Kate thought it looked as good today as it had in those far-off times when she and Megan had made their cubbyhouse under the brilliant magenta spill of the bougainvillea, which grew at the back, beside an underground tank dug by the pioneer who'd started the farm.

Tank and bush were both still there – well, the old-fashioned hand pump was. She couldn't say about the rest. Nobody had used the old tanks for years, for the farms mostly had bores, but she dimly remembered being stung by a bee once that had come to drink from the pump. *She couldn't have been more than seven or eight*, she thought, and as if plucked from some hidden place, the memory was suddenly sharp before her – a warm day like this and a game of hide-and-seek through the garden. It had been her turn to hide and she had run with heightened senses, finding and rejecting hiding places until the great swathe of bougainvillea caught her eye.

It was perfect. They had not yet made their cubbyhouse there, so Megan would never suspect her presence behind the awesomely armoured bush. Ignoring the gold-banded insects crawling into the pump's spout, she'd slowed her steps to look for the best way under the thorny branches, and her bare foot had found the bee in the grass.

She'd shrieked at the sudden pain, and then again, louder, panic mounting with the fiery intensity of it. Megan's mother had come running and Kate remembered the ineffable comfort of standing, hiccuping sobs within the circle of her arms as she scratched the sting out and applied a blue bag from the laundry to the swelling. Smiling now at the memory, Kate got out and stood by the car, waiting for the barking collie racing towards her to slow, then sniff at her and wag her tail.

'Good dog.' It was a bitch, her dugs loose and heavy. She barked again, then fell in behind as Kate followed the winding path beneath the trellis that served as an entrance, through the garden to the front door. It was open, only the screen door shut to keep out flies. The cowbell still hung from the rafter under the deep verandah and discarded workboots lay tumbled by the bench seat against the far wall where a geranium flourished in a large clay pot. Kate pulled the bell strap and called, 'Anyone at home?'

'Is that you, Benny?' a woman's voice answered and Heather Wantage came briskly down the long hall, wiping her hands on a tea towel. 'Ken's just gone. He said to leave —' She broke off and pushed the screen door open. One hand went to her throat and her eyes widened. Something leaped in them and was gone again, swift as the shift of light on water, then her brows drew in and she was staring at Kate.

'Katie?' she said uncertainly. 'My God, it is you! Katie Doolin. Where did you come from? I haven't seen you since —'

'My wedding,' Kate supplied, hugging her. 'Well, I've come back for a visit, so you're naturally first on my list. How are you, Mrs Wantage? And Ken?'

'Oh, we don't change.' She held the girl off for a moment, then hugged her again. 'But come in, come in. I was just about to make some tea. I thought you were young Benny over from Halls' . . . ' She ushered her guest down the passage, still hung with familiar pictures, and through the doorway into the green and cream kitchen, saying an automatic, 'Mind the step,' as the floor level suddenly dropped. Kate's feet had remembered anyway. She glanced about.

'It hasn't changed a bit,' she exclaimed as the carriage clock on the mantel chimed. 'You've still got the old slow-combustion stove, even!'

'Yes, we keep it the same.' Heather Wantage's voice sounded suddenly tired. 'In case – well, I wouldn't want her to find it different. Not how she remembered.' Kate swallowed uncomfortably. After all the years, the woman was still hoping, still waiting, just as the Pringles had said. Kate remembered the way Heather's eyes had looked at the door. Of course – any strange vehicle, particularly with a young woman in it, could be bringing Megan back to her.

'Come. Sit down, Katie.' Heather Wantage smiled, her face gaunt, older than it should have been. The brown hair had faded and she wore glasses, but behind them the blue eyes, the same colour as Megan's, were as caring as ever. She had been a pretty woman once, full of fun and laughter, and Kate had adored her. 'I'm so glad to see you again. It's been so long.'

'Yes. I'd have come sooner if I'd known, if I'd thought —' Shock forced the words from Kate. 'Oh, Mrs Wantage, I had no idea you were still expecting Megan to come home. I suppose I shouldn't say this, but —'

'It's all right. I know what everybody thinks.' Her knuckles pressed down on the table but her voice was unemotional, like one restating an old, old argument. She even smiled a little. 'I'll believe she's dead when I see her body. And until I do I'll keep waiting. Now – tea. And talk. And lots of it, my girl. You can start by telling me why you've come back. It wasn't to see your folks.'

'No.' It hadn't been a question. There was no need for pretence between the two women. Heather had dried Kate's tears often enough to know how matters stood between mother and child – and sister and brother. She said, 'I suppose I'll have to see them some time because we're bound to bump into each other in town, but until then —'

'So it's not just a visit – you're staying?' Her hostess had laid a lace cloth in her honour. Now she poured the tea, then passed milk and a plate of rock cakes still warm from the oven.

'If I can get work. And according to what the Pringles say, that's going to be harder than I was counting on —' Kate drew a deep breath and lowered her tea cup, hearing it rattle against the saucer. Eyes down, she smoothed the pretty cloth with trembling fingers. 'Guy left me. And I've lost my job. I had nowhere else to go. That's why I came back.' Her eyes stung and she gritted her teeth, forcing the moisture back. 'I didn't mean to tell you.' She tried to smile. 'But I always did, didn't I, Mrs Wantage? Haring across the paddock to you at least twice every week, looking for comfort. And here I am getting on for thirty and still doing it.'

'You can't be!' Her hostess sounded startled.

'Well, close enough. Twenty-eight this year.' The age Megan would have been; the knowledge hung unuttered between them.

'Truly? Then it's high time you started calling me Heather.' She reached across the table to pat the younger woman's hand and cocked her head. 'So, Guy – what happened? Just a fight you can recover from, or was there some other reason?'

Kate's laugh was sudden and bitter. 'Oh, there were – are – reasons! Three I know about – and who knows how many more I don't? This one's a blonde. It's my own fault. I should never have married him. Before the first twelve months were over I knew that I'd made a dreadful mistake. But I still thought we could work it out, you know? Though he'd already committed adultery within twelve months of our wedding. He swore it would never happen again – but even back then I think I knew it would. And it has! Heaven knows how many times. When it comes to women he's like a kid in a sweetshop, wanting them all.'

'But you stayed?' Heather's brows rose above the cup she held near her lips. 'Most women wouldn't, these days.'

'Believe me, I've asked myself why. Plenty of times. And it always comes back to personal failure.' She gave a small unhappy smile. 'Dad always said I was pig stubborn. I kept asking myself if it was somehow *my* fault. If there was something lacking in his makeup that I wasn't perceptive or – or mature enough to see and somehow help him overcome.' She swallowed and the hand that had been distractedly smoothing the tablecloth suddenly clenched on it. 'Dad always said you married for life – and *he* had enough to put up with, but he stayed. He wouldn't think much of me now, bailing out like I have.'

Heather shook her head. 'Trust me, he'd want you to be happy above everything. Anyhow, surely it's Guy who's, as you put it, bailed out?'

'Call it mutual, then, because it's over. I've always forgiven him before, but then he's never actually physically left me. The affair would run its course, then he'd be bringing me flowers and begging forgiveness. But not this time. I told him I was sick of his playing around. We had a row.' Her eyes fell and Heather watched the girl's hand rise to touch her face. 'He – hit me.' Kate's voice wavered between outrage and disbelief. 'It was – I couldn't – Anyway, he packed his stuff and walked out. Later I discovered he'd cleaned out our joint account, too. If I never see him again, that's soon enough for me.'

'I should think so! And you did the right thing, pet. What about the house?'

'Rented,' Kate said. 'As for the furniture, I stored the pieces Dad made me and left the rest. Everything else I own is in the car. I dare say he would've taken that too,' she added bitterly, 'if the blonde hadn't owned a better one.'

'You're well rid of him,' Heather said briskly, before adding worriedly, 'He's not worth crying over unless – You don't still love him, do you, Katie?' She sounded horrified by the prospect.

'No – not for years.' Kate sniffed and caught a tear on her finger. 'It's just – well, it's like I've *wasted* so much of my life. Between Guy and my job – nothing's turned out the way I planned.'

Heather smiled sadly. 'Yes, I remember you were always a great one for plans. So what about the job? You weren't sacked? I find that hard to believe.'

'I was. And I could be deregistered yet.' Another tear spilled. 'I – oh, dammit,' she sniffed, groping in her pocket, 'that would mean I could no longer teach.'

'But – why? What happened? Here.' Leaning back in her chair, she plucked a box of tissues from a shelf. 'You don't have to talk about it if —'

'Might as well.' Kate said dispiritedly. 'It can't make it any worse. There was an accident while I was on playground duty. Gross negligence, according to the department inquiry – and I've no excuse. I *was* responsible for the child's safety. The parents were going to sue so of course the board had to come down hard on me. The inquiry was the same day Guy walked out. It was like – I don't know – a message that there was nothing left worth staying for.'

'Well, that tells me everything and nothing.' Heather frowned. 'What sort of accident? How were you responsible?'

'An eight-year-old boy left the school grounds during lunch-break to ride home. A car knocked him off his bike at the first intersection. Like I said, I was on playground duty that day. But I was starting a migraine and I went back to the staffroom for some Panadol. ("Abandoning your trust" was how the principal put it.) Russell, the boy who was hurt, had told me he had to go home, and I'd told him he couldn't. Well, *none* of the kids are allowed to leave the grounds during school hours. They all know that. But he went anyway. And was hit by a car.'

'But surely – if he disobeyed you when your back was turned —?'

'It's not *supposed* to be turned. And Russell – well, he's Aspergic – not bad, I mean, he's quite able to cope with school and normal life – it just makes him very stubborn, very focused on what he wants to do. It wasn't like I wasn't aware of it so I should've been watching him.'

Heather's face was troubled. 'Was he badly hurt?'

Kate blotted her eyes. She looked drained and tired, Heather thought, and the clear morning light showed shadows, like faint bruises under her grey eyes. 'A broken arm. The point is, he could have been killed.'

'But he wasn't. That's the important thing.' She reached across to clasp the girl's hands. 'It was no more than an error of judgement – hardly a hanging offence. You're too hard on yourself, Katie – you always were. And right now you look an absolute wreck. You're too thin, you've got dark smudges under your eyes, and when did you last sleep through the night? Still, it's nothing that a few days' rest won't fix. That's all you need, love. A bit of a breather and several nights' proper sleep. Let's get your stuff from the car. You can have the bluebell room. It'll be so good to have you and such a lovely surprise for Ken. He's missed you too, you know.'

'Stay? Oh, but I couldn't put you to that trouble —' Kate began feebly, standing up as her hostess rose. 'You'll be harvesting any day now —'

'Then you can help me with the cooking.' Firmly, Heather cut her off. She hugged the slender figure again. 'Of course you're staying. This place has always been your home. Time to say welcome back to it.'

3

The bluebell room was the spare bedroom with the double bed that Kate and Megan had shared as children whenever Kate slept over. The door to Megan's old room stood open, allowing Kate a quick glimpse as she passed. Nothing had changed – the same frilly curtains with the matching ruffled bedspread on the white-framed bed with ceramic flowered knobs. It had been those knobs that had inspired their young artistic efforts on the walls of the spare room. Looking at them now, Kate saw instead two young girls, ginger-haired and tawny, kneeling on the polished boards with the poster paints between them, faces intent as they transformed the plain cream background with splashes of colour. She shook her head.

'What little vandals we were! You never thought of repainting?'

'I rather like it.' Heather bent down to run a hand over the lop-sided blobs meant to represent a bluebell wood with a fairy perched on a toadstool in the foreground.

The colours have faded, Kate thought. Mercifully, they had kept the fairy small; she and her seat now resembled a strange fungus. But the flowers weren't actually bad – for nine-year-olds. 'You didn't at the time,' Kate reminded the older woman. 'I'd never seen you so cross before, but Megan said —' she cut herself off. 'I think I might've stayed away for two whole days afterwards.'

'Well, you got enough disapproval at home,' Heather said gently. 'And it was only a bit of paint. I probably shouldn't have lost my rag. Do you ever look back, Katie, and notice how things that were once desperately important hardly matter at all?' She laid down the towels she'd brought with her, and plumped a pillow. 'And don't be afraid to speak of Megan. Nobody does, you know. Ken let her go years back. Martin too. They're convinced she's dead – what about you?'

Kate hesitated. 'I don't know, Mrs – Heather. If she isn't, she'd have come back. I know she would – unless for some reason she couldn't. Trite as it sounds, people do lose their memories. And she was very young. You hear of children suppressing bad experiences until, as adults, they won't believe that they ever happened.' She winced, wishing she hadn't brought that up, and finished hurriedly. 'She – I mean, any youngster might lose her identity that way. Enough to be confused and not know where home was – or even who she was. I suppose it's possible.' Her face clouded, she said simply, 'It's strange. I spent eighteen years of my life in the Mallee but it's those first nine with Megan that I remember best. They were the happiest for me.'

Heather's eyes moistened with the memory of old pain. 'Bless you for that. I missed your visits, you know – after it happened. It was like I had two daughters and then suddenly I had none.'

'I'm sorry.' Kate bit her lip. 'Mum wouldn't let me come at first. And then when I realised she was really gone, I was afraid you'd blame me. Because I wasn't on the bus that day. I never told them that at home. I said I'd been playing in the creek – to cover up being late. Maybe if I'd told the truth, it might've made a difference.'

Heather shook her head. 'No, Lamb.' The old pet name slipped out unnoticed. 'Don't think it. You're not to blame.' She sighed, twitched a curtain straight and achieved a smile. 'Well, it's old history. I'd best get on with lunch and you'll want a look about the place. There's new ducklings in the yard. And Fly's had pups. I remember how you two used to love the baby things. I'll be in the kitchen. Just wander about to suit yourself.'

Glad to take Heather at her word, Kate fetched her hat from the car and was soon in the garden, following remembered paths to the back of the house. There was the big pepperina tree by the stand of the rainwater tank, with the stepping-stone path that led to the vegetable section and the sudden burst of colour that was the bougainvillea patch beyond. She reached for the trailing tree leaves, pulling them through her hand so she could sniff her palm, savouring the bitter scent as she had done as a child. There'd been a pepper tree behind the smithy at Stones Place too. It had been her refuge when she wanted to get away from Doug. He was five years older and nastier, she had thought even then, than any boy ought to be. Certainly he was unlike Martin Wantage, whom both she and Megan had adored.

Well, you couldn't choose your family. Brushing her hands off on her jeans, Kate continued her exploration, pausing often as remembered lines and vistas of sheds and machinery were overlaid with memories from childhood. In the feed shed redolent with the sweet smell of past hay harvests, she lifted the lid from a familiar drum and scooped a handful of grain to bring the mother duck and the brood about her feet. The ducklings were fluffy, soft as velvet against her skin. Roosters strutted amid their tidy wives, and half a dozen geese appeared in the hope of a handout, weaving their necks as they walked.

She found Fly and her litter in the mallee barn, a structure whose walls were built from mallee timber rails and topped with a high, hipped roof of iron now spotty with rust. The collie she'd met earlier eyed her mistrustfully as she approached the pups but soon settled back down beside her squirming brood. There were five of them, about six weeks old, Kate judged, their eyes already open, and she was on her knees beside them when the motorbike swooped into the shed and drew up with a final sputter behind her. The collie riding behind the driver jumped down and ran over to sniff at Kate.

Ken Wantage kicked the bike stand down and stepped off, obviously surprised by her presence.

'Mornin,' he said. 'Help you?' He was tall with a chunky spread of shoulders. He'd thickened a trifle around the girth, Kate saw, but not much else had changed. He wore a cotton work shirt with the sleeves rolled up, a pair of stained shorts, a floppy felt hat and workboots. He poked his hat brim up with a callused finger, disclosing once sandy hair now faded to steel grey, and squinted at his unexpected visitor.

'Uncle Ken.' Kate shook her head. 'You don't look a bit different. I swear it's the same hat, even.'

His jaw dropped. 'Kate – Katie Doolin? Well, I – Bugger me! When did you arrive?' He stepped forward to catch her in a hug as warming as it was strong.

'This morning.' She breathed in the smell of him. 'It's so good to see you again – and Heather too. Have you been round the paddocks?'

'Just out to Nelly's to check on the sheep. We still run a few, though God knows there's not much in wool these days. So – you quit Queensland or you just back on a visit?'

'It wasn't Queensland, but I'll tell you all about it at lunch,' she promised. 'Heather's asked me to stay a few days.'

'Good. She'll enjoy that. We've missed you, girl. I always hoped you'd come home for visits but I suppose, after your dad went, that wasn't likely.'

'No,' Kate agreed, 'only I should have made it sooner. I never realised – well, that Heather still thinks – still hopes, that Megan – I mean, she *has* to be dead, Ken, surely?'

'Probably within two days of her being taken,' he agreed heavily. 'That's what the police told us when they stopped searching. She's long gone, poor wee lass, but Heather just can't accept the fact.' Abruptly he added, 'I should've sold up that same year, started some place fresh. It might've given her a chance to grieve properly, to heal —'

Kate touched his arm. 'How could you know? Don't blame yourself.'

He sighed. 'That's what I tell myself. Anyway, enough of that. How's your husband – Gerry, was it? Is he with you?'

'Guy,' she corrected. 'I'll tell you everything at lunch.' As their steps turned towards the house the bell rang and she smiled. 'I remember how that used to bring us flying from all over the place – Martin too. How's he doing?'

'Not bad.' Ken Wantage, like most Mallee men, veered to the lower end of optimism in his outlook and opinions. 'He seems to get enough work. We don't see that much of him but he visits a couple of times a year – mostly.'

'Not a family man yet?'

'Nope.' He pondered the matter. 'Shame about that. A couple of grandkids might've helped Heather. Could even be the means of getting her off the farm. If he had a mortgage and kids, we could sell up, move closer – but it doesn't seem likely to happen.'

'You'd give up farming altogether?' Kate was surprised.

'Not much point going on, is there? It's not like Martin's going to follow me. I suppose a man could get a hobby – take up fishing . . . '

The idea of a dry-land farmer turning to such a watery pursuit in retirement made Kate laugh. The sound preceded them as Ken pulled open the screen door and ushered her in to the kitchen, where the table was spread for lunch.

* * *

Dusk came slowly to the farm. Kate, who'd gone out in the ute with
After the meal Ken vanished into the office while the two women
washed up.

'He still works a full day,' Kate commented, picking up a plate,
'but he looks well for his age. I know it can't have been easy with
the drought years, and wool prices so low.'

Heather smiled faintly. 'Oh, the office is for looks. He's gone
there to nap in his chair for twenty minutes. Wouldn't do to admit
he's slowing down.' She wiped the sink and hung up the dishcloth.
'Would you like to rest too? It'll be cool enough in your room if you
use the fan.'

'Thanks, but I'll settle for one of your verandah chairs. I'll
read a bit and just enjoy your garden.' She needed time to think, to
sort out her future – part of which, she knew very well, meant a
visit to Stones Place. She remembered something else. 'That can't
be the same Fly? She was old when I was a kid – but I did enjoy
seeing the pups. If I can find a job and a place to settle, I've decided
I shall have to get myself a dog. Dad's Tam was the last I had anything to do with. I can't believe that I've gone so long without a
pet of any sort. Only Guy was never interested, so . . . ' She
shrugged.

Heather nodded, adding, 'You're right about Fly, though.
That's the daughter with the litter. Ken's only ever thought of the
two names – Fly and Flash. I don't think even he knows how many
of either we've had. I know that most of the pups are taken but you
could ask Ken if there's one still unclaimed. If there is, I know he'd
be happy for you to have it.'

'That'd be wonderful,' Kate said. 'I'll have to wait and see how
things pan out for me first, but thanks anyway.'

It was cool on the verandah – or as cool as you were likely to
be in the dry hot air of October, so different to the damp humidity

of the northern coast. The squatter's chair with its canvas sling and padded headboard was deep and comfortable, and the garden's shade broke up the glare. Kate pulled off her sunglasses and, putting them down on top of her unopened book, lay back with a sigh. Currawongs quarrelled somewhere under the trees at the side of the house, and from inside came the soft intermittent whir of a sewing machine. Patchworking was Heather's passion and Kate had already seen the heritage-patterned double-bed quilt she was working on.

Long ago she had begun to teach the two girls. Kate smiled now to remember how proud she'd been of the half-dozen patches her childish hands had joined. She'd chosen stripes for her first attempt – unwisely, for they'd simply shown up her clumsy seams. But Heather had praised them anyway. As a child Kate had adored Megan's mother. Looking back now, she even wondered if, subconsciously, Heather was the reason she'd made Megan her best friend – along with proximity, of course. With the pine plantation on the other side of Stones Place, The Narrows was their only real neighbour, the next closest being Halls', some ten miles distant by road.

Flash, the dog that had been on the bike with Ken, padded across the verandah to Kate's chair, tail wagging in amiable greeting. Sprawling on his belly on the cool concrete, he closed his eyes and she let a hand drop to fondle his ears. So had she sat many times as a child in her father's workshop, with the collie Tam at her feet, sniffing the enticing smells of wood shavings, oil and glue. Kate's father had been a craftsman, a painstaking maker of beautiful furniture and smaller pieces, either turned or carved, depending, he told his daughter, on the shadow of the object that his mind's eye saw in a particular piece of wood. The small girl had accepted the literal truth of this explanation and had awaited the inception of each project with breathless excitement. 'Is it a horse, Dad?' she would ask. 'Can you see a horse?' From the age of six she had wanted a pony quite desperately, but this ardent desire had never been granted. 'You'd have to have two, Katie,' Brian had pointed out. 'One for Megan as well.'

Instead he had done the next best thing and out of a tiny chunk of Tasmanian blackwood he'd carved a pony in the round, small enough to hang on a thong around her neck. She'd worn it all through primary school, to the envy of her classmates. Megan had done the same with hers, a dog – a collie so like Tam that the little girl had christened it with the same name. Tam and Blackie – Kate smiled. No prizes for originality there. The leather thong had long since broken but she still cherished the carving, now safely packed away in her jewel case.

But Brian's main work had been the cabinets, chests of drawers and chairs with hand-carved legs. However, none of these, beautiful though they were, could, to Kate's mind, touch the small oblong box with the hidden catch that her father had called his graduation piece. He had crafted it as a young man and to the casual eye it appeared to be a solid block of polished timber, save for the careful dovetailing where the sides joined. So perfectly did it fit together that you had to examine it very carefully indeed to spot where the lid ended and the lower part of the box began. No hinges or catch were visible and there were no handles to lift it by.

As a child the box had fascinated Kate. Its silky timber had drawn her like a magnet and she would sit on her stool at the end of the workbench with the box on her lap – it was not large, thirty centimetres square, perhaps – while her fingers felt for the hidden catch. She never found it. And however much she teased and begged her father to tell her the secret, he only shook his head.

'When you're older, Katie.' His grey eyes, a darker shade than hers, twinkled.

'But I'll have to wait forever and that's not fair!'

He pursed his lips and seemed to think about it. 'I don't suppose it is. Well, tell you what – when you've got something really precious to put in it, then I'll show you. And mind – not just a toy you don't want Doug to get. It has to be something that really matters. Deal?'

'Okay.' They had shaken hands solemnly on it, her small fingers enveloped by the calluses and scarring of old chisel nicks on his. She had sighed, too, knowing she would have to stick to their agreement and dolefully aware that none of her possessions came anywhere near *really precious*. So she would have to either wait, or continue to seek the solution herself.

It wasn't until she was ten that the answer occurred to Kate. Megan had been gone for a year then and as a result she was spending more time at home – much of it, between chores and homework, with her father. The idea came to her as she perched on her stool, scuffing at the wood shavings with her feet, while Brian used a fine piece of glasspaper on the slider of a rocking chair he was making for Mrs Quickly.

'Dad.'

'Mmm?'

She felt for the clasp of the thong about her neck and slipped it open, then pulled the freed ends to bring the little pony amulet out the neck of her dress.

'Blackie is *truly* precious. But if he goes in your box, can I have him back again?' she asked hopefully. Her father smoothed a hand over his work, then laid it down and regarded her. His brown head was cocked a little and there seemed to be a glint in his eye – or perhaps it was just caused by the bright shafts of sunlight coming through the dusty windows.

'Of course you can, colleen.' It was a special term he used whenever she especially pleased him. Without further ado he rose and brought the box to the bench. Blowing aside the sawdust he set it down and took her right hand in his. 'Okay, put Blackie down. Now slide your fingers along the dovetailing here on your right, a gentle pressure – just a bit – right *there* – and at the same time put your other hand here on the opposite bottom corner. Just like you would if you were holding it steady. Now push on that too and – presto!' A click sounded as he spoke, then a short wooden rod slid out of the end of the box.

'Wow!' The child's eyes widened. She lifted the top and peered into the box, trying to see where the rod had come from. 'How does that work?'

'That bit is the lock. There's a hidden spring that pushes it out, and a catch to hold the spring.'

'But I've pressed there lots of times,' Katie objected, staring at the sunken point where her finger had been, 'and nothing happened.'

'That's because you have to open the catch first. From here.' He tapped the bottom corner.

'Smart,' she grinned, front teeth like tombstones. 'Can I take the stuff out?'

'If you like.' Brian had picked up the length of varnished timber again. He found his bit of glasspaper and bent his head, rubbing the silky grain in gentle, even circles.

Kate, remembering the scene, blinked wet eyes. Her father's presence had been so real for a moment that she intuitively understood what he had been thinking. She must have read it in his face, she thought, and been subliminally aware, even at ten, that while watching her a part of him had wished that his son could also have shared and understood his passion for fine timbers and the artwork he produced from them, as none save his daughter did. And that even as he wished it he had known that it would never happen.

4

Kate moved restlessly in her chair. She didn't want to think about Doug but sooner or later she'd have to. She'd always feared him. Her 'big' brother was just that – stronger, bigger and slyly cruel in ways that even her father took a long time picking up on. And it had never helped that he was an uncommonly beautiful child with his mother's dark curls and blue eyes and an adorably dimpled cheek. The sort of little boy old ladies doted on, and whose face brought a proud smile to Edna Doolin's whenever her eyes rested upon it.

Even as a child Kate had known that her mother and brother were paired in affection, just as she and her father were. The difference was that Brian Doolin had tried to love his son. Edna had made no such effort with her daughter. Kate didn't matter to her – or not in the same visceral way that Doug did. Part of it was the farm. Edna was the last of the Stones, the sole remaining bud of the sturdy sapling old Joshua Stone had planted back in 1884 when he took up land in the Wolly River area, building his original homestead some dozen miles from what would become the site of Laradale.

Edna's uncles were lost in the First World War, her brothers to the Second, and when her own parents died two years after the war's end she had married Brian Doolin, not so much to have a man for the farm, but to breed one of her own blood. She and her new husband's first row had occurred when he refused to change his name to Stone. Brian, whose own family were tribal, gregarious and went where the wind blew them, missed the full significance of her strange request, which he had in any case refused, on the grounds of outraged manhood.

With Doug's birth, Edna's participation in the marriage began the slow decline that effectively ended when Kate was a toddler. By then husband and wife shared little more than a room. Brian, with a doggedness that was part of his nature, had tried to make it work, had even fancied he was succeeding, until he realised that Edna was simply keeping up appearances before the neighbours. Separation and divorce were still uncommon in rural communities in the seventies – at least among farming families – and there was his daughter to consider. They had gone past rowing into indifference by then, their emotions no longer engaged, but Brian never stopped protesting Edna's differing treatment of the children.

Kate could still hear the exact tone of his voice, exasperation edged with anger, and the hopelessness of a gentle man for whom reason was the only recourse. *Can't you see that you're spoiling the lad, Edna? He has to be taught, not indulged. It's no kindness to let him think he can have everything* – but of course Doug always could because he was the future, the one born of Stone blood who would inherit the farm. There had been no spoiling of Kate, rather a brisk handling allied to a strict code of good behaviour from which, most unfairly from her point of view, Doug was mainly exempt. Kate had learned very early not to expect the caresses that were his lot or the goodnight hugs. Neither did her mother's gaze ever seek first for her on days when she met them off the bus.

Accordingly the young Kate had learned to hold herself aloof from Edna. If she didn't care, then her mother couldn't hurt her. But it had been wasted effort, her older self thought wryly now, for Edna Doolin had never noticed. Obedience was all she wanted from her daughter, that and a show of manners that her world might see she had brought up a respectful and dutiful child who would do nothing to disgrace the family. After the farm, respectability had always been Edna Doolin's first care. *It was all about show*, Kate thought. As long as her socks were clean and her hair tidy, there could be nothing wrong. Happiness, not being a requirement, was beside the point.

* * *

Dusk came slowly to the farm. Kate, who'd gone out in the ute with Ken for a look around the country, watched the long shadows whip past along Mooky Lane as they drove back to The Narrows' gate.

'I'll get it,' Ken said as she thrust her door open.

'Don't be silly. Farm girl, remember? I can open a gate.' The dying day had cooled but the air rustled dryly through the mallee, smelling of dust and sadness, she thought, as she undid the chain. It was just her, of course – well, her and the past, heard even in the mundane sound of creaking metal. Down the shadowy avenue of trees she could see the lighted windows of the farmhouse, and the last glint of silver on the mill beside the dam. Fly's warning bark sounded and from somewhere near at hand an owl hooted in the timber. And at that moment it all seemed to Kate unlike anything actual but thin echoes of memory tinged with tears and loss.

Back in the vehicle shed, Ken switched the motor off and spoke into the silence broken only by the tick of the engine block and the slither of Flash's feet going over the side of the ute.

'You're thinking about home, aren't you?'

Kate, who'd been collecting her hat and sunglasses, paused in surprise. 'How did you know?'

'Guessed. You stopped talking the moment we turned into Mooky Lane. Same as you used to when you were little. You'd go all quiet and your face'd screw up whenever it was time to go back home.'

'Did I?' Almost defensively she said, 'Dad loved me, you know.'

'I know.' It was dark in the shed but she sensed he was looking at her and knew that his face would be concerned. 'You're a grown woman now, but – you want some advice, Katie?'

'I don't know.' And she didn't. 'Tell me anyway.' The signature tune of the news came faintly to her from the house, tinged with the smell of hay and poultry.

'Go over and see them. Half an hour in and out and then it'll be done with. Like a visit to the dentist.'

'Meet expectations, you mean?'

'Why not? Saves talk. You came home, you saw them, then you went on with your life. Just like your mother would want.'

'So she gets her own way – like always?' Her tone was bitter.

'Does it matter?'

Kate sighed and slumped back into the seat. 'Probably not. Tell me something, Ken. And I want you to be straight with me because you're not going to hurt my feelings. What do you truly think about Doug – as a person, a neighbour, if you like?'

He deliberated a moment, prompting her to speak again. 'An honest opinion.'

'Right. Well, he's good to the land, a first-rate farmer, but I wouldn't sell him a dog of mine.' His fingers tapped the steering wheel before he added, 'And I wouldn't want him for a son-in-law, either. There's something rotten in him. That plain enough for you?'

'Thank you.' In the dark Katie touched some part of his arm. 'It's just – well, sometimes I think it's only me – that because it was personal, maybe I blew it all out of proportion and he's really not so bad. But I trust your judgement. And yes, I think I'll take your advice and get it over with. I'm not a child now, and I no longer have to fear him.' She pushed the doorhandle down. 'Thanks for showing me round today. I enjoyed it. Really. It gets under your skin, doesn't it? There's a part of me that's always missed the Mallee.'

'Well – born and bred to it, lass.' His voice was gruff. 'Let's go see what's on for dinner.'

* * *

Kate had made the decision to visit her family but the next morning Heather unwittingly delayed it.

'I'm going into town,' she said as they cleared the breakfast table. 'Would you come? I've decided it's time to change the curtains in the front room. They've been there forever. We probably won't find anything today but Lasson's have catalogues – you could help me choose.'

'Of course I'll come. Be glad to,' Kate responded. 'But you've got a wonderful eye for colour, Heather; you don't need help.'

'I do too,' Heather said fervently. 'You have no idea – even Ken will have his say about house furnishings, and he's hopeless, just to get me to decide one way or the other.'

'Well, in that case —'

It was just past ten when Heather turned the big Ford out of Mooky Lane and onto the stretch of gravel that preceded the sealed road into town. 'If we do the chores first,' she said, signalling the next turn, 'then we can take our time at Lasson's, and maybe fit in a coffee after that. I shall need it, I know. And we mustn't forget Ken's motorbike part. Maybe we should call in there before we go to the bakery.'

'Tell you what,' Kate gazed down the street at the clearly visible clock tower as Heather parked in front of the bike place, 'give me the box key and while you're doing that I'll walk up to the post office and collect the mail. Then I'll head over to Lasson's and we can meet up when you're ready. Don't hurry – I'll have a walk around till you get there. See what's changed and what's new.' Releasing her seatbelt, she pulled her sunglasses down and stepped out of the car, wishing as she did so that she'd brought her hat.

Kate didn't recognise Clover. Had, in fact, walked past the young woman holding the toddler's hand, and it was only when she heard her name that she glanced back, uncertain it was she who was being called.

'Kathryn – it is you! I thought – what are you doing here?' Clover's brown hair was scraped back, secured by a large grip. She wore a long-sleeved blouse over three-quarter length pants, there were sandals on her feet and she carried a large shoulder bag. Her face was pale and pinched-looking and there were shadows under her eyes. She wore no make-up or jewellery, save for a gold watch that had slipped sideways on her wrist as if she'd recently lost weight. Well, the Pringles had said she was pregnant again. *Three or four months, perhaps*, Kate thought, looking assessingly at her body, as she found a pleasant smile for her sister-in-law.

'Clover! How nice. I'm sorry, I didn't recognise you. Oh, and this must be –' she made a frantic search of her memory, 'little – Adam? How old is he now?'

'Andrew,' Clover corrected. 'Nearly three. Say hello to your aunt, Andy.'

'Harwow,' the little boy said, then hid his face against his mother's leg.

'Hello, Andy. Sorry I got your name wrong.' Kate touched his fair silky hair. 'I suppose his brother's at school? Are you – who's in town with you?'

'Just us. I brought Jeremy in as I was coming anyway. He usually catches the bus. And you – just a visit, is it?' She stepped aside into the recess of a building set back from the pavement.

'For the time being,' Kate agreed. 'I'm staying with Ken and Heather at The Narrows.'

'So you aren't – coming home?'

'I'll drop in some time, yes – to say hello,' she said coolly. 'Probably tomorrow. While my time's my own.' Ken was right, get it over with. Steeling herself to be pleasant, she added, 'How's Mum – and Doug?'

Clover bit her lip. She had been glancing left and right throughout the conversation as if keeping her eye out for other acquaintances, but now she raised strained brown eyes to Kate's own. 'I'm —' she began, then blurted, 'Can we talk?'

'Well, yes. I —' Kate stared in surprise, but the other woman had averted her face. 'Is something wrong? You're trembling.'

'Not here.' Clover visibly got a grip and bent to pick up her son. 'Let's cross to the park.'

Once there, she set Andrew down in the tiny playground and stood opening and closing her hands while the child ran to the swings. Her nails, Kate saw, were bitten to the quick. 'This – you won't tell her, will you, Kathryn? Your mum, I mean?'

'Tell her what?' Kate was mystified. Realising the other woman wouldn't answer without assurance, she added, 'You must know my mother and I barely speak. So no, I won't. That's a promise. Now, what's up?'

Clover pressed a hand to the base of her throat as if helping the words out. 'I'm leaving him. I can't – I have to get away.'

'Oh.' Kate blinked. It was the last thing she had expected. She thought of the boys. Doug's sons. Knowing that was exactly how her brother would view them – his sons – his and the farm's future. 'Have you told Doug?'

'No!' Clover's voice was shrill. 'He'll never let me go – or the boys. He mustn't know, or Mother Doolin either.'

'They won't hear it from me,' Kate said pacifically. 'Where will you go?'

'To Ballarat, to my mum's – for starters.' Her expression hardened. 'I notice you haven't asked why. You know, don't you?'

'I know he's cruel. He always was – to me anyway, but —' Her glance flicked to the other's body. 'This – well, the timing's a bit – unexpected, isn't it?'

Clover looked down at the slight curve under her blouse. 'You think I had any say in it?' she asked bitterly.

Kate's lips tightened. Anger, tempered by the old fear, rose in her. So her instincts had been right – neither maturity nor parenthood had changed Doug's nature. She said roundly, 'Then you should have gone ages ago. I'm sorry, Clove.' It was the first time she had ever used the family diminutive. 'I'd help if I could but I've no money and no job. Guy walked out on me – after cleaning out our account. That's why I came back. Does he – hurt you? Or the children?'

In answer Clover pushed a sleeve high to disclose a fading ring of bruises above her elbow. 'Only where it doesn't show. And no, not the boys.'

'Then report him,' she said. 'The police can't help until you do. If he's abusive, they can file for a restraining order to keep him away from you.'

'A piece of paper! Yeah, like he's going to take notice of that.' Clover's fingers worked nervously and she gulped, thin and afraid in the sunlight. Her face was tight with strain and held none of the rounded prettiness that she had had as a bride, when her hair had fallen softly about a face bright with belief in her love.

'He can be arrested if he doesn't. Trust me, he won't risk that, Clove. Mum'd see to it he didn't.'

'Probably, if it came to it,' Clover agreed, 'but it wouldn't. The police are his pals, Kathryn. Doug goes duck hunting with Greg Simpson, the district inspector. Greg brings his wife out to the farm for barbecues. He and Doug, they're both Rotarians. No copper's going to serve any sort of order on Doug Doolin. Not in Laradale, anyway.' Andrew came running back on unsteady feet, calling,

'Leaf, Mummy, leaf,' and Clover picked him up, hugging him to her. 'Yes, I see, darling. A pretty leaf.' She drew a shuddering breath and Kate saw that she was on the verge of tears. 'I wish I'd known the truth before I married him. Why didn't I? Why didn't you tell me, Kathryn?'

'Oh, call me Kate. *Kathryn* reminds me of my mother. And would you have believed me if I had?' Kate's voice cooled, remembering. 'You weren't exactly friendly.'

'No – well, it wasn't long after your father died, was it? Doug said I should expect you to take against me. He told me you were upset about the will. He said you'd always been your dad's favourite so you'd have naturally expected to share in the farm, whereas everything went to Doug —'

'What a load of rubbish!' Kate interrupted hotly. 'He told you that? Clover, the farm never even belonged to Dad! It's Stone land. The deeds were held by my mother. All Dad owned was his tools – apart from his clothes and his dog. And his box.'

'Oh,' Clover said blankly. She gave Andrew a pat and set him down again, ignoring his pleas to be pushed on the swing. 'Not now, darling. Mummy's talking. So he *doesn't* own the farm?'

'I don't know.' Kate shrugged. 'He probably does by now because of inheritance tax. Mum would sign it over to avoid that. I've never cared one way or another. But he didn't own it then – that was a lie. He always lied, though.'

'So I've discovered.' She looked across to check on her son. 'What box?'

'Something Dad made. He kept personal stuff in it – his marriage certificate, his war medals, little things he'd carved or turned. It had a hidden lock. I could open it but he'd never shown Doug how. I suppose that made him jealous.' She spoke woodenly but the hurt still lingered. 'No matter how much he had, Doug always wanted more. Dad left me the box – not because it was valuable, though I suppose it was, he was a master craftsman after all – and Doug couldn't stand that. Before the funeral he went out to the workshop and smashed it open. I found it with the axe still buried in the lid.'

'I'm sorry. *God!* What an awful thing to do.' Clover put a tentative hand on Kate's arm.

'Yes. Well, he shot Tam, too. Said he was old anyway, and that a masterless dog was no good on a farm. He knew I was going to take him.' She shook the painful memory aside. 'When you leave him, Clove, make a job of it. Go somewhere other than your mum's – some place he doesn't know of. And get police protection. He won't give up his sons, you know – he needs them for the farm.'

Clover swallowed. 'I know. He – I'm terrified – but I have to go – for them, for me.' One hand moved to press her body, 'And the baby I didn't want – but it's still my child.' She brushed an impulsive kiss on her sister-in-law's cheek. 'I'm glad we met up today. I wish I'd got to know you. Maybe we could have been friends. I'd have liked that.'

'Doug wouldn't have,' Kate observed. 'He had a way of finding out things you took pleasure in and – destroying them. He could break up a relationship before you knew it was happening. I should know.' *But never with Megan*, she thought, *as hard as he'd tried*. 'Dad kept saying he'd grow out of it, and when I went away to college I thought so too. That one day he'd find someone to love more than himself, and it would make him kind and thoughtful, and all the things he isn't. I *wanted* it to happen, believe me I did. But after Tam – I've kept as far away from him as I can.'

Clover twisted the loose watch until she could see its face. 'I've got to leave. Andy,' she called, 'come on. We're going now.' She hesitated. 'If – tomorrow, don't let on we've met, will you?' Her eyes pleaded. 'I just don't think he'd like it if he knew we'd talked.'

'Okay.' Kate tousled her nephew's hair, feeling the first pang of regret for the absent years – Doreen Pringle had been right, she'd missed out on a lot not being here to watch the boys grow. 'Bye, Andy. Be good for your mum. I'll see you tomorrow then, Clove. Good luck.'

'Goodbye, Kate.' She gave a quick, strained smile and was gone with the child in her arms, shoulder bag swinging as she crossed the road.

5

'It's about the colour of mallee foliage,' Kate said.

'I think it will do,' Heather said judiciously, draping the swatch over the net. 'The walls are cream too, so between them both it should lighten the denseness of the green. It is nice, though, isn't it?' she said, feeling the sample.

'I think we've done a great job,' Kate agreed. 'Are you going to order it? I don't know about you, but I'm dying for a drink.'

She hadn't yet told Heather of her meeting with Clover but over tea and fresh scones in a new-looking café opposite the post office – 'Oh, not the Pringles',' which Heather had immediately understood – Kate said, 'I told her I'd call tomorrow.' She pulled a face. 'I'm following Ken's advice. Get it over with, he said.'

'Best way.' Heather set down her cup. 'Edna Doolin's not my favourite person but – would it help if I went along too?'

'Thanks, it's sweet of you, but no. Best if I do it myself.' She hadn't, nor would she, mention her sister-in-law's plans, but the thought of her prompted the question, 'Do you see much of Clover?'

'Not really. She's dropped out of things a bit the last few years. Edna still comes to the various meetings, but I suppose with the children —' She broke off, her eyes widening in sudden recognition of the man approaching their table. 'Why, Max! Fancy seeing you here.'

'Hello, Aunty.' The tall stranger bent to kiss her cheek. 'I've been meaning to drop in on you – just haven't got round to it yet.' He winked, eyes crinkling into a laugh. 'Biding my time, see? Reckoned I'd make it about Sunday for your roast dinner.'

'I'll hold you to that now,' she promised. 'Six o'clock. I'll tell Ken you're coming, so don't disappoint him. Max,' she touched his arm, 'this is Kate Doolin. She's staying with us at present. Katie, meet Max Shephard.'

It wasn't a name Kate knew. She shook hands, seeing a tall farmer type in jeans and boots, shirtsleeves rolled up with a felt hat, which he'd removed, baring a wiry brush of brown hair. He wore a suntan like a second skin. In his thirties, she judged. He had an angular face with a long nose and hazel eyes set under spiky brows. His front teeth were slightly crooked.

'How do you do?' she said. 'Shephard – are you from round here?'

'In a manner of speaking.' He grinned, taking in the soft, figure-hugging blouse and skirt on the young woman with the tawny-gold hair and grey eyes. Smart and a real looker, despite seeming a tad washed out, though it could have just been city pallor. 'My mother was a Quickly – a pioneering family round here – she married away. But my work brings me back. So where are you from, Kate?'

Heather laughed. 'Sit down, Max. Stop looming over us. Kate's family settled this country. Their land adjoins ours – Stones Place? You've seen it – the gate before ours on Mooky Lane.'

'Oops.' This time the grin was rueful. '*Doolin*, of course. You just don't look like a local.'

'It's been a few years,' Kate replied, wondering if his remark meant that she looked citified. 'And anyway, Heather forgets – it's Gilmore now, not Doolin. Your work brings you back, you said. So what do you do?'

'Machinery contractor. I'm here for the harvest, just getting things organised now; the early crops will start coming off next month.' His glance moved over her left hand, catching the glint of gold. 'What about you – visiting, are you?'

Kate lifted a slender shoulder. 'Sort of permanently, if I can find a job. If I can't,' she let the shoulder fall, 'I'll have to try somewhere else.'

'You'll get something,' Heather said comfortably. 'Max talks to heaps of people. He can keep his ear to the ground too.' She patted his arm, 'You will, won't you?'

'Sure thing.' He checked his watch. 'I've got to pick up some gear so I'd better keep moving.' He stood and fitted his hat. 'Nice meeting you, Kate. Tell Ken hello from me, Aunty.'

'Yes, and we'll see you Sunday,' she reminded him. 'Don't forget.'

'As if I would.' The tall figure strode away down the street and Heather reached for her bag.

'We'd best be going too, unless – is there anything you'd like to do while we're here?'

'I don't think so, thanks.' Kate pushed her chair in, her brow crinkling. 'How exactly is Max your nephew? I thought your brother only had girls?'

'Oh, he isn't, of course, he's – let me see.' Heather, trim in a cream dress with a boat neckline and a pleated skirt, which she'd teamed with red open-toed shoes, led the way to the parked car. 'His grandfather on my mother's side was my great-uncle, so he's really my cousin – second, or third, I'm not sure. Anyway, I'd see him occasionally when he was growing up and because of the age difference his mother had him call me Aunt. And it stuck – though it's more name than title now. He had a brother, or maybe two, I forget. They were right little wretches – practical jokers, you know. But Max had such a winning, gappy-toothed smile . . . He always got round one.' She smiled, remembering.

'Ah,' Kate pulled her seatbelt on. 'I don't remember him from high school.'

'You wouldn't. He was born in the wheat belt but his family shifted east – somewhere in western Victoria, I think. Now,' she had the car moving down the street towards the edge of town, 'what shall we do with ourselves for the rest of the day?'

* * *

The following day Kate went home. She dressed carefully for the occasion: tan shoes, khaki pants and a butter-yellow shirt with three-quarter sleeves. She opened her jewellery box to find a chain, threaded it through the swivel on the little carved horse and slipped it round her neck, where it hung in the open V-shape of her shirt. She'd been a child the last time she wore it but it gave her strength now, as if its maker stood behind her. Lipstick in hand, she studied herself in the mirror. 'That'll have to do.'

Heather, who had come to the open doorway, offered a raffia hat. 'It's hot out there – you want to borrow this?'

'Good idea. Thanks. I knew I'd forgotten something yesterday.' She put it on, tried a couple of angles. 'What do you think?' She felt the same nervous dread as at her first day at college.

'You look wonderful.' Heather reached unsteadily to touch the pony charm. 'I haven't seen that since —' she blinked and swallowed. 'He was a true artist, Brian – and so good to you girls.'

'Yes.' Kate hesitated, then asked anyway. 'Have you still got Tam?'

'No,' Heather turned away. 'She was wearing it when we lost her. She never took it off.'

'Neither did I – back then.' Kate gave a rueful smile. 'I put it on today for courage. Well, I'd better go. Back for lunch – or probably sooner.'

Outside, just when she would have welcomed a delay, the car started first try. Kate made the turn and headed for the gate out to Mooky Lane. She wished it was further but all too soon the familiar entrance loomed up and beyond it the well-known track, the clump of lightwood trees at the first bend, the dip where the wattle grew, and then the gravelled section that led on to the first of the out-buildings, none of which she had seen since the day before her father's funeral. Then she was pulling up beside the line of mallee trees that sheltered the house, fingers shaky on the keys as she switched off the engine and looked around.

Nothing much had changed. The sturdy farmhouse built of natural stone had weathered the years well, its black verandah shade a haven from the heat. Dusty oleander bushes, grown huge over the years, fringed the browning lawn. The single garden bed carried the usual hardy cactus varieties – together with a few geraniums. Tough vegetation that could look out for itself. She thought of The Narrows, the love and dedication that had gone into the garden there. If her mother had possessed a tenth of the nurturing skills Heather Wantage had for children and plants, how different her own life might have been.

Quickly, keen to get it over with, she glanced at the sheds, finding the usual clutter of equipment, diesel tanks and parked vehicles. Her gaze skipped over them, the shearing shed and quarters, the hip-roofed garage, the hay barn, the old smithy, the holding silos along the paddock fence, the fowl house, empty now, its inhabitants scattered about the place in little groups of russet, red and black, and finally the old workshop. The front had been taken out, she saw, and replaced with a sliding door, open to display drums of oil and grease. The rack where her father's tools had hung now held an array of funnels, pumps and grease guns. Stifling the pang the sight caused her, she stepped around her car and headed for the house.

There was a metal swing in the shade of the pepper tree and a plastic three-wheeled trike on its side on the verandah. A child's laughter from within the house meant that Clover was probably there. So she'd have one ally, if no overt support. Kate needed no lessons in her mother's ability to stifle and overawe weaker natures. Her shoes made no sound on the boards and, in common with most farmhouses, there was no bellpush. 'Hello – anybody home?' She pulled her sunglasses off to peer through the dark mesh of the screen door, then started to see her mother standing silently behind it, watching her.

'Kathryn.' Edna pushed the door open and stood for a moment, blocking the entrance as she looked her daughter over. There was to be no display of affection then and Kate, who had tensed herself to return a kiss, relaxed. 'I heard you were back. Staying at The Narrows, I believe?'

'Hello, Mum,' Kate said quietly. 'Yes, I'm welcome there. I always was. How are you?'

'Nothing to complain about.' The dark hair had greyed, she was a little stooped, and there were more and deeper lines in the weathered skin of her face, which seemed to be set in a look of automatic disapproval. 'Come through.' She moved her head to indicate the kitchen at the back of the house. 'Does that mean you consider yourself unwelcome here?'

'I didn't come to fight, Mum.' Kate followed her past the front room with its wide fireplace and along the hall where sepia portraits showed off dead Stones headed by a daguerreotype of the original Joshua. Clover was buttering scones at the big pine table and she greeted her, then the child who was pushing a truck around her feet. 'Hello, little man. Who's this?'

'That's Andy. Say hello to your aunty, Andy.' There was gratitude in the look Clover sent her.

'Lady,' Andy obliged, 'in town.' Amazingly, he recognised her.

'Aunty,' Clover corrected, adding hurriedly, 'He equates ladies with town. That's where he sees other women, you see.'

'Haven't you made the tea yet?' Edna cast an eye over the preparations. 'Gracious girl, the date loaf needs butter. It'll be dry as chips without. Here, give me the knife.'

Nothing, Kate saw, had changed, save that her sister-in-law was now the focus of Edna's impatient contempt. Feeling sorry for her flustered state, she nodded at Clover's expanded waistline. 'When's the baby due?'

'March, or thereabouts. Sit down, Kat – Kathryn. No, Andy!' She lifted him away from the chair he was in danger of toppling. 'You shall have some cake in a minute. Wash hands first. Sorry,' she grimaced at Kate, 'I'll just be a minute,' and with Andy yelling in outrage, she carried him from the room.

'Where's Doug?' Because it was a Saturday, Kate had been hoping all along to find he'd gone to town.

'He'll be back shortly. And speaking of people's whereabouts,' Edna said, as if she'd just noticed his absence, 'isn't your husband with you?'

'Guy and I have separated,' Kate replied. 'End of story. So how are they all? Clover looks tired – I suppose it's the pregnancy. Can't be easy with two others to look after.'

'The boys are no problem. A credit to their father and the farm. So – why are you here, Kathryn? Because your marriage has failed? We don't hear a word for years and then suddenly you're back. Why? You surely don't expect your brother to take you in? He's in charge here now, you know.'

Kate's laugh was without humour. 'Hardly! I can look after myself, thank you. And communication's a two-way street, after all. I'm here to be polite – keeping up appearances before the district, if you like. You set such store by the look of things, after all – you always did. Maybe it's the only thing you taught me.' She kept her voice down and her expression pleasant as if defusing a classroom confrontation. *Lose your cool, you lose everything – you have to stay in charge.* A teacher's adage that also worked in the world beyond the classroom.

'Now you're being ridiculous,' Edna said sharply. 'And that's no way to speak to me. There's nothing wrong with good manners. Sit down, Kathryn. You were always one to dramatise things, to imagine the world revolved around you.'

'Really?' The word was laden with irony. 'I can't think why when it was being disproved every day.' She accepted the cup handed to her as Clover and her son returned and were seated.

'Some cake, darling?' Edna served the child first, then offered the plate to Kate. She accepted a piece of date loaf, brown and moist-looking, and raised a friendly brow at Clover sitting silently beside her.

'Did you make it?'

Edna snorted. 'I'm sure poor Doug wishes she had. Clover's no better in the kitchen than you ever were, Kathryn. I do all the baking. I feel sorry for young men these days. When I was a girl it was a woman's duty to learn how to cook. We prepared for marriage.'

And much good it did Dad. Kate bit back the words. Then the outer door that led into the laundry and the backyard opened, and Doug entered the room. Kate felt herself tense the way she did when the dentist said, 'Open wide, please.' He was bigger than she remembered, thicker through the shoulders but still trim-waisted; his dark curls as riotous as a child's. He was a very good-looking man. The blue eyes were as brilliant as ever and when he smiled, the dimple gave his square face its familiar boyish appeal.

'Well, if it isn't my little sister!' Doug said. The note of gladness in his voice rang as false in Kate's ears as a cracked bell.

'Hello, Doug.' She responded woodenly as he dumped his hat on the sideboard and came around the table behind her to thrust his cheek against hers and hug her where she sat. She tried not to stiffen at the strength and nearness of him. Despite herself, her head made a small involuntary movement to break the contact of their skin and for a second he held her tighter, laughing because he could. Then she caught sight of the boy staring at her from the door, and leaned forward so that Doug had to release her.

'Hello,' she said brightly. 'Who are you?'

'That's Jeremy. Proper chip off the old block.' Doug's voice overrode Clover's hesitant introduction before it was fairly begun. He spoke in a proprietary tone and as far as appearance went it was true. Jeremy was tall for his age with dark curls and a look of his father about him that went deeper than the brightness of his blue eyes.

'Have you washed your hands, Jerry?' Clover asked.

'Don't start nagging him the minute he comes in, woman.' Doug sat, scraping his chair forward as he waited for Edna to pour and sugar his tea. 'Thanks, Mum. So, how long have you come for, Katie?' He knew exactly, she thought furiously, how much she resented the use of that name in his mouth.

Jeremy saved her from answering. 'Who are you?' He took the seat beside his father and inspected the scones disparagingly. 'Isn't there any jam?'

'Of course there is, dear,' Edna said, and passed it to him. 'Manners, please,' she chided.

'Thanks, Gran.' He stabbed the knife into the jar, his eyes turning again to the stranger. 'Who's she?'

'I'm your Aunty Kate,' Kate informed him. 'I came from Mr Wantage's farm and I'll be going back there when I've had my cup of tea.'

'You're just next door, then,' Clover said, as if this was news to her. 'How are they keeping, the Wantages?'

'They're well, thanks. I'll tell them you asked. Do you see much of Heather, Clove?'

'Not really.' She wiped jam from her son's fingers. 'Finish your milk, Andy. She's not very – social, I suppose. I find it hard to talk to her.'

'She lost a child,' Kate said evenly. 'Megan was only two years older than Jeremy when she was taken. You've been here what – ten years? You must've heard about it?' But Clover was shaking her head.

'Nobody's ever mentioned it to me. What happened?'

Kate lifted her palms. 'That's the problem – nobody knows. It's a mystery that's never been solved. Megan left the school bus one day and that was it. She hasn't been seen since. Somebody took her, but the police never found out who did it.'

'They always had a pretty fair idea,' Doug interposed. His voice held the same maddening tone of superiority that Kate had heard, over the years, in all their arguments, which she'd always lost. 'And there's precious little mystery involved. It was old Pete, the gyppo pedlar. He died when his wagon caught fire about – what, Mum? – twelve months later. They always had him down for the job, just couldn't prove it. Then he topped himself and they didn't have to. The cops were keeping up the pressure and I suppose he couldn't face jail, being a gyppo – rootless and restless, that lot – don't fancy being locked up. Besides, he must've known what happens to kiddie-fiddlers once they're inside.'

Kate raised her brows. 'Really? I've never heard that before – that he was a suspect. And I don't believe Heather Wantage has either. She still thinks Megan's alive somewhere.'

Doug rolled his eyes. 'Oh, come on, Katie – the woman's batty. Has been for years. And why would you have heard? You were a bratty kid. The adults were making damn sure you didn't hear anything about it. Little princesses and their innocence, you know.'

He grinned but his eyes sent a different message and with a sudden jolt, in a barbed flash of understanding, Kate thought, *Good Lord! He's jealous. Of Dad and me, of what we had. All this time and I didn't realise* . . . It scattered her thoughts. She watched her hands slip her cup and saucer onto the bread-and-butter plate and align the cake fork with her teaspoon.

'So how did you learn? You weren't that much older. Or,' she added dryly, 'is all this just schoolyard speculation grown into accepted truth?'

He grinned again, his eyes on the talisman at her throat. She almost raised a protective hand to it. 'Ooh, there's the teacher showing. Speaking of which, you ought to know that five years is quite a stretch at certain ages. I was fifteen – or near as. But as a matter of fact it's something Greg told me last year.' He paused, waiting for her to ask.

'And he is?'

'District inspector of police. Course he was just an ordinary cop back then, but he worked on the case, so I guess he knows.' He stretched, tilting his chair back, eyes never leaving hers. 'So what are you doing back here anyway, Katie? Sick of Queensland?'

'Byron Bay is not in Queensland,' she snapped just as Edna spoke.

'She's left her husband.'

Well, thanks very much, Mum, Kate thought. *I really wanted that spread around.* Though of course there was no way she could have kept the news from Doug. *Oh, what did it matter, anyway?* Abruptly she pushed her chair back and stood.

'Actually he left me. And now I have to go too. Thanks for the cuppa, Mum. No doubt we'll run into one another in town some time. Bye, boys.' Doug, she decided, could take that to include himself or not, as he chose.

His dimple showed as he smiled at her. 'You're so restless, Katie. You haven't changed a bit; you were always dashing about. Was that the problem with what's-his-name – he couldn't keep up? We haven't even been down memory lane yet.'

'Perhaps it's best we don't,' she retorted. 'I'll see myself out.'

Nobody suggested she should stay longer or call again, so she swooped a sudden kiss onto Andy's upturned face and smiled tightly at Clover. 'I might see you round.' Jeremy's expression forbade the hug she'd like to have given him so she contented herself with twiddling her fingers and blowing a kiss in his direction.

'I'd like that.' Kate barely heard the softly spoken words but the memory of her sister-in-law's pale, unhappy face followed her from the house.

6

'In here,' Heather called as the front door clacked. She glanced up as her guest came into the long slate-tiled area known as the sewing room, the borrowed hat swinging in her hand. 'There you are. How did it go? I was about ready to mount a rescue attempt.'

It was a narrow room full of light, which poured in through the banks of open louvres along the outer wall. Filmy curtains covered them, their white ruffles pleasing against the pale-green paint and the bright-yellow cushions piled on the deep cane sofa. Heather's sewing machine and cutting table, a large cupboard open to show shelves of folded material, and two cane easy chairs completed the furnishings. A couple of quilts hung out of direct sunlight on the facing wall: one a vivid shifting kaleidoscope of blues and greens, the other more subdued – a pattern of russet and gold that Kate knitted her brows over before giving a little gasp of surprise. 'Oh, I see! It's a wheat paddock with the fence and everything, or –' she moved her head, 'a geometric pattern in – what d'you call those shapes?'

'Arrowheads.'

'Yes. It's brilliant, Heather! Like something an artist would paint.'

'Thank you.' She smiled. 'Well, how did it go? Did you see them?'

'Oh, yes. But it didn't take all this time. I've been down to the forestry block – the pines. Only I don't remember it being so large before.'

'They've more than doubled the area in the last ten years.' Heather bit off a thread and laid the work aside. 'But what on earth were you doing there?'

Kate shrugged. 'Cooling down. I let Doug get my goat. It's quiet amongst the trees – a good place to think.' She sat, taking off the sunglasses she'd pushed up onto her head. 'Jeremy's the image of his father. Clover asked after you, by the way. As for Mum —' She screwed up her face. 'It was like being ten again. She wanted to know why I'd come back. As if I was looking for a handout! She actually asked me if I was – did I expect Doug to —' She jumped up from the chair she'd taken, gritting her teeth in remembered outrage. 'She made me so mad. I defy *any*body to get on with that woman. She does it to Clover too, you know – that long-suffering exasperation because nothing she can do is good enough, or ever quite comes up to *her* standards. I suppose I was lucky – I never had to live with Guy's mother.'

'And your brother? Was he pleased to see you?'

'As a snake with a bird,' Kate said wearily. 'No pun intended. But I finally worked out why he dislikes me. It's jealousy. I can't believe I never saw it before. He always despised Dad, you know. Forever belittling him, sneering at his work. He never saw what talent Dad had. To him it was just time-wasting, nothing to do with farming. Because he is a good farmer – at least the place *looks* well run. The sheds are maintained, the sheep yard's been kept up, even what passes for a garden looks okay. But getting back to Dad – he must've been desperate for his approval all along – or maybe he wanted a share in what Dad and I had.' She shook her head. 'It wasn't as if he ever shut him out – Dad, I mean – but he wouldn't give him his *exclusive* attention. I think that must've been what he wanted.' Kate thought back over her words. 'I'm sure of it. He didn't want to share. He wanted the lot – like he's got with Mum.'

'Families,' Heather sighed. 'Listen, do you fancy taking the ute down to Salter's Tank? You know where it is, don't you?'

'Yes, of course, back paddock – across the road from Halls'.'

'That's it. The trough there has sprung a leak. I've already loaded the gear Ken wants. He'll be waiting there for it. You don't mind?'

'Don't be silly! Okay if I borrow your hat again?' Kate kicked off her shoes. 'I'll just grab my trainers, then I'm out of here.'

The driver's seat cover in the ute had a large hole worn in it and the cab smelled of dog and sheep dip, an odour that took her straight back to childhood. The road followed the fence, which was banded either side by strips of mallee scrub, their leaves glinting in the brilliant light. Not a cloud broke the broad expanse of sky and nothing stirred in the heat save the rippling air above the crop, and a single crow that sat on a mallee branch, cooling itself with widened beak, wings raised like black shoulders and lifted away from its body.

Kate hummed as she drove, glad to be useful, feeling her spirits lift after the encounter with her family. She hadn't expected anything more from her visit but it had been hurtful for all that. Driving away, she'd been torn between a welling fury at Doug and pity for her sister-in-law. Despite the disillusionment of her own marriage and its pathetic end, at least she was free and there were no children to muddy the issue. She tried to be glad of that, though it felt like a betrayal of the worst kind for the baby she'd lost. If Clover ever escaped her husband, it would be without her sons, for Doug would never let them go.

At the gate into Mooky Lane, instead of turning left towards The Narrows she'd impulsively swung right and taken the rutted road beside the fence that separated the Forestry block from Stones Place. She'd pulled up after only a short distance, not liking the sound of the loose stones hitting the chassis. As it was too hot to sit in the car, she'd climbed through the fence into the trees, revelling in their shade and the springy layer of pine needles underfoot.

There, sitting with her back against a rough pine trunk, breathing in the resinous scent, she'd let the calm of her surroundings flow into her. The thing to remember, she'd told herself, was that she was in charge now. Her mother's disapproval didn't matter, and it was past time she stopped letting Doug get to her. He might have frightened her as a child, and he still knew how to push her buttons, but that was no excuse. The farm had ceased to matter to her from the moment her father died, so as of today she need never return there.

That settled, she had sat on, isolated within the stillness where no bird sang. It was a long time since she'd felt so much at peace. Idly she wondered if what Doug had said about the old gypsy tinker was true – and if so why the Wantages didn't know. Unless they did and Heather had refused to believe it? *It wasn't impossible*, Kate thought. With typical cruelty Doug had called her batty. She wasn't; but her refusal to face the possible truth – all right, the highly probable truth – was hardly realistic either.

Gypsy Pete, or Petro Pardocci to give him his right name, had been a common sight about the district when Kate was a child and it was strange, she thought, that she hadn't noticed his absence if he had indeed died only a year after Megan's disappearance. Or perhaps not – because so much else had changed that year. And he had moved around a lot. She could see his van now in her mind's eye – the brightly painted panels on the sides, the high seat across the front with the little door behind. And the big bay horse with the crooked blaze and feathery feet that had pulled between the shafts, chains jingling as his hoofs clopped along the dusty roads. The same one that had broken his leg and been destroyed outside their farm gate a few months after Megan was taken.

Pete had sold homely things – copper pans and combs and ribbons, dishmops, scrubbing brushes and straw hats. There were lollies in glass jars – peppermints, and toffees that oozed in the heat – and chamois leathers and coloured pencils. Looking back, Kate wondered how he had ever made a living from such items. Everybody knew the gypsy tinker and his van. He visited all the farms, wheedling cups of tea or fresh vegetables from the gardens of the women who purchased his goods. His van could be seen rolling slowly through the back streets of town, or more frequently on the common, with the shafts down and the little door open to the mysteries within while the bay horse, unharnessed, cropped the grass beside it.

The tinker had been a swarthy man, dark-haired and hook-nosed with brown eyes and deep creases running down from each nostril to the corners of his mouth. He'd sometimes eaten his lunch in the park beside the school and when he had he'd wave and call out to the children. Kate and Megan, warned of stranger danger, had never waved back (although he wasn't really a stranger, Megan had argued). Some of the other children had done so, though. The two girls had seen him urinating once against the trunk of a tree and when he'd noticed them staring in giggly, guilty fascination at his organ, he'd given them a smile and a big wink. They'd run away then, Kate, at least, more disturbed by the wink than by what she'd seen. Too young to analyse it, she'd nevertheless felt dirtied somehow by the complicity of the man's response. That feeling had stopped her talking about it, even to Megan. She had never mentioned it to anyone and now, frowning in recollection, she wondered if the man's lewdness had been a symptom of a greater ill. Perhaps the police were right and he had been responsible after all. Getting up to go, she made a mental note to ask Ken about the gypsy's death.

* * *

It wasn't the trough that was leaking at Salter's Tank but the inlet valve. Ken, accepting her appearance without comment, unloaded the oxy bottles and effected repairs, felt hat discarded for the welding mask. A farmer, as Kate knew, had to be a jack-of-all-trades. Shielding her eyes from the glare of the oxy torch, she watched a flight of swifts whirl out of the air into a nearby wattle. Its branches, dusted with fallen blossom, dipped under their weight, causing them to shoot skywards again, twittering in alarm. She sat under the tree waiting for their return, remembering other times when she and Megan had squatted stone-still in the long grass by the creek watching the fairy-wrens nest-building, and later, feeding their chicks. So still, in fact, that once a snake had slithered between them, its tail actually sliding across her toes while she watched, petrified, too frightened to even think of moving. Megan hadn't even seen it.

She'd never spoken about that at home either, she reflected, though she'd told Megan's mum, flesh goosepimpling at the memory of the reptile's touch. But if Doug had known, he would've gone hunting for the spot, not resting until he found and smashed the delicate nests. Experience had taught Kate that anything precious she cared about was better kept secret from her brother. Because, challenged after the fact by his father, he would lie so convincingly that even Brian would doubt her tearful accusation. Edna naturally took his part, and Doug himself would smile forgivingly upon her even as his eyes promised to make her pay, later, in sly pinches and Chinese burns.

'Penny for them.' Ken's voice startled Kate from her reverie. She looked up to see him frowning at her. 'That's a heavy thought, whatever it is.'

'What? Oh, sorry.' She laughed dismissively. 'I was miles away. You've finished, then?'

'Yep. I'll just load the four-wheeler up, then we can go. How was your visit home?'

She pulled a face. 'You know Mum. Fatted calf wasn't on the menu.' Standing, she dusted herself down. 'I don't know about you but I'll be glad of lunch. You want me to back the ute up for you?'

He'd left the four-wheeler parked at the end of a gravel pit where, a quick glance had shown, it could be ridden onto the tray of a vehicle reversed into the hole. Ken clicked his tongue, wagging his head admiringly.

'You ought to be farming, girl. You're wasted in town.'

'Yes, well – it might come to that yet,' Kate said dryly, 'if I can't find anything else.' So far she'd done nothing about getting herself a flat or a job, but that would have to change. Apart from needing the money she couldn't take advantage of the Wantages' hospitality forever. She'd stay on till Monday, she decided, then shift into town for a couple of days and if, during that time, she was unable to find anything, then she'd best call it quits and move on. There had to be something, somewhere, that she could do.

7

As it turned out, her faith in finding a job was not misplaced. It was Max Shephard who relayed the offer over the roast lamb and mint jelly on Sunday evening. He'd come later than six, his white Toyota roaring up the track just on sunset. Kate, sent to the door by Heather to welcome him, stood on the dim verandah as he walked through the garden, silhouetted against the band of pale-yellow light that ringed the horizon. Up close he looked strong and brown, in jeans and a freshly ironed cotton shirt, its sleeves rolled up to display powerful forearms. Day's end smelt of dust and water, for the sprinkler was turning on the lawn, and a whiff of aftershave as he came to a halt beside her.

'Hello again, Kate. I'm late, I'm afraid.' He wore a hangdog expression and carried a bunch of flowers that dripped onto his jeans.

'Heather will forgive you – especially with those.' She bent to smell them, 'Mmm, clove carnations. Come in, Max. She's just starting the gravy.'

He grinned. 'Well, at least she hasn't tossed it out.' His glance went over her. 'You look nice tonight.' She had dressed for coolness in cropped khaki pants and a lacy singlet top, her wristwatch and the pony pendant on a gold chain her only adornment.

'Oh, thanks.' Surprised at the compliment, she passed it off with a laugh. 'It's Heather you have to pacify, remember. I'm just the guest.'

Ken's voice boomed over hers. 'Come in, Max. There's a beer here with your name on it.'

They talked about the district over the meal, and Max's work, which amounted to the same thing, and it was then that he said, 'That reminds me, Kate. Are you still looking for a job? Doesn't matter if you've already found something but if you're interested —'

She put her fork down. 'No – no, I haven't. And yes, I am – very interested. Whereabouts and what is it?'

'Not in town,' he said quickly. 'So it's maybe not what you're looking for. I mean – Ken told me you're a teacher, but this —'

'Stop whittering, Max,' Heather admonished sternly. 'Just tell the girl.'

'Right,' he said, 'well, it's housekeeping-cum-carer, I suppose. Old Harry Quickly. He's a great-uncle of mine and he lives by himself out in the mallee, on Rosebud Farm. The old boy's ninety and he's been doing for himself ever since Aunty Edie died about ten years back. He doesn't need nursing or anything. Just somebody in the house to cook his meals and keep him company, really. To be there, you know, in case he's ill, or has a fall. There's a bit of a lad comes and goes but most of the time he's by himself. And before you ask – nobody's shifting him off the place. He was born on that farm; he intends to die there, too.'

'I'll take it,' Kate said without further thought.

'Are you sure?' Max frowned. 'I mean, it's a job but I don't want to dragoon you into anything – it's a pretty lonely place. The Hollens, they're the sharefarmers who work the land, live six or eight kilometres away and they're not very . . . sociable. And you won't see too many other people.'

'Don't his family visit?'

'Ah,' Max rubbed his head, making the hair stick up, his eyes not quite meeting hers. 'I'm about the closest he's got left. The rest are sons and daughters of second cousins type of thing and he's quarrelled with most of 'em. I won't pretend he's easy to get along with – unless he takes a fancy to you.'

'Umm.' Kate gave him a suspicious look. 'He does know about this? I'm not going to turn up there tomorrow and find out it's been organised without his knowledge or consent? Because if it has, I can't see it working.' She looked at Ken. 'Do you know him?'

He nodded. 'I've met him. But I haven't seen him for, oh, twenty years or more. About the time he got the sharefarmers in. He was a good farmer but he quit when his wife got sick.'

'It was his idea.' Max looked at her through the carnations, which Heather had placed in the centre of the table. 'He was telling me how fed up he is with his own cooking and I said he ought to get somebody to do it for him. Told me he'd hire anyone that'd take on the job.'

'He's not totally alone, then, if you go to see him?'

'Yeah, but I have to admit I never know from one visit to the next if the stubborn old devil will still be breathing. Don't get me wrong,' he added hastily, 'he's a grand old bloke. Just a bit crusty – but I'm sure he'd like you.'

'Really?' Kate raised her brows. 'Well – let's hope you're right. Could you write down some directions for me later, so I can find the place? I don't think I was ever out that way.'

'I can do better than that,' he offered. 'I'll take you over.'

'That's all right. I've got my own car —'

'It's no trouble,' he assured her, 'and it'll give me a chance to see him again. And for you to size the place up. After all, you mightn't like it – or him.'

'Now you've got me worried,' Kate said, 'but thank you. It's very kind.'

He grinned. 'My pleasure. Eight o'clock in the morning suit you?'

They had coffee after dinner and then played Scrabble, Ken winning the first game and Kate the second.

'I'm outclassed here,' Max grumbled. 'Schoolteacher. Not fair.' His eyes glinted with laughter, the light catching the tiny wrinkles at their corners. He ran his hand through his hair so that it stuck up and Kate had a mad momentary impulse to lean forward and smooth it down. Despite his homely features and with that quizzical grin, he was an attractive man – and married with six kids, for all she knew to the contrary. If she was interested – which she wasn't.

She said lightly, 'Must be luck because I've not had much practice. In fact, I haven't played since Heather used to beat us both. You said it was good for our spelling, remember? But it never did much for mine. It was Megan who won all the spelling bees.'

Max looked at his watch. 'It's late.' He pushed his chair back and rose. 'I'd better leave and let you people get to bed. Thanks for the dinner, Aunty, and the company.' His glance fell on the girl. 'Nice meeting you again, Kate. I'll pick you up about eight, okay?'

'I'll be ready.'

They all went out to see him off, welcoming the coolness of the night air. Max tripped on something near the archway and they heard him swear. 'Sorry,' he called penitently, then the door slammed and the engine fired. Headlights flashed across the garden as he turned, the horn bipped once and the red tail-lights receded down the track.

Heather sighed with tired contentment. 'That was very enjoyable.'

'And a great dinner,' Kate agreed. 'Look at those stars.' The sky was frosted with them, as if somebody had tipped a truckload of diamonds onto a sheet of black velvet. A fox called from across the paddock, its sharp wild cry startling them all.

'Did you lock the henhouse?' Heather asked through a yawn.

'Yes, dear,' Ken said. 'Same as I do every night. But it never stops you asking.'

'Well, you might forget.' She turned indoors, heading for the kitchen.

Kate followed her. 'You did the cooking. I'll see to the dishes. Go on, put your feet up. You've earned it.'

'But you're a guest,' Heather protested.

'No, I'm not. I'm family.' Firmly Kate took the apron from her and tied it about her own waist. 'Just leave it to me.' They compromised in the end, Kate washing and Ken drying, though he declined to put away.

'She'd never find 'em again.' He wiped a plate, carefully setting it down gingerly as if afraid he'd break it. 'Thanks, Katie. Your being here has done Heather a load of good.'

'Oh, nonsense – the shoe's on the other foot. I feel so much better than when I arrived. And I will come back when I can – if you'll have me, that is.'

'You're taking the job, then?'

'Unless I get a better offer. Even if the wages aren't much, I'll be living in and that's worth a bit these days. What do you really know about the old man, Ken?'

'Not much more than I've already told you.' He chuckled. 'He's a Quickly, so he's bull-headed, but he must still have all his marbles to manage alone at his age. They're a long-lived tribe. His sister, old Granny Hendon, has already made a hundred and two.'

'I remember her! She scared me witless. Megan too. We were positive she was a witch. Poor old thing,' Kate rinsed off the silver and tackled the roasting pan. 'Remember that black shawl she wore in winter? Like a cape. I suppose it was that and her bent-up shape. We used to reckon she got it from riding a broomstick. So, old Harry's her brother. Let's hope he's not as crabby.'

'If you don't like him or the job, just come back.'

'Thank you,' Kate said huskily. Her eyes had filled at his offer. It seemed lately that any kindness brought her to tears. She was like a leaky sponge, she thought in disgust – an emotional wreck. Sniffing them back, she laughed shakily. 'I don't know what's wrong with me. Except –' She turned then, hugging him fiercely, wet gloves and all, 'that you give me somewhere to belong. We never really belonged at Stones Place, Dad and I. It was like we were always interlopers.'

'Well, you're family here, girl. Never doubt that,' he said gruffly. 'We all done now?'

'Yes.' Kate wiped the sink down and stripped off the gloves. 'By the way,' she added, remembering, 'that old gypsy tinker with the van who used to visit the farms – whatever became of him?'

'Old Pardocci? He burnt to death, oh, years back. Got caught in a bushfire, poor bugger. One of those deliberately lit blazes. The general opinion was that his horse cleared out. He had a young one, not as well trained as the old bay. Course he shouldn't have stayed with the van but the truth of it is, he wouldn't have got far on foot anyway. It was no better than murder. Still – what can the police do? Anyone can drop a match. Proving it's a different thing.'

'When did this happen? Was it one of the big fires?'

Ken pulled at his earlobe. 'You got me there, Katie. Some time in the early seventies – '72, maybe '73 – but no, it wasn't a particularly bad fire, 'cept for poor old Pardocci. Somebody's woolshed burnt down, I believe, and there were the usual stock deaths but no other loss of life. What made you think of him anyway?'

'I don't know,' she said untruthfully. 'Being here, seeing the roads again. Bits of the past come floating back. It just amazes me how many things I'd – not forgotten – just not thought about for so long. Pete was one of them. It doesn't matter.'

So, she thought, preceding Ken from the kitchen, what Doug had told her wasn't true. He had always lied. It had driven Brian

Doolin wild to know it, and Doug himself must have realised he wasn't believed, but he still did it, even when the evidence against his words was blindingly obvious. And she remembered he didn't even need to have something to gain. He had always lied – simply because he could.

'Well, I'm going to call it a night.' Ken was shutting the front door and switching off lights.

Katie caught back a yawn. 'Me too. I'll see you in the morning.' Their goodnights followed her up the passage to bed.

8

Kate had been tired enough when she went to bed, slipping almost immediately into sleep only to wake an hour later, heart thudding in the silent house. Vague wisps of dream, too nebulous to catch, filled her with foreboding and she lay straining to remember them, but it was no good. *It was going back to the farm today*, she thought morosely, *seeing Clover's tense, unhappy face again, and my mother's unforgiving eyes*. Well, there wasn't much she could do about Clover, while she and her mother . . .

Damn it all! Kate punched her pillows, bundling them together to support her head. Why couldn't she just forget her family? Wherever she went, whatever she did, they lurked in her subconscious, their silent disapproval like a weight on her soul. It had been the same at her wedding. She grimaced, remembering the ceremony that had occurred a scant ten months after Brian's death.

'So soon? How can you even think it, Kathryn? What will people say? You might as well dance on your father's grave.'

'Don't you talk about Dad,' she had yelled, the blood hot in her face. 'I don't give a damn what they say. If you don't like it, don't come. You aren't invited anyway – or Doug. It's MY wedding and I'll have it when and how I want. And what about Doug? He got married eight WEEKS after the funeral, but that was all right, wasn't it?'

'It was already arranged,' Edna had said, as if that settled matters.

Kate shut her eyes on the scene as if that could block it from her head. But even after nine years the anger still remained, only larded now with regret for youthful folly. The timing alone should have told her it wasn't right. She hadn't even married to get away from home, for her training years had already accomplished that, but in terror of the aching void Brian Doolin's death had created. She had tried to fill it with Guy – and how bright had that proved to be?

'Idiot!' The fierce whisper was loaded with self-loathing. But there had been love for a while. And a contrary voice in her head sneered, *Yes – about ten months' worth – just as long as it had taken his gaze to wander.* Part of her mourned for the pretty young bride with the woebegone eyes marrying defiantly in the Quickly Park with a marriage celebrant officiating and a high tea served afterwards in the lounge of the Railway Arms. Nothing flash. She and Guy were paying for it themselves. Her insistence on that had puzzled him, for his nature was to take whatever was offered.

'If your old lady's willing to cough up for it, why not have a proper shindig, hey? So you two don't get along – what's it matter? We're talking money here, babe. In the scheme of things that's what counts.' He'd winked then, smooth and smiling. 'Gotta look out for number one, you know.'

That was Guy to a tee, she thought bitterly now. Always out for what he could get. And though she'd tried to explain about her mother and the antipathy that lay between them, it had plainly mattered less to him than the expense of catering for their guests – not to mention the expected tally from the bar.

Her friends had meant nothing to him. But why should they? They were strangers to him after all, for he'd met and courted her in the city. So it was galling that the only one to make an impression on him was Doug. 'Hey, your brother's a really nice bloke. I'm having the evening with him and a couple of his mates, babe. He's been telling me about this farm of yours. You never said it was so big. You never know – might be handy to have a brother-in-law with deep pockets, eh?'

'Guy, please.' She had felt her heart shift and thud. 'He's not a nice bloke. I can't explain but – don't, please, honey, don't tell him anything about us. Promise me you won't?' Eyes wide with uneasiness, desperate for him not to betray their secrets and knowing he would, because Doug was so charming, when he chose to be, so bloody clever at ferreting out what mattered to her.

'What sort of thing? Oh, you're shy.' He'd grinned then, pleased with himself, and kissed her. 'Mmm, come here, babe. I daresay he wouldn't care anyway – seeing we're practically married.'

'I mean anything – not just that! Where we met, the streets we walked in. . .' Knowing as she spoke that he would, he'd give it all away because he didn't understand the power Doug would then have over even this part of her life.

Kate moved restlessly, willing her churning thoughts away. She shifted the mound of pillows and threw the sheet off. He had the sensitivity of a brick, Guy. He wasn't a bad man, just selfish. Which was another way of saying self-centered, without Doug's cleverness to disguise his naked wants and the blatant manner in which he served them. And Doug was mean with it. *The smyler with the knyfe beneath the cloke.* The words drifted aptly into her mind. One of the Canterbury Tales but she couldn't remember which. Well, make that the boy who baits the rabbit trap for one of the farm cats, then arranges for his young sister to find it.

Kate flinched, remembering. That three-legged ginger tom had haunted her childhood. Farm cats were half-wild and adept at slinking from sight but she had gone in fear of glimpsing him, visiting on the cat itself the horror of finding him, snarling and bloody-masked, in the cruel steel jaws.

She had come around the corner of the smithy, which was left over from the days of horse teams working the paddocks, to her special tree, the big old pepperina with its widespread, comfortable branches and dense screen of hanging green foliage that would hide her from the world, though she could (if she chose) part the leaves with a careful finger and peep through. Since Megan's disappearance the previous year, Kate had often spent time in the cradle of its boughs – dreaming, or reading, or simply missing her friend. Megan's absence was an ache that never left her. There were other girls at school with whom she had been friendly but none had lived close enough for her to know them outside of school hours, and she was a little. . .not afraid exactly, that wasn't right – but awkward, abashed even now, when she was with Megan's mum. Not that Mrs Wantage didn't make her welcome, but there was a heaviness about The Narrows these days that subdued her spirit. It was as if not only the people but the farm itself grieved for the missing girl. It felt wrong to laugh, and Martin was no longer the merry, indulgent companion he'd once been.

So her tree had become more than a hiding place. It was her refuge from loss, a place where Kate could still imagine the day when Megan would return, or dream of the things she might do when she grew up. She could be a nurse like her beautiful Aunt Ginny, or an actress perhaps, or go to Africa and dig for diamonds that she would have made into rings and necklaces and wear every single moment, even for the washing-up. It was a magical place, the tree. Nothing was impossible there, until the day she'd pushed, stooping, through the outer canopy and found the rabbit trap wired to the trunk of it, and the big yellow tomcat crouched above his front paw, mouth bloodied from gnawing his own flesh.

Kate's cry of horror was followed by a rush of pity so intense it was a pain. Tears started to her eyes. Crying, 'Oh, poor thing, poor thing!' she rushed to release it. The tom snarled. His fur stood up and with a ferocious yowl he leapt at the girl, the force of his lunge tearing apart the remaining fragments of his trapped flesh. His claws raked her forearm as he shot past her and vanished from sight as if he had never been, save for a foulness in the air from where terror had loosened his sphincter. Kate had clutched the bright ribbons of blood leaking from her wounded arm while staring in sick fascination at the stump of paw he'd left in the trap, then doubled over and vomited.

She felt her gorge rise again now and sought to banish it. Moonlight was a pale square in the window. The curtains fluttered as a breeze arose and simultaneously came the slow creak of the mill blades from the dam, responding to the wind. Outside, Fly's pups slept against her enlarged dugs, and the poultry, beak down, in rows upon their roosts. The small things of the night would be scurrying from cover to cover while the hunters – owl and fox and cat – went about their murderous work in the shadow-haunted dark. She heard the rods draw up as the mill blades spun and sighed. Perhaps if she thought about the job interview tomorrow, or the man who'd brought the offer of it to her, she could forget the past.

Max Shephard – a shoot of the multitudinous Quickly tree – or would that be a branch? Shoot or twiglet implied somebody young – younger than thirty-odd anyway. And he must take after his father's people, she decided, because it was a given that a Quickly was foxy – and not only in their physical appearance. They all seemed to be sandy-haired, freckled and narrow-faced. Kate yawned, reflecting that there were no proper redheads among them. Not even a decent ginger like Megan had been. Her friend had had freckles too – not a fine rash but large generous ones that had shown off her creamy skin . . .

The curtains moved again as the breeze sighed against them, but Kate was away in a dream paddock with Megan, following after a Quickly whose russet coat and lolling red tongue flickered before them through the wheat.

* * *

In the morning the day spread like a blue canvas above the crops, its vastness touched here and there with flecks of white.

'Wind sky,' Max said, pulling the Land Rover door open for her.

'Yes.' Kate tipped her face up before getting in. 'I always loved the skies here. We'd lie on our backs in the wheat and ride the clouds wherever we wished. Even the tiniest bit, like that,' she indicated a wisp that could have come from the flick of an artist's brush, 'could take us anywhere. You only needed enough to grab hold of.'

'Who was the "we"? Your brother?' Max engaged the gear and turned the vehicle.

'No!' Her vehemence surprised him. After a moment she said more calmly, 'I meant Megan, Heather's daughter. We were like sisters up till the day she vanished. I spent almost as much time here as I did at home. I still came afterwards but it was never the same.' She shook the thoughts away and donned her sunglasses. 'Farm kids. We made our own amusements. What about you?'

'Oh, the usual stuff, I suppose. Plenty of boy cousins so push-bikes, forts in the mallee, that sort of thing. We came over most summers for a camping holiday at Lake Summers – if Dad could manage it. Occasionally he'd have to stay home and work but he could usually take a couple of days. We went canoeing, had sing-songs round the fire, cooked spuds in the coals – pretty good times really. I suppose most of us used the lake.'

'I know. All the farmers round here did. Us, Wantages, Halls. I don't remember you, though.'

'Probably because we stopped coming when I was about twelve when Dad had his accident. Tractor,' he added briefly, 'it crippled him. Pity – it was the only time I saw my cousins. That made it special.' He reflected a moment, then gave a wry grin. 'Well, most of them did. Some family members you can do without.' He stopped for the gate. 'Don't worry, I'll get it.' He was out before Kate could finish opening her door.

She got out anyway. 'Country girl, remember? Passengers open gates. I'll close it.'

'So,' he said when they were moving again, 'how did a country girl end up in the city?'

'Town.' She shrugged, deciding to keep it short. 'Work. Schools are in population centres so I didn't really have a choice until now. And I might still end up back there,' she added lightly, 'if your uncle doesn't take to me.'

'I'm sure he will.' They were skimming along Mooky Lane through the early shadows, disturbing a family of happy jacks hopping about on the verge. They flew just in time, their camouflage colours perfect for shadows and the early morning mallee foliage through which the light splintered in golden shards. Without looking away from the narrow road Max said, 'Was your husband a local too?'

'No.' She was going to leave it at that but he was putting himself out for her, so continued. 'I met him in the city. And it was just like the song – you probably know it. The one about being too young for love. Well, they were right. I married at nineteen. Big mistake. So now we're separated.'

'Ah, that song. Though I seem to recall it had a different ending.' A sideways glance showed him she thought he'd missed the point and he nodded. 'I do get it. It's happened to more than you – one of my cousins . . . though love had little to do with it, on his part anyway. She has Down syndrome, and a child now to complicate matters. I take it you haven't —?' A lift of the eyebrow finished the question.

'No.' They were coming to another gate. She got out and when they were moving again he continued as if there had been no interval. 'Well, you'll possibly see young Maxie around Harry's place.

He lives with his mum at the Hollens' but he wanders a lot. He and the old man are as thick as thieves.'

'Maxie? Was he named for you, then?'

'Yeah, well, Connie's fond of me. I sort of looked out for her at school. She's never forgotten that. You know what schoolyards are like if you're . . . different.'

'Yes. So he visits Mr Quickly?' This struck Kate as odd. Hadn't he said the farm was isolated, that the sharefarmers lived some distance away? 'How old is he, this boy?'

Max pondered. 'I dunno – nine, ten? Bit more, maybe. Women seem to know these things; I don't.'

'And he just wanders?'

'Oh, he's fine,' Max said cheerfully. 'He's got a pushbike and can look after himself.'

Kate swallowed the retort that leapt to mind. It would be unfair, she reminded herself. After all, she had gone for years without once thinking of Megan, and only coming back had changed that. Max knew the child and the area, and presumably the circumstances that allowed unchecked roaming about, so jumping down his throat, footwear included, would be a poor return for his helpfulness. A flash of colour in the scrub ahead caught her eye and she sat forward.

'Is that it?'

'Yep. Gate's just up here past the grid.' They rattled over it onto a potholed track. A rusty mill was visible first, then, in gaps between the trees, glimpses of sway-backed sheds and ancient machinery and beyond the mallee, a thick mass of light-green foliage that proved to be a belt of pepper trees about the farmhouse.

'Plenty of shade,' was all Kate could think to say as the vehicle came to a stop. Her heart sank. All she could see of the house was not promising – a warped verandah reached by a set of crooked steps that had seen better days, none of which had included oil or paint. The gate before them sagged, the chain overgrown with weeds, as if it hadn't been opened for years. The whole place looked as inhospitable and unwelcoming of change as she feared its owner would also prove. A section of rainwater tank showing at one side of the building bore ominous brown stains, as though holed, and a downpipe jutted crazily, obviously partly detached from its gutter. She drew a breath, deciding to make the best of it. It wasn't forever, after all. She could handle it – she would have to.

Max seemed to take her remark as approval. 'The old boy's pretty forward-thinking. He's been banging on for years about replacing some of the timber the pioneers cleared to control salinity in the soil. He started with a windbreak for the house, then gradually moved outward through his paddocks, planting the fence lines. His neighbours laughed at him – but he just told 'em he liked having birds around him. His land has never had a problem with salt, so I guess he's proved he knows his onions —'

'From his spuds,' Kate finished the quote. Her sudden whole-hearted smile startled Max, lighting her face as it did with gamine charm. 'As my father used to say.' She pushed the door open. 'Well, let's go and find him. See what he thinks of me as a prospective employee.'

'Smile like that and you'll knock him off his feet,' Max quipped and caught her quick look of surprise as she turned away. He was still wondering about it when they reached the steps and a gaunt old man shuffled out onto the verandah.

Harry Quickly had a full, curly beard. It fell to his chest and was as white – *Rinso white*, Kate thought, bemusedly remembering the ads of her childhood – as his hair. With his thin features and large ears he looked like an elf, if skinny, six-foot, bearded elves were possible. He had a narrow face with eyes of washed-out grey embedded in wrinkled skin and, behind the steel-framed glasses, alarmingly sharp for his age. White eyebrows jutted hairily above them. He had large teeth, worn down and yellowed from tobacco or possibly coffee, and a nose with a definite sideways lean as if at some time during its owner's lifetime it had been broken.

His voice was firm if slow, not at all the old man's quaver she had been expecting.

'Max?' He raised a hand against the brilliant morning light. 'Who's that with you. Do I know her?'

'Morning, Harry. And nope, she's a stranger. This is Kate —' he had obviously forgotten her married name, 'Doolin. A Stone descendant. You said you were sick of cooking for yourself, remember? Well, Kate's volunteered for the job. Providing you pay her enough, that is.'

It wasn't how Kate had planned to approach him but she trod up the steps, hand out. 'How do you do, Mr Quickly? I believe I can run your house and provide meals for you, if that's what you want.'

'Can you?' The glasses glittered below the quiff of white hair above his deeply lined forehead as he eyed her up and down. 'You one of these tidying females who can't leave papers alone?'

'I shan't interfere with anything you tell me not to,' she answered.

'Humph. Stone, eh? How many generations between you and the first Joshua?'

The question startled her. 'I have no idea,' she said frankly, then made the connection with the papers she wasn't to disturb. 'Are you interested in history, Mr Quickly?'

He humphed again, creaking slowly, about to lead the way indoors. 'Only a fool isn't. Well, come in if you're going to. Max, you better sort her out a room she can use. And show her the kitchen. I've got work to get back to.'

'Hold it, Harry —' Max began but Kate put up a hand and stepped forward.

'Mr Quickly, I'm happy to work for you but we need to establish parameters first. What you will expect from me, what wages I'll receive, and when you wish me to start.'

He blinked behind his glasses, suddenly owlish and bewildered. 'What's wrong with now? You can make my dinner.'

Remembering his age, she said gently, 'Look, I'm just here to see you now. Max will take me home again, because he has his own work to do, you know, and if you want me to I'll come back. To stay, I mean. Is that what you want?'

'I want my dinner cooked, Missy. I'm sick of doing it myself,' he whined. The eyes that had been so sharp a moment before looked vague and lost. Kate drew in a breath.

'Right,' she spoke crisply. 'Just so we understand each other, Mr Quickly, you needn't try the frail old pensioner act with me. I'm a schoolteacher. I can spot a fake a mile off. I want the terms and conditions of my employment – if you intend to employ me – finalised. Then Max can get on with his day and there might even be some chance of dinner. It's up to you.'

The old man grinned, quite unabashed. 'Worth a try, Missy. You'd better come with me, then. And when you do get round to dinner, I like bread pudding. Think you can remember that?'

'I'll try, Mr Quickly. With jam and raisins?'

'That's the one. There's a place in town makes it but they never put the raisins in. Well, if you're going to be working for me, you better drop the Mister. I'm Harry.'

Kate smiled, offering her hand again. 'And I'm Kate. And speaking as your employee, I think we'll get on. I actually make quite a good bread pudding.'

* * *

Driving away again, Kate was moved to apologise. 'Sorry.' She glanced first at the sun and then at the man beside her. 'Half your day will be gone by the time we get back. But the old are like the very young – hurrying them is counterproductive.'

'It's not a problem,' he assured her. 'I was right too – about you and old Harry. And you didn't even have to smile.' He wagged his head admiringly. 'All guns blazing – you handled him a treat.'

She laughed. 'I like him, old rogue that he is. I'll bet he uses that act to good purpose. What's this work he talks about?'

'He's writing a history of the district, been at it for years.' Max grinned back at her. 'Some of my mob are a bit worried about what he might be including. Apparently one of the Quickly great-grandfathers wasn't as upright as he could have been. He'll be after your family details too, if he hasn't already got them sorted, so be warned.'

'He's welcome to anything he can find out about the Stones,' Kate said absently. Her eyes caressed the passing scenery, taking in the shifting shades of the mallee and the rusty gold of the wheat and barley. Here and there between the crops sheep grazed, their new wool already darkening, and over all stretched the endless reach of the sky. *A day for whistling, Katie.* Another of her father's sayings. She was home, she had a job and her future was, for the moment, assured. A smile curved her lips as she thought of the old man. *He might be a challenge*, she conceded, *but no worse than twenty-odd kids, all ready to follow the lead of the one or two who saw all teachers as fair game.*

Max caught the smile. 'Penny for them?'

Somebody else had said that recently, but she couldn't remember whom. She evaded the question. 'Just thinking we must be near the first gate.'

'We are.' He slowed down for it. 'Think you can find your way back all right?'

'I've been memorising it. Thank you for your help today, Max.'

'It's my pleasure,' he said, meaning it, as she pushed the door open but he could tell from the little nod she gave that she took his stilted disclaimer as nothing more than politeness. He was intrigued by her, a little attracted too, he admitted, perhaps because she so plainly wasn't interested, continually withdrawing into her own thoughts. He wondered about the absent husband. Perhaps the split-up was new, the emotions still raw. In which case he should take it slowly. Maybe drop in on old Harry more frequently, get to know her that way. He wondered how old she was – guessing at mid- to late twenties – and why, after a reportedly long absence, she should be staying not with her family, but their neighbours. That was odd. He'd tried to pump Ken last night over their beer, but the latter had given nothing away. They treated her like family so loyalty had to be involved but over what? Mentally he shrugged. If he got to know her, perhaps she'd tell him herself. It surprised him just how much he wanted that to happen.

Back at The Narrows Kate thanked him again briskly and went indoors to pack.

'You got the job, then?' Heather was pleased for her. 'I shall miss you, though. But you can pop back for a visit, maybe stay over on the weekends?'

'We'll see,' the girl promised. 'He looks in good shape. I'll just have to work out how much support he really needs. He's not a bit like a Quickly – tall, to start with, though he's got the narrow face. He might've been ginger once, I suppose. Impossible to tell now with his hair snowy-white. Still, Max isn't foxy either.' She looked around the room. 'That's all, I think. Where's Ken?'

'Out in the paddock somewhere. They'll be starting on the crop next week. I'll tell him you said goodbye, shall I?'

'Yes, and give him my love, Heather. You've both been so wonderful. I'll drop by whenever I can.'

'I shall look forward to it. And here – a few salad vegetables for lunch. There mightn't be much to choose from in the pantry. You know what men are.'

Kate hugged her in gratitude. 'He wants bread pudding. But you're right, I'll probably have to shop first.' They kissed at the door, then Heather stood under the arch watching and waving until the red car was out of sight. Turning back, she pulled a weed or two from a border and plucked off some dead roses before returning indoors to a house that felt suddenly empty.

9

It didn't take long for Kate to settle into her new job. She was pleased to find that the dilapidated appearance of the old house was not echoed inside. It was built of stone, save for the laundry and the front and side verandahs, obvious late additions now as badly in need of paint as its cracked and splintered boards were of oil. But decades of heat and cold had left the interior untouched, except the kitchen, which was hopelessly outmoded. For the rest Kate found a degree of comfort and elegance she had not expected, though somewhat lost under the grime and cobwebs. Once the clutter was sorted and the stained floorboards and neglected furniture restored to a proper gloss, it would be a different place. She wondered how men could live just pushing stuff into corners and adding to already full shelves until the items crowded each other off and the shelves themselves parted company with the wall, as had occurred in the kitchen. It was like sweeping dirt under the carpet – it solved nothing, and the carpet never lay flat afterwards.

For the first few days she cleaned, stopping only to prepare meals for herself and the old man. The heavy drapes at the sitting room windows were dusty and, she judged, too fragile to risk in the tub, but she washed the lighter curtains, scrubbed and polished the timber floors, and beat the rugs vigorously.

'You know, girl, if that was a dog you were laying into, you'd have killed it.' Old Harry spoke as she climbed the verandah steps, flushed from her efforts.

'Well, if you kept a vacuum cleaner, I shouldn't need to do it,' Kate retorted. 'You could have grown a crop in the dust that came out of it.'

'Don't believe in 'em,' he replied promptly. He had said the same about gas stoves, an electric heater for the bathroom, and the television that sat mainly unused in the sitting room, affecting to believe that the latter stole your brains. 'Curse of the modern world. Take wireless, now – it gives you the words, which is all you need. Your imagination can supply the rest. What happens when it atrophies from underuse, eh? We'll all be like sheep – no imagination, no language. Bleating at each other,' he cackled, highly amused by the vision.

Kate couldn't decide whether he believed his more preposterous statements or simply used them to stir. He was by turns provocative, maddening, unpredictable – but she liked him. He seemed very self-sufficient but she suspected that his brusque manner covered a deep well of loneliness. She had glimpsed it only twice – once when he pronounced judgement on the promised bread pudding: 'Thank you, girl. My Edie couldn't have made a better one.'

The second time was when he first wandered out into the clean hall and sitting room, where the timber floors were newly polished and the furniture gleamed with beeswax. Kate had washed the neglected jardinières on the mantelpiece, the rose-coloured globes of the table lamps and the grimy glass in the breakfront bookcases. She had picked what greenery she could find to arrange in a vase, and pulled back the drapes to let the light in. Harry had stared for long moments, then turned away, but before he did so she had seen his eyes well. 'It looks like Edie kept it,' he'd said, then shuffled back to his office, where most of his time was spent.

Max, on his first visit, had been more outspoken. 'My God! What have you done to the old place?' Hat in hand he'd walked from room to room, marvelling. 'I can't believe – you must've worked like a navvy. The floors —' Confronted with the change he'd looked, for the moment, abashed. 'I suppose a man could've done a bit more. You tend to sort of not notice. We were mostly in the kitchen anyway.'

Kate rolled her eyes. 'That's straight out of the dark ages. I don't know what I'm going to do when the cut wood runs out! That range simply gobbles it by the armload. I have to keep it lit all day, that's the problem. Why he couldn't have installed an electric one . . . And as for the sink – you could wash sheep in it. Talk about wasting water!' The only modern appliances in the house were the electric jug and toaster, and an elderly washing machine. *It could be worse*, she supposed. *There might only have been a laundry tub.*

Max had arrived in time for lunch so she had set a plate for him and later he and Harry had carried their tea into the office, where the old man had something to show him. She had not yet set foot in the room, judging it politic to await an invitation. No doubt it badly needed a broom and duster but her employer was unlikely to agree to that. *Well, a bit at a time*, she thought, surprised to find that she was enjoying the task of bringing the house back to a semblance of itself. It had obviously been a prosperous place once, with a large garden and a tennis court at the back; nothing left of the latter now, of course, but rusted netting and weed-grown asphalt. Years of neglect had seen only the hardiest trees and two outsized stumps of purple bougainvillea survive in the garden. The branches of one had completely covered a timber seat and the remains of a collapsed wishing well, while the root system of the other had heaved up sections of the tennis court, allowing the weeds in.

'Not worth worrying about,' Max said, appearing suddenly at her elbow, as she stood beneath a pepper tree surveying the wreckage. 'You weren't thinking of taking on the garden too, were you?'

She shook her head without turning. 'It's a shame, all the same. It must've been quite a place once.'

'I believe it was – though well past its best before I ever saw it. Great-Aunt Edie was crook for a long time before she died and things just slipped into ruin. Wool prices were falling by then, and between a sick wife and increasing age the old boy didn't have the energy – or the money, I suspect – to keep it up. Then when Edie died he just lost interest. Handed it over to sharefarmers. I don't believe he's been down to the sheds once since.'

'They must've been happy, then – he and Edie – or he wouldn't have cared so much,' Kate said, turning back to the house. 'You're off now?'

He followed her. 'Yes. Thanks for the lunch.'

'You're welcome,' she said automatically, then laughed. 'It's Harry's food anyway. I only cooked it.'

'Well, it tasted pretty good.' Passing the wayward downpipe, he tried to force it into alignment but it immediately sprang out again. He squinted at the gutter where the problem lay and shook his head. 'Maybe next time. This place could use a part-time handyman and that's a fact. I'll be seeing you, Kate.'

'Yes.' It was a standard goodbye, no more than that, she told herself, watching his dust power away up the track. He must be fond of the old man, or perhaps he felt that having got her here, the occasional visitor might help to see that she stayed. It was very quiet with old Harry forever in his office, and Max, so far, their only caller. Luckily there was plenty to do – she had barely scraped the surface of the house. With this in mind Kate returned indoors to make a start on the kitchen cupboards.

* * *

The boy turned up that afternoon. He arrived silently, slipping as was his custom through the open front door, and the first Kate knew of his presence was the sound of his voice in the office when she went to tell Harry that afternoon tea was ready. For a moment she thought he must be reading aloud and tapped before opening the door to poke her head through.

'Harry,' she began and saw the slight figure seated beside the old man fling itself towards the corner of the room.

'It's all right, Maxie.' Harry rose slowly, his voice unalarmed. 'It's just Missy. I told you about her, remember? Come and have some cake.' He cast an enquiring glance her way. 'Are there cakes?'

'Yes,' she said composedly. 'Chocolate ones, with sprinkles. And a glass of cold milk if it was wanted.'

'Maxie likes tea,' Harry said. 'Suppose you get an extra cup out and we'll be along presently.'

'Don't let the pot get cold,' Kate warned.

Max's guess as to the boy's age had been good, she thought, assessing him. He was about ten and undersized with it, or bred from small stock. He was thin-faced, with nervous, darting eyes, knobby wrists and sharp elbows. His hair was dirty-blond, his eyes possibly blue, though it was hard to say for he'd stolen only quick sideways looks at her and, anyway, her attention had been taken up by the fading bruise on his right cheek; it covered his face from eye socket to jawline. Anger filled her at the sight of it. No childish tumble had caused that much damage.

When she returned with a mug and another plate (onto which she'd slipped a couple of extra cupcakes) to the dining room, where they now took their meals, Harry and the boy were seated, the latter on the edge of his chair, looking ready to bolt.

'Well,' she said cheerfully, 'I'm glad you came to visit, Maxie. I'm sure Harry will be tired of chocolate cakes if we have to eat them all ourselves.' She passed the mug to Harry, figuring that he would normally attend to the boy's needs, and took a seat across the table from them. Maxie made no reply to her greeting and in fact said nothing at all beyond a brief 'Ta' when receiving his tea. He concentrated on eating instead, polishing off four of the cupcakes before draining the mug and wiping his mouth on his wrist. Her gentle questions as to where he lived and what his parents did were ignored. Then Harry, meeting her eyes over the child's head, shook his own and she talked to him instead. Afterwards the two returned to the office but when, having made extra sandwiches, she went to call them for lunch, the old man was alone.

'Where's Maxie?' Kate glanced about as if the desk might be concealing the child.

'Mm? Oh, he's gone. Don't worry. He'll think about you for a bit, then he'll come back.'

'Today, you mean? It's just – I made him some lunch.'

Harry rose and rubbed his hands together. 'Let's eat it, then. But not in that damn-fangled dining room, girl. He didn't like that, Maxie. What's wrong with the kitchen, anyway?'

'Nothing, if you can stand the heat,' she snapped. 'It's thirty-nine degrees outside and around forty-two in there with the range going. We can have it on the verandah if you wish. A salamander couldn't eat in that kitchen.'

'Outside it is, then.' Harry led the way and munched contentedly at the egg and tomato sandwiches she'd made. He poked through them, avoiding the ones with the crusts, which she'd intended for the boy. She ate them instead and when he made no attempt to broach the subject did so herself.

'Why didn't Maxie like the dining room? And what did you mean, he'll think about me? Where does he come from, Harry?'

Instead of answering, the old man snapped his eyes to his wrist and gave a sudden cackle. 'Damn me if you haven't just lost me a bet, girl! I said to myself you'd ask the first question inside five minutes and here it's nearer nine.'

'You're impossible, Harry Quickly.' His pleased expression drew an answering grin and she laughed herself. 'All right, then. I admit it, I'm curious. That child looks half-starved, and that bruise on his face – he's not being cared for as he should. And it's Monday. Why isn't he in school?'

'He's a bit different, Maxie. He's got something . . . ' Harry was sharp enough but he sometimes searched for words. Kate waited and he produced it now triumphantly. 'Dyslexia, that's it. He's never learned his letters, but he's smart enough in other ways. Kinda shy, and he don't trust easy, especially strangers – but he'll come round to you if you give him time. You ever,' he asked, breaking off to fix her with his faded eyes, 'tamed a wild thing, girl? Then you'll know you mustn't startle 'em, or change things too quick. The boy's like that. He knows me, knows my routine and we sort of suit each other; he comes over, spends the day, stays the night sometimes. I'm teaching him about the stars.'

'But he can't just wander. His parents – don't they worry?'

'There's only his mother, and Connie's flat out caring for herself. She was born with Down syndrome – should never have had a child. Her mother was a Hollens, dead now, so she lives over at Macquarie with her two uncles. They sharefarm Rosebud; a rough pair, but good workers.'

'Rough enough to have caused the boy's bruised cheek?'

'Very likely.' Harry, alerted by her tone, shrugged defensively. 'Boys get clipped around the ears, Missy. I did, my brothers too. Matter of fact we were thrashed more than once and I daresay we deserved it. It never harmed us.'

'No simple clip caused that bruise,' Kate retorted. 'And whatever happened eighty years ago, Harry, it's now illegal to hit a child. Let alone not sending one to school.'

'Now, don't be stirring things, Missy.' Harry looked alarmed. 'You're a teacher. Just use your head for a minute. Everyone knows about his mother's problems, so you think about what he suffers at school. *That* sort of thing is what ought to be illegal. You report him and like as not they'll take him away from Connie, who loves him as well as she can. His clothes are clean, you've seen that, he's fed – all right, he's skinny and hungry. Boys are, in my experience, and he bikes eight kilometres to get here. Enough to make anyone hungry. But in his own way he's happy enough, so why not let him be?'

'But he can be taught,' Kate said. 'There are teachers who specialise —'

Harry snorted. 'In the Mallee? It'd mean sending him away from all he knows. Just let him alone.' His voice was suddenly fierce.

She shouldn't upset him, Kate thought with sudden compunction; the old man's hands were trembling and the tendons of his neck were taut. Besides, one shouldn't meddle without knowing more than she did. The boy's father had obviously cleared off. Hadn't Max said something about it? And if, despite her disability, Maxie's mother loved him, then surely that counted for much? So she smiled at her elderly employer as she rose to collect the detritus of their lunch. 'I won't interfere, Harry. That's a promise.'

10

It was another week before Maxie returned. This time Kate saw the slight figure bicycling up the track. She stepped behind the old hen-house, where she could watch unobserved. The boy dropped the bike in the shade and looked carefully about before vanishing from sight. When she returned indoors with her armful of wood, she heard the murmur of voices in the office. She stoked the firebox and turned the pages of a recipe book, printed in the 1940s, looking for cakes and slices.

This time she set lunch on the verandah, where they now took all their meals. The band of pepper trees might have cut the view down to the width of the yard but their thick foliage cooled the hot winds, and anything was preferable to the kitchen. She tapped on the door, calling, 'Lunch, Harry,' and was already seated at the table when they arrived. Maxie slid a look her way and nodded at her greeting. She went on serving the salad, leaving the shredded lettuce off Harry's, saying in an absent tone, 'Did you wash your hands?' and was gratified when the boy started, then went obediently to do so. Over the meal she talked only to Harry, for the first time asking about his work. 'Is it about the people, or the country? And at what point did you begin?'

'With a villain called Joshua Stone.' He gave his old man's cackle. 'He was the first settler in the district, so course I started with him. It's the history of the Mallee so I thought I might as well start with the first Mallee man.'

'Not with the explorers, or the Aborigines?'

'Nope. Mind the latter come into it – briefly, I might add. Old Joshua saw to that.'

Kate was genuinely startled. She laid down her knife and fork. 'You don't mean he – shot them?'

'Shot, poisoned, whatever. It's not like the pioneers bought the country, girl. Did you never hear the term *land takers*?'

'Yes, of course. You just don't think,' she said blankly. She had another thought. 'What about the Quicklys, and the Halfords?'

'All guilty as charged,' Harry said cheerfully. 'Don't look so tragic. It's history. You can't mend it, but you shouldn't hide it either. There's blood on the land but it's old blood now. Best we can do for the dead is to tell the truth – though not many are going to like it.'

'You've got that right,' Kate said with feeling. 'My mother pretty near worships old Joshua. Doug won't be best pleased either.'

Harry was unperturbed. 'There's more Quicklys to upset than there are Stones, let alone our lot married into the Halfords and the Hollens, and there was a Kelly man way back ran off with a Quickly girl – without benefit of clergy.' He cackled. 'I ever get finished, most of the district'll be after my hide.'

Kate smiled, liking the old man's spirit. 'I don't suppose that most will worry. I've met people proud of their convict ancestry. Though theft, I suppose, and fraud, are a bit different to murder. Well, I must get on. What would you like for dinner?'

'Whatever I say, you're going to tell me you haven't got it,' he retorted smartly, 'so make what you want. It all tastes pretty good. You should be married, girl. Your skills are wasted on an old fart like me.'

'As to that, I'll need to go to town tomorrow.' Kate ignored the rider. 'The store cupboard's low, so you might think if there's anything I can pick up for you – unless you want to come too?'

He refused, as he always did, and she went off, compiling a mental list for which she would have to coax a cheque from him. Harry professed to disbelieve that supermarkets refused to let their customers run accounts. Perhaps, if she rang Heather, she would be in town too, and they could meet for coffee.

* * *

In the event it was Clover she met, not Heather, literally bumping into her as she stepped out of The Hair Place, the only salon in town. She had her head bent to a grizzling Andy and recoiled, apologising.

'I'm so sorry – oh, Kate. I didn't – how are you?'

'I'm fine, thanks, Clove. Hello, Andy.' The child who had clutched the door frame and was refusing to move made no answer. Kate switched her gaze to her sister-in-law. 'Your hair looks nice.'

'Thank you.' Clover gave a brittle laugh. 'It was past time I had it done. Two months since it was last cut but I've been saving every cent for – I've no money of my own, you see. Come on, Andy!'

'Let's have a coffee,' Kate said brightly, 'and perhaps Andy would like an ice-cream? My treat,' she added quickly.

'Thanks.' Clover's expression was grateful. 'We'd love that, wouldn't we, Andy? Say thank you to your aunty.'

When they were established at a table on the pavement under the deep shade of a tree with their coffees before them, and Andy, settled in a plastic chair at his mother's side, absorbed in his cone, Kate looked around at the leisurely pace of the main street, where the occasional vehicle rolled by and half a dozen figures moved slowly along the pavement. She grinned. 'Could be Paris, eh? Another dozen tables, a bit more traffic and exhaust fumes, a few extra people . . . of course the pace is a bit lacking.'

'You went there – Paris, didn't you?' Clover observed, sounding not so much envious as sad.

'A fortnight's honeymoon,' Kate said. 'It rained for the first week and Guy had his passport stolen.' She grimaced. 'Symptomatic of our marriage, I suppose. The timing was always off and my expectations were probably too high. I was very young. How old are you, Clove? I don't think I've ever asked.'

'Almost thirty-one.' She put her hand down on the slight curve of her stomach. 'I will be when this one's born. I'm scared, Kate. I don't know how I'll live. How can I hold down a job with a newborn to care for?'

'I don't know.' Kate glanced across at her nephew but he was too young to follow their conversation. She touched his mother's arm. 'But others do. There is help available for abused women – shelters, welfare assistance. Nobody can make you stay in a relationship that threatens your health and the wellbeing of your kids. Not if it involves rape and physical abuse.' She indicated Andy. 'What's that going to do to him, and his brother? They'll turn into men like Doug because he's the example they'll have to copy.'

'I know. It frightens me. But,' she added hopelessly, 'everything does. I did love him, you know. It seems inconceivable now because he's taken everything I had and twisted it, the way he's twisted our marriage into something hateful. I have no confidence left, Kate. I tell myself I can do it, that I held down a job and managed my money and had a social life before I met him, but when I start to think about doing it again with the kids to provide for, I'm paralysed with fear. If you're constantly told you're stupid, you start to believe it.'

Kate nodded. 'I know how it works. I grew up believing I was plain and awkward and useless, because Mum never missed a chance to tell me so. If it hadn't been for Dad . . . You know, I even asked him once if I was adopted. Doug put that idea into my head and I came to think it might be why she didn't love me, you see. And of course I don't have the Stone colouring, or even Dad's.'

'Nobody else's got fair hair, and my face is a different shape too,' she had explained earnestly to him. Adoption would account for everything wrong with her, she had thought. But it would also break her heart because it would mean that Brian Doolin was not her real father.

'Hey,' he'd said gently, 'your face is fine, Katie. You're growing every day and there's no saying who you'll look like when you finish. At the moment you're very like my sister when she was your age.' She had never forgotten that, or the loving look with which he'd spoken.

There had been a photo of Aunt Ginny in her father's box and that night Kate had compared it with her own reflection, examining her big front teeth, and the thick fair hair strained back into plaits as tight as Edna Doolin could pull them, leaving her face as bare as a scrubbed tabletop. But it didn't matter because Aunt Ginny was beautiful, which must mean that her father thought she was too. She had bought a cheap frame for the photo and kept it by her bed but some time during her high school years it had disappeared. Doug, she had supposed at the time. He had a way of taking things she valued, but now she wondered if her mother had been responsible.

'At least you had the evidence of your own eyes to refute it,' Clover said, 'about your looks, I mean. No amount of saying it can take that away.'

'No, you're only beautiful if you believe it.' Kate smiled sadly. 'I envied you, you know. When we first met I thought I'd never seen anyone so pretty. Look, I have to run, Clove. Harry likes his meals on time and I've the cold stuff to pick up yet. I wonder – would you care to come over one day? We could have lunch. I'm sure Harry wouldn't mind.'

'No.' Clover's face tightened. She rose and crossed to Andy to mop his chin with a tissue from her bag. 'Thanks, but I couldn't. I'd have to explain why I wanted a vehicle and Doug . . . ' She kneaded her hands, whispering, 'It's so hard. He wouldn't let me, not without a fuss. It's why I've given up on the meetings and committees I used to belong to.'

'Then perhaps you shouldn't have,' Kate admonished. 'You've a perfect right to visit anyone you want to. Heather said she never saw you at the meetings, even though Edna goes to them. Next time just tell her you're going too. Think of it as a practice run for getting away.'

'I-I'll try.' Clover leaned over to kiss her cheek. 'I'm not as strong as you, Kate. Thanks for asking, anyway. Say bye-bye, Andy. Bye-bye to Aunty.'

She picked him up and the little boy smiled angelically and waved a pudgy fist, which Kate captured to kiss. 'Take care.' She watched them cross the road, then put her chair in and tucked the paper napkin under her cup. And looked up to see Max striding towards her, his angular face splitting into a smile.

'There you are, Kate.'

She tipped her head up, smiling back in sudden pleasure. 'I didn't expect to see you in town. Were you looking for me?'

'I was.' He poked a finger at the brim of his hat, lifting it and letting it drop again. 'Harry told me you'd come in.' His eyes twinkled. 'I hear you've refused to serve meals in the kitchen. What's staff coming to these days, eh?'

'Staff,' she said firmly, 'shouldn't have to work in a sauna, let alone eat there. It's unbearable with the range going. The old wretch – what does he expect you to do about it, anyway?'

'Address the problem by changing stoves. I'm here to buy a gas job and he thought you ought to choose it. Have you got ten minutes?'

'I suppose.' She was laughing. 'And I also suppose you get to cart it out and install both it and the gas bottles? That old man's got a front as wide as Myer's! Still, I own I'll be happy to have it. I shan't have to worry about wood then.'

'Then shall we?' He swept his arm towards the Railway Arms, which stood next to the only shop in town selling whitegoods, and she fell into step beside him. Movement across the street caught her eye and glancing over at a truck unloading boxes outside the bakery, she was startled to see Doug standing in front of Pringle's watching her. He turned away almost at once, leaving her to wonder just how long he'd been there. A quick backward glance showed no sign of Clover but he could still have seen them together. Uneasily she worried about what capital he would make of it, before common sense dismissed the idea. Max had noticed her frown. 'Something wrong? I'm not keeping you from . . . Look, I'm sorry. I just assumed —'

'No, no.' Her tone banished his suddenly stricken look and she tucked a hand through his arm. 'Let's see these stoves. How does Harry know I won't pick the most expensive one in stock? Or do you get a veto in lieu of service charges for the installation?'

'Now, *that's* an idea.' His hazel eyes glinted lazily and she thought again what an attractive man he was, for all his long nose and spiky brows. Perhaps she should have married a farmer, someone kind and dependable like Max, who could find time in his day to drive into town to buy and fit whitegoods for an old man who, she was sure, could perfectly well afford to pay a tradesman for the same task.

* * *

The new stove was a big success, though the installation wasn't as simple as Kate had believed. Fortunately, for the old range was the large, double-oven type, Ken Wantage turned up in time to help Max lift it out, bringing with him a pup for Kate.

'The runt of the litter,' he'd said, lifting the roly-poly black and white bundle from the ute into her arms. 'The rest were all spoken for. You got a name for him?'

'Oh,' she gasped, 'thank you, Ken!' She gave him a one-armed hug, the fingers of her spare hand caressing the pup's ears standing comically at half-cock. Lifting him from Ken's grasp, she said, 'A dog, too, lovely. So, a name – let's see now – what about Flash?'

He grinned. 'You're as bad as Heather. And I'll tell you the same as I tell her – it saves me learning a new one. What about Flip instead?'

'I like it. Right, I'd better just square it with old Harry first, though he's been a sheepman so I'm sure he'll agree. But Flip it is. He'll need his shots. When should I take him in for that?'

'Already done. How's the job?'

'It's good, thanks. There's plenty to keep me busy, and he's an interesting old chap. Used to his own way, of course.'

Ken grunted. 'Not too lonely? You know you're always welcome at home. Get Max to bring you for a meal, or come for the weekend some time.'

'Max has his own business to look after,' she said. 'He's only here now because Harry dragooned him into installing a new stove. Go in and see him. I'll make a cage for the pup, then I'll put some lunch together for us all. You'll stay, won't you? Harry seems to enjoy visitors.'

The chimney, disconnected from the stove, had disgorged a load of soot over both stove and floor, so they ate as usual on the verandah. The pup, fenced into a cage made of camp stretchers, yapped disconsolately at his isolation, then fell asleep.

'What'll you call him?' Max asked. Beside him, Harry and Ken were deep in the history of The Narrows, which apparently had consisted of two leases combined some time back in the twenties.

'Flip. It seems appropriate; his parents are Fly and Flash.' Something moved in the corner of her eye and she turned her head.

'It's just Maxie.' He spoke lazily, his eyes on her face while he marvelled inwardly at the perfect curve of cheek and eye arch. 'I saw him before. He won't come in with strangers here. I'm afraid we've made a bit of a mess in your kitchen. I went at it arse about – should've put down the cement pad for the bottles first. It won't dry in time now. Could you manage without the stove tonight? There's a primus somewhere I could set up for you. Means you could fry a chop or cook some vegies at need.'

She thought a moment and shook her head. 'It's fine. I can manage without, thanks all the same. There's cold meat. We could have salad, and a tin of fruit, I suppose. Coffee and cake if more's needed. I hope Harry appreciates your efforts, Max. This business is taking up your whole day.'

'I don't mind if you don't.'

'Anything,' she said positively, 'is better than chopping wood.'

'Ouch,' he muttered, and she was stricken with laughing remorse.

'I'm sorry. That was most ungrateful of me. I'm the one who benefits, after all. Don't worry. I'll feed us all, whatever state the kitchen's in. And if you need it, I can make up a bed for you.'

'I don't want to put you to any trouble.'

'Don't worry about it,' she said lightly. 'I'm a housekeeper. It's what I'm paid for.'

II

Ken took his leave after lunch, Kate walking to the ute with him. 'Give Heather my love,' she said, kissing him. 'It's been lovely to see you. And thank you so much for Flip. I'll get him a collar next time I'm in town. I hope old Harry didn't wheedle too many promises from you? He's absolutely shameless when he wants something.'

Ken pulled a face. 'It's just a bit of research. He's interested in the original survey lines. Course, the field markers are long gone but the descriptions ought to be written into the deeds and I have them somewhere. It's just a matter of finding them.'

'Shameless,' Kate repeated. 'He's already got Max chasing round the country mapping bore sites and looking out for the stumps of dead woolsheds.' She waved him off and returning to the house found the boy sprawled on the verandah petting the pup.

'Hello, Maxie,' she greeted. 'Have you been to see Harry yet?'

The boy's gaze met hers fleetingly, then returned to the pup. 'Is he yours, Miss? Can I play with him?'

'You may – after you've seen Harry. That's only polite. Have you had lunch?'

'No, Miss.' His tone was suddenly hopeful.

'Well, go say hello, then wash and I'll make you a sandwich.'

* * *

Maxie stayed until evening. They ate an early tea in the dining room and when it was over Kate, who'd finished clearing up, suddenly missed his presence.

'He's gone,' Max said. 'Ducked off a while back.'

'I don't know, that child seems to come and go as he pleases.' Kate's brow creased. 'It's an eight-kilometre ride in the dark.'

'He'll be okay. There's a full moon,' Max responded.

'I wasn't thinking about him falling off,' Kate responded tartly, then bit her lip. 'Sorry, it's just that I can never forget how Ken's daughter vanished – and she had nothing like that distance to cover. Just from where the school bus stopped to the farmhouse. You could walk it in ten minutes.'

'I remember that,' Harry said. 'First incident of its kind in the district. Oh, there was the Lipp killings back in the thirties but they got the feller did that. No, that little girl – that was bad. It upset my Edie, that did. I forget the family's name now.'

'It was Wantage – that was her father who came today,' Kate said gently. Harry's mental slips were so few that she found it disconcerting when they occurred.

'Yes, of course. Stupid of me.' His eyes sharpened. 'Your family's place neighbours his, so you must have known her.'

'She was my best friend.' Kate's hand, lying on the table, unconsciously closed. 'But the one time it mattered I wasn't there with her. Some friend!'

'There might have been two deaths if you had been,' Max pointed out.

'Or none,' she said flatly. 'How can I know for certain? We never quarrelled, you know, Megan and I. Not once – until that day . . . '

* * *

It was the last period, the final fifteen minutes before the bus came, when the teacher normally read to them, but today they were colouring in instead. Golden Fleece was holding a competition, the first prize a Super Elliott bike. There'd been a picture of it at the bottom of the competition sheet, two models, one for boys, one for girls. The girls' one had a basket and pink ribbons on the handlebars. Since giving up on the longed for pony, Kate had never wanted anything so much.

The picture to be coloured was an extravagant basket of flowers and they had planned it to the last bloom, because each entry had to be different, and anyway, it gave them two chances, Megan said. She was to have blue daisies and Kate yellow; her sweet peas would be pink and Kate's violet. Whichever of them won the prize would share it with the other – *our* bike, they'd agreed. They'd worked so carefully, mindful not to colour over the lines; brown stems, green leaves, yellow centres, and the large rose in the middle a beautiful pink. Both roses, because that was the only colour a rose should be. When they'd finished it down to the raffia handle on the basket (a mixture of brown and yellow), Megan had suddenly wet the tip of her pencil with her tongue and darkened the rose. It looked so striking that Kate had darkened hers too . . .

* * *

'That's what we quarrelled about,' she recounted. 'The colour of a flower. When the bell rang she ran out spitting mad. It was the last time I saw her – climbing onto the bus with her head turned away. Probably crying. I handed my paper in and hid in the cloakroom until I heard the engine start, then I walked home through the pines. I was still angry, it was so *unfair* of her. We always shared, you see, and did everything the same, and I couldn't see it mattered because all the rest of the bunch was different . . . I knew I'd get into trouble for missing the bus but I didn't care. If I was going to be punished anyway, I thought I'd do something I wanted first – and I'd always wanted to walk through the pine plantation.' She sighed ruefully. 'Such a little thing – a colouring competition – to alter so many lives.'

Max nodded sympathetically, asking as if it really mattered, 'Why the pines? What was it about them you liked? I take it you *didn't* win the bike?'

'No, some kid in Adelaide got it. As to the pines . . . I don't know.' Kate shrugged, fiddling with her placemat. 'I thought they were mysterious. The silence, I guess, and the way the needles mat down so it's like walking on carpet.' She looked at him, daring him to laugh. 'I used to think – I don't know why, but I did – that the cones sang. I wanted to hear them, by myself.'

'Sounds perfectly reasonable to me. *Did* you get into strife at home?'

'Oh, yes. Mum always came down hard on me over the least thing. Of course, Megan had been missed by then and everyone assumed we'd be together so when I finally got home the Wantages – Heather and Martin anyway, Ken was off somewhere, a sheep sale, I think – were waiting there for me. So I lied about walking home. I said I'd stopped by the creek to play and I only saw Megan on the bus and going through The Narrows' gate. And all the kids on the bus said the same when they were asked – that she went through her gate, I mean. I never even told Dad the truth, and I told him most things. It was just too awful, because I knew it was down to me that she was lost.'

'Of course it wasn't,' Harry snorted. 'It was down to whoever took her.'

'The gypsy hawker,' Max remembered.

'*If* he did,' Kate said. 'Yes, I know suspicion fell on him, but it was never proved. His being dead is convenient for the police, don't you think? But look at the facts. The bus driver didn't see Pete's turnout on the road, and short of going into one of the farms there's no other way off Mooky Lane.'

'He could've been on foot.'

Kate said positively, 'He couldn't, or how would he have got her away? And whoever it was must've taken her out of the area because they turned the district upside down before they quit searching. Old man Hall was still making haystacks back then and they hauled them apart with pitchforks, to see if she was in them. They dragged the dams and looked in every culvert. The kids at school said they even dug up the newest grave in the cemetery to see if she'd been put in it. It probably wasn't true, but I believed it then.' She shuddered. 'It was a terrible, terrible time.'

Max yawned and immediately looked stricken. 'Sorry. Look, it's history, Kate. You were – what – nine years old? You couldn't have changed anything then and it's pointless worrying now. Let it go. We have to believe that whoever was responsible will get his deserts in the end.'

'I hope so,' she said. 'And I hope Maxie's safely home. I'd best check on Flip and then I'm turning in. It's been a long day.'

'Sensible female,' Harry said approvingly as she went out. 'Not one of those silly flappers who think dogs belong inside. Nothing as destructive as a pup, or as easily spoiled.'

'She's a farmer's daughter, old timer.' Max stretched until his shoulders cracked. 'I'll fit the gas bottles first thing, then get going. I've got to be across the lake tomorrow for a job at the Junction. I'll drop in when I get back.'

'Good. We'll expect you then; and don't forget about my wool sheds.'

Max grinned. 'As if, you old slave driver.'

***

Kate rose early next morning, spurred by the thought of the pup who would, she knew, be both lonely and hungry. Besides, the early morning with the first rays of sunlight backlighting the mallee, and the air cool and clear, was the best part of the day. She heard a magpie carolling behind the house and the clink and tap of metal, which proved to be Max hooking up the gas bottles. They stood on their newly created slab, secured by a chain, while he crouched alongside fiddling with the thin copper connecting pipes. His hat lay beside him and his unruly hair had acquired a patch of dust from its contact with the kitchen wall. He saw her and grinned.

'About ready to go, if you want to pop the kettle on. When the bottle's empty you just swap this connection over, but remember it's a left-hand thread.' He gathered his tools. 'All it takes is a shifter and a screwdriver for the plug. There'll be a spanner that'll fit in the shed – I'll find it before I go. I don't think Harry's ever got rid of so much as a worn tyre off the place.'

'I can believe it. I found a hand mangle in the shearing quarters last week. What will you have for breakfast? I'll just check the puppy and then I'll start on it.'

'I have to get going, but a cuppa would be good. As for the pup —' he jerked his head sideways, 'young Maxie's got him. Probably slept with him, too.'

'He was here all night?' Kate was startled. 'I thought he'd gone home. What sort of mother —? Good grief! I'm going over there to see her today.'

Max picked up his hat and fitted it, saying deliberately, 'It would be best if you didn't, Kate. Look, Connie Hardy's intellectually impaired. She does her best by Maxie, believe me, she does. But it's not easy for her. She gets a disability pension and the rest is down to the generosity of her uncles. They own the van she lives in and they keep an eye on her but they've got no time for young Maxie. If you go over there stirring things, suggesting she's incompetent, they'll jump at the chance to have him put in foster care. That would be a tragedy.'

'Actually,' Kate said firmly, 'it might be the best thing that could happen to him. He's running wild, missing school. The holidays don't start for weeks yet. Harry said he's dyslexic, so he needs specialist help. Perhaps a foster home would give him the chance to make something of his life.'

'No,' Max contradicted her. 'That's the schoolteacher talking. What would happen is that he'd lose his freedom and his sense of place. He'd be among strangers in an environment totally foreign to him, away from everything he knows. He deserves better than that.'

'He deserves an education,' she said sharply.

'And he's getting one! Why do you think he spends so much time here? Harry's teaching him. The boy's a natural artist and Harry's working with him on the rest of it. It might be unorthodox but Maxie's neither neglected nor unschooled.'

'Harry is?' she said incredulously. 'What does an old farmer know about the problems facing dyslexics?'

Max's expression hardened. 'Rather more than you know about him, obviously. Why suppose that Harry's just a farmer? Didn't your own father have a trade, Kate? Something outside the property?'

'He was a cabinet-maker,' she admitted, beginning to bristle. 'A very fine one, too.'

'I'm sure. Well, Harry and Edie had a dyslexic son back in the days when the problem was barely recognised. He grew up to take over the farm and both of them, thinking of grandchildren, and fearing it might be hereditary, went off to study the condition, to learn what could be done for it. Their own son was illiterate but they were determined that his children wouldn't be. But in the end there weren't any. Josh Quickly married but he got leukemia only a year after the wedding and died childless. There were no other sons so Harry moved back to work the place until Edie died, then he leased it to the Hollens brothers. So I would appreciate it, and Harry would too, if you didn't meddle. There's no need – Maxie's fine.'

'Very well,' she said stiffly. 'You see yourself as responsible for him, then? Why? Who's his father, anyway?'

'Nobody knows. Some low-life who took advantage of Connie. But she's family – sort of. Daughter of a third cousin, I think.'

Maxie appeared then, Flip lolloping beside him, and Max waved at the boy. 'Morning, Maxie. Perhaps you'd better give Kate back her dog.'

The boy gave her one of his fleeting glances and wriggled bare toes in the dust. 'He were crying, Miss. Lonely like.'

'Good morning, Maxie,' she said sternly. 'I know; it was his first night away from his family, but he won't be going back so he has to get used to it. Where did you sleep?'

Flip rolled over, panting at his feet, and the boy ducked down to rub his belly, ignoring the question. She waited, then said resignedly, 'Well, go and wash for breakfast. And the pup stays outside, do you hear?'

'Yes, Miss.' He ran off and Max chuckled.

'He's getting the message. You sounded quite fierce then.'

She opened her mouth, couldn't think what she wanted to say and settled for, 'Breakfast in five minutes. And thank you, in case Harry hasn't, for fixing the stove. Everybody seems to act pretty much how they wish round here, but that's no excuse for bad manners.'

Marching off, Kate felt seriously ruffled, though which of the three of them was to blame for it she couldn't have said. You could expect irresponsibility from a ten-year-old, so it was either Max's blind assumptions about the care of children, or Harry's slyness . . . Well, what else *could* you call it? she raged, clattering cups and plates onto the table with one hand while stuffing bread into the toaster with the other. The boy must've slept in one of the sheds. Max hadn't been surprised to see him; nor, when he arrived in the kitchen, beard spangled with the drops of his morning's ablutions, was Harry. While Connie, she supposed – if she had spared a thought for Maxie's whereabouts – wouldn't even have a phone on which to ring and enquire.

After breakfast Kate put the washing on, then returned to the kitchen to bake before the day heated up. The gas oven was a joy after the wood range and she finished as cool as she'd begun, though she'd scorched one tray of biscuits, having overestimated the temperature. Edie's recipe books with their beautiful copperplate writing used terms like *a smart, a quick* or *a slow* oven, which, while adequate for wood stoves, were difficult to translate into the degrees her new oven worked by.

Well, she'd get the hang of it eventually. She hung the washing on the length of line raised in the middle by a prop cut from the mallee, a device that had been old-fashioned in her childhood. She played for a while with Flip, teaching him to come to his name and gently pressing his wriggling body down to the command of 'Sit!' Then she watered the little colony of pot plants she'd amassed on the side verandah. Some had come from the Wantages', but the ferns she had bought in town, drawn by the cool green of their fronded stalks. Some day, she thought, looking out at the dried weeds furring what had been garden beds, she might do something with them, just for interest's sake. Given Harry's age, her job could only be viewed as temporary but she refused to look ahead. Starting a garden was not making a commitment to a place – not necessarily. If the job ended and the house fell empty, there would be heirs, or a caretaker anyway, to see to the upkeep of the place.

Kate glanced at her watch. Harry would be wanting his morning tea. An opportunity to talk to young Maxie, then. She went in to put the kettle on, but when it was time to call them she found the old man alone.

'Oh, he's gone home,' Harry dismissed her query. 'Smoko time already? All right, girl. I'm coming.'

'What's that?' Kate had not been beyond the door of the office before but now she stepped across to look at the artwork thumb-tacked to the wall. It was beautifully done, a pencil drawing of a mallee hen's mound with the bird atop and a young bushy tree filling part of the foreground.

'Not bad, eh?' Harry's pale eyes gleamed through the steel frames of his spectacles. 'There wouldn't be too many youngsters these days that'd know what a mound was. Young Maxie studies things, though. See the way it's drawn, the detail of it? There's dried leaves, seed cases, bits of stick – so clear it's like you could pick up the pieces in your fingers.'

'Has he done more like this?' Kate asked.

'He's always drawing.' Harry shooed her from the room. 'Ask him about it some time. Not that he's likely to tell you much. Now,' he rubbed his hands, 'did you make me some more of that cream cake, girl? Man gets to my age, he ought to be able to indulge himself in what he likes.'

'Even if it's bad for you?'

'Good, bad – that's for the young to worry about. Does that mean you haven't?'

'I've got a nice date loaf instead. Kinder to your arteries.'

'Bah!' he snorted. 'You want me to be immortal?'

'I want,' Kate said tartly, 'to keep my job, which means pre-serving my employer's life. Harry, can you manage if I take a few hours off this afternoon? Don't worry, I'll be back in time to make your dinner.'

'My Edie,' he said pointedly, 'got to town once a fortnight if that.'

'I'm not going to town. Just to The Narrows, the Wantages' place,' she added, for his memory seemed to come and go. 'It's the anniversary today; I thought Heather might appreciate a visit.'

'Anniversary?' He gave his cackle of laughter. 'Ten to one Ken's forgotten and your turning up will make it worse for the poor sod. But do as you please. In my experience women mostly do, for all it's supposed to be a man's world,' he grumbled.

'Thank you,' she said quietly. 'It's not their wedding anniversary. Her daughter went missing nineteen years ago today.'

'Ah.' His pale eyes blinked at her as his age-spotted hands lowered the delicate cup. 'I'm an old fool, Missy. You take as much time as you need. Poor woman. At least Edie and I never suffered that.'

But they had lost a child. She remembered the heartache of her miscarriage and thought how much worse the loss of a living child must be. Harry was so old it was hard to think of him as a parent, to remember that children had once shouted around this house, and caused their share of worry and exasperation. She offered him more tea and when he refused piled the cups together and carried them out, pausing in the doorway to say, 'I'll leave about two; mind you don't do anything silly while I'm gone.'

12

After two weeks at Rosebud the road was becoming familiar; Kate could now anticipate the gates. She drove slowly with the fan turned high and the wonky air conditioning off, watching galahs rise in pink and silver clouds from amid the stubble of the occasional harvested paddock. Most of the wheat was still there, paddocks of tawny gold spread below the baking heat of the sun. A wedge-tail took off from his perch on a post and winged heavily away, and through the open window she smelled sheep and dust and the sweetness of new-made hay. No haystacks now, of course, just the lines of round, rolled bales staggered across the paddocks not sown to crops. Mooky Lane drowsed in afternoon heat. She saw a rabbit crouched in the shade of a mallee tree, coloured junk mail flapping from the open mouth of a Brathway mailbox, and the solid dark green of the pine plantation looming beyond the entrance to Stones Place. The Narrows gate was just short of it. She had a sudden vision of herself and Megan jumping off the bus, and calling farewell as they skipped off to their respective homes, plaits and satchels bouncing against their backs. She blinked, steering the car into the turn-off, and stopped at the gate.

A wilting posy was tied to it. Kate swallowed and gently touched the dying flowers: celosia, cockscomb, carnations – all in shades of red; all, she guessed, from what had been her and Megan's garden plot beside the trellis. Heather must have kept it going with the same flowers. She pictured her each year, on the anniversary of her daughter's disappearance, leaving the posy of her child's favourite blooms on the gate that led to home. A memento? Or in the vain hope that one year the hands it was meant for would take up this token of remembrance and welcome, and bear it back to her? Kate pushed the gate wide, appalled by this fresh evidence of Heather's lifelong Calvary. She would never give up; only the discovery of her daughter's body could end the torment of hope and despair that consumed her days. And that was not going to happen, not after so many years.

Heather greeted her with a hug, her eyes bright. Ken was out, she said, as Kate patted Fly, who'd come nosing busily about her skirt.

'She can smell him on me, I expect. Flip.'

'Is that what you called him? How is he? Come in and I'll put the kettle on.'

'He's settled nicely. Seems to have his mother's brains, which is good. That flowerbed is so lovely.' Kate looked about her. 'Is that gypsophila? And they must be clove carnations – I can smell them from here. What's the vine over there? It makes a great shade.'

'Jasmine, pretty when it blooms. Thank you for coming today, Kate. It is why you're here, isn't it?'

'Yes,' she said simply. 'I thought you could probably use some company. I saw the flowers on the gate – still from that same old bed we used to grub about in?'

Heather nodded. 'I have to do it.' She led the way into the kitchen, setting the tea things out with the ease of long practice. 'It irritates Ken; hurts him too, I think, but I can't help myself.'

Kate nodded. 'Men move on more easily, I find. Perhaps they have to. I've never told anyone,' she swallowed, remembering, 'but I got pregnant the year after I married. Just for three months, then

I miscarried. I was utterly devastated. I felt – I don't know – so empty, so broken. The baby had been so real to me, whereas for Guy, after a week or two, it was like nothing had happened. Like I'd had the flu, perhaps. I still dream about it sometimes – that I'm pregnant again and I'm so happy – then I wake up and I just ache with loss.'

'I'm sorry, Katie. I never guessed. So you want children?'

'Not in my present circumstances, thank you. But some day . . . ' She sniffed, shaking her head as Heather put down the teapot. 'No, I'm all right, truly, just parched. Let's have that tea. And tell me what you know about a woman called Connie Hardy.'

'Connie,' Heather mused. 'Why ever . . . ? Well, not much at all, and that only by repute. She's a bit simple, they say. Lives with a couple of men – uncles or cousins, family anyway – on the old Macquarrie block and draws a disability pension, I believe. Why do you ask?'

Kate told her about Maxie. 'Harry seems to be the only one to take any responsibility for him. He comes and goes at all hours, even spends the night at Harry's place, though I haven't discovered where yet.' Her search of the sheds had failed to turn up anything. 'He draws very well. A quite amazing talent for his age; and apparently Harry's teaching him to read. I wanted to visit his mother but Max – Max Shephard, I mean – wouldn't have it.'

Heather's interest quickened. 'Oh, so you've been seeing him?'

'He comes and goes too, visiting Harry. The old man uses him for whatever he wants done – he's quite blatant about it – but Max doesn't seem to mind. He said they're related – he and Connie, I mean – so he keeps a sort of an eye on the boy, but the school seems to have given up on him and I just . . . I suppose it's none of my business really,' she finished in frustration. 'Schoolmarm-itis run mad.'

'If it's working, don't meddle.' Heather patted her hand. 'You were always conscientious. I finished the quilt.'

'Did you?'

They talked about that for a while, then Heather's eye turned to the carriage clock on the dresser. 'The bus would've just been pulling up,' she said quietly.

Kate, too, glanced at the clock's face, hearing the suddenly loud ticking of time passing. 'The next fifteen minutes,' Megan's mother continued, 'that's when it happened. I sit here on the anniversary and try to imagine . . . Where were you that day, Katie? I'm not blaming you, never think that, but the bus was on the road and it's just a ten-minute walk, *somebody* must have seen. How far away were you?'

'I don't know,' she answered wretchedly. 'We had a fight at school. It was the *stupidest* thing because you know we never argued! The bell went and I hid in the cloakroom until the bus left so I wouldn't have to get on it, then I walked home. It took longer than I thought it would. When you're a kid distances seem so short in the car. I was halfway through the pine plantation before I realised just how far it was. I ran most of the rest of the way. It had been going to be so special being in the pines . . . '

Only the row with Megan had soured the day, and her own boldness in walking had begun to scare her. Doug couldn't tell on her for missing the bus because like most high school kids he biked it, but even though her mother no longer waited at the gate, she'd still notice what time Kate got home. And it was going to be late – she'd be for it and no mistake. She had run then, her satchel growing heavier as her face crimsoned with effort. It was a long way through the pine plantation, a very long way for nine-year-old legs. The soft bed of needles made running harder while the sunlight, striped into golden bars between the shadows of the long, straight trunks, no longer delighted her. And the silence that hushed the birdsong and had seemed so enchanting had somehow turned creepy. She had burst from the edges of the trees with a feeling of relief, as of one escaping danger, scratching her legs on the barbs as she climbed through the fence, intent only on getting home.

The shadows had been long on Mooky Lane where the bus tracks lay in silent accusation. The shrill-voiced peewees had walked over the top of them, and she saw the thin line of Doug's bike wheels coming behind, the tracks of his boots around the gate and where he'd wheeled the bike and dropped it in the dry creek bed a little further on. Intending to spy on them, she'd supposed. They were usually home within five minutes of each other and he was always sneaking around watching the two of them. Then she'd run again as far as her pepper tree, and paused until her breathing steadied, then sauntered from there, readying a lie about stopping to play.

'I must have been at least an hour behind the bus,' she said. 'Anyway, you were there when I got home – you and Martin. Then the search started and pretty soon somebody – Dad, I think – called the police.' She looked down at her hands. 'I was desperate to say sorry to her by then – Megan. It was such a stupid thing to row about. Mum was mad at me, of course, but she never found out I wasn't on the bus. All the fuss distracted her and nobody talked of anything else for days, so I suppose she forgot to give me the usual third degree. And the policeman didn't ask. Heather,' she clasped the other woman's hand, 'does this do any good? Why don't you leave a note for Ken and come for a drive somewhere? We could go across to the Lake, or into town – wherever you want.'

Heather shook her head. 'No, Katie. Thanks all the same but not today. This is the day I keep vigil for my girl. It's the one time that I let myself think she won't ever come back, although tomorrow the hope will return. Does that seem mad to you?' Her eyes were dry but tears bled in her voice. She looked at the clock again. 'You'll have to be starting back; that old man will be needing you, and there's Flip as well. I'll work in the garden for a bit – I feel closer to her there – then Ken will come home and we'll pretend it's just another day. Martin might even ring this evening but he doesn't always remember.'

Kate hugged her and picked up her keys, saddened by her friend's pain. 'You're right. I must go, but I hate to leave you like this. How long can you mourn, Heather?'

'When it's your child?' she said. 'Forever.'

* * *

Next morning a strange Toyota pulled up before the farmhouse. Flip barked and Kate, looking through the curtains in the front room, called through the open door of the office, where Harry's tall frame was moving about.

'Visitor, Harry. Were you expecting someone?'

'No,' he said crankily, 'and I don't want to see whoever it is. Have you touched my papers, Missy? I can't find the sheet listing the district's bores.'

'Huh!' she said wickedly. 'You mean like Bert and Doreen Pringle, and —'

'Water bores,' he snapped. 'Well, have you? It was right here . . .'

'Then it probably still is. I haven't, but I'll help you look. Your visitor's coming this – Oh, God, it's Doug.'

'Who?'

'My brother. What does he want? I'll be right back, Harry.' She went out and Flip, who'd been barking at the stranger, ran thankfully to her side as she stepped down from the verandah to confront the tall, dark-haired man.

'What do you want here, Doug?'

'Katie,' he said lazily, 'is that any way to greet me, little sister?

I just wondered how you were, how you're getting on here. You haven't been back to see us and it's not like it's that far. You were at The Narrows yesterday; I was working the Pigeon paddock and saw your car. You could have dropped in. Aren't you the faintest bit interested in the farm?'

'Why should I be?' she asked bluntly. 'You don't want me there and neither does Mum.'

'Katie, Katie – always on the defensive. We're family, aren't we? Isn't that reason enough?'

'Hardly. Dad was my family. After him it's Ken and Heather. That's why I go there.' She stared suspiciously at him. 'How did you see my car anyway? That paddock doesn't overlook Ken's farmstead.'

'Unless I shifted the fence to improve the contours for plough-ing,' Doug suggested, 'which I did.' He smiled, the dimple flashing in his cheek. 'You're talking to a farmer now, you know. My left foot knows more about land than the old man ever did. The pup's one of Ken's, isn't it?' He squatted down and reached to click his fingers at the watching pup, who sat with cocked ears beside her. 'Waste of a likely working dog, really. Here, c'mere, boy.'

Flip tensed, then uttered a sharp yap and edged behind Kate's heels. 'Leave him,' she said sharply. 'You should know better.'

Doug laughed, the superior, pitying laugh she had always hated. 'Oh, training a worker, are you? Don't kid yourself, Katie. You're what? A cook, a glorified housekeeper to a pensioner? What do you want with a working dog? Where is the old man, anyway?'

'Mr Quickly is inside. He doesn't want to see you; he expressly said so. Neither do I, so you'd better leave – and don't bother com-ing back.' With Flip at her heels she mounted the steps, her back stiff, and lifted the pup into his temporary cage. She had grasped the doorknob before he spoke again.

'Temper, Katie. You're such a spitfire. Maybe things

are different now, or could be. Don't you even want to see your nephews? Young Andy was asking why you don't come visit him. Seems he's taken a shine to you, which is odd after only seeing you the once. Am I to tell him you don't consider yourself his aunt?'

She wavered, knowing it for a lie and wondering at the purpose behind it. 'I'm a housekeeper, remember?' she said coldly. 'I have meals to cook, a house to run. But there's nothing to stop Clover bringing the children for a visit. Andy and his mother can come any time they like; after all, with Mum still running things at Stones Place she must have time on her hands.' She didn't wait for an answer but went in, shutting the door behind her. What had he meant by *only seeing you the once*? Had somebody mentioned the meetings in town? Clover had begged her to keep them secret.

Kate's hands were trembling and she felt a little sick. It dismayed her; she thought she'd outgrown her fear of him, but the mere sound of that hated voice had reduced her to jelly. The old sick dread of childhood surfaced, mixed with the remembered impotent fury of knowing that he would get away with whatever stroke he'd pulled – because he always did.

'You all right, girl?' Harry asked. He'd come out of the office and was giving her a concerned look. She heard the Toyota start up and drive off, and blew out her breath.

'I'm fine, thanks.'

'Edie used to say that when she had one of her migraines coming on,' he said unexpectedly. 'You're shaking. Here, sit down. What did he say to you?'

'Oh, Harry.' Inexplicably she felt like crying. She sat where directed and managed a smile for the old man. 'Family baggage. My brother and I don't have a good history. Did you have brothers?'

'Two, and six sisters. All redheads. All gone now, save Gloria. She's more than a decade older than me and nutty as a fruitcake.

They've got her in a home down in Elizabeth. So what'd he come for?'

'Specifically? I don't know.' She lifted her arm, tracing the invisible scar about her right wrist that Doug's hands had imprinted on her memory. 'When I was little he'd catch me and give me Chinese burns. He was always watching me – us,' she corrected. 'He's not a very nice person, my brother. I don't understand him. I never did. I was scared of him when I was a kid and now I find I still am. Isn't that pathetic?'

'Sounds intelligent to me. He comes back, I'll warn him off for good.'

Alarmed, she caught his arm. 'No, it's all right. Please, don't do anything to – to get his notice. I've already told him not to come back.'

Harry snorted. 'It's my property. I'll tell him again. What's he going to do to me?'

'I don't know. Something.' She looked wildly at him, aching for him to understand and believe her. 'Everybody's fooled by him. They think he's a reasonable, civilized man. They've even voted him onto the council, for heaven's sake! That shows you. He's a Rotarian, too, and his wife says he's got pals on the police force. He beats her up, by the way, but nobody would believe it. You don't want to annoy a man like that.' She remembered his missing paper and rose, thankful for the diversion. 'Now, let's find this list you've misplaced before I make a start on lunch.'

13

Harry's papers were a mess. Kate, turning over piles of pages filled with looping longhand marred by crossed-out sections, shook her head in disbelief. 'How long have you been working on this?'

'A long time,' he grumbled. 'It'd go faster if the bit I wanted wasn't always getting mislaid.'

'You need a system, Harry. This —' she shifted a pile of paper, bent to pick a dozen sheets from the floor and sought for somewhere to put them on the crowded desk, 'is hopeless. Why not have each chapter typed as it's finished?'

'Because it may not be,' he said irritably. 'Finished, I mean. There's always something more turns up. Like with these bores. Did you know that Joshua Stone's grandson William put down the original bore for the district? Your family was the first round here to go off tank water.'

'Really? And that matters enough to be included?'

'Well, of course it does,' he said testily. 'William also started the old market gardens that fed Laradale in the early days. Think, girl! How much small cropping can you do on a rainwater tank? Or a river that's dry ninety per cent of the time? The Victorian goldfields had their Chinese market gardens but they had permanent water, too. Back then, prior to the bores going down, every spud and onion the pioneers ate had to come from Adelaide. You think about that. They used to say about the Stones that they could smell an opportunity across a paddock. They were smart, got the pick of the land and never missed a chance to improve it. Your brother's sitting pretty today because of it – and because he's reckoned to know his job, of course.'

'Really?' Kate repeated, genuinely surprised. 'I thought all farmers were doing it tough?'

'The ones with no padding behind them are. I wouldn't count the Doolins amongst them. It's why your coming here was, well —' He paused, then bent to pick up a sheet. 'Ah,' he exclaimed unconvincingly. 'Wondered where I'd put that.'

'What?' Perching herself on the corner of the cluttered desk, she raised a brow, a quelling action she had perfected in her first year in the classroom. 'Not the paper, the other. You might as well tell me what you started to say.'

'You bully a man, Missy. It's just, I never expected a Doolin would *need* a job. Not with the money your family's got.'

'That's them,' she said briefly, 'not me. Can I say something, Harry, about this project of yours?'

'Huh! Can I stop you? That's the question. What is it?'

'If you really want to make sense of all this,' she swept a hand over the littered desk, 'to finish it, produce a proper manuscript, then you need a computer. It's the only way you're going to do it.'

'You're wrong there. I wouldn't know how to turn it on. I was going to get a typewriting machine,' he confessed regretfully. 'Edie would've learned to use it – she had that sort of patience – but it was about the time she fell sick . . . '

Kate shook her head. 'Typewriters only type. With a computer you can organise and file, even print out your pages, given the proper equipment. Trust me, all this – this mess – could be a neat file you could access in a moment. No more papers to lose. You can cut and paste to swap sections around, you can —'

'And how long's it going to take for me to learn to do all that, hey? You think I'm immortal, girl? When I close my eyes at night it's not like there's a guarantee they'll ever open again.'

'You don't have to learn,' Kate said. 'If you get a computer, I'll type up whatever you produce and you can bin all this. Anything you want to check on, or amend, will be there in the files. A couple of hours a day should cover it; I'd expect a bit extra for my time, of course.'

'Ha!' Harry crowed as if spotting a catch. 'What'd I say about Stones and opportunity? I swear you're in league with the electricity company with your stoves and your computers. You'll be wanting a new washing machine next.'

Kate grinned. 'A vacuum cleaner,' she said. 'And the stove runs on gas. Talk to Max about it. I'll bet he uses one to do his accounts. Here,' she glimpsed the corner of a sheet behind a copy of *Dry Land Farming* and waved it, 'is this what you're looking for?'

'Ah, yes,' Harry felt for the chair back and lowered himself into it, 'that's the one. Now, where'd I put those dates . . . ?' Humming to himself, he leafed slowly through the nearest pile. Kate left him to it. There was ironing to be done, meat to defrost for dinner, and lunch to get on the table.

* * *

The days went by, and the weeks. Maxie came and went and Flip's roly-poly shape turned leggy, his outsized feet and clumsy antics a cause for smiles. Maxie produced a drawing showing Flip standing prick-eared with a lolling tongue, and left it in the kitchen for Kate to find. She bought a frame and kept it by her bed. Doug didn't come again, nor did Clover visit. Kate had not expected her to, and running into her again in town, found that Doug hadn't told her of their meeting or her invitation.

'So, how are your plans for getting away?' she asked. They were in the library at Clover's request, Andy one of the half-dozen youngsters being read to in the Children's Circle.

'I'm saving,' her sister-in-law said. She twisted the ring on her finger. 'Even when I've got the money, leaving the farm will be the hard part. I'll have to wait until he's away for a couple of days.'

Kate nodded at her expanding waistline. 'You can't afford to wait too long, Clove. What are you now, five months?'

'And a bit. I know. Could I – if I could arrange for a friend to pick me up – could I send her to you, Kate, just to have somewhere to wait? I mean, she can't come to town. You know how strangers stick out in a place like this. Doug would find out.'

'How?' Kate asked practically. 'Don't be paranoid, Clove. He's a nasty piece of work but he doesn't have supernatural powers.'

'He doesn't need them,' Clover said bitterly. 'His copper mates would just have to ask who'd been booked in at the Railway Arms or the Melbourne. Or they'd look at the CCTV tapes at the roadhouse and he'd know. So can I?'

'Yes, of course.' Kate hesitated. 'Does your friend know what sort of man Doug is? I mean, he's going to be very angry when he learns — It's only fair that she knows what she's getting into.'

Clover's face showed a rare animation. 'I met Bea at uni. She's a lawyer now; she specialises in divorce and custody cases, and does pro bono work for a women's shelter in Adelaide. She'll be handling things for me. I imagine she's dealt with plenty of abusive men.'

'Good for you,' Kate said warmly. 'A lawyer's just what you need.' A thought struck her. 'Does Doug know about her? Would he guess you'd contact her?'

'I don't think so. I mean, I haven't kept up with my girlfriends from back then. I meant to but Doug didn't like most of them. They were too mannish or assertive, he said; by which he meant that they dared to argue with him. I was so besotted that I thought he was jealous of them and wanted me all to himself, and was stupid enough to feel flattered,' she confessed. 'I was right too, only not in the way I imagined, because I mistook ownership for love. Mary and Rog came to visit once but your mother didn't make them welcome, and Doug ignored them – when he wasn't making fun of Rog. It was horrible! I was so embarrassed and ashamed . . . I never asked them again. I never asked any of the others, either – I couldn't. When I wrote to Bea it was the first contact we'd had in years.'

'All to the good.' Kate fished in her bag for a pen. 'Give her my name, and this is Harry's number.' She scribbled it down. 'I'll make it right with him. He can be an old bear, but he wouldn't refuse to help.' She glanced at her watch. 'Now, I must go. I've still got plants to pick up from Greenthumbs.'

A flash of remorse crossed Clover's face. 'I never even asked how you're getting on with old Mr Quickly. It must be lonely stuck out there with an old man. I suppose a gardenbed will help fill your time.'

Kate laughed. 'I'm acting as his secretary as well as his cook and housekeeper; between Harry, Maxie and my pup, I don't *have* any spare time to fill. I like it.'

'You look better than you did when you came to visit,' Clover conceded. 'More content,' she said enviously, as if it was a state she could no longer aspire to.

'I am.' The realisation surprised Kate. 'Got to run, Clove. Take care.' She brushed a kiss onto her sister-in-law's cheek and left, the automatic doors sighing shut behind her. Crossing the street with the sun in her eyes, she failed to see the man get out of the Toyota, parked a little way behind her, and stand watching her walk away.

Clover, gathering up handbag and toddler pack a few minutes later, ignored the sound of the electronic door opening. Then she raised her eyes to the figure approaching her and froze as they found her husband's face. 'W-what are you doing here, Doug?'

He glanced around at the book-filled shelves and scattered chairs, at the busy desk and the filled seats before the rank of computers against the far wall. 'Meeting my wife,' he said, relishing the panic in her gaze. 'It seems to be what you do here, meet people. Have a nice talk with Kathryn, did you?'

'I – she – we ran into each other.' Clover's voice jumped nervously.

'Funny,' he said, 'she didn't seem to carry any books out. That's what libraries are for, isn't it? Lending books. You haven't been having a girlish heart-to-heart, by any chance?' His hand closed firmly about her wrist, squeezing the bones. 'Because I won't have that, Clover. You do understand that, don't you?' It took an effort of will not to crush the bones within his hand. He could feel the desire pumping in his blood – the need to hurt; it had always been this way with him. He had never wondered why, or why satisfying the need was so essential, but maturity had at least made him careful. If the act was viewed as wrong by the rest of the world, then it must be done in private.

Her brown eyes shifted from his and panic drove her to inspiration. 'She was checking her emails, for heaven's sake! I brought Andy in for the storytelling and saw her. She said you'd visited her and she'd invited me to bring the children out there. Why didn't you tell me, Doug?'

'Because you're not going. If she wants to see her family, she can come to Stones Place. I'll not have my sons making a second home someplace else the way she always did.'

'That's ridiculous,' Clover said faintly, then blanched at the sudden flare of anger in her husband's face. Her soul shrank within her, for she had learned early in their married life never to criticise.

'*What* did you say?'

'N-nothing. Only one visit isn't – besides, her friend lived at The Narrows. You can't keep your children from having friends . . . ' She swallowed, saying tightly in a quivering voice, 'You're hurting me, Doug.'

'Just remember that I can. Get my son. We're going home.'

'But I haven't finished the shopping.'

'Too bad.' He shoved her urgently. 'Get him now. We're leaving.'

* * *

November fled into the arms of December. Kate, dividing her time between office, kitchen and garden, scarcely noticed the days passing. Maxie had ceased to view her as an enemy and cheerfully minded the household rules she introduced. He wiped his feet and washed his hands, and whenever he turned up went first to the kitchen. He never asked but his gaze moved hopefully from her to the cake tin and she seldom disappointed him, even if it was in the shape of a sandwich or a piece of fruit rather than the preferred cake.

'It'll save you visits to the dentist,' she said, while privately acknowledging that there would very likely be no one to take him.

'Yes, Miss. Thank you, Miss,' he invariably replied, following it with one of two questions. 'Can I play with Flip?' or 'Can I have a go on the computer, Miss?'

'Ask Harry,' she always answered to the latter. Despite having made the suggestion, she had been surprised when Max carried the bulky carton into the house. She'd never really expected Harry to follow through. Max, however, had been enthusiastic about the whole thing.

'It's a great idea, Kate. I should've thought of it myself. Most old blokes'd never manage but Harry's always been a forward thinker. He'll wind up knowing more about it than me.'

'I don't think that's likely.' She had sat on the floor with him amid the discarded plastic and styrofoam, watching as he unpacked the leads and read the booklet. He crawled about on his knees locating sockets and squinting at symbols on plugs and outlets.

'Here —' She'd taken the multilanguage pamphlet from him. 'I'll read, you do it. You want the red lead next, for the printer. Look, there it is.' In this fashion, hands touching and their heads occasionally bumping, they'd got the monitor and hard drive connected, the set of tiny speakers sorted and the electrical cords taped out of the way of elderly feet. She'd made coffee for them then while he ran the disks to install the various programs. He'd even stuffed all the packing back into the boxes and slung them onto the Toyota tray. 'I'll get rid of them in town,' he'd said. Guy, had he known, would have lectured her about not using the incinerator during the height of the fire season, but Max assumed she already knew. It was strange what a bond shared knowledge created. She felt at home with him in an undemanding way that was both warming and comfortable, like a favourite jacket – and had to smile at the absurdity of the comparison. Straightening the mouse on its pad, she'd booted up, then gone to find Harry, nervous now and wondering if this was going to work. How many men of his age learned computer skills?

She needn't have worried. Both the old man and the boy took to it like cats to cream. Over the next few weeks Kate typed up his manuscript, but Harry rapidly progressed to the point where he could open the file and search through it to check on points, and even add a shaky sentence. 'There's just one rule to remember,' Kate said. 'Always hit *save* before you close.'

'And if I don't, Missy? Does that mean it's lost?'

'No, because I back it up – make a copy – every day. It just means you'd have to put the sentence back in. Don't worry, you're doing great. You and Maxie both. Games won't hold him for long. He's going to really want to read now so he can do more.' She hesitated. 'If you like, I could type in a lesson for him – whatever it is he's working on at present. You can do it in different colours, you know, and change the size of the letters, make little pictures, put it in columns. It would add some novelty to the task. Kids like that.'

The white bush of his brows pulled together. She said hastily, 'It was just an idea, Harry.'

'Max told me you're a teacher,' he said. 'I'd forgotten. Hell – why not, if you want to? Only you won't be screwing more wages out of me for it, Missy.'

'Perish the thought.' She grinned at him. 'I'm still hanging out for that vacuum cleaner.'

* * *

A day or two later Maxie brought her a sketch of the old harness shed with the pepper tree beside it and two of the half-wild bantam hens in the foreground. It was a beautifully balanced work spoiled only by the clumsily shaped *Thanks* across the bottom corner where the artist's signature would normally be. The S and the A were back to front. Kate examined it carefully. 'It's beautiful, Maxie. The writing too. You know what it says?'

He gave her an affronted look. 'Course I do, Miss. I wrote it, din' I? Says *Thanks* – for the story, like. Harry said maybe you could do another one, if I asked?'

'I certainly will.' She could surely find some educational software in town.

'Harry said I should give you a hand for a bit. He's having his nap,' Maxie explained. 'So maybe I could help you train Flip?' It was said so hopefully that she had to smile.

'I was actually going to work in the garden bed while it's in the shade. It's full of old grass, and the borders are all broken. If you wanted to help with that . . . ?'

He looked disappointed but nodded manfully as she pulled on gardening gloves and led the way to the side of the house, where the patch of ground she'd been soaking with the hose waited with its burden of old weeds. There'd been rusty gardening tools in one of the many sheds, along with the leaky hose she'd mended with a bit of plastic tape.

In her case, Kate thought wryly, nurture had won out over nature. Save for the cactus plants along the front of the house, and a hardy oleander or two, there'd been no garden at Stones Place, but if she put her energies into a single bed, she might achieve a shadow of what Heather had created. Megan's mother had taught them both to cherish growing things and wherever Kate had lived she had always grown something, if only pot plants. Rosebud's barren yard was a daunting task, but then so were Harry's efforts to change the future of the child beside her. The old boy was as pig-headed in his way as Brian Doolin had always accused his daughter of being. She smiled at the thought, and then at the quiet boy with the net of shadow across his face, standing awaiting her direction.

'Right, let's get started. Do you want to have a go with the fork, or the digger?'

14

The garden bed took shape slowly. Kate borrowed books from the gardening section in the library and started a compost heap with household scraps and whatever old leaves and rubbish she could rake up. Max, calling in for a visit, cast a knowledgeable eye over her efforts and said, 'You want a bit of manure, both for that and the garden bed.'

'Oh, yes?' Kate sleeved sweat from her face, then pulled off her hat and fanned herself. 'How much gardening have you done?'

He grinned. 'I'm a farmer. What's that but gardening on a large scale? Tell you what, there's the old sheep yards at Crow Creek only three k's from here. I could clear out the back of the vehicle and bring you a load.'

'Would you? I mean, it's a kind offer, very kind, but have you got time?'

'Yeah, I'm between contracts at the moment, for a day or so.' He looked dubiously at the narrow-bladed shovel Maxie was using. 'You got anything bigger than that?'

'There's probably something in the sheds; Maxie will know.'

He did. The two went off together and Kate returned to the kitchen to make morning tea for herself and Harry, then type up his previous day's work. 'Max is here,' she told him. 'He's gone for a load of manure just now but I expect he'll stay for lunch. What's this word here? I can't quite make it out. And you haven't given a name to that farmer who concreted the drums of petrol into his underground water tank during the war. Did that really happen, Harry? Or was it something you made up?'

He peered over her shoulder. '*Judgement* – plain as a shearer's duds, girl. Of course I didn't make it up! I'm writing history, not lies. It was Vic Brathway from Roadsend farm. Stubborn old coot but sharp enough in his way, though you didn't have to be Einstein to know that with a war on, fuel was going to be short. Stood to reason the armed forces'd have first call on it, and the further out you were the less you were likely to get. So he took his own measures, but he didn't know the whole story, because the drums were all numbered. And when the fuel companies finally called in the numbers, he had to dig them out again. He was done for hoarding. Serious offence that, back in the forties.'

Kate laughed. 'This book'll see you hanged, Harry. But I'm really enjoying it. I wonder if Max has learned anything about your lost woolshed yet?'

He had, and he'd marked the position on the big pastoral map that was slowly filling up with pencilled notations so that it now contained two layers of information – the present configuration of the properties, and as they had once been.

'It's fascinating,' he'd said, studying the scores of notations. 'The original boundary lines and the old roads – they're all so different. There were a dozen more farms then than exist now. Not to mention the old tin mine workings, and at least four more woolsheds. There must've been twice the population then. It's like a different landscape. All the old stuff's gone now and pretty conclusively too. I damn near did a tyre on the one I was looking for. The grass had covered the stumps and there was nothing else around but rotted timber and a few sheets of tin.'

'What about the grave?' Harry asked then. 'It ought to be near.

According to the stories, he hanged himself in the shed, so he should've been buried somewhere close.'

Max had shaken his head. 'I couldn't find anything. Of course the grave fence, if there was one, might've rotted away, or been burnt in a bushfire. Maybe it happened at another shed? Or the body was carted away after all?'

'I'll think about it.' Harry's gnarled fingers combed through his splendid beard. 'I can't be the only old bugger left alive round here. There's got to be someone still breathing who knows something about it.' He pottered off and Max gave a mock groan. 'Five to one he'll recall somebody's second cousin's aunt – probably senile at that – and have me chasing after her.'

'You're very good to him,' Kate said. 'Have you got the name of the dead man? I might be able to google it at the library.' Her eyes twinkled. 'Save you some fuel, perhaps. I owe you one for the manure.' She sniffed then and he grinned.

'I dusted myself down and flogged my shirt on a rail but the stink tends to cling, doesn't it? Your plants'll shoot ahead, though. Look, I was wondering if you could help me out with something, Kate?'

'Of course, if I can. What is it?'

'No big deal – except,' he added ruefully, 'Aunt Rita definitely is. It's the annual Growers' Dinner on the fifteenth and she expects me to escort her and I thought – well, I wondered – if you'd accompany me instead, so I've got a legitimate excuse? Because I'm sunk if you won't, Kate.' He looked at her with the same hopefulness with which Maxie eyed the cake tin.

'You mean Stanley Quickly's widow – *that* Rita?'

He nodded.

'And she hasn't changed? She's still —'

' . . . the same obstinate, loudmouthed terror, with the cow-caller's voice,' he said gloomily, 'that gets louder by the drink.

Which she still puts away like a teller packing bank notes ahead of a flood.'

'You could always stay home.'

He sighed. 'Not really. Bad for business. A fair bit of it gets done at the dinner. Next season's contracts, that sort of thing. Put a heap of farmers together in one room and —'

'I know,' she said dryly. 'Teachers suffer from the same problem too. I expect spies are the only professionals that don't. Thank you, then. I will come.'

'Thank *you*. You've saved the evening. And no strings, Kate. I mean,' his gaze strayed and for a moment she almost thought he coloured under his tan, 'I'm taking you out as a friend – I'd like to think we are friends now. You don't have to dance or – or anything.'

'Is it a dinner dance?' Fleetingly she wondered what *anything* covered. 'I haven't been to one of those for a while. I'll wear something appropriate then, and we'll see, shall we – unless you don't dance?'

'I learned.' He grinned. 'I have talents that amaze, Ms Doolin – gasfitter, dung loader, dancer – you haven't seen the half of them yet.'

'I believe you,' she said, and was still smiling when he left.

* * *

The fifteenth was a week away. It had been several years since Kate had attended a function that included dancing. She spent the afternoon wondering what she could wear and next day took the problem to Heather, along with a shiny scarlet top, the only item in her wardrobe remotely like evening wear.

Ken was leaving the shed on the four-wheeler, Flash riding up behind, as she pulled up. He roared off without seeing her. She followed the smell of baking into the kitchen, calling, 'Just me,' from habit as she entered, then winced at her choice of words. Like an echo in her head chimed the childish treble, *'Just us, Mum.'* She hoped Heather hadn't noticed, and to cover it inhaled deeply as the door swung to behind her. 'Mmm, what's this? The national bake-off?'

'Hello, Katie.' Heather smiled at her across the top of the ginger cake she was turning onto a cooling rack. A filled sponge sat beside it, and a score of partly iced patty cakes. 'Martin's coming for a visit later this week. I thought I'd stock up the freezer. If you've time for a cuppa, we can sample the baking.'

'Always,' she assured her. 'It'll be lovely to see Martin. How long's he staying?'

'He didn't say. A few days, I expect. Ken's as pleased as punch. You must come for dinner one night; he'll want to catch up, I know.'

'I'd like that,' she said, taking cups from the dresser. 'Does the sugar still . . . yes, I see it does.' She got it out, went to the fridge for the milk. 'Are you planning on going to the Growers' Dinner?'

'Probably. It depends on Martin, really. Why?'

Kate explained as they drank their tea. 'He's been so helpful I couldn't really refuse. I mean, I pity any man stuck with Rita Quickly, aunt or not. But I really don't have anything to wear except this – half an outfit.' She lifted the top from her bag.

'It's lovely.' Heather stroked the shimmery fabric. 'Just your colour. So you'll be Max's excuse. Trust him to think of something like that.' She smiled faintly. 'So, you want to go shopping for a skirt to go with this?'

'Waste of time in Laradale. No, what I hoped was that Lasson's might have some suitable material that I could prevail upon you to make up for me. The dinner's a week away. What should I look for, Heather? Better still, could you come in with me and help me choose?'

'What about we see what I've got first? Ken always says I could put Lasson's out of business. Let's have a look. It could save a trip to town.'

Heather was as good as her word. Driving home again with a bunch of flowers and a box of vine-ripened tomatoes on the seat beside her, Kate thought that Ken was right. Heather's capacious material cupboard was augmented by plastic storage boxes filled with every style and type of fabric, and it had taken her no time at all to choose something to complement the red top.

'It's so good of you to do this,' Kate had said. 'I'm hopeless at it. Harry's got an old machine I could probably use but I wouldn't know where to start.'

'I shall enjoy it. Sewing for a daughter is one of the things I've missed.' Heather blinked suddenly and hugged Kate. 'It's lovely to have something special to work on. Thanks for asking me.'

'What about Martin? I feel bad that I'm taking away from your time with him.'

'Nonsense. I'll bring it over Thursday. I'd like to see what you've made of the old place. It was a lovely farmhouse in its day, you know. Harry ran sheep all through the boom years of the fifties. It was only when the prices got so bad that he started cropping. Edie Quickly had money to work with but she had a real flair as a homemaker anyway. They gave tennis parties, oh, forty years ago, the like of which the district hasn't seen since. People came and stayed over using the shearers' quarters. They pulled down the shearing shed when wool went bad – sold it off, I believe. The garden was beautiful; I thought it was the most glamorous place I'd ever seen. That big bougainvillea arch that covered the tables of cold drinks – oh, and sponges, and fairy cakes and mince pies – I've never forgotten that. All the different colours planted together. It was like some magic, extravagant rainbow and so wide you could get a table under it with shade to spare.'

'There's not much left of it now,' Kate said. 'A couple of stumps that have collapsed over some old features. It still flowers but it's just the one colour now and hasn't been pruned or watered in twenty years. Everything else's gone but Harry's trees.'

'It shows what can be done, though,' Heather had said as she'd waved Kate off from the garden where a sprinkler turned in the shade, and blue and yellow daisies made a bold splash of colour – *a bit like one of her own patchworks*, Kate thought, with the brilliant sky behind her and the rust red of a shed roof peeping through the pendant green foliage of the pepper tree.

As the days passed Kate found herself looking forward to the dinner. It had been a long time since she'd attended anything more formal than a coffee with her fellow teachers after school. Occasionally she'd accompanied a friend to a film she'd wanted to see, or spent an hour or two at the beach, but never with Guy. She couldn't remember when he'd last taken her out. If his firm had dinners, he'd either lied about it, or escorted his current girlfriend to them in her place.

She had left him once for three months when she'd discovered he was sleeping with the office receptionist. They'd been married four years then, and her biggest mistake – apart from the marriage itself – had been letting him sweet-talk her into going back. She should have cut the tie then instead of sticking it out. Marriage without trust was a sham; she had despised herself for it at the time, but even when she knew he was trying (and he did try for eight months or so) she could never fully believe that he wasn't seeing someone else. She'd felt guilty then for not trusting him, telling herself that her actions were pushing him into the arms of another woman. But trust wasn't something you could command. It had to be built, the logical side of her argued. In a way it had been almost a relief to uncover his next lie, because it meant her instincts had been true and proved that her inability to trust was not a character defect, but sound common sense.

Kate sighed, remembering. She should have left for good then, but it had taken another five years of struggle and rows before she'd finally given up. *You could give lessons to mules, Katie.* Brian Doolin's exasperated tones echoed in her head and her own smart, seventeen-year-old rejoinder: *And I wonder where I got that from?* But he'd had children, she reminded herself. He'd stayed married for them – for her. Her only excuse was an inability to publicly admit to a mistake. Well, it was all last year's crop now, to further quote her father. Rage had propelled her journey south but even that had faded. Guy was a part of the past and, if she was honest, the loss of her career grieved her more than his absence.

* * *

On Thursday the Wantages' dusty Ford pulled up at the gate. Flip barked and Harry, returning to the office where Maxie was doing his lessons, paused mid-step.

'Who's that? It's like Rundle Street round here lately.'

'What, at midnight?' Kate asked. 'It'll be Heather Wantage. She's bringing me something to wear for tomorrow night.' Not sure that she'd told him, she said, 'I'm going to the Growers' Dinner with Max so he doesn't have to take Rita. You remember Rita – Stanley Quickly's widow? But don't worry, I'll see to your dinner first.'

'Huh!' He looked at her under his brows. 'I might be old, Missy, but I've still got all my marbles. Maybe I'm slow on names but facts are different. And the fact is Rita moved away and remarried years ago.'

'What?' She paused, hand already pushing the screen open. 'But —' Heather waved and she waved back, calling a greeting. Ken was with her. She said quickly, 'I'll make some tea, shall I, Harry? It's a little early but —'

'Yes, yes. I'll come out and do the polite presently. This place has become a madhouse,' he grumbled just loud enough to be heard. She grinned, knowing he didn't mean it, and hurried down the path to meet her friends.

It was Martin, not Ken. Kate stopped in surprise, then went forward to hug him with unreserved pleasure. 'I thought you were Ken. Your walk's the same. Well, how are you, Martin? You don't look a bit different to last time, only bigger.'

'You do.' He grinned down at her. 'You've got prettier, Katie.' He winked, his easy lopsided smile carrying her back to childhood, when he had called her Princess and devised endless games for her and Megan's amusement. It was no wonder, Kate reflected, that they'd adored him.

'And Heather tells me you're still walking around unclaimed?' She grinned back. 'A handsome guy like you? No girls where you work, or are they all blind?'

'Nope, just none from the country. Still, now you're here . . . '

'Martin,' Heather protested, 'behave yourself!' She gazed around, taking in the rickety shape of the old verandah, the leggy pup at Kate's side and the flourishing green of the bed she and Maxie had laboured over, where the first cosmos flower shone like a gold penny on a stalk. 'My, Kate, your plants look so well! And just see the size of that pup. What have you got in the pots?'

Kate recounted their names, then ushered the Wantages inside, where Harry and Martin soon found common ground. Maxie had vanished again. In the kitchen Kate switched the gas on under the kettle and turned to her friend.

'What's it like? Can I see?'

'Of course.' She pulled it from her bag and held it up, a soft ripple of some synthetic black material that fell straight to the hips, then flared into a gathered skirt that came to just below knee-length, ending in a fall of frothy black lace.

'It's beautiful, Heather.' Kate held it against her, admiring the invisible zip at centre back. 'It'll be just perfect with that top. Oh, thank you! And I've a very fine wrap, like a black spider web, in case —'

'What? It gets cold?' Heather laughed. 'You know I've had that bit of material for years. Can't even remember where I got it, it was so long ago. It was a real treat to make it up at last. I can't wait to see you wearing it.'

'Then you're coming to the dinner?'

'All three of us. It'll be fun.' She looked about the kitchen with its timber cupboards, and the old settee against the wall. The pine table was scrubbed to a creamy yellow, and the glass-fronted dresser displayed standing plates and flowered milk jugs. A glowing copper pot containing a bunch of reddened mallee tips sat on top of the cupboard beside Maxie's framed sketch of the shed.

Heather touched it. 'That's a nice drawing; simple but homely. It's a lovely room – perhaps a new sink wouldn't be out of place, but the rest looks great.'

'The gas stove helps, but I've seen younger fridges,' Kate agreed. 'Still, everything works.'

'That's the main thing. Old Mrs Quickly would be pleased if the rest of the house is as well kept as this. How long did it take you to shine that pot?'

'Quite a while.' Kate picked up the tray. 'Can you bring the tea? And by the way,' she fixed her friend with a mock frown, 'when were you going to tell me that Max's aunt, the one I'm supposedly protecting him from, had left the district?'

'I wasn't,' Heather said serenely. 'I wanted to see you in that skirt.'

15

The following night Kate left a cold supper for Harry and Maxie, who was still present when she set it out. Dressed and ready, she came in to the old-fashioned sitting room, only used for watching TV, to remind them to rinse the dishes afterwards.

'And no sneaking Flip indoors,' she admonished Maxie.

'No, Miss.' He stared at her wide-eyed. 'You look real pretty, Miss.'

'Thank you, Maxie.'

'He's right. You're a picture.' Harry got up. 'I like the red earrings. Enjoy yourself tonight. I reckon it's about time you did.'

Touched, she said, 'Why, Harry, I'm fine, but thank you anyway.'

The eyes under his bristling brows were wise, and sharper than she liked. 'There's no fooling an old fool, girl. Forget your troubles and have a bit of fun. You got a key?'

'Right here. You two behave yourselves.' On an impulse she kissed his whiskered cheek. 'There's Max now. I'll see you in the morning.'

Max, his rangy body encased in grey trousers and a cream shirt fastened at the neck with a maroon tie, looked very different to his workday self. He came forward smiling to greet her, his wiry hair carefully combed and a shine on his town shoes. 'Evening, Kate.' He caught the whistle before it reached his lips as his appreciative gaze took in the slim shape in the shimmering top and frothy skirt. There were strappy sandals on her feet and she carried a small red clutch purse and a filmy black wrap. 'You look beautiful,' he said reverently. The shining bell of her hair, the angle of her cheekbones and the rich red of her lipstick held him so spellbound that she had almost reached the vehicle before he sprang forward to open the door.

'Good evening, Max. Thank you. You're very smart yourself.' The Toyota had been washed inside and out and a cover stretched over the seats. His suit jacket lay folded on her seat and she lifted it onto her lap as he pulled the seatbelt down for her and carefully closed the door. Behind the wheel he inhaled her fragrance and smiled for no reason – save that she was there with her slender legs and sweetly curved body, and that quick, infrequent smile that lit the grey eyes he would do anything to rid of the sadness he'd sometimes glimpsed there. But right now they sparkled with happy anticipation.

'Do you think you'll wear it?' She meant the coat and he pulled his thoughts into order.

'Maybe. The dinner's at the Civic Centre,' he said, and by way of explanation, 'new air conditioning.' He glanced across at her as they started off. 'Did you ever go to the old hall in Delia Street for the Christmas plays, Kate?'

'Oh, yes. It was always the same – first the play, then Santa's visit. We loved it when we were little. It was quite our favourite entertainment, despite always being so hot. No ceiling fans, remember? I was a kitten in the play one year. I must've been five, I think. I fell in love with the costume but it was so hot I sweated my whiskers off, then sat on the stage and bawled about it. That's child actors for you.' She laughed. 'I thought you grew up somewhere else?'

'I did but a couple of times I was staying with my Quickly cousins and we all went.'

'Maybe we even met?' she said. 'I don't remember.'

'No.' He was positive about it. There was no way, he thought, that he could have forgotten.

* * *

The Civic Centre had wood-panelled walls that sported an honour board, and a dais from which the band played soft dinner music. The tables were arranged in a half-circle about it, and the local member headed a shortlist of speakers. The MP was a farmer and kept his words short, perhaps the reason he had been clapped to the echo by his fellow diners. *There's a good crowd*, Kate thought, twisting about in her chair. All the tables were taken if not filled, and the waiters had worked hard to serve them all. She'd seen the Wantages, and wriggled her fingers at Bert and Doreen Pringle in the corner, and recognised at another table the woman who worked in the library but who was obviously, judging by her leathery-skinned companion, a farmer's wife. Now, folding her napkin and laying it beside the glass bowl in which the *crème brûlée* and peaches had come, she touched the stem of the vase holding the dried wheat and silk flower arrangements. 'That's pretty. It was a lovely meal, Max. Thank you.'

'Not bad, was it? I'm glad you enjoyed it.' He lifted the bottle. 'More wine?'

She shook her head, saying mischievously, 'Maybe you should – before you explain about Rita.'

He set the bottle down without pouring, his expression suddenly glum. 'Somebody told you?'

'Harry,' she agreed. 'Unwittingly, though.'

'Damn!'

He looked so much like Maxie caught in some misdemeanour that she had to repress a smile, saying sternly to cover the fact, 'So why?'

'Because I didn't think you'd come if you were just going out with me,' he said frankly. 'I like you, Kate – a lot. Rather more than that, even, but I don't think you want – I mean, you told me you'd just separated and it seemed too soon to . . . Damn it all,' he interrupted himself, flushing. 'I asked you as a friend. No strings, I said – so do you care to dance? It's okay if you'd rather not.'

Flustered, Kate rose. She could feel the heat rising to her face but was unaware of its brightening effect upon her eyes, or the delicate blush of colour it put in her cheeks. She had not tried to attract Max but had she really, a tiny voice enquired, been as unconscious of him as she'd pretended? 'In for a penny,' she said lightly, though feeling shy now of his gaze. '*Somebody* was talking up their skill. Let's test it, shall we?'

'Why not?' He said it like a challenge and she laughed and let him lead her out, finding him light on his feet for a big man. He hummed as he held her and she was able to relax, following his lead easily without thought. Other couples began to rise and join them but the striking blonde in the black and flame-red outfit took everybody's eye. Realising it, Max grinned down at her. 'I love your dress – did I say? You look like a million dollars.'

Kate laughed in genuine amusement, the sound of it winning a sympathetic smile from Heather, seated at the edge of the floor, and turning Doug Doolin's head from his table against the wall. 'No, really, Max – I got the top for nine dollars from a Rockmans bargain bin, and Heather made the skirt for me. Stick to farming, that's my advice. You'd soon go bust in the retail trade.'

They returned to their table again. Max held her chair, a courtesy she had not experienced from Guy, then she saw Martin's lean form approaching.

'Katie,' he stooped to kiss her upraised cheek, 'you look gorgeous. How about a dance? So I can skite I was with the best-looking sheila in the room.'

'Martin, you're as bad as your father! Do you know each other?' She glanced between the men. 'Max, this is Martin Wantage, the boy next door when I was a kid. Martin, Max Shephard.'

The two shook hands and exchanged greetings. Martin was an inch taller. He wore a lightweight suit jacket but no tie, and dancing pumps with paper-thin soles. He'd discovered ballroom dancing at university, Kate remembered, and placed in several minor competitions before giving it away. Cocking a pale eyebrow at the other man, he said, 'Okay if I borrow your girl for a bit?'

'Of course.' Hiding irritation, Max sat down and watched the man glide expertly onto the floor. *He was well built*, he thought grudgingly, tall and fit-looking, his red hair (worn rather long for Max's taste) flicked back from a face dominated by high cheekbones. He wondered if Kate found him attractive. He could certainly dance. Max saw the way their steps matched, as if they'd moved together this way a hundred times, and Kate's animated face as they talked and laughed. He wished he could hear what was being said.

Kate was actually scolding her grinning partner. 'I'm not his girl. I wish you hadn't said that, Martin. It's embarrassing.'

'You reckon, Princess? He wasn't best pleased to have me walk off with you.'

'He's just a friend who found me a job when I needed it. And a very nice man,' she added warmly.

'I'm sure. So am I. So what went wrong, Katie? How come you're back? I thought when your father died —'

'Oh, Martin, so did I.' She looked up at him, grey eyes shadowed with old pain seeing the adored older brother he'd always been to her. 'I thought I'd leave all the sorrow behind, start a new life, but I chose the wrong man to share it with. And when it all goes wrong, where is there left to run to but home?'

He murmured something and she said wistfully, 'I have missed it, you know, so much. Mostly your parents, but the country too, and all the good times we had growing up. My happiest memories were made in the Mallee.'

'I wouldn't come back to live, but I know what you mean,' he agreed.

'Yes, well – enough about me. It's you I want to hear about. I expected you'd be married with a family by now. You're what? Thirty-three?'

The dance was ending. He grinned. 'Late starter? We can do all that next time. I'm here for a couple more days yet, so what say we spend Sunday together? We could take a trip down memory lane – visit the lake and the lookout, even the old school if you like. It's no good going to those sorts of places alone, that's Sadsville. How about we take a picnic and make a day of it? How long is it since you had a squash at the Chinaman's, or a game of tenpin?'

'How long since you drove up Delia Street? The bowling alley's gone, you great nit. There's a warehouse there now. And the China-man's place is a boutique.'

'Well, we can look at that too, and quaver at each other, *I remember when* . . . ' He dropped the falsetto that had made her laugh and smiled engagingly, pale eyes twinkling. 'What do you say?'

She smiled back and hugged the arm she still held as he walked her to the table. 'You're on. Sunday, then. Not before eight, though.'

'Got it.' He stooped swiftly to kiss her cheek. 'I'll be there, Prin-cess; thanks for the dance. Nice meeting you, Max.'

'He seems very fond of you,' Max said, watching the tall figure depart.

'As I am of him. When I was nine I was sure I was going to marry him. He's a nice guy. An engineer by trade. Shame, really. It means there's no one to follow Ken on the farm.'

He smiled. 'You're bred to the land, aren't you? You think like a farmer.'

'Oh, well,' she responded lightly. 'You can take the girl from the Mallee . . . '

'But you didn't want to make a career of it? Stones Place is surely big enough for two.'

'Not if it was twice the size it is,' Kate said flatly. 'My brother doesn't share anything.' She'd noticed him from the dance floor and could almost feel the speculation in his gaze. Clover was with him but not her mother. She'd be home with the boys. Clover, dressed in a bunchy dark-blue outfit that didn't suit her colouring, looked pale. Kate had made no attempt to speak to her, warned off by one quick, frightened look. Giving herself a mental shake, she rose and held out an inviting hand. 'It's a crime to waste that music – let's dance.'

* * *

The farmhouse was dark when they got back. Max coasted the vehicle quietly to the gate and killed the engine and they sat for a moment letting the dust settle before cracking the doors. Flip barked once and his chain rattled. The vane on the mill head creaked as it turned and the vagrant puff of wind brought the scents of the night, of eucalypt leaves and summer grass, and the distant smell of Hollens' silage.

'I had a lovely time, Max,' she said. 'Thanks for asking me.'

'Thank you for coming.' He walked her to the front door, peering into the darkness. 'Your garden bed's coming on well.'

She chuckled. 'As if you can see it!'

'I can smell the greenery and the damp soil.' His teeth glimmered. 'Goodnight, Kate.' He made no attempt to kiss her cheek but stood watching until the darkness beyond the door swallowed her slim form.

'Night, Max.' The call drifted after him as he turned away, then the screen door clicked shut and he was alone in the night, with the tick of the cooling engine in his ears and the shapes of mallee limbs, elegant as posed dancers, caught in his headlights.

* * *

Sunday morning Kate prepared a cold lunch for Harry and put up sandwiches, a wedge of fruit cake for Martin, a thermos and a plastic box of grapes for the picnic. She gathered her hat, protective cream and sunglasses and chained Flip again, then sought out Harry. 'You will remember to let him go again when I'm gone?'

'I'm not senile yet, Missy.' He glowered at her, put out by her defection. 'Gadding about. I should be docking your wages for this.'

'Yeah, yeah, you're a regular tyrant. Just don't forget to eat your lunch.' She blew him a kiss from the doorway as Martin's Mazda arrived ahead of its dust, catching the corner of his grin as she turned away. 'Remember: dog, lunch.' Then Martin in jeans, cotton shirt and a rag hat she would bet was one of Ken's was stowing the Esky in the boot and handing her into the car.

'What's the old boy like?' Martin asked as they slid away. 'A tough boss?'

'Well,' she pondered, 'think of some naughty ten-year-old and give him whiskers and a pathetic look. Nothing a seasoned teacher can't handle. He's an old dear, really, but you have to make the rules.'

'Ah,' his blue eyes smiled, 'you'd be good at that. When you were a kid you had a very strong sense of justice.'

'Thanks to Doug,' she said dryly. 'There wasn't much to be had at home – save from Dad.'

'So you haven't made up with your family?'

'Let's just say they're happy enough without me. Except for Clover. I see her in town sometimes, poor thing, and little Andy. He's too young yet to be turned against me.'

'Why poor?'

'Oh,' Kate shrugged, 'I sort of gathered things aren't too rosy between them. But maybe it's just the pregnancy.' She trusted Martin but Clover's story was not hers to tell. To get his mind off the subject, she said curiously, 'You were in high school together, you and Doug – how did you find him?'

'Underhand, mostly. And bloody scary.' He spoke without having to think. 'We were never friends. He was better at sport than me, and not dumb; he should've been popular but he never was. Most of us boys tended to be wary of him. Maybe because he was always, you know – getting at people. He seemed to be able to weasel out whatever you were ashamed of, or wanted kept quiet, and use it against you.'

Kate nodded, 'I know *exactly* what you mean.'

'Like he had a . . . a divining rod to find your weak spots,' Martin agreed. 'The underhand bit was his lying. He'd lie about anything.' He shrugged. 'So I wasn't an angel either, teenagers aren't, but Doug had a mean streak as wide as a house. He liked to hurt. He got off on it.'

'I know.' Kate was staring ahead through the window. 'He told me I was adopted once, that I didn't belong at Stones Place. Siblings don't always get on, especially when there's such a big age difference, but you and Megan did. I don't ever remember Doug being nice to me, not even on a birthday, or at Christmas.'

'I always thought he was a bit mental,' Martin confessed. He didn't add that right after his sister's disappearance Doug Doolin had paused beside him in the school assembly area to whisper, '*I hear someone took your sister, Wantage. Congratulations! Pity he didn't get mine as well.*' Martin hadn't been able to believe he'd said it until after Doug had sauntered off. That night down in the hayshed he'd told his father of the incident, blubbering like an outsize baby, all knobby joints and big ears, his heart breaking for his baby sister. 'I didn't even hit him,' he'd confessed. 'Oh, God, Dad! Poor little Megs.'

Ken had hugged him to his chest. 'I know, son. And I'm proud you didn't. It won't bring her back to us.' Nothing had. Time had blurred them but those terrible days full of despair and the slow death of hope were engraved upon his youth. There had been a bombing in London at the time, an IRA attack on some tower or other, and listening to the media reports he had thought that the survivors must feel as he and his family did. Stuck in a nightmare that should never have happened. The Post Office – that was it – the bombing of the Post Office Tower in London, October '71, a date he would never forget – any more than he would ever forgive Doug Doolin's words. He grimaced. 'He was a proper nasty bastard. Everyone at school knew it. No surprise he married a stranger. No local girl would've been fool enough to take him.'

'You're probably right.' Kate smiled ruefully. 'But then, I married out too, and that didn't prove such a good idea either.'

He glanced across at her and his voice was gentle. 'What went wrong? But if you don't want to talk about it, then we needn't.'

'It's all right,' she said, 'just not very interesting. I was too young and too unhappy after Dad died to know what I was doing. Rushing into marriage was a way to stop being lonely, I thought. Maybe even a way to hit back at Mum. If Dad hadn't had his heart attack, there'd have been a long engagement that I'd probably have broken off. But it wasn't all Guy's fault. I used him. When Dad went there was no one to love me and I grabbed at Guy – he wasn't really ready for marriage. Maybe he never will be. He's not a strong person and it's possible the farm influenced him too. He was very full of it at the time – marrying into the land. I thought he was joking. I never realised he believed I had a share in it. That came out when things started to go wrong and money was tight.

Even when I explained, he kept insisting I was legally entitled.' She smiled weakly. 'Crazy townies, eh?'

'Yeah. There's a few about.'

'Well,' Kate gave herself a mental shake, 'that's enough Mooky Lane history. We seem to have missed the school and the warehouse, so where's the lake got to?'

''Bout thirty-five kilometres this way.' Martin turned onto a side road. 'Shortcut,' he explained. 'Should bring us out behind Roadsend onto the highway.'

She chuckled and he looked at her, 'What?'

'*Should*,' she said, 'and *shortcut* in the one sentence. It gives me great confidence.'

'Hey,' he responded, 'this is me, Princess. Guaranteed fixer of all problems. How many kites did I mend for you two? How many dolls? Trust me. I'll get you there.'

16

Lake Summers, known to the locals as Lake Sometimes for its often dry bed, had changed in the twelve years since she'd seen it last. The dirt road had been sealed, and the stretch of sand and scrub where the farming families had pitched their tents and built their camp fires in the sixties and seventies was now a railed park with tables under shelters, and barbecue facilities, and a brick ablutions block labelled *His* and *Hers* in place of the two tin-walled long-drops Kate's father had helped dig when she was three.

'Did you bring your bikini?' Martin eased into a bay in the car park, where the skinny shade of a young athol pine fell obliquely across the vehicle. Before them, the wide surface of the lake glittered brightly.

'Well, a costume. It's nearly full.' Kate's eyes had gone to the old willow they'd always called the marker tree. Its leaves trailed in the water, which came almost to the fork in its trunk. 'I haven't seen so much water in it for years. But everything's different. The park, the buildings . . . When did this all happen?'

'While we were gone,' Martin said. 'Sounds like the title of a song, doesn't it? Do you remember where we used to get changed?'

Kate grinned. 'Oh, yes. Boys to the left, girls to the right. The bushes used to be about where that second table is. I wonder where they took the big boulder?'

He gestured at the gravelled foreground. 'That's probably it. But where's the canoe tree?' His eyes searched the foreshore. 'That must be it – though it looks a bit on the small side. I used to think it was huge. Janice Pringle fell out of it one year, remember? Broke her wrist.'

'Yes. Megan put a stick along it and tied it up in her shirt. We were going to grow up and be nurses that week. Poor Janice yelled her head off.'

'So she did. Well,' he blew out his breath. 'The water must be cooler than the air. Want to swim now or later?'

They swam, then searched the lake shore until Kate found one of the tiny, almost translucent spiral shells that were a lake specialty. She and Megan, she recalled, had collected them obsessively one year, scouring the lake shore at all hours in their bathers and sun hats. It had been the year they'd learned to swim; Kate remembered standing waist deep and screwing her courage up, then launching into the water with a death grip on the floatie as she kicked for shore, Megan beside her. They had practised for days, gasping encouragement to each other and squealing with delight when they managed to stay afloat. Megan's pale skin had pinkened the first day and she'd had to wear a shirt over her bathers. Kate could see them both now, building sandcastles with elaborate gardens made of grass stems; drinking homemade lemonade in the shade; giggling on the air mattress in the tent after lunch for the mandatory halfhour before returning to the water. She couldn't remember what they'd eaten but it had always tasted wonderful, and the days had never been long enough.

'We had some good times here.' She slipped her blouse and skirt on over her rapidly drying costume and spread her towel along the wooden seat. 'I got my first kiss just over there, the summer I was fifteen.'

'Really?' Martin was working the cork from a bottle of sparkling wine. 'Who was it?'

'Spoggy Pearson. An incomer. You'd have left for uni by the time he came. His dad managed the farmers' bank in town. He used to follow me around and a girlfriend dared me.'

'And how was it?' He fished two plastic wineglasses from the cooler.

Kate grinned reminiscently. 'Pretty disappointing, really. I mean, he was just a boy – spotty, and his breath smelled. It wasn't as if I fancied him or anything. I was just curious, I guess, and Mary Kelly dared me. Besides, we were all doing it, pairing off, however briefly, experimenting, choosing careers. I decided I'd be a vet.' She laughed, remembering. 'Your poor father. I was always after him to find me sick and hurt sheep I could practise on. What about you?' She wondered if he'd tell her, though she'd guessed long since. It made no difference to her feelings for him. He would always be her comforter and champion. 'Was there anyone special in high school?'

He shook his head. 'Slow starter. Glass of wine, Princess?'

'Thank you.' She spread the food out and handed him a paper plate and they talked as they ate. 'There used to be more ducks, I'm sure.' Kate broke off a bit of sandwich and tossed it, an action that brought half a dozen gulls flying in. 'Oh, look – there's Pogo.'

'Pogo?' Martin paused mid-bite.

'The one standing on one leg at the back. The first time we saw a gull do that, Megan and I, we thought it only had one leg so we called it Pogo – for the jumping stick, you know. She tried to catch it so we could take it home but it put its other leg down and flew off. They've been Pogos for me ever since. I'm still amazed they come so far inland, but they always did.'

'Black swans some years, too. And pelicans,' he added as they watched a flotilla of the stately birds sail past. There were shags drying their wings and plovers here and there, neat grey wings folded as they uttered their clinking calls. It was very peaceful with the moving pageant on the water and the tiny hush of the waves meeting the shore.

'Nice having it all to ourselves,' Kate said. She eyed the NO CAMPING signs. 'No more summer holidays, then. Just daytrips now.'

'If they come at all – the locals, I mean. Different world for kids these days.'

'Well, it has been for a while,' she pointed out. 'You talk as though we weren't part of the digital age.'

'Yeah, but I'm older than you.' He took a large bite. 'Nice sarnies, by the way. I remember when the digital watch was cutting edge.'

'Fool,' Kate said amiably. 'Anyway, it's not age, it's attitude. We – Guy and I – came here once, before the wedding. I should have seen then it was never going to work. I was sharing my world with him, you know. We went to the lookout and round the farm, and into the Chinaman's for a squash. He said that was quaint and I never realised he was laughing at me.' Her hands lying on the table knotted and Martin covered them with his own large ones.

'The guy must be a jerk.'

'He's that, all right. Anyway, I brought him here. Made him close his eyes from the last bend and promise not to look and then *Ta-da!* the big surprise. I suppose it wasn't fair, really. It was a dry year and most of the water was gone. I'd told him we called it Lake Sometimes. City-bred.' She shrugged, but couldn't keep her eyes from turning to the spot where they'd made love in the shadow of the boulder that was no longer there.

'So what happened?' Martin prompted when the silence stretched.

'He sat there, sort of puzzled, and after a bit he said, 'And . . . ?' I told him about all the good times we had here: the canoe races, learning to swim, the raft you boys made that summer when there was barely enough water to splash in – remember?'

'Yep. It got bogged on a mud bar. That was another dryish year.'

'It was all a big yawn to him. He teased me about being a country bumpkin, wondered if waiting to watch a train pass was the highlight of our week, and how my life was going to be so different now. If I hadn't been so unhappy, so desperate for comfort, I would've seen he was all wrong for me. Don't you sometimes wish you could go back and start over, Martin?'

'Why? We'd just make the same mistakes. Unless we're going to be allowed to remember our previous incarnation, of course. That, I'd vote for.'

'So would I. Sorry. We're meant to be enjoying ourselves. Have a grape – or would you rather try the cake?'

'Both, thanks. You know how to feed a man, Princess, and it's okay, you know. Pretty girls are allowed to moan. It brings out the protective cave man in us.' He beat his chest and roared convincingly.

She said, 'You don't have to pretend, Martin. About being gay, I mean. Do your parents know?'

His face had stilled for a moment, then he smiled, somewhat ruefully. With his dark-auburn hair and high cheekbones he was very handsome, despite the dusting of freckles that covered his skin. 'I haven't officially come out to them but Dad worked it out, years ago. It was him who encouraged me to go for another career and he was right. I daresay there are gay farmers but I wouldn't want to be the first one in the district. I just never expected you to figure it out – stupid, I suppose, but, kid sister and all that – otherwise I'd have told you.'

She said, 'I live in the modern world, Martin. I guessed ages ago because you were always so different – but it's not a crime to be that. And your mum? Does she know?'

He lifted big shoulders. 'I dunno, though I wouldn't be too

surprised if she did. I couldn't tell her, because if she's hoping for grandchildren . . . It'd be just too cruel, after Megs.'

'Yes, I see. She's never mentioned it. So – have you found somebody?'

He nodded. 'Alec's an accountant, a beautiful man. We've been together for five years now. He understands how things are here so I come back alone.' He shrugged. 'We're not ashamed of it, you know. In the city we don't hide what we are, but for Mum's sake —'

'Discretion is best,' she finished. 'Believe me, with Doug for a neighbour it is. Did he never guess?'

'How could he? I didn't work it out myself until I was eighteen and by then I was at university. Just as well. It's blokes like Doug that go out queer-bashing. He was always on my case in high school; it was like he knew there was something, but he couldn't quite put his finger on it.'

'I used to think he could smell secrets,' Kate confessed and gave a little shiver. 'It's strange but I think I'm more wary of him now than I was as a child. Of course I had Dad and you to run to, and I must've subconsciously known there were limits he couldn't pass. Temper helps, too – it banishes fear, and I couldn't be in his company without getting mad.' Her laugh was rueful and held more sadness than mirth. 'Dad always said he was spoilt, and that's how I saw him too. It was only after Dad died that I began to think he was . . . unbalanced. I wondered —' She broke off and when Martin raised his brows interrogatively, shook her head restlessly.

'Why are we wasting a perfect day talking about him? He's not worth it. Tell me about your career. I don't have one any more but I want to hear about yours. I might drive over one of your bridges one day and not know you built it, or designed it, or whatever. And that'd be a pity.'

***

It was late when they left. Martin was heading back in the morning, his duty visit over.

'They'll miss you,' Kate said. 'It's a shame about the farm.'

He didn't pretend to misunderstand. 'The choices we make never suit everyone. Dad should sell up while he can still enjoy retirement, but Mum would never agree.'

'I know – she's still waiting. You don't believe she's still alive?'

'No.' The shadows of Mooky Lane whipped across the windshield as they drove, dust rising to coat the hanging mallee leaves. 'She was most likely dead before nightfall, certainly by the following day. So the police said – afterwards.'

'After Gypsy Pete died, you mean?'

'What had he to do with it?'

'Wasn't he their chief suspect?'

'No more so than any other man who couldn't account for his whereabouts that day. They probably gave him a hard time because he was an itinerant, but I think in the end they had nothing on him. Far as I know the inquest verdict still holds. *Taken by a person or persons unknown* . . . You were just a kid, Katie. Why ever did you think that Pete —?'

'Oh, well, Doug said the police were satisfied it was him. And Megan and I thought he was creepy. God damn him!' she said with sudden anger. 'He'd lie about his own mother's death to score a point.'

'And we're back to talking about Doug,' Martin observed wryly.

'Sorry,' Kate said penitently. She smiled at him, a wistfulness behind the shadows in her smoky eyes. 'I shall miss you, Martin. I wish you could stay longer.'

'You and Mum both, but your friend Max wouldn't be pleased if I did.'

'Now you're being ridiculous,' she scolded. 'He comes round because he's a relative of the man I work for. He's good-hearted and very kind to the old chap,' she said defensively.

'And that's why he has to go dancing with you? Tsk. But I suppose you do what you must to keep the help happy these days.'

She smacked his arm and he grinned.

'You're a good-looking gal, Princess. I daresay he doesn't need much bribing.'

'I'm married. And even if I wasn't, it's not a trap I'm falling into twice.'

'It wouldn't be twice if you weren't,' he pointed out. The farmhouse appeared within its sheltering belt of timber and he pulled up in a swirl of dust and prancing legs as Flip rushed to greet them. Leaning across to open her door he kissed her cheek. 'Sweet Katie – thanks for your company today. I enjoyed it.'

'So did I, Martin. Tell Heather I'll be over soon.'

'I'll do that.'

She stood holding the thermos with one hand and patting Flip as he left, then noticed the bike lying by her garden bed. At least old Harry had had company; and Flip, she thought, eyeing his belly with suspicion, had probably wolfed an extra feed. She'd have to tell Maxie off about that. Again.

17

Christmas passed in a blaze of heat that had even the crows hunched, slack-winged and panting, in the mallee shade. Magpies crowded the old drinking trough under the rainwater tap and Kate searched through the sheds to find other receptacles she could fill and spread around for the smaller, shyer birds.

'I've seen 'em drop dead out of the sky in weather like this,' Harry observed, peering through the front door at the shimmering sky. 'Bushfire weather if ever there was.'

'Don't even think about it.' The air was so dry that Kate's hair crackled and stuck to her fingers when she combed it, and by ten in the morning even the verandah plants drooped in their pots. Walking, as she liked to do, in the cool of dawn, she had felt the brittle grasses cracking under her feet, and heard the tired creak of the mill rods, a sound as desiccated as the rattle of eucalypt leaves stirring in the dry wind. It was like every summer of her childhood, she thought, only the years away in the lush, northern climes had made her forget how stark and dry South Australia could be. Well, January would be worse – and at least Christmas was over.

* * *

Kate, after due thought, had rung Stones Place to deliver her Christmas greetings. She had always sent a card, addressed to the family with a bland greeting: *Merry Xmas to all, from Kate and Guy*, but that would hardly answer now. It was her mother who picked up the phone. She'd been hoping for Clover and dreading getting Doug, so made the best of it.

'Hello, Mum. I called to wish you all a happy day tomorrow.' She found she'd unconsciously crossed her fingers.

'Kathryn! Well – it could've waited till you got here.' Edna sounded surprised and disapproving, as if she were paying for the call. The sharpness of her tone scratched at Kate's memory – it was how she had always spoken to her daughter. 'Dinner's at one,' she said. 'Try not to be late.'

'I'm not coming, Mum,' Kate said coolly. 'That's why I rang. Enjoy your day, have fun with the children.'

'Not coming?' Edna sounded incredulous. 'Why ever not? It was reasonable to be absent when you were a couple of states away, but you're here now and you can't pretend that distance is an issue. We'll expect you at one. Christmas is an important tradition, Kathryn. One that families are supposed to respect whatever their differences. I suppose you'd go to the Wantages fast enough —'

'Maybe I would,' Kate snapped, her ire rising, 'and who's fault's that? But I have a position to fill here and it includes cooking Christmas dinner for Harry. That's what he expects, what he pays me for. I'm sure you'll manage just fine without me. You always have.'

Edna's voice rose, 'There's no point in being child —'

'Goodbye, Mum,' Kate said crisply and hung up the handpiece, then stood holding it in place, struggling to contain a howl of frustration while her thoughts settled.

'Who said I needed Christmas dinner, Missy?' Harry demanded gruffly behind her. 'You want to go home, you go. *I'm* not keeping you here.'

Kate turned, 'Well, need it or not, you're getting it. We're having cold roast chicken and a cheese and walnut salad. I bought grapes and cherries and a bottle of wine, we've got crackers and bonbons for the table, and if you insist you can even have a bread pudding with your tea. Harry, wild horses couldn't drag me back there for Christmas – so you'd better get used to the idea.' She had spoken so fiercely that he blinked.

'All right, girl,' he said gently, his old eyes peering from under their startling brows. 'What's wrong?'

'Nothing,' she snapped, gathering anger like a weapon against threatening tears. She dreaded further questions and wished he'd stop looking at her like that.

He sniffed at the rebuff. 'What about a cuppa, then? I suppose I can expect that too?' He followed her into the kitchen and took down two mugs from their hooks on the dresser, before seating himself at the old pine table. He didn't speak again until he'd blown across the top of the tea and shaken his head at the cake Kate automatically offered.

'Have some yourself,' he said. 'You could do with a bit of meat on your bones.'

'Oh, yes?' But her expression relented. 'You'd be an expert in that department, would you?'

'Nope. I dunno much about women but I was married for sixty years. And one thing I learned, girl, was that when Edie said nothing was wrong she meant just the opposite. Truth is you're a great cook, Missy, and like a . . . a flower in the house.' He thought about that and nodded. 'Yep, like wattle in bloom, girl. You've brought the place alive again with your rules and your chatter and your little kindnesses. But you're not happy, and I wish I could change that for you.'

'Oh, Harry.' She laid her slim hand over his gnarled knuckles. 'Your Edie was a lucky woman. I just let my mother get to me, that's all. Mostly I know better, but ever since Dad died this has been a hard time for me.'

'She wants you to spend Christmas with her – what's wrong with that?'

'It's why she wants it, not the fact that she does. So people won't talk. All my mother cares about is appearances – oh, and Stones Place. She married to get a son for the farm, and my brother and the property are all that's ever mattered to her. And what people think, of course,' she said bitterly. 'It wasn't a problem while Dad lived. *He* was where I belonged, and after he died it was The Narrows, Ken Wantage's place. So really, I've nothing to complain about. It's just,' she burst out as an afterthought, 'that the hypocrisy of it drives me wild.'

'I can see it would.' He sipped his tea, bright old eyes lidded under the white bridge of their brows. 'A good property, Stones Place, always has been. Old Joshua had an eye for country, and by all accounts your brother's a good farmer. The land's in good heart.' It was high praise from a Mallee man.

She said dryly, 'I doubt Joshua's passion for it was greater than my mother's. It's an obsession with her. Anyway, how do you know what it's like now?'

'I get to town occasionally, and I've got eyes. But land gets in your blood,' Harry agreed, 'speaking as a farmer, that is. Still, it takes second place to parenthood.'

'Not with Edna Doolin. Not as far as I was concerned, anyway. She's spoiling my nephews too, the little bit I've seen of her with them, just the way she did Doug. And look what he's turned into.' Kate hesitated but she knew Harry would have to be told some time and preferably before Clover's lawyer friend turned up. 'I found out that he abuses Clover, his wife. She's going to leave him but she's terrified of him – he won't let her go so she's planning to skip when he's not around.'

'Sounds sensible.'

'It's the only way, believe me,' Kate said soberly. 'She's got a lawyer friend in the city who's coming up to help her escape. That's what she's doing, Harry, escaping. The thing is, she asked if she could meet her here, and there wasn't time to check with you first – so I said yes.'

'Did you, Missy?' The deeply engraved lines of his face that looked stern in repose stretched into a smile. 'I'm glad you think so well of me.'

'Then you don't mind? He's going to be very angry – Doug, I mean – when he finds out.'

'He should've thought, then, 'fore he lifted his hand to a woman. It's a poor sort of a man that does that. Anyway, she'll be safe here – and if you reckon he won't listen to me, you just give young Max a call. He'll come if you ask. I take it there's a good reason she hasn't gone to the cops about it?'

Surprised again by his quick grasp of things, Kate nodded. 'According to Clover, Doug and the district inspector are thick as thieves.' She wrinkled her brow. 'My brother can be very plausible, you know; very charming too, when he likes – especially if he wants to pull the wool over someone's eyes. And he can lie black into white. I'm sure his mates on the force think he's a perfect husband. If they saw Clover's bruises, he'd convince them she'd somehow done it herself – might even get her locked away for psychiatric evaluation. I wouldn't put it past him.'

Harry made a soothing noise and Kate sighed deeply, feeling the tension drain from her with the exhalation of breath. The clock with its yellowed painted dial ticked from the mantel and she thought how often Harry and his wife must have sat there in the past through winter and summer mornings with breakfast on the table, and the unregarded background tick of time measuring their days. Sixty years was a long marriage and he loved her still in death. She was pierced with envy for the woman who had known such constancy, and had a sudden desire to know more about her.

She said, 'This is a lovely house, Harry. Did you build it for your wife?'

'Not me – well, only the laundry and the verandahs. The rest was down to my father. Thought you'd have recognised the material, girl. Your own family used it. Matter of fact, it was William Stone opened the quarry it came from.'

'Really? My mother's story is that Joshua built the farmhouse at Stones Place.'

'And that's what it is, girl – a story. William dug the first stone. The farmhouse isn't even built on the original eighty acres. Joshua would've put up a timber hut, probably with a bark roof, and the family would've lived there while he got a crop in and his fences up and all the rest of it. It was hand-to-mouth in those days – nobody had the time or resources to be building flash houses. That sort of thing happened in the second and third generation when they'd had time to expand and consolidate their properties.'

Kate stared in surprise. 'But – he's buried there, old Joshua. He's in the graveyard at the farm, along with William and the rest, right up to my grandparents. Not Dad, though. He's in the town cemetery.'

Harry shrugged. 'Then they dug him up and shifted him. I can show you the map but take it from me, everybody started with eighty acres. I suppose the thinking was that back in England a man could make a living on that. But this is the Mallee. You needed more to survive and those that did, knew it. Joshua for one – and William. It was him added what's your home paddock now, which is proof, if you like, that Joshua couldn't have built the house. He had a partner for a bit, did William, man called MacPherson, but when they started the quarrying business their ways diverged. William stayed farming and Mac took over the quarry.' He sniffed, eyes bright with enthusiasm for his subject. 'He did all right for himself, too. I found some old receipts from the works. A wagonload of stone cost more than a good draught horse – and *they* weren't cheap, Missy!'

'I imagine they weren't.' Kate was revolving something else in her mind. 'The place they call Macquarrie, where your sharefarmers live – would that have started out as Mac's Quarry, by any chance?'

He beamed. 'That's it. You see why history, especially local history, is important? Names and places get lost and as for the truth —' he lifted his hands, palms up '–there's people everywhere passing on so-called facts to the next generation, and you just try telling 'em they're wrong!'

Kate thought of her mother. 'I can imagine. Look,' she said impulsively, 'after lunch tomorrow, what about coming for a drive? Could you find Joshua's original grant, do you think? And the quarry? It's my history too, in a way, and you've piqued my interest. Oh, come on, Harry. Surely you can take Christmas Day off!'

'All right.' His sudden acquiescence surprised her. 'But if we're going to waste a day gadding about, you need to get caught up with yesterday's pages first. At my age a man's got leisure enough – the one thing he doesn't have is time.'

'It'll get done,' she promised, as he rose creakily to his feet. And they'd fit in a visit to The Narrows as well, she decided, her spirits rising. It might turn out to be a better day than she'd hoped for, after all.

* * *

Christmas was another hot day. By the time Kate returned from her morning walk with Flip, the sheep in the paddock behind the old shearing quarters were already settling to rest in the long shade of the mallee trees. She stood for a moment watching one little group of them, slim legs folding at the knees as they plumped down, the half-closed, faraway look of their eyes as the cud slid smoothly up their throats and the jaws began their rhythmical champing. Their woolly overcoats, thin still, for they were barely three months off shears, were a dirty grey in contrast to the slender white legs below, and red and blue plastic car tags defaced their pointed ears. They smelled the way her father's shirts had done at shearing time, and their occasional bleats sounded soft and absent-minded, like a group of women murmuring among themselves.

She grinned at the thought and made the same sound, varying the pitch the way she and Megan had done when they fed the poddy lambs. They'd always come running and it was only now that she knew it was because their childish presence, and not their amateur calling as they'd believed, had signalled feeding time. Today's lot ignored her – as they should, she thought, heading back. Flip cocked his ears and looked hopeful – he was already rounding up the hens whenever they strayed more than a few metres from their coop – but she made the hand signal for *stay* and the tension went from him. He was smart, and deserved to work; perhaps Ken would make a few sheep available to them both if she asked? Meanwhile she'd make pancakes for breakfast. The day demanded something better than tea and toast to mark it.

Kate entered by the back door and walked slowly through the house, setting the front door wide to let the air flow through, and switching on the ceiling fans. She would serve lunch in the dining room today. She looked with satisfaction upon the gleaming surfaces, making a note to change the greenery in the tall jardinières before she set the table with the good china. She'd use the linen napkins too, slightly yellowed though they were with age, and for dinner tonight the silver candlesticks she'd found in the back of the big old sideboard. It was probably a little silly for just the two of them, but she felt that Edie would have done so and it suddenly mattered that this should be something of an occasion for Harry.

18

Max ate the Christmas dinner the Railway Arms provided for its guests along with the complimentary glass of sherry. Fruit fool had (sensibly) been substituted for the traditional pudding, and a tray of tea and coffee things accompanied by brandy-snap biscuits awaited in the sitting room, where a small silver tree had been strung with red and green streamers. Christmas carols played softly on the speakers. The air conditioning hummed, and the only other guests, a middle-aged couple with little to say to each other, were sunk into the opposite corners of a long couch; him with a newspaper, her with a book. Max poured himself a cup of tea, glanced at the long-case clock in the corner and wondered how soon he could leave for Rosebud Farm.

He supposed he could have gone home. His parents had certainly expected him to, and he had heard the disappointment in his mother's voice when he'd rung to say he couldn't make it.

'But it's only a four-hour drive, Max. And we've been looking forward to —'

'I know, Mum, but I've a job on tomorrow and it's more like five from here, you know. I'll try to make it for New Year. You have a good day, now. Give my best to Dad.'

'But what will you do? You can't spend Christmas alone!'

'Oh, I'll be right. The pub I'm staying at will bung on a flash feed, and I'll have a drink with the boys later, maybe. I'll see you when I can. Merry Christmas, Mum. Love you lots.'

No need to tell her that the 'boys' were scattered to their various homes and that by hanging around Laradale he hoped to spend the evening at Rosebud in Kate's company. In Harry's too, of course, and possibly even Maxie's, but as long as he could see her, that didn't matter. He wondered when exactly mild interest had changed to hunger for her presence. And gloomily acknowledged that it was unlikely to be reciprocated. The absent husband, of course – he'd either turned her off men, or worse, still claimed a part of her heart. Realising he'd drunk his tea without tasting it, Max set the cup down and, glancing again at his watch, picked up a paper. He should wait at least until two. Wriggling deeper into his chair, he composed himself to while away the time with yesterday's news.

At twenty minutes past the hour he braked the Toyota to a stop before the farm gate in time to meet Kate's old Commodore being driven towards him from one of the sheds. He got out and walked to the gate, disappointment turning his voice flat.

'G'day, Kate. Merry Christmas. You off somewhere?'

'Oh, Max – merry Christmas to you too. I thought you'd have gone home for it. I'm taking Harry for a drive, that's all. It can wait a bit, if you'd like to come in?'

His spirits instantly restored, he said, 'Where to? The drive, I mean.'

'Oh, a few places, a sort of history crawl, you know?' She smiled. She looked good enough to eat in a pale-blue shirt with her tawny hair sitting on its collar and the glint of a gold chain about her slender neck. 'I'm interested and I thought it'd do him good. It's a holiday, after all, and he hasn't left the house since I've been here.'

'Great idea,' Max said heartily. 'Tell you what – what if I drive you both? The Toyota's got good aircon and I know the roads better than Harry does, though I wouldn't tell him so.'

'We'll see what he thinks,' Kate said diplomatically, getting out of the Commodore. 'Come on in.'

'Right.' Max fished through the window for the gift he'd brought and followed. In the front room and suddenly uncertain, he proffered the ceramic pot with its arrangement of dried waratah and protea between the two of them. 'I thought it'd suit the house,' he said. 'Call it a thankyou for all the meals I've eaten here.'

'Flowers.' Harry looked, and sounded, astonished.

'Dead ones,' Max said desperately and Kate, swallowing a laugh, rescued him.

'They're lovely, Max. Aren't they, Harry? Very artistic, and the colours will go so well in here. Wait.' She opened a drawer to remove a doily and spread it on the table. 'There,' she said, setting the pot carefully on the scrap of lace and turning it until she was satisfied. 'Perfectly suited. And they'll last forever. Just right for summer. Now – Max has offered to drive us, Harry. That okay with you?'

'He has? Well, least he'll be able to change a tyre. That's something you didn't think of, Missy. Let's go, then. You young people have more time to waste than me. If you've got a camera, you'd better bring it. I might need pictures.'

'Already organised.' Kate picked up a soft shoulder bag from a chair near the door. 'Come on, then – and mind the steps.'

* * *

Driving back to the pub with the shadows lying long across the road and the dust drifting gold-tinged through the dying sun's rays, Max whistled contentedly, pleased with his afternoon. It had been a good one and he'd had Kate seated beside him for much of it, close enough that his hand brushed against her knee whenever he changed gears. They'd located the original eighty-acre grants of several farms and peered into the overgrown pit that was the old quarry – the first time he'd ever done so. It was big and surprisingly deep but Harry – give the old boy his due, he knew his stuff – explained that the eight or ten farmhouses built from it hadn't been the only use for quarried stone.

'Water tanks,' he'd said cryptically, squinting into the hole the Hollens brothers had made their personal tip. 'Twenty, thirty thousand gallons capacity. The early farms all had 'em. Dig the hole, line it with stone – or brick, some of 'em used brick – put your boxing in, then pour the concrete. Do it right, it'll last a lifetime. Barring earthquake,' he'd added thoughtfully.

'So who's over there? Your sharefarmers?' Kate waved a hand at a patch of iron roof glimpsed through the scrub – more, Max thought, to get Harry back from the edge of the quarry than because she cared.

'The Hollens' place. It's a dump,' Max said frankly. 'Connie, Maxie's mother, is here too. We could stop by but she's painfully shy, not much at ease with strangers.'

'But she doesn't mind you?' Kate hooked a blowing wisp of hair behind one ear. 'I bought a little Christmas present for Maxie – a paintbox. Maybe you could give it to her, then?' She glanced at Harry heading tiredly back to the vehicle. 'And then I think we should call it a day. I'd planned to drop in on the Wantages, but he's probably worn out.'

'Okay, then.' Disappointed but liking her the more for her care of the old man, they had bypassed the rundown Hollens' place, where a black dog barked aggressively on a chain from amid a jungle of dead vehicles and rusted farm junk, and stopped briefly at the caravan where Connie Hardy and her son lived. There was no sign of the boy but Kate, waiting in the car, saw the shadowy bulk of a woman come to the door, and heard her squeal of glee as she embraced Max. It was too far to hear what was said. Harry, his head canted at an angle against the door, mumbled something and snorted, and she realised he'd been napping. She touched his arm.

'We'll be heading home after this, just in time for a cuppa.'

'Where are we?' His eyes narrowed and he grunted, remembering. 'Ah, must've nodded off. Well, this was your idea, Missy. Where's our driver?'

'Just coming.' She watched Max's tall figure approach, wondering where the boy could've gone on Christmas Day. She felt for the thermos in her bag and poured a capful of chilled water for Harry. 'Here,' she gave it to him, 'you don't want to dry out.' Beyond the cab the light shimmered cruelly, glistening off the leathery leaves of the mallee and painting phantom pools across the distant track. 'Must be hot in that caravan,' she murmured, watching Max's tall figure approach. 'All done?' she asked as he got in. 'You want a cold drink?'

He accepted gratefully. 'Fry an egg out there. And that caravan – phew!'

'She seemed happy to see you.' Kate screwed the cap back on and stowed the thermos.

'Connie's a simple, affectionate soul.' Chin on shoulder, he steered them backwards, then changed gears, 'and she's fond of me. Maxie was off somewhere. Home now, Harry?'

'Seems to be the idea,' the old man mumbled. 'It's got me thinking, though. Maybe next time we can visit the site of that woolshed. The stumps are still there, you say? Man should be able to work out the number of stands from the size of the shed. And then there're the cemeteries – one at your place, isn't there, Missy?' He rubbed his hands. '*That'd be useful.* I could crosscheck the dates on some of my findings. Let alone the original boreholes there somewhere too. Might not be what they're using now, but the more reason to check if it's not. I'm damn glad you talked me into this, girl. Best Christmas I can remember in a long while.'

'I'm glad you've enjoyed it,' Kate said, the words at odds with her expression. She looked frankly dismayed by the idea, Max thought.

Assuming the driving to be the cause – her old car looked about ready to quit – he said helpfully, 'I'll be gone for a few days over New Year but that apart I'd be glad to take you around. Just give us a call anytime, Harry.'

'Good. That's settled, then,' Harry said happily.

'Thanks very much,' Kate muttered, sotto voce in a tone that suggested the opposite.

Max blinked, startled. 'What'd I do?'

By the time they pulled up at the farmhouse gate to Flip's welcoming bark, she'd forgiven him. They shared a late cuppa on the verandah, then Harry went off to his room to rest. Kate mentally simplified the dinner she'd planned. Something quick followed by an early night would suit him better.

'The old boy enjoyed himself,' Max commented. 'I haven't seen him so lively for ages.'

'Yes, but it's tiring at his age.' She stacked the crockery. 'Well, I must get on. There're the hens to feed, and the eggs to collect, and I like to take Flip for a run about now. Will you be staying for supper, Max? Just leftovers, I'm afraid. I hadn't planned on company.'

'No, I'd best be off.' He said it firmly, though he'd rather have stayed – if the invitation had been differently phrased. He replaced his hat, looked at the dishes. 'Can I give you a hand with those first?'

'Don't be silly. They can wait till tonight. Thanks for everything, Max, including the flowers. He really enjoyed the day and I did too. You never think of your own family history as being part of a district's, do you?'

* * *

It was better than nothing, he thought now, eyes squinted against the glare down Mooky Lane, then his whistling cut short as he jammed the brake pedal down and slid to a stop beside the farm Toyota sitting with its door open and back wheel elevated. The driver squatting beside it working the jack handle looked up at Max's approach. His hat lay on the dusty road, disclosing a spill of dark curls as he glanced up.

'How you doing?' he greeted. 'Great day for a flat, eh?'

A boy's dark head popped up in the cab at the words. He stared at the stranger as Max nodded. 'Yeah. Holidays are fair game. You need a hand?'

'Think I'm pretty right, thanks.' He stood up, eyeing Max and the logo on the Toyota door: *Shephard's Harvesting*. 'Seen you somewhere before.' He snapped his fingers and smiled, activating a dimple in his cheek. 'That's it. The Growers' Dinner. You were with my sister. She should have introduced you. I'm Doug Doolin, and that's my son, Jeremy.'

'Max Shephard.' They shook hands. 'Must've missed you at the dinner; there was a fair crowd that night. It was a good do.'

'It was that. Katie seemed to be enjoying herself, anyway; good to see after her trouble,' Doug said heartily.

Max let the invitation pass but Doug continued as if he had asked. 'Bit of marital strife but they'll work through it.' He laughed gently. 'Women, eh? Never know what they want and I guess we spoiled her, my father and I. Kid sisters – they're like dolls. You just want to make them happy.'

'I can understand that,' Max said, 'though I never had a sister. Matter of fact, we were just talking about your place today. You know of course that Kate's working for my great-uncle, Harry Quickly? A grand old boy, very interested in history. Well, we took him for a drive this arvo and it seems he's cracking his neck to get a look at your family cemetery. You think that could be arranged?

It's a matter of cross-checking dates with those he already has.'

'No problem.' Doug had unclamped the spare as they were speaking and bounced it down onto the gravel. 'Tell Katie – I take it you'll be seeing her again soon? – tell her any time. Not that she has to ask; she knows that,' he added indulgently.

Max nodded his thanks. 'Thanks. I'll do that.' He hesitated. 'She's does a great job, you know, with the old fella. He might be sharp as a tack, but he's in his nineties. He's come to depend on her. Be a shame for him to lose her now, but by what you said . . . well, how likely is she to go back to her husband?'

Doug looked up, the muscles of his forearms clenched as he levered the tyre onto the wheel studs. The blue eyes in the handsome face were guileless. 'Who can say? It isn't the first time she's run off, but poor old Guy always takes her back. Maybe . . . seventy per cent likely? Let's say you might be wise to line up a substitute for your uncle. Hey, Jerry,' he called, screwing wheel nuts on with deft fingers, 'fetch us the wheel brace, son. I put it down somewhere at the back. Well,' he wiped his hands and grinned. 'Seeing it's Christmas I reckon I can leave fixing the flat till tomorrow. Nice meeting you, Max; we do our own harvesting at Stones Place but it never hurts to make new contacts.'

'Yeah, well, compliments of the season to you. It looks like you've got a great crop, if that's your land?' He waved a hand at the paddock fronting the lane.

'It is – a fine bit of country. Always yields well,' Doug said. He shook hands genially again.

Max's voice sounded glum in his own ears. 'Might see you round, then.' Dusk had fallen while they talked, bringing the half-light to blur the outline of paddock and trees. He waved at the kid, slammed the Toyota door and drove off wishing the encounter had never happened.

19

Next day Doug Doolin played golf with his long-time partner, the district inspector of police, who also had public holidays off. On the first green, dotted with the pleasing shapes of pepperina trees, he said casually, 'How would you go about locating someone in another state, Greg? If you only had the name of the town, say, and a vehicle registration?'

His companion paused to set up his ball and address it with his club; he watched the result with satisfaction. 'The Shark couldn't have done that better.' Replacing his club, he grabbed the trolley handle. 'Depends who you'd want to find, mate, and why.'

Doug sighed and fell into step. 'It's that sister of mine. She's bolted from her husband again and I think she's about to get involved with another man. If I had his address, I'd give Guy a ring. The poor bugger'll be gutted. He loves her, for all she leads him one hell of a dance. Don't suppose you could get it for me? Somewhere in Byron Bay.'

'What's he do for a living?'

'Insurance assessor. I reckon that's half the trouble – always away from home. And Katie's spoilt. My father saw to that. You know how it is with men and their daughters. Reckon you can help?'

Greg pondered. 'Write down the details, then. I'll see what I can do.'

'Thanks, mate. You're a prince,' Doug said. 'My shot, I think.'

* * *

Back home Doug lifted the bag of clubs from the vehicle and gazed with proprietary pride about him, captain of all he surveyed. He'd been aware from an early age of his Stone heritage; it had come to him, it sometimes seemed, with his mother's milk, and he cared as much for his inheritance as Edna ever had. Sentiment was a stranger to him, love not a concept he understood. He didn't love his wife; he possessed her, as he did his sons. They were his, as the land itself was his – a heritage that had come down to him through a line of hard-grafting men who had understood, as he did, the needs of the land. Happiness was not something he wasted time thinking about, but if forced to define it, he would have done so by the feelings he had, the catch at his heart when his gaze rested on the shine of the curving furrows of new-ploughed earth. Or the sight of a paddock filled with the packed ears of a crop ready for harvest. Pride flamed in him then and nothing else mattered. This was what he was born for, what he worked for, and what his son would some day inherit.

Now, as he stood contemplating the painted, orderly buildings about him, his eye fell to the lube shed that had once been Brian Doolin's workshop, and which inevitably brought his sister to mind. She'd always be in there with him, chattering her rubbish by the hour, in her flutey little-girl voice. He'd hear her laughter and watch her come out with him when the dinner bell rang, holding hands more often than not. Sawdust all over her shoes, smiling that secret smile that said she was his and he was hers, and there was nothing that Doug could do about it.

It had hurt him in a way that he'd never understood. Not then, and not now. God knows he'd had no time for the whittling old fool himself – he wasn't a farmer's bootlace – but he had owed Doug something. All his life the younger man had mistrusted what he didn't understand, and that included the love between Kate and her father, for Doug had never seen Edna's support of him in that light. He was owed service by virtue of who he was – it was as simple as that. His mother's petting he had to endure. Her indulgences were no more than his due. Though blind to his own tragic lack of feeling, he was astute enough, once he began school, to don the mask of conformity, while going his own way behind it. It had worked, too; he could, he found, fool most of the people, most of the time – but he had never fooled his sister, or her irritating little friend. He could scare them, dismay and upset them, but he couldn't manipulate them the way he could everyone else – and he had never forgiven Kate that.

Remembering it now, his hand closed with painful force over the bag strap. Men had always been fools for Kate – her father, Ken Wantage, that idiot she'd married . . . And now her newest conquest seemed as besotted as the rest. Well, Max what's-his-name could talk it over with her husband – just as soon as good old Greg delivered the goods.

* * *

In the kitchen Edna turned from the stove to smile lovingly at him. 'Good game, son?'

'Useful.' Knowing she expected it, he kissed her cheek. 'What are you wearing yourself out with there, Mum? Surely Clover could be doing that? You've more than done your share on the farm.'

'She's giving the boys their music lessons.' Edna's tone was carefully noncommittal but the downturning of her mouth spoke volumes.

Doug winced with irritation for the wavering notes sounding clearly through the house. He should have got rid of that damned piano years ago. Clover, who used to lose herself at the keyboard for an hour at a stretch, no longer played – he'd seen to that – but she'd proved unusually obstinate about teaching the boys, despite his displeasure. What use, he'd demanded, would piano playing be to them? His sons would be farmers, not poofter musicians. She'd accepted his decree without argument, but now it seemed she'd carried on behind his back. Anger swelled in him.

'Well, that can stop. She'll be sending them to ballet next.'

Edna said, 'She claims Andy's got a gift for it.'

'Is that what she calls it?' Abandoning his clubs where they fell, he stalked from the kitchen. Edna, continuing to stir the mixture in the double boiler, heard the notes stop and the crash of the lid descending over the keys. Clover's nervous voice protested and was silenced by Doug's harsh tones, then Jerry whooped and came pounding down the hall.

'Hey, Gran, can I have a biscuit? And guess what? Dad says I don't have to do that stupid music no more.'

Edna looked lovingly into the vivid face with its sparkling eyes so like his father. 'Course you can, lovie; and one for your brother too.'

'Him!' Jerry sneered. 'He's crying. He *likes* that stupid stuff. I'm gonna play in the 'chinery shed.' Another whoop and he was gone, taking both biscuits with him.

* * *

Harry rose late on Boxing Day, an unusual occurrence for him. Kate eyed him as he sat at the pine table amid the breakfast dishes, making no effort to finish his second cup of tea.

'You feeling all right, Harry?' She suspended the action of

wiping the neck of the marmalade jar to set it back down. 'Did you overdo it yesterday?'

'I'm fine,' he grumbled. 'Man can be a bit tired if he wants, can't he? What you going to do about it, anyway?'

'Nothing. But maybe you should just take it easy today. May as well, because I'm on strike. It's a holiday, after all, so – no typing.'

That raised a small smile. 'Knew you were trouble, Missy. I might just lie down for a bit, though.'

'How about the couch in the sitting room, then? If I turn on the fan? Or would you rather go back to bed?'

'Why?' he snapped. 'I'm tired, not dying. The couch'll do me.'

'Good. I'll have a bit of company, then, you old grouch. And Maxie might turn up today. I'm surprised he hasn't already done so. But maybe his presents are keeping him busy.'

'Huh!' Rising, the old man plodded through to the long couch with its view into the dining room. 'I doubt he'll get many.'

'Doesn't his father even do that much for him?'

'Probably doesn't even know he exists – whoever he was.' Harry sat and laboriously raised his legs, then sighed as he lay back. 'Ah, that's good. Maxie doesn't know who his dad is. Asked me once if I did. Think I'll have a bit of a snooze.' His crepey old lids closed and as Kate stood uncertainly watching him, one opened again. 'Don't worry, girl, I'm not going to croak on you just yet.'

She flashed a smile. 'You old faker. I'll get on, then. Sing out if you need anything.'

She was worried all the same and debated ringing the Railway Arms, but that was to panic, and what, anyway, could Max do? Rest was the obvious answer and that was happening. She was making too much of it, she decided. All that jouncing around yesterday would tire any ninety-year-old, let alone the heat and excitement – well, hardly that, but stimulation certainly. If she stopped to think about it, she felt a little tired herself – flat, anyway. She was, she admitted, missing Max's genial presence. Of course, she always felt down at this time of year, although most of yesterday had passed without her thoughts once turning to her father's death. That had occurred two days before Christmas, on the one year she hadn't already returned home.

Putting things straight in the kitchen, Kate paused to stare sightlessly through the window above the sink, remembering how she'd stayed on after college to attend a friend's wedding when she could have already been home. She would never forget it had been her decision to do so, or her mother's accusatory voice on the phone.

'I told you you should have come home, Kathryn, but oh no, some chit of a girl I've never even met is more important than your own family. Well, I hope you're satisfied now that your father is dead.'

The words, hitting with the cold hurt of hailstones, had shocked the breath from her, making her stammer. 'W-what? What are you saying, Mum? He's not . . . he . . . he can't be! I was coming tomorrow – tell me he's not —?'

'Well, there's no hurry now, my girl,' Edna had said sourly. 'He died in his shed an hour ago – of a heart attack, the doctor said.' Then as an afterthought, 'He'll be buried in town.'

It was the final straw for Kate. That after a lifetime's service to Stone land Brian Doolin should not be deemed worthy to lie among the family he had married into. Her own pain mingling with a terrible anger, she rang the girl for whom she was to have been bridesmaid that afternoon, threw her gear into a bag and with shaking fingers dialled the number of The Narrows.

It was Martin who had met her off the train, his freckled face and copper hair a beacon of comfort on the busy platform where returning family members, laden with gay parcels, waved at waiting friends and relatives. His comforting arms had swept her into a hug. Even as a boy, displaying emotion had never bothered Martin.

'It's a sad day, Princess,' he said softly, 'a sad, sad day. Come home. Mum's got your room ready.'

Afterwards, white-faced and as numb as if she had been anaesthetised, Kate sat at the kitchen table, hands cradling the cup of tea she wasn't drinking. She said blankly, 'How can he have had a bad heart? He never told me about it.'

'Perhaps he didn't want you to worry,' Heather Wantage suggested. 'It was a massive attack, we heard. He must have died very quickly.'

Kate's head turned. 'Who was there? He wasn't alone, then?' The thought had haunted her ever since she'd heard the news.

'Young Ron Hall. He'd come to pick up the chair Brian made for his granny. He'd only just got there when he heard the shouting. He thought it was Brian but when he went across to the shed it was Doug. He was with your father. He yelled at Ron to ring for an ambulance; Ron ran for the house then but your dad was gone long before they came.'

'Gone,' she echoed while the silent tears slid unregarded down her cheeks. She couldn't stop them. It was as if there was a dam inside her and Brian's death had torn a great hole in the bank to loose the liquid flood of pain and regret. She should have been there! If she hadn't agreed to be Jenny's bridesmaid, she *would* have been there, and he needn't have died alone. Doug must have come along afterwards and seen him on the ground amid the sawdust. He *never* set foot in Brian's workplace so he certainly wouldn't have been with him. She thought of how it must have been – the crippling pain like a bolt from the blue followed by the terrible knowledge of what it meant, and his inability to help himself.

Desolation swamped her. She cried until her eyes were sore and her throat choked and tight with pain while Heather Wantage stroked her hair, saying helplessly, 'There, Lamb, there,' and Martin rubbed circles with the tips of his fingers on the back of her hand.

The holidays had delayed the funeral until two days after Christmas, by which time the family solicitor had been out to Stones Place to reassure Edna and her son on the matter of probate. Had Brian owned a share in the farm, it might have seriously jeopardised the day-to-day running of the place, let alone next season's planting. The reading of his will had been almost incidental. Brian had bequeathed a little money and his graduation box to his daughter, together with half a dozen pieces of furniture and his carving tools. It was all he had to leave, apart from his dog and his workshop stuff – the benches, saws and other tools for which she had no use.

'I'll take Tam back with me – after,' she had said tightly and left the room, without a word of thanks to the solicitor, Edna noted indignantly, but Alec Forsyth, of Forsyth, Grainer and Son, sought her out before he left, to express his private sympathy.

He found her in some sort of workshop, stacked with wood and various tools with a ratty old dog at her side, both of them sitting on the floor amid mounds of sawdust and . . . *keening*, the solicitor thought, was the word that would apply, had there been any noise involved.

'This is where he died,' she said by way of explanation, her grey eyes wandering across the floor. 'I wish I was a dog and could talk to Tam – he must've been with him.' The old collie looked up at his name, whined in his throat, then dropped his head back onto her thigh.

'I am truly sorry, Miss Doolin. If there is anything – legal, personal, anything at all I can help you with – I hope you will call on me.'

'Thank you, but I don't expect there is. I'm going back straight – after.'

Again he noted she could not bring herself to say *funeral*. 'Well, I'm in town at the end of a phone,' he said as he left. When he glanced back she was still sitting there, calves folded beneath her, rocking gently in the sawdust with the dog beside her.

20

It was mid-afternoon with the worst of the heat over when Maxie came pedalling through the mallee, skinny brown legs working overtime as the bike swayed along the dusty track. He dropped it with a crash as Flip came bounding to meet him. Kate tutted to herself, half vexed, half amused. As a child she had been taught to ignore other people's dogs; the allegiance of a working dog belonged solely to its master. It was the golden rule of training but it was not as if Flip was really meant for the paddock, she told herself, and Maxie plainly had little of his own to love. It would be cruel to deny him the pleasure of playing with the pup.

With Flip pouncing playfully at his bare heels the boy came to the verandah, where Kate met him to dismiss the dog, which had never entirely conceded defeat in the matter of sneaking indoors.

'Out.' She lifted a minatory finger and Flip ducked his head and turned aside. 'Hello, Maxie. I've made some lemonade. Would you like some?'

'Oh, yes, Miss, please.'

'I thought you might.' She smiled. 'Wipe your feet first. Did you have a nice Christmas?'

Maxie considered. 'It was okay. Where's Harry?'

'In the sitting room, watching the cricket – he's having a quiet day. Go and say hello. You want Christmas cake with your drink?'

'You bet.' Maxie forgot his customary caution so far as to grin at her. 'Thanks, Miss, and for the paints. They're super.'

'I thought you'd like them. Off you go, then.'

But the boy hovered uncertainly, one hand clenched in the pocket of his raggy shorts. 'I brung you something, Miss.' He produced it bashfully, a small screw of Christmas paper (recycled, Kate saw, from the paintbox wrapping) that had been thoroughly sealed with sticky tape, and was about the size of a mallee nut. He proffered it on his open, grubby palm. 'It's for you – a present, like.'

Kate was touched. 'Thank you, Maxie.' She picked it up, saying as she had a hundred times before with children she had taught, 'This is exciting! I wonder what's in it? I'll open it later, and I do think you'd better wash your hands before you transfer all that dirt to the cake.'

He grinned and slid into the sitting room where the commentator's voice *a splendid hit. That'll be a four . . .* was quickly overlaid by his eager chatter. Getting the cake tin out, Kate smiled to herself. Maxie's company was just what Harry needed; he'd napped most of the morning but she didn't know how much longer the despised television would hold his attention. She put the kettle on and cut a second slice of the rich cake. Might as well make afternoon tea half an hour early – save doing the job twice.

She was filling the cups when Flip barked and Maxie's head came up. The boy's ears fairly quivered as he lowered his glass to the pine table. 'Vehicle coming.'

'It'll be Max.' The rush of warmth she felt surprised Kate. She had not expected to see him today but unacknowledged at the back of her mind the desire for company – not his, specifically, she told herself, just anybody's really – had been there.

'No.' Maxie was already sliding off his chair. 'Somebody else.' Flip barked to add verisimilitude to the statement and Kate put out a hand to stop Harry getting up.

'I'll see who it is.' She heard the back screen door slam as Maxie made his escape, then her quick steps brought her to the front door and the sight of her brother strolling towards the house, looking leisurely about him as he did so. He paused to prod the fallen pushbike with his foot and click his fingers at the bristling Flip barking at him from a judicious distance.

Lips compressed, Kate stepped out onto the verandah. 'What are you doing here, Doug? Has something happened to Mum?'

His brow creased momentarily. 'Why should it? Oh, I see – that's the only reason you can conceive of for a visit from me. What an unnatural sister you are, Katie! It's the Christmas season and as you didn't see fit to come to us, I thought I'd just drop in and make sure that everything's okay with you. Head of the family and all that, you know. I'm sure Dad would've wanted me to.'

Kate's eyes flashed. 'Don't,' she said angrily, 'mention him.'

'He was my father too. You weren't even there when he died, remember.' He snapped his fingers again. 'Seems ages ago but I guess it was only what – five or six years?'

She wanted to yell at him that it was eight years and four days but ground her teeth on the impulse, moved to fury by his cavalier attitude. He hadn't forgotten. He had said it to hurt. Something moved in her side vision and she caught a brief glimpse of Maxie ducking behind the pepper tree at the side of the kitchen and cravenly wished she could join him. Doug, who missed little, had seen it too, and his attention turned to the rusty bike on the path. 'You still collecting strays, Katie? You want to be careful with that one. Max Shephard's by-blow might prove a bigger risk than a fallen fledgling. He's not right in the head, that kid. Not to mention he's likely to nick the place clean.'

Stunned, she demanded, 'What did you say?'

'That he's light-fingered. Come on, Katie. You surely know what *nicking* means?'

'Not that. You said —'

'Oh, his parentage. It's no secret. Well,' he grinned, 'dead giveaway, the girl calling him after his father, but then she's a halfwit too, fall for any story. No, a bloke called Max Shephard did the dirty with her. He runs a harvesting business in the district. He's not a local man so you wouldn't know him. But that's old history and beside the point. You going to ask me in or not?'

'No,' Kate said coldly, 'I'm not.' *He lies*, she reminded herself. You *know* he lies – about everything. Because he'd surely seen her and Max together at the Growers' Dinner. 'I want nothing to do with you and I can't see why you won't believe it.' She stepped back inside, slamming the screen door, and heard him laugh with what sounded like genuine amusement. Her hands were shaking as she clicked the snib across, and she felt sick. *It's a lie,* she told herself fiercely, but the phrase *did the dirty* danced before her like graffiti on a soiled wall, and for the life of her she couldn't stop remembering the way Connie Hardy had squealed with delight and flung herself at Max. *Doug always lies.* That was a fact. Another was the boy's name – but hadn't Max said he and Connie were cousins of a sort and that she was fond of him? A mean little voice whispered: *Just how fond, exactly?*

It's just Doug, she answered. But why say it when he thought she didn't even know Max? But they'd been at the dinner. He *must* have seen them together. They hadn't spoken, though, so how had he found out who Max was? Of course he could always have asked – Max had greeted enough of those present for her to know that he harvested paddocks for many of them. So getting his identity wouldn't pose a problem for Doug, who, she reminded herself, had always been an expert at planting little poison darts of doubt. The only ones impervious to them had been Brian Doolin and Megan. Brian had known his son too well. *And Megan*, Kate thought painfully, *had been too loyal to believe a word against her friend*. Doug had caused mischief between them only once; after that, believing as only children can in evil, they'd made a pact to trust each other forever, so that it could never happen again.

Kate almost smiled then, remembering the two of them crouched in the wheat, the heavy-headed grain nodding about their absorbed faces as they'd each shrinkingly pricked a finger with a long thorn snapped from a cactus plant in Edna's no-frills garden. They'd rubbed their punctured skins together, and she wondered now wherever they'd got the idea from – what story or childish legend had brought it to mind. It had worked, though. Doug had never again managed to shatter their faith in each other and when he'd tried, their habit of chanting 'Liar, liar, pants on fire' had driven him wild. It was, she reflected, probably their only victory over him.

'Well, Missy?' Kate blinked and found Harry approaching creakily from the kitchen. 'Who was it?'

'Nobody. Just my brother sticking his nose in again. I sent him away. Did you finish your tea?'

'Yes. Yours is cold and the boy's gone. Shame, I was hoping for a game, too.' He had taught Maxie chess and they played what seemed to Kate, who knew nothing about it beyond the names of the pieces, to be long silent games punctuated with terse murmurs that made no sense to her.

'I'm sorry.' Distractedly she whisked the crockery into the sink and put the uneaten cake away. 'I daresay he'll be back tomorrow.'

The shrewd old eyes surveyed her. 'He's upset you again, hasn't he?'

'It's nothing. Just *seeing* him upsets me. What I truly don't understand and never will is how he could possibly be my father's son.' But the utterance put her in mind again of Doug's idle – well, *seemingly* idle – remarks about Maxie, and she thrust the cake tin onto its shelf with unwarranted vigour. 'It's cooling off; I'll feed the hens, then take the dog for a walk.'

* * *

Max turned up the following afternoon. Kate, catching sight of him coming through the gate, had little time to ready herself, but her normal greeting still sounded constrained in her own ears. She coughed to cover it and found herself comparing his looks to Maxie's. His hair was darker, but then that happened with age (but not from blond to brown, surely?) and anyway, she didn't know Connie's natural colour. The boy had light eyes – *a bluey sort of grey*, she thought – but a ten-year-old's face was unfinished, a work in progress, and all she could call to mind was its thinness. Perhaps there was a similarity in the jawline? She looked away, flushing slightly as Max's big knuckled hand rose to rub at his mouth.

'Have I got dirt on my face?'

'No,' she managed. 'Why do you ask?'

He chuckled. 'I had a teacher used to look at me like that when I hadn't turned in my homework.'

'Don't be silly. Maybe I was just wondering what you're – Look out!'

He jumped aside as Maxie came barrelling past on his bike, legs pumping madly. The boy wheeled about in front of them, jammed on the brakes and let the bike fall in one continuous motion. He grinned at them both. 'Hey, Max! Hello, Miss. I brung this to show you.' Fishing down the front of his cotton shirt, he pulled out the paper that had lain flat against his ribs and handed it to Kate.

She took it, saying, 'You brought it, Maxie. There's no such word as *brung*.' Her gaze fell to take in the painting he had made of a wheatfield with a fence in the foreground and an old tree railed into the corner. The perspective was a little out, she saw, but the tree was beautifully done and the wheat, harvest-ripe, a sea of tawny heads touched with gold. 'It's very, very good,' she said. 'You have a gift for drawing and painting. One day people will pay you to paint pictures like this.'

'You reckon, Miss? I'd like that.' His face lit up; he took the drawing back and studied it proudly. 'I'm gonna give it to my mum. Did you like your present, Miss?'

Kate had forgotten all about the tiny parcel. She'd put it down to do something, then – Her mind was blank, but mindful of his expectant gaze she said heartily, 'I did, Maxie. It was lovely. I'm going to keep it forever. It was very clever of you to know I'd like it. Why don't you show Harry your picture? And I'm sure we can find an envelope for you to carry it home in.'

When he had gone Max said, 'Are you busy, Kate? I thought we might take Harry out again – see that cemetery at your place. He enjoyed the last trip, and guess what? I ran into your brother going home that night. He was pulled up with a flat tyre on Mooky Lane. I mentioned about Harry wanting to visit and he said any time. So what do you think?'

'No,' Kate said baldly, while a flush of something like triumph went through her. So Doug had met Max and within twenty-four hours he was there at Rosebud spouting his poison. Max had unwittingly let something slip, perhaps just her name, but it was enough for Doug to act on. Which meant she could disregard everything he'd said. Her heart felt suddenly lighter for the knowledge. 'Look,' she added as his face fell, 'it's a kind thought and maybe Harry will want to go but I'd be happier if he didn't. Not today, anyway. That last trip wore him out and I think he should have a couple more days of rest before trying it again. Maybe you could take him on Wednesday, say? But I won't be going with you – not then, not any time. We don't – I have nothing to do with my family.'

'Right.' Max rubbed his jaw and cleared his throat. 'Well, in that case, Wednesday's no good, I'm afraid. I promised my mother I'd go home for New Year so I'll be on the road that day.'

'Some other time, then. Come in and I'll make some tea.'

'Thanks.' He hesitated. 'I suppose I shouldn't ask why . . . ?'

Kate sighed and shook her hair back, unaware of the catch in Max's breathing as he gazed at the slender line of her jaw and throat the action revealed. 'It's not something I want to talk about. You don't know my brother, do you?'

'Like I said – met him in Mooky Lane. First time I've set eyes on him but he seems a decent enough bloke.'

'Most people think that – at first. He lies, Max. About everything. He was here yesterday. Do you want to know what he told me – about you?'

She was staring at him, the dappled shade of the pepper tree, beneath which they stood, masking her eyes. He shrugged. 'Can't be very dreadful. He doesn't know me. So, let's have it.'

'Maxie was here,' she said. 'He told me that you were his father. Oh, and that Maxie himself wasn't right in the head, and that you'd taken advantage of his mother, who was a halfwit.'

Stunned, Max stared at her while his face slowly reddened. 'He said that? The bastard! I'll kill him!'

'I'm sorry.' Her voice was steady, unsurprised by his vehemence. 'But I've found people won't believe the simple assertion that he lies. They need to hear it firsthand. So gauge whatever he told you, about anything at all, against the truth of that.'

'Right.' She watched his right fist, which had unconsciously clenched, loosen as he thought back over what had been said. 'Does that mean you aren't going to be quitting the position here, because you're – how did he put it? – seventy per cent likely to return to your husband?'

'He said that?' A slow flush climbed Kate's cheek. 'You needn't worry. I'll be here as long as Harry needs me. But now you know what he's like you can see why I keep away.'

Max grimaced. 'I can. What I can't see is why somebody hasn't flattened the bastard before this – or have they?'

'He's too clever for that,' Kate said tiredly. 'You see, he didn't say I *would* go back to Guy, only that it was seventy per cent likely. That's his opinion, and anyone can have an opinion, even if it's wrong. It's still a lie. Only repeat it and it becomes gossip and innuendo, the sort of thing you can't shake, but you can't pin on him either.'

'Well, thank God for honesty, then.'

'You're like Megan.' Her beautiful smile lit up her face. 'That's how we beat him when we were young. We told each other everything he said, no matter how hateful. And because of it he never managed to hurt our friendship.'

'Good for you.' He touched her arm for the pleasure of it. 'Did I hear something just now about tea?'

21

Wednesday afternoon Clover's lawyer friend from Adelaide arrived. She drove cautiously up the road, the fire-engine red of her car vivid as a shout amid the pale dust and the dull green of the mallee leaves. Galahs burst raucously out of the paddock where the sheep were camped in noonday shade, and the tall woman in the lightweight pantsuit ducked, then whirled reflexively to stare at the tumult of rose and silver against the blinding light of the sky. The hot, breathless air shimmered above the iron roof of the farmstead as she shook her head, hoisted her shoulder bag and marched towards the house. Marching was her style; the gate gave her a moment's thought and Flip's appearance met with a commanding stare that stopped him in his tracks. Her heels rapped across the dry verandah boards towards the opening screen door, while her left hand pulled off the heavy sunglasses. The right one, shapely, the nails polished but unpainted, was extended to Kate.

'Good afternoon. I'm Beatrice Collins, Clover Doolin's friend. Am I right in thinking this is Rosebud Farm?'

Kate's eyes ran over the smart, no-nonsense attire and slightly bony face, and approved of the determination she read there. 'Yes, it is. Won't you come in? I'm Kate, housekeeper for the owner, and Clove's sister-in-law. So she's finally going?'

'That's my understanding, given her last communication two days ago. She instructed me not to ring her at home, at Stones . . . er, Place? Peculiar names these properties have.' She glanced back at the white glare irradiating earth and sky beyond the verandah's edge and raised an interrogative brow. 'Why Rosebud?'

'Why not?' Kate said lightly. 'They're pretty hardy bushes, roses. Come through, Beatrice. Harry Quickly's in the kitchen. He's the owner. How does a cold drink and a cuppa sound, then I'll show you your room?'

'Very welcome, thank you. And please, it's Bea.' She was looking around at the graceful lines of the front room, at the high ceiling with its moulded corners and the elegant mantel above the fireplace. The tapestry seats of the ladder-back chairs added faded colour, and Max's bowl of dried flowers was reflected in the polished surface it stood on. 'What a lovely room. Is the house very old?'

'A couple of generations. Harry's father built it and Harry's in his nineties. He's something of a local historian; he can tell you all about it.'

About to follow her, Bea hesitated. 'And my car? Is there a shed? Somewhere it can stand out of the sun?'

'Good idea. It should be out of sight. Better if nobody knows you're here,' Kate agreed. 'We'll find somewhere, even if I have to shift mine to make room.'

Bea raised one pale brow. She had sandy-coloured hair twisted back into a chignon. 'I was thinking of the paintwork.'

'I,' said Kate grimly, 'am more concerned that my brother never finds out you were here.'

Harry, whom Kate feared might have forgotten all about Bea's expected arrival, accepted her presence without fuss. 'From the city, eh? Then you'll not be used to the heat.'

'No. Is it always this hot, Mr Quickly?'

'Times it is, times it's hotter.' He cackled maliciously. 'Fire summers are the worst. Mind you, couple more degrees, this could be one. Back in '51 I remember . . . ' He was off on one of his favourite stories, words and facts ready at his tongue's tip. *His mental faculties are amazing for his age*, Kate thought, listening with half an ear as she prepared meat for the oven. Later when Bea had gone off to rest, her offer to help refused, Harry grasped the back of a chair to haul himself to his feet.

'Might have a nap myself. Nothing but visitors these days, Missy. They wear a man out.'

'I'm sorry. I should have thought of that.' Contrite, she looked searchingly at him, only to find a twinkle in his deep-set eyes.

'Rubbish, girl. I was turning into an old fossil before you came. I like it. How long's this one staying?'

'Could be one night or several – until my sister-in-law gets here. Which depends on Doug. She'll come the moment he leaves on whatever trip he's taking – that's my guess. And knowing Clove they'll not hang around here either. She's terrified of him.'

'He might've met his match in this lawyer woman. Got an eye on her like a gimlet. Had an aunt with that same look once. She was a holy terror.' His bony shoulders shook with sudden laughter. 'Me and my cousin Lenny set fire to the dunny once, with her in it. We were just burning the grass behind it, never thought it'd catch, but it did and Aunt Roma came out like a charging rhino – she wasn't built skinny like this one, but she had the same eye.' He shook his head. 'Petticoats or not, and she had plenty, I reckon we'd have preferred the rhino.'

Kate smiled at the image he'd conjured. 'How old were you?'

'About ten. My cousin was a few years older; I remember he had the matches.'

'Born to be hanged, the pair of you. What happened to Lenny? Did he go on to bigger and better arsons?'

'In a way,' Harry said. 'He shipped to France in 1918, the hinder end of the war. Never came home.'

'I'm sorry,' Kate said gently. He had lived through so much history, it awed her. She watched him shamble from the room and, lifting the hair where it curled damply against her neck, went out to water the pot plants on the verandah.

* * *

The worst of the heat was past and Kate was scattering grain for the hens when, for the second time that day, she heard a vehicle on the road. Clover. She wondered if her sister-in-law would stay overnight and mentally reviewed how far dinner would stretch. Some extra potatoes should do it, she decided. The children wouldn't eat much and Clove would be as nervous as a cat – if she even agreed to stay. Fleetingly she wondered how the woman could have been certain that Bea had arrived, then considering the emotional state she'd have to be in, abandoned the eggs for later collection and hurried towards the gate. But the green Datsun pulled up there, its engine still running, was unknown to her, unlike the figure wrestling busily with the gate in an attempt to drive into the yard. The feed tin fell unnoticed from her hand.

'Guy!' It had to be some sort of nightmare. Expecting her brother's runaway wife, she had got instead her own absconded husband. Memory of their parting, the cleaned-out account, the smack of his fist connecting with her face, banished the shock, replacing it with a healthy dose of rage. 'What the *hell* do you think you're doing here?'

'Kate – baby.' Leaving the gate, Guy walked towards her, arms out, his good-looking face, with its rather weak chin and indeterminate gaze that slid guiltily from hers, twisted in contrition. 'Baby, I've been so wrong and I'm so sorry. I can't tell you, Kate – perhaps I had to lose you to realise how much I need you. You've got to forgive me this one last time and I swear that I'll never look at another woman. I mean it, Kate. This time I really do.' As she stepped back his arms slowly fell. 'I *need* you, baby,' he reiterated.

Kate's lip curled. 'Luci dumped you, did she? Well, that's too bad, but I can't say I blame her. Did you beat her up too? I don't know what you think you're doing here, or why you've come, but you can turn right round and go again. You left me, remember? It's over, Guy. I'm filing for divorce.'

The intention to do so crystallised as she spoke, as if she had suddenly blinked awake from a drugged stupor. All those weeks and months of rudderless unhappiness, convincing herself she'd failed in some fundamental way – over a man not worth the dust on her shoes! While at the same time she'd scorned Clover's lack of effort to free herself from a much more dangerous situation. When she compared their relative positions, Kate found her own suddenly much less admirable.

She spoke wearily. 'Go home, Guy. I can't think why you ever came. Someone will be in touch later about the divorce.'

'I can't,' he said sulkily. 'The house at Byron's gone. You think I've got the sort of money that —'

'Your problem,' Kate said. 'You left me with it and I didn't even have a job – or any money after you cleaned out our account.'

He flushed. 'I'm sorry; I shouldn't have done that.'

'Like you shouldn't have hit me either, I suppose? Marrying you was a mistake, Guy. I've known it for years, but it's only now that I've come to my senses enough to know I'm better of without you. It's over.'

She meant it. Guy, whose persuasive tongue had seldom failed him, couldn't believe it. Kate had always compromised for him, believed what he'd told her – or pretended to – and if not forgiven outright, then at least come round enough to allow him time to work on the side of her nature that *wanted* things to be right between them. That couldn't have changed, not in just a few months. He shouldn't have hit her – that was the sticking point here – but perhaps even that could be overcome if he grovelled enough. But it would take time. He sighed heavily. 'Look, I'm really sorry, Kate. But it's late and I've been driving all day, and I've nowhere to go.'

Her voice was cold. 'Try the Railway Arms in Laradale.'

He hid a flash of irritation. 'I'm short of dough. Couldn't I just stay here for the night?' His gaze went past her to the solid outline of the farmhouse and the verandah, where Bea now stood watching them. 'It's a big house, and it would give me a chance to explain. If you'll just let me explain —'

'No to both. You can't stay and I've heard you explain before. It's never your fault, is it? Besides, it's my employer's house. I work here, I have one room – which I'm not about to share.'

'Is that Mrs Farmer, then?' He nodded at Bea and Kate saw that the woman had come out to lean on the verandah railing behind them. 'Supposing I ask her? Country people are famous for their hospitality and it's only one night.'

She shook her head wonderingly. 'You always were a tightwad, Guy. Something for nothing, that's your motto. No, she isn't, as you put it, Mrs Farmer. She's my guest. In fact,' she added maliciously, 'she's a lawyer who specialises in divorce. Now go! And if you're thinking of hitting me again,' she warned as his expression tightened in frustration, 'she'll also make a fine witness.'

'Baby, you can be a bitch,' Guy snarled, his fair skin suffused with blood. 'I should've known better than to come. All right, rot here then with your paddocks and your crows. You always liked the sticks. I hope your fancy man falls into his own combine.' He strode back to the car, slammed the door and roared off in a cloud of dust.

Kate's feet took her automatically to the gate; she heaved it shut and chained it while his parting shot echoed in her head . . . *falls into his own combine*. Part of her brain wondered how Guy even knew what a combine harvester was. The rest was filled with a spreading sense of disaster. Her heartbeat had quickened and her sweaty palms felt suddenly cold. If he went to Stones Place and repeated her words – and if Clover had already left . . . or even if she hadn't . . .

Her brain spinning, Kate couldn't decide which scenario would be worse. She found herself on the verandah with no recollection of climbing the steps, and Bea's bony face, thin lips pursed, studying her.

'Are you all right? You seem a little upset.' The clipped tones were dispassionate.

'Yes – no. I think – I think I may have given us away to my brother. *If* he's home, and my husband – that was my husband, legally anyway – goes to him, which I think he might. He was being awkward and to get rid of him I told him you were a divorce lawyer. It'll take Doug about two seconds to work it out.'

Bea's long fingers came together and tapped her lips. 'Why should he go to your brother? Isn't he supposed to be away from home? Anyway, what makes you think they're connected?'

'He said something only Doug could have told him. Doug must've contacted him as soon as —' *The Growers' Dinner*, she thought numbly. He'd seen them together there, she and Max, and saw a chance to make mischief, for her, or for him, though for the life of her she couldn't see what he gained by it. Tiredly she wondered at the way Doug's mind worked. He'd told Max she'd go back to Guy, and he'd told her that Max and Connie . . . all just to make mischief. 'If Guy were to see him he'll be forewarned. She'll never get away then.' Would he do that, she wondered, head to the farm in the hope of a night's accommodation? Her mother had never made much effort to disguise her opinion of him, but Guy could be thick-skinned when there was an advantage to be gained.

Piecing Kate's disjointed phrases together, Bea crinkled her brow. 'Well, let's wait and see – and prepare for a quick start. There may be no need but if you had a thermos ready and something for the children to eat?' She tapped her teeth thoughtfully. 'We could be gone at once. Just throw her stuff in the car – I've hung a few things, perhaps I'll just repack them – in case. Oh, and I found this.' Reaching into her pants' pocket, she handed Kate the sticky-taped little packet Maxie had given her. 'It was in the bedside drawer.' Bea gave a smile that illuminated her pale eyes and made her rather plain face suddenly attractive. 'It looks like somebody meant it to stay unopened.'

'Oh, yes, thank you.' Kate dropped it into her own pocket as they turned indoors. 'I can't think how it got there. Thermos and food – that's no trouble. But we never actually worked out what to do with Clover's car. Ideally it shouldn't be found here. I'd rather not involve Harry in any . . . unpleasantness. He *sounds* robust enough, but he's not really. If Max – but he's not here.' She remembered Ken Wantage then and her face cleared. 'It's okay. There's a friend I can contact. I'll drive it off somewhere, the old quarry maybe, and he can pick me up and bring me back. That way we might keep Doug off the scent a bit longer.'

'Even if it doesn't, there'll be nothing he can do,' Bea said calmly. 'Once she's safe in the refuge, the law will see to that.'

Kate smiled wanly and pinched nervously at the bump in her pocket. 'You don't know my brother.'

'No,' Bea's eyes flashed and her crisp vowels hardened, 'but I'm looking forward to prosecuting him. I haven't seen Clover since her marriage, and the emotional wreck who contacted me was *not* the feisty woman I remember. She had a good mind when I knew her, and strong views about women's rights. That Clover would've walked out the door the first time he raised a hand to her.'

'She didn't have children then. And the one she's carrying now – she told me it's the result of rape.'

'The bastard!' Bea hissed vehemently, then recovered her professional poise. 'Hard one to prove, that.'

'I daresay,' Kate agreed. 'The point is, she's in a pretty fragile state, and with good reason. You'll need to be patient, Bea, and careful. He shouldn't, but if Doug gets within physical reach of her, he'll be dangerous. His whole future is tied up in his sons.'

'Then I'm happy to think I'm going to help him lose them.' She zipped the bag shut with a flourish. 'There. Ready when she is.'

22

Clover arrived just before sunset, driving not the town car but Doug's four-wheel drive. She slewed to an erratic stop outside the gate and struggled awkwardly from the high cab, her hair falling across her pale, red-eyed face. Moving jerkily as a puppet, she rounded the vehicle and released Andy, also tear-stained, and clutching a clown doll, from a seat belt that had been cobbled about to fit his small size. He was fretful and clung to her, shrinking from the unfamiliarity about him.

'Don't like it, Mummy. Want to go home. Want Gran.'

'Hush, sweetie.' Clover swallowed and kissed his forehead. 'It's all right. We're going to see Aunty Kate – you remember her? She's nice. Look, here's her puppy come to meet you.'

Clover set him down amid the gathering shadows as the last of the sunlight glinted off the windscreen and three crows flew cawing above the mallee. Andy squealed 'Doggy!' as the pup's tongue found his face. The mill turned sluggishly and the smell of roasting meat and damp earth mixed in her head with a wave of sudden dizziness. She clung grimly to the seat back until it passed, trying to still the clamour of grief and indecision that all but paralysed her, then hooked out the two bags that were all she'd brought, and stooped to take her small son's hand.

'Going to see Aunty Kate,' she chanted, like a mantra of

hope, and led him towards the gate.

Kate had heard Flip's bark and was flying to meet her. Wordlessly she opened the gate and seized the bags. 'Come inside. We've been waiting,' she said. 'Bea's here.' And then, stopping in her tracks as she noticed both Clover's silence and his absence, 'Where's Jeremy?'

It was enough to shatter her sister-in-law's precarious control. The sobs came, thickening her words until they were almost indistinguishable. 'Doug took him. He never said – I didn't know – and then they were gone. I've been going mad. How can I get him back if I leave – but if I don't – and there's the baby . . . '

'Stop! Clove, you must stop it now, for the baby's sake.' Kate dumped the bags and picked up the wailing Andy, upset by his mother's distress. Bea had come out and was hurrying towards them; Kate signalled her with her eyes, mouthing, 'The bags.'

The woman nodded and Kate, her spare hand firmly guiding her sister-in-law's steps, got her inside, Bea following. 'Hello, Clover,' she said.

'Oh, Bea, you came. I'm sorry,' she took the tissues Kate handed her and mopped her eyes, 'and Mr Quickly, it's g-good of you to —' Manners gave way in the face of grief. 'Oh, Kate – did I do right? What if I don't ever see him again? Doug's never taken the boys with him before, not overnight. He'll be gone two days. Do you think he suspects? Is that why he took him?'

Kneading the wet tissues, she raised a blotched face to the two women. Kate explained in a rapid undertone. 'Her eldest son – Doug's taken him along on the trip.'

Bea considered for a moment, a tapered finger once again tapping her mouth. 'Could you return home now?'

'What?' Clover stared at her, unconscious of the contrast between the slim, neat figure of her old friend and her own swollen, rumpled, tear-stained state. 'Go back? No. Mother Doolin knows

I've left. She'd never believe anything I could make up to explain it, not this late. He left this morning; it took me all day to decide to come.'

'Then we carry on as planned.'

'But Jeremy, my little boy —'

Kate patted her back as she sobbed, Andy clinging to her leg with one hand as he peeped past her at Harry, sitting in his usual chair, silent amid the feminine uproar.

'Stop it, Clover,' Bea said crisply. 'We'll get him back. I promise you we will. Pull yourself together or this whole thing will go pear-shaped. We don't need a miscarriage now.' Clover blinked at this brisk handling but Bea, hefting the two bags, carried on. 'This is all your stuff? Then I'll take it to the car. You're going to wash your face, then we'll eat something and we're leaving.' Her heels tapped decisively away across the floor and in the sudden silence as Clover caught her breath on a final sob Andy said plainly, 'Mummy, that man's face is hairy.'

Harry winked at him, placed both hands under his beard and flipped it up to eye level. 'Bet you can't do that,' he said with satis-faction when his face reappeared. Andy crowed with delight, and let go of Kate's leg.

'Gain,' he cried. 'Do it 'gain.'

They followed the program Bea had outlined. A comb and some time in the bathroom restored a fragile calm to Clover. By then Harry and Andy were firm friends. Fascinated to see the fork-fuls of food vanish into Harry's beard, Andy was easily persuaded to match each mouthful, and when his eyes grew heavy Kate wiped his face and lifted him into the cushions on the kitchen settee while the adults finished. Five minutes later he was fast asleep. Clover's composure held up until she glanced across at the angelic little face with its double curve of lashes lying gently on the tender cheeks. Her lips trembled and Bea reached across to grip her hand.

'You've done the right thing. Victims don't have choices but you made one today. Work it out – you had a good brain once.'

Clover smiled weakly. 'And you were always abrasive. I'm glad you're here, Bea. I'd be ecstatic if only Jeremy was too.'

'We'll get him back. Now, loo stop, then it's time to go.'

'Yes.' To Harry she said, 'I'm afraid it's been a terrible imposition, Mr Quickly. I can't thank you enough for —'

'That's all right. Sad to see a marriage go wrong, but if bolting's the only way . . . What about your vehicle? Seems to me you're expecting your husband to chase you, and the getaway car's a good starting point.' Gruffly he added, 'I don't want him blaming the girl.'

Touched by his concern, Kate said swiftly, 'I'm taking care of that, Harry. I'll drive it away somewhere – up to Macquarrie, I thought.' The customary name for the old quarry came automatically to her lips. 'I'll ring Ken first, see if he can follow and bring me back.'

Harry's eyebrows bristled. 'Where's the sense in that? You can bet your life the police'll want to know who put it there. Ask the lawyer here.'

Kate looked at Bea, who reluctantly nodded. 'If it's not stealing,' Harry said, 'it's Taking and Driving Away, or some such foolery; if they can't charge you for it, they'll sure as hell make a fuss. You don't want that.'

'No.' She chewed her lip. 'But it can't stay here either.'

'Well, use your loaf, girl – what do runaways do? You can't catch a plane from Laradale, but there're buses, trains —'

'Of course.' She flashed him a smile. 'I'll park behind the bus station. *Much* better. He'll never know she was here.'

'Unless your husband says something,' Bea reminded her. She had picked up the sleeping child and was shepherding Clover, very much as Flip did with the hens, towards the door.

'Says what? That I'm consulting a lawyer about a divorce? It can be the truth any time you care to send me the papers, Bea. But get Clove sorted out before you start on my mistake.' She hugged her sister-in-law. 'Be strong, Clove. And don't worry. The court'll never let him keep Jeremy. You'll be safe too – you and the baby.'

'I'll see she is,' Bea said brusquely. 'I'll ring when we get there. And you can ring me in a week or so with the details for your divorce. Thank you, Mr Quickly. I'm sorry about the intrusion. I'll make sure it does some good.'

'Don't worry yourself.' Harry was making his slow way to open the door for them. He cackled happily. 'Haven't had a peaceful moment since Missy here arrived. I'm quite getting to enjoy it.'

When they'd gone with the still-sleeping child strapped into the car seat and the headlights carving a bright track through the silent mallee, Kate came back up the steps and tucked her hand companionably through his arm. 'You're an old dear, Harry. I'm sure your Edie would be proud of you. Now, I'd better ring Ken. I've just thought, it's New Year's Eve. I hope he's home.'

He was, if a little puzzled by her timing. 'Happy New Year, Kate. A little early in the evening, aren't you?'

She glanced at the clock, startled to see it had barely gone eight. 'Yes, well I didn't call about that. Could you – I hate to ask, Ken – but I wonder if could you do me a big favour?'

'If I can,' he responded simply. 'What is it?'

'Could you meet me in town?'

'Tonight, you mean?' Now he sounded startled.

'In, say, an hour? Wait for me —' She thought rapidly. It needed to be somewhere out of sight. 'At the back of the library. If you meet anybody, don't say why you're there. Can you do that?'

'Yes,' he said, mystified. 'Mind telling me why? You're not in any sort of trouble, are you?'

'No, but it has to be secret, Ken. Trust me. I'll tell you everything when you get there.'

She'd overestimated deliberately in allowing an hour but it took her fifty minutes. She found the gears difficult and the Toyota sat much higher on the road than the Commodore so she drove carefully, avoiding the direct way up Mooky Lane to come into town from the opposite end. The pubs were a blaze of light and there was a party going on in The Chef's Place. She kept to the back streets, and sighed with relief as she slipped neatly into a parking bay behind the high-roofed depot at the bus station and killed the motor. That end of town was quiet; after a moment's thought she locked the vehicle and pushed the keys behind the front wheel, then set off quickly for the library.

Ken was waiting in the car with the windows down and the fan running. His body was in shadow but she sensed as much as saw him before opening the door and sliding in. 'Thanks for coming, Ken. We can go now.'

He reached to turn the key. 'What's going on, Katie?'

She had thought carefully about how much to tell him. The less he knew, the less he'd have to keep quiet about. Because as sure as Doug would first suspect Kate of complicity in his wife's escape, his attention would turn next to her friends. She said, 'Did you know that Doug beats Clover? I've seen the bruises. He's been terrorising her for years and nobody's done anything about it. She was too scared to, and Mum, if she knew – and she *must've* – would never admit it happened. Well, I've just helped her get away. I swear, Ken, if she'd stayed, he'd have wound up killing her. What sane man belts up a pregnant woman? Anyway, she's gone. And when he returns from wherever he went, he'll find his Toyota at the bus station.'

'So you need a ride home?'

'You've got it. I'm sorry to involve you, but there was no one else.'

'You know,' he said simply, 'there doesn't need to be while I'm around.'

She felt her eyes fill and blinked the tears back. 'Thank you.'

'So,' he said practically, 'when's he due back?'

'Clove didn't know. She was in a bit of a state because at the last minute he took young Jerry with him, so at present they have one son each. Clove's devastated, but with the baby due in three months she had to seize the chance. It could be her last one.' With bitter passion she added, 'Mum's always been one-eyed about him but she loves her grandsons. How she could stand by and let it happen is beyond me.'

'They certainly kept it in house, as it were.' They were running through the quiet streets past lighted homes. 'Heather and I had no idea. I mean, we knew she wasn't happy – you only have to look at her – but that there was physical abuse – of course, we didn't see much of her. She'd dropped out of most things the last few years anyway. It was mostly your mother who turned up for the various committees. I hope,' he added with an abrupt change of subject as he slowed for the turn into Mooky Lane, 'that some silly bugger back there isn't planning on fireworks come midnight.'

'They'll be banned, surely?'

'Doesn't always stop 'em. They head out into farmland to set them off, then scoot before the cops arrive – and before they notice if they've started a fire.' He grunted angrily. 'Stupid bastards. No more brains than God gave geese.'

'You're right there.'

His shoulders lifted in a shrug, then he stood on the brakes and doused the light as they came to a stop.

'What was it?'

'Bandicoot, echidna – didn't really see. We'll give him a minute. Have you thought what you'll do when Doug returns, Kate? He'll see your hand in this. I mean, if the abuse has been going on for a while, Clover could have gone ages ago. The only difference now is that you're here. You see the reasoning?'

'I know. I'll act surprised. He'll be angry.' She rephrased the statement, glad the dimness in the cab hid her shiver of apprehension. 'He'll be *furious* but he can't prove I was involved. Nobody saw me at the depot – I made sure of that.'

Ken grunted again. The night sped by, drenched in starlight that threw no shadows; the cool air carried the smell of dust and dried feed, and she ducked involuntarily as the shape of a nightjar fled, half glimpsed, across their windscreen. The corners of split fence posts and the trunks of the mallee wavered in the moving beams and once she saw a little huddle of sheep facing outwards from the corner of a paddock.

'Fox's been among 'em, or a dog,' Ken muttered. And then, 'How's the pup?'

By the time she'd told him they'd reached Rosebud. She hugged him at the gate, promised to call at need, then stood watching while Flip yapped on the chain as Ken's headlights swung about and moved off down the track. She rubbed her arms, went and spoke to the dog, then entered the house. A light burned in the kitchen and she found Harry sitting on the old settee in the corner listening to a radio program.

'There you are, girl.' He turned a knob and the voices faded to a murmur. 'Everything go all right?'

'Yes. Only I've just realised we didn't check a timetable. So we don't even know if there was a bus running today, let alone when it left.'

'Should've been. Every day, save Easter Friday, Christmas, and New Year. Trains are twice a week, but it's eight p.m. on the dot for the bus. It carries the mail, see?'

'Good,' Kate said. 'Mind you, he's only to speak to the booking clerk to realise she didn't take it.'

Harry nodded, his faded eyes shrewd. 'Of course. But is he likely to broadcast the fact she's left him? I knew a fella years ago, had country up the northern side of the Wolly. A regular savage – there was no other way to describe him. Shockingly cruel man. Hit a horse with an axe once because it wouldn't stand to be harnessed – almost took the poor creature's foot off. He beat his wife, too, and when she left him he never breathed a word. Kept up the pretence she was still there for – oh, five years or more. When his neighbours finally realised she wasn't, he was arrested for her murder and they would've hanged him if the truth hadn't come out.'

Kate was scarcely listening. She said, 'You cleaned up, you old dear. You shouldn't have! I'd have done it when I got back.'

He shrugged. 'I'm not useless, Missy. I can still wash a few dishes. The scraps are over there.' He nodded to Flip's bowl. 'Kettle's ready to go if you want a cuppa.'

'Thank you, I do.' She was touched to see that he'd set out cups and sugar bowl, and the pot was already charged with leaves. 'I'll be straight back, soon as I've fed Flip.'

Standing under the stars surrounded by the smell of dog and damp earth, she tipped her head to seek the brilliance of the Cross, while Flip gulped his food, the rapid rattle of his chain a counterpoint to the long drawn clank of the rods spilling water into the tank, and thought fondly of her employer. She wished she could have known him ten or even fifteen years ago, before his days hung by the gossamer thread that tethered any ninety-year-old to life. He was nothing like her father but he still resembled Brian Doolin in that he exuded the same rugged wisdom, as if life with all its tragedy and disappointments was something he'd long come to terms with. Unlike herself . . . The bowl, thrust by Flip's energetic tongue, hit her foot. She bent to pat him, then turned back to the lighted kitchen and the waiting tea, suddenly weary from what had been an emotionally charged day.

Harry had already poured for her. 'Take the weight off,' he invited and she sank thankfully onto the other end of the settee. Something dug into her thigh and, exploring her pocket, she retrieved Maxie's gift which she'd dropped in there earlier and then forgotten about. Smiling at his enthusiastic sealing of the little package, she rose, fetched the scissors and snipped the tape free, then carefully unfolded the paper to reveal a scrap of raw sheep's wool with something hard at its centre.

'Well, he certainly didn't mean it to get bro—' Her voice died in her throat as she stared down at a carving that had once been as familiar to her as the one that presently hung on the chain about her neck.

Harry's voice broke the silence. 'Something wrong, Missy?'

'It's Tam.' She whispered. Her face had paled and she was suddenly cold. 'My father carved it for Megan. He made me this.' She pulled the carved pony from inside the neck of her blouse to show him. 'That's Blackie. Then he made Tam for her. She had it on when she disappeared.' Kate stared as if mesmerised by the miniature likeness, then raised wide eyes to Harry's bearded face. 'She was wearing it, Harry, but the search parties never found so much as a thread of her clothing, so where on earth can Maxie have got it from?'

23

Kate sat turning the exquisite little likeness of Tam over and over in her fingers. There was no visible damage. The points of Tam's ears were as sharp as ever, his nose as round, the ruff at his nape perfect. The dark wood shone – although Maxie could have buffed it up, she supposed, and the little brass findings through which a chain would go must certainly have been polished. *If*, she thought uneasily, *blood had ever stained it, then only a forensic examination could tell*. She thought of the care and skill that had gone into its making, and the ache of her father's loss was as fierce and sudden as it had been at the time of his death. Closing her hand over the carving, she let her brow sink onto it, remembering as she did so the next time she'd returned to the farm after Alec Forsyth's visit.

Ken had wanted to drive her, Martin had offered to accompany her, but she'd elected to go alone, walking across the paddocks as she and Megan had always done. Her friend was on her mind that day, partly because that loss was an old wound lacking the raw hurt of this newest one. She had sat in the wheat for a long while, hunched over, her arms about her knees on the little rise where, as children, they'd believed the fox had denned, and from there she'd progressed to the old pepper tree behind the shed that had been her refuge as a child. But whatever solace it had once held was missing that day, as it had mostly been since the maiming of the ginger cat, and in the end there had been nothing for it but to enter the house and feel the emptiness of his departure.

There had been one other stop to make first, but the second she pushed open the door to expose the curled shavings underfoot she had known this sanctum too was lost to her. It had taken her a moment to comprehend the ugliness of it – the carving tools that had fitted so sweetly to his hand hurled from their places, scattered blade-down wherever they had landed. The stacked and weighted timber kicked apart, and in the middle of the floor her father's box hacked open and left, with the axe blade still buried in its ruined end.

Weeping quietly, she had gathered the contents: his army discharge, his marriage certificate, drawings of furniture he would now never make . . . The box was beyond salvage, its opening mechanism sheared through. She found an old black-and-white snap of a Doolin family group, her own report cards from primary school, the program from her high school prom. She collected his tools, and placed them in the box but made no attempt to lever the axe free. Let whoever next came upon it see what he had done; let him dispose of the evidence of his own shameful act. Once the funeral was over she would never set foot on the farm again.

Hands filled with the collection of salvaged items, Kate had greeted her mother at the house, then gone immediately to her room to begin packing. That done she took string from the kitchen drawer and cardboard from the one in the dining room sideboard where Edna had always thriftily stashed items that could be useful, and cut labels to tie to the furniture – the bookcase and chest of drawers, and the curly-backed chair and dressing table – that over the years her father had crafted for her.

At Stones Farm they had never had a proper Christmas tree or strung Christmas lights the way the Wantages had done. But there'd been a small tree, brought out each year to stand on one end of the sideboard in the largely unused dining room. Brian Doolin had carved the exquisite little ornaments that hung on it – bells and stars and pot-bellied Santas whittled from scraps of lumber. Kate's favourite had always been the reindeer with their splendid branching antlers. She was taking them down, packing them carefully between layers of tissue, when Doug walked past and saw her there.

'What are you doing?' They were the first words he'd spoken to her since she'd refused to greet him.

She looked up, meeting the gaze of a stranger. He had always been different but what he had done had made him into something alien, a force she could neither control nor understand – not that she had ever done either, but it was somehow more disconcerting to meet with it in the large man's body he had acquired since she'd left to begin her training. Yes, he'd always been older, five and a half years, to be precise, and would shortly be married, while she remained, in effect, an inexperienced teenager – at least until her next birthday. Towering above her, intimidatingly close, his sheer physical bulk seemed to emphasise her youth and helplessness, and the more so when he shrugged, saying carelessly, 'It's not going to matter to him whether they're up or down, you know, Katie. He's dead. Boxing up decorations won't bring him back.'

'Don't call me that!' she flared. 'I'm taking them, and the furniture he made me, and Tam. If I never set eyes on you again, it'll suit me fine! You and Mum can fester together —'

Doug threw back his handsome head and laughed. 'What a little hellcat you are! If you could see yourself – like a baby shrew on its hind legs. Take the stuff. It's junk anyway. But I'm afraid you'll have to do without the old mongrel. I shot him – a masterless dog has no place on a farm.'

She had screamed at him then, the noise bringing Edna from her work, and for the first time in her life, Kate thought now, she'd had a shouting match with her mother, yelling out her fury and accusations against them both. She had not cared what she said – in truth she could not say anything bad enough about her brother, but neither had Edna escaped her censure. They deserved each other, but she cursed the day her parents had met to make their farce of a marriage, as she was certain her father had also done . . .

'Stop it!' Edna never shouted, but she had then, pale face patched red with anger. 'Listen to yourself,' she said furiously. 'Have you learned nothing of respect and proper behaviour? I might as well have tried to teach a rock! Your father's dead and here you're brawling to raise the roof. As a widow, I could be afforded some respect. And Doug was right to shoot Tam. How were you going to keep a farm dog in a flat anyway? I've already —'

'I'd have found a way, or left him with the Wantages. Uncle Ken wouldn't —'

'He's not your uncle,' Edna said shortly. 'As for your father's precious box – as I was saying, I've already spoken to Doug about that. But perhaps you should examine your own behavior there. It wouldn't have hurt either of you to have shared it with him years ago, then the situation would never have arisen.'

'Oh, yes,' Kate's eyes stung with tears of sheer fury, 'give him everything he wants so the monster won't be nasty – is that it? Then I hope you never get in his way, or you might find out what it's like to be Tam.'

'Go to your room, Kathryn,' Edna said icily. 'You can apologise when you come to your senses.'

The familiarity of the command had pulled Kate up. She blinked and the room that had seemed, moments since, to be the centre of a hurricane, stilled. She saw her mother's stiff figure and white face; her brother's bright, almost clinical gaze; the known lines of family portraits; the heavy, well-polished furniture. The sudden realisation that now she need no longer obey, or even stay, or ever set foot in the place again, was like a gift from her dead father's hand.

'I wouldn't hold your breath,' she said. 'You might smother.'

Then with the little box of ornaments in her hand she'd walked across the room, down the hallway, through the front door and over the paddocks to The Narrows. She'd returned the following day with Ken's ute, and Ken himself wooden-faced behind the wheel.

Edna met her at the door but she'd brushed past her, saying only, 'I've come for my stuff. This way, Uncle Ken.'

It wasn't possible (she'd counted on the fact) for her mother to make a scene before a neighbour. Ken, embarrassed beyond words but stalwart as always, had bade Edna good morning, then played his part silently, carrying the heavy pieces and packing them carefully for the short ride back. Clover, her sister-in-law-to-be, was arriving that morning and Doug had gone to meet her train. Kate was thankful for that. She scarcely knew Clover but anything that kept Doug away was good. When the last bit of luggage was stowed Ken nodded gravely to the silent woman. 'He was a good man, Brian. A good neighbour. I'm going to miss him. We'll see you at the funeral.'

Kate had said nothing, climbing into the cab and slamming the door, refusing to look at her mother as they drove away. Remembering it now, she regretted that. Ken had tried to tell Kate she would, but she'd known better, of course. She sighed. Nothing had ever gone right between her mother and herself. With a child's simplicity and innate sense of what was right, rather than what was forgivable, she'd blamed Edna for everything. But it was possible, she thought now, that her mother too had cause for complaint. Kate had been a stubborn child, never relenting once her face was set against something. Even her championship of Brian might have hurt, for what, after all, did any child know of the complexities of their parents' marriage?

She sighed again; it was too late now to worry over the past. Besides, the carving was the immediate problem. It was evidence – she would have to take it to the police, but first she needed to speak to Maxie, and Ken would have to be told.

'Not tonight, though,' Harry said when she sought his opinion. 'It's been how many years? Another night won't make a difference, unless it's to how much sleep he and his wife get.' He ruminated on it before adding, 'Course there's another option. You could just put it away and say nothing.'

She almost recoiled from him. 'This is important, Harry. Megan was wearing it that day. It's a direct link between her and whatever happened.'

'Yes,' he growled, 'and you're proposing to drag it all up again; the heartache, the grief and loss. The parents have lived through it once – is it right to make them do it again?'

'I can't say. But I do know that Heather would never forgive me if she found out I knew something and hadn't told them. For her it can't get any worse. For Ken . . . ?' She shook her head. 'I don't know. But I'm sure he'd agree there are some things in life you can't dodge just because it hurts.'

'God protect me from sanctimonious women,' he muttered crankily. 'Well, you'll do as you like, Missy. It's something your sex is good at. I'm going to bed.'

'I'm sorry to disappoint you,' she said contritely to his back as he shuffled off. 'But when a parent loses a child —' Too late she remembered that his son, too, had died. 'I'll sleep on it,' she finished quietly. 'You're right about that. It would be cruel to call them tonight.'

* * *

In bed Kate tossed restlessly as the hours crept by on sticky flannel feet, marked at each quarter by the single chime of the hall clock. With a start she remembered Clover and her dilemma over leaving

Jeremy. It seemed like something that had happened last week, not mere hours before. She dozed and dreamt of fireworks exploding over the Seine, while she and Guy watched from the tiny balcony of their hotel. 'That's for us, babe,' he'd said, toasting her with his glass. 'They're doing it for us.' It had been one of the few spontaneous hours of pleasure they'd enjoyed in Paris, where the weather had been bad, the prices exorbitant and the people unfriendly. A holiday to forget rather than dwell on. An omen perhaps for the years ahead?

The dream faded then and she was a child again, riding home from school in the bus, watching the road with a rising sense of dread as they neared their stop on Mooky Lane. 'Don't get off, don't!' she pleaded, grabbing Megan's hand, but her friend had laughed and done so while Kate knelt on the seat, palms flat against the window glass staring back at her as the bus rolled on. Grey mist swallowed up the lane, out of which, with shocking suddenness, Gypsy Pete's horse had burst, eyes rolling wildly and great shards of bone protruding from his shattered leg.

Kate jerked awake with a cry, her pulse thudding in her ears. She sat up while the fragments of dream faded, and her heartbeat slowed, then went to the kitchen for a glass of water which she drank standing at the sink. The moon had risen, flooding the sheds and yard with light. She heard the slow thump of marsupial feet in the sheep paddock, and the rattle of Flip's chain as he stirred and barked.

Back in bed Kate took up the tiny carving from her bedside chest and held it, thinking about what the day ahead would bring – apart from the start of 1991. Megan had vanished on the twenty-third of October 1971, and twenty years later (if you counted the difference a day made) a part of her necklace had turned up. If she didn't tell the Wantages, then certainly the police would – and they had to know. Wasn't withholding evidence of a crime a chargeable offence? It was possible that the little carving might help uncover the enduring mystery of Megan's fate. Equally it might not, but she hadn't the right to decide. Somebody out there had taken her friend, and then hidden all traces of his act, but somewhere along the way he'd overlooked this vital piece of the puzzle. The little carving could be the one thing needed to help the police find the truth. And that, Kate thought sleepily, must be worth any pain its appearance produced.

Folding her hand carefully over the wooden amulet, she slept, to dream that she walked beside her father through a paddock of silver stubble splashed with the crimson of blowing poppies, while a young Tam ran, nose down beside them. She woke refreshed, with a smile for the new year heralded by the liquid call of magpies in the mallee.

24

Once having made her decision, Kate could not decide on how best to carry it out. Should she ask Ken to visit her, or risk the increasingly feeble battery in the Commodore and go to The Narrows? It would come as a terrible shock, so should she see them together, or leave it to Ken to tell his wife? And whatever she did, the next question was when? When was a good time to shatter their peace on New Year's Day? She grimaced across the table at her employer.

'The closer I come to it, the more I see your point about forgetting the whole thing. Only the thought of him getting away with it stops me doing so.'

Harry raised his bristly white brows. 'Who exactly?'

'Whoever killed her. She has to be dead.'

He spread marmalade with maddening deliberation and took a bite before answering. It was a ploy, Kate knew. His brain worked quite as fast as her own; he might speak slowly but that was a regional thing and nothing to do with age.

'Maybe so, but that doodad didn't come off a dead body.'

Strangely the thought had never occurred to her, but instantly she knew that he was right. Remembering the fears and taboos of childhood, she realised that Maxie would never have touched anything connected with a skeleton. Which meant he had found it somewhere else. So did that improve the odds? Was it even possible

Megan still lived? If nothing else it helped Kate decide. She must definitely tell Ken, alone. And it would be best if she did it here rather than at his home. Once the dishes were done she'd phone, ask him to come over, tell him – she sought for inspiration . . . yes – that it was very important, a favour to do with last night. And with that thought the phone rang, its abrupt summons shattering the cool peace of the house.

Harry was looking at her; it had become accepted between them that she answered the phone, but she hesitated, wondering wildly if by some osmosis it was Ken sensing that something momentous had happened. Hesitantly, like one approaching a snarling cur, she reached to pick it up, then in a rush of relief remembered that of course, it was New Year's Day. Somebody – Max, or Heather, perhaps even Martin – was ringing to wish them a happy new year.

'Rosebud Farm, Kate speaking. Happy new year.'

'Kathryn!' Her mother's voice sharp with worry caused her to jerk the handpiece back from her ear. 'Is Clover there? Have you seen her?'

'What?' She recovered herself. 'No, of course not, Mum. Why? Isn't she there with you?'

'Would I be ringing if she was?'

'She won't be far,' Kate said carelessly. 'Ask Doug. He keeps her on a pretty short lead. I invited her, weeks back, to bring Andy and visit and he never even passed it on. She didn't even know about it when I saw her in the library.' She forced an indignant note into her voice.

'Doug's not home.' Edna might not have heard the rest. 'I phoned him, of course, when she didn't bring Andy back for his tea last night. Where can that stupid girl have taken him?'

Any sympathy Kate felt for the worried woman on the end of the phone fled. She said, 'I don't know. Ask Jeremy. Try her friends in town. Look, I've got to go. I'm expecting a call.' She put the phone down and blew out a shaky breath. 'Okay, the hunt's officially on. Mum rang Doug last night at wherever he is. Maybe I should've asked, got a clue to how long they've got before he's back? Too late now.'

'Nothing more you can do.' Harry carried his cup and plate to the sink. 'Any road, my money's on that lawyer woman. That was an eight-cylinder car she had,' he added somewhat obscurely, then paused to squint down the hallway where the sunlight lay bright beyond the screen door. 'There's Maxie, just arriving now.'

Instead of dropping his bike and leaping up the verandah steps, the boy came carefully, one hand cradling a small bulge inside his ragged T-shirt. His thin face was animated as he let the screen door slam behind him and greeted them eagerly, ''Lo Miss, Harry – look what I found.'

It was a possum kit, a small bundle of fur and huge eyes cowering in the cage of his hands. 'Its mum was lying right by the road about a kilometre back.' He stroked the tiny creature's head. 'Hit by a car. We've gotta save it, hey?' Kate found herself the focus of his pleading eyes. 'It wouldn't take much and I'll do all the feeds – promise! It just needs milk and somewhere soft and dark, like a shoebox maybe? Please? The uncles'll kill it if I take him home. Biggest pests, they reckon, after rabbits.'

'Don't look at me,' Harry said helpfully into the silence. 'She's in charge here.'

Kate gave in – not that she had any choice, she thought. She couldn't let it die, and there were no animal refuges in Laradale. 'We'll need an eye-dropper. And —' her eyes roved the kitchen, wishing the house possessed a plush cushion, 'I expect the tea-cosy will have to do.' If not furry, it was soft enough for the kit to cuddle into. She sighed, 'And they're nocturnal, night creatures,' she amended. 'Of course you can't do all the feeds.'

'I can. I'll stay here, Miss.'

'That's your mother's decision to make,' Kate said gently. 'It's all right. I'll take care of it. We'd best fix it up now but later there's something I want to talk to you about, Maxie.'

He looked wary. 'I haven't done nothing wrong, Miss.'

'I know. You're not in trouble; I just need your help.'

'Oh.' He straightened, visibly pleased. 'Anything, Miss.' Generously he added, 'You can name the kit, too, if you want.'

While feeding and bedding down the little creature, they settled on the name of Vegemite, after Kate had explained *Possum Magic* to Maxie. Then with the dishes still in the sink Kate sat him down and produced the carving.

'I want you to tell me about this, Maxie. Where did you get it?'

'If you're thinking I pinched it, Miss, I never!' His eyes jumped nervously away from her. 'I brung it for you. I thought you liked it – you *said* you liked it.'

'Yes, I know.' Kate sighed, there was nothing for it. If she expected truth from him, then she must give it in return. 'I did say that, but it was what's called a white lie. One you tell to spare people's feelings. You see, I didn't open it straight away and then something came up and I forgot about it. So when you asked me I said that. Because I *knew* I would like whatever you chose. And it's true – it's lovely.' She turned it in her fingers, then pulled on the chain about her neck. 'See, I've got the other one here – you must have seen me wearing it? It's Tam you gave me, and this is Blackie, the pony. My father carved them when I was younger than you. But Tam was lost long before you were born. Somebody . . . took it. So I want to know how you came to have it.'

'Oh.' The fright had gone from his face. He looked towards Harry, who stood by the refrigerator as if he'd forgotten what he wanted from it, but was really there to support the boy. 'That's okay.' Expansive in relief, he said, 'I found it – near home. You ain't been there yet, but it's near the quarry they dug in the old days – that's a big hole in the ground, Miss. I think it was my mum's maybe, or,' he added doubtfully, 'the uncles? I wouldn'ta noticed him in the dirt, only for his ears. They stuck into my foot,' he explained. 'Course he was all dirty like, and the metal bits was green. But I polished him up good.'

'Yes, you did, Maxie. He looks as good as the day he was carved.'

'And your dad made them both?' He eyed the tiny pony with respect. 'I reckon he's dead clever, then.'

'Yes,' Kate said, 'he was. Thank you, Maxie.' Over his head her eyes met her elderly employer's. 'Well, I'll clean up, then make the call. Of course the police must've searched the quarry at the time. It's the first place they'd look; but I expect they'll go back.'

Maxie looked alarmed. 'You aren't telling the pleece, miss? The uncles'll kill me!'

'No, they won't,' she said firmly. 'I'll make sure of that.' Something about her mien must have convinced him, for he visibly relaxed at her words.

'Okay,' he murmured. 'How soon are we gonna feed Vegemite again?'

Harry harrumphed a sound that could have been a laugh. 'You're a dangerous woman, Missy. When you're through running the world, I'll have some pages ready for you to put in that computer.'

* * *

It was afternoon before Ken arrived. Heather had answered the phone and Kate, who had practised her pitch for Ken, was initially thrown, then found herself talking at random, pretending the call was simply that. She wished Heather a happy new year, asked whether they'd stayed up to see the old one out, and with Ken's words in mind expressed the hope that no fires had been reported.

'Thankfully no,' Heather said. 'Are you coming over to see us? Come for lunch, bring Harry too if he'd like it. Ken'll be back by then and they can have a beer and pore over the old maps. Ken said he was very interested in the lease here.'

'I can't today, Heather, I've other plans, but what about tomorrow?' *She would need someone tomorrow*, Kate thought guiltily. 'Would that suit you?'

'Of course, Lamb. We'll look forward to seeing you.'

'Thanks – and Heather, when Ken gets home, would you ask him to give me a ring. It's . . . rather urgent.'

'Yes, of course, Kate.' There was a brief silence before she continued delicately. 'Is it about last night?'

'In a way. I just need to speak to him.'

'I'll tell him. Till tomorrow, then. Bye.'

* * *

The morning ground endlessly on while outside the leathery grey-green of the mallee leaves hung motionless in the still air. A magpie, perched in the shade on a verandah rail, cocked his head to warble his song, and the iron roof made little cracking sounds in the heat. Maxie hovered over the shoebox until it was time for the possum's next feed, then vanished into the office where Harry was working. Kate heard the occasional murmur of voices as she swept, and watered the pot plants, then sat on the back steps to talk to Flip. It was too hot even for him; he sprawled belly down on the cool flagstones there, having learned his lesson about seeking coolness in Kate's flower garden. At one moment she wished that the morning were gone, and at the next that there were hours to go before she needed to speak to Ken. She served lunch and had cleared up before the call finally came.

She kept it short. 'Something's happened, Ken. I need to see you – alone. Can you come?' The handpiece crackled as she waited.

'Is it about last night?' he asked. 'Because —'

'No. There's something you need to see. Just come, please.'

A sense of the suppressed urgency she felt reached him. He said curtly, 'Very well,' and hung up. Kate's stomach fluttered as she put down the phone. For good or ill, it was done. How different would all their lives have been, she wondered, if Maxie had just worn shoes?

Ken was prompt. Kate had hardly thought he must be close when she heard the vehicle and a few moments later he was pulling up at the gate. Harry, emerging from his office, met her eyes. 'Do you want privacy or —'

'No, stay.' Maxie was already eeling from the room. He vanished through the kitchen and then Ken was at the door. Kate kissed his cheek.

'Thanks for coming.'

Wiping his feet, he said, 'What's this about, Kate? You were very mysterious. Hello, Harry – how's it going?'

'Because of Heather,' Kate said, ignoring everything else. 'Sit down, Ken. Just to prepare you – it's about Megan.' She saw his sudden shock and opened her hand. 'This has turned up.'

'Jesus!' he breathed and raised a stubby trembling finger to touch it. 'Where? How?'

She told him. Wordlessly he listened, then held out his hand and she tipped the little carving into his work-hardened palm. For a long moment he stared at it and she looked away, made uncomfortable by the gleam of unshed tears in his eyes.

'You've told the police?' Suppressed emotion roughened his voice.

'She said not before you knew.' It was the first time Harry had spoken.

'Then they have to know now.' He got up. 'The old quarry – they must've checked it before but they can damn well look again. He might've buried her there, made it look like a rock-fall, perhaps? There might be fissures in the rock left from blasting. He could —'

'Ken.' Kate touched him arm, then said it again louder, 'Ken, what about Heather?'

'Heather?' He frowned, his thoughts still seeking possibilities.

'Don't you see? This will be proof for her that Megan's alive.'

He stared at her, and pain flickered in his eyes. 'I can't not tell her, Kate. This – it's too important.'

'I know, but she shouldn't get her hopes up. It could have fallen from her body. He might have taken it for a souvenir – some killers do that, don't they?' She drew a breath. 'You know I almost didn't tell you. I thought that maybe, after all this time, it would be kinder not to – because of Heather. I hope,' she said hesitantly, 'I've done the right thing?'

'You did. You have.' His voice roughened. 'No matter how much it hurts – and Christ, it still does, even after nineteen and a bit years – this could end it for us. No more lying in the dark, thinking, imagining. I want that more than anything – for Heather.'

'Then I'm glad I rang.' The relief she felt lessened her sense of urgency and she remembered it was a public holiday. 'Look, don't go tearing off. The police aren't going to call a search today, not for a case this old. Think of the overtime they'd have to pay. I'll make some tea. If we had a map, we could look at the roads, find out how he could have got from Mooky Lane to Macquarrie unseen. It might help to have some constructive ideas to take to the police.'

'Yeah, maybe.' Ken frowned as he pictured the district as a whole. He knew his way around the properties, yes, and where the boundaries of each were, but could he be certain of where every farm track led? He doubted it, then Harry, who had wandered off at mention of a map, was back carrying a roll of them. They spread them on the dining-room table, pushing Max's dried arrangement to the edge, where Kate rescued it as she brought out the tray of tea things. Outside Flip had begun to bark, then they all heard the vehicle roaring up the track. It slewed to a halt as the brakes were jammed on, and the door slammed and moments later boots crossed the verandah at a run and a heavy fist pounded the door.

Kate swallowed. 'That'll be Doug.'

Ken had followed her across the room but stood back as she passed through the door into the narrow hallway, leaving him unobserved by the angry man outside, who snatched the opening door from Kate's hand and crowded inside, forcing her back with his presence. There was a tic in his cheek and his eyes were murderous.

'Where are they, you interfering bitch? Where's my wife?'

Kate forced herself to stand her ground, saying frigidly, 'She's not here, Doug. I've already been through this with Mum. And I'll thank you to mind your manners; you're not at home now.'

'What have you done with her, then, my sweet little sister? I know you're behind it. She'd never have had the guts to do it alone. You will tell me, Kate, so it might as well be now.'

'Or what – you'll beat me up like you do Clover? Guy tried that. Divorce courts take a dim view of wife-beaters, Doug. If she's really gone, I expect her lawyers'll be in touch.'

Doug's hands closed into fists and Ken stepped into view, speaking in a flat, hard tone. 'Settle down, Doolin. You're already trespassing; threaten your sister again and holiday or not, I *will* call the police. Maybe I should anyway, then you can explain your actions while you list your wife as missing.' To Kate he added, 'We could get this investigation underway a few hours sooner, because even if the inspector's not there, they'd have somebody on duty. The cop shop's never shut.'

'Perhaps it's an idea.' She followed his lead, seeming to ignore her brother, knowing that a witness to his behaviour was the last thing he'd want, particularly one of Ken's rectitude. 'At the very least they could log the carving into evidence, or whatever it's called, and dust off the file.' From the corner of her eye she watched Doug's aggression melt from him. In the heat of rage he had not even noticed Ken's presence until he spoke; now he would be scrambling to undo the mistake and pretend he hadn't meant a word of it. Right on cue she heard his rueful little laugh.

'Is that you, Ken? I'm in such a panic I didn't even see you. God! What a day. Look, I'm sorry, Katie. What was I thinking? Truth is, I'm about off my head with worry. Clover was diagnosed as a diabetic just last week and it's really freaked her out. And now she's taken off and I've no idea whether she's got her medication with her. She could slip into a coma if she isn't careful, and there's only young Andy with her. He'll be no help if – if anything happens.'

Kate admired the artistic break in his voice, but Ken, to whom he addressed these words, said gruffly, 'Sounds like you do need the police, then.' He was too straightforward – easy meat for Doug, she thought, as he glanced sideways at her, an interrogative twist to his brows. Already it seemed he was at least half convinced by the tale.

'In that case you'd better search the place and go,' she said bitingly. 'You don't want her escaping you via a coma, do you?'

'Katie,' he said sorrowfully, 'I've said I'm sorry, and I am. Worry makes a man say things he later regrets, but when it's your family . . . Of course I don't want to search but the police might be a good idea at that. You were going to call them, you said. Why's that?'

Ken held up thumb and forefinger to display the carving. 'Because this turned up near the old quarry. Megan was wearing it when she disappeared.' Doug reached out his hand to examine it but Ken, suddenly possessive, closed his fist over the little dog and looked across at Kate. 'Before I turn it in, I'll show Heather. I wasn't going to but I reckon it'd be cruel not to.'

Kate, the corner of her eyes pinched down with concern, nodded her understanding. It was the last link between mother and missing child. Of course Heather needed to see it, however upset it made her. Thinking of this, she crossed to Harry's side.

'Can you manage for lunch if I go with Ken? It's going to be an awful shock. I could stay with her while he sees the police; I'd try to be back by dark.'

'So a man's too old to feed himself now, Missy?' She grinned at his pretend indignation and he scowled back. 'Course I can manage. You think that brother of yours is going to beg my pardon for bursting into my house without a by-your-leave?'

The last sentence was uttered loudly. 'I doubt it,' she said calmly. 'He's accustomed to doing what he wants. He always has, you see.'

Doug shot her a furious look but he came forward into the room like a penitent boy and apologised, stressing the worry his pregnant wife's absence was causing him.

'If you treat her like you do your sister, I'm not surprised she's gone missing,' Harry said. 'Diabetes, is it? The sort that involves a lot of walking into doors, I suppose? I've heard a bit about you over the years, boy, and there wasn't much of it a man'd want to repeat about himself.' His white head jerked at the door. 'Now, clear off and do your bullying somewhere else. You're not welcome here.'

Rendered speechless, a tide of furious red suffusing his neck and face, Doug glared at the old man but common sense triumphed and he'd folded his lips and got out of the room. They heard the clomp of his boots across the boards, the sound of splintering as he kicked the verandah railing, and Flip's retreating growl. Then the car started and he was gone.

'Wow!' Kate said in simple admiration. She clapped her hands and felt a bout of giggles coming, releasing the tension that had been building ever since the vehicle, now speeding away, had roared to a stop outside. 'I have never heard *anyone* handle him so well. You were brilliant, Harry!'

The old man looked pleased but shook his head. 'Nah, what I am is old, girl. That's a weapon too, gives me licence to say things that'd land a younger man in a fight. All the same, I wouldn't have said it without witnesses. He's got a liar's soul, that boy. It was peeking out of his eyes even while he was trying to flannel me. I pity that lass he married.'

'And had you heard he ill-treated Clover? I thought it was a secret.'

'Nothing's secret in the Mallee,' Ken said. 'You should know that. There's been talk about Doug Doolin ever since Ronnie Hall broke his elbow that summer at the lake. You probably don't remember —'

'I do too. Come on, Ken. I was twelve. Of course I remember. He fell out of the tree because he was trying to see over the boulder the girls changed behind,' Kate interrupted. 'We all giggled about it – and talked of nothing else for weeks.'

'You're partly right, only it was Doug up the tree. Ronnie caught him there, so Doug smashed his arm with a cricket bat to stop him telling. Martin saw it happen. He told me – oh, weeks afterwards.'

'And you didn't do anything?' Kate was incredulous.

'He begged me not to. Doug had threatened Ron, told him he'd cripple Benny if he ever so much as hinted it wasn't Ron up the tree. He could've, too – a cricket ball to the ankle or knee. Given his bones, that's all it would've taken. An unfortunate accident – who could say otherwise?'

'Yes, I see.' Ron's young brother Benny's chalky bones – he suffered from some deficiency that made them as brittle as sticks – were common playground knowledge; he'd broken both wrists and a collarbone going through primary school. 'I wonder if Dad knew? It would have sickened him. 'I didn't. But who else did?'

'They were high school boys and you were a little kid. Some of those boys are now the young farmers round here, so yeah, the farming mob know about him. It's different in town. They might vote him onto the council, but the men who grew up with Doug Doolin know what he's really like.'

Kate picked up her hat. 'And here I was thinking he had you fooled.'

'Not for a minute,' Ken said, opening the door. 'See you later, Harry.'

25

It was cooler in the moving vehicle. Kate said out of silence, 'Doug was in his car. He can't have checked the bus depot yet.'

'No.' Ken adjusted the air. 'Funny old turn the world's taken. We jog along for years, then in just a matter of a few months after you arrive, Clover's broken free, and now this lead on Megan. I'm not getting my hopes up but if it brought the truth . . . '

'What would you do? If her body was found.'

'Sell up.' He wrestled the wheel to dodge a pothole. 'Get shot of the place. Go somewhere new where Heather couldn't keep seeing her. It's like she's always watching for her round the farm. If I could take her somewhere else —'

'Adelaide, then – near Martin?' Kate suggested.

He slanted her a look. 'Could be, but Martin's got his own life – he might prefer to keep it that way. I expect you've realised he's gay. Heather doesn't know, bless her.'

'I wouldn't be so sure,' Kate observed. 'And Heather's heart is bigger than most. She always had room for me, even knowing what my brother was like. Talk to her, Ken. It's possible she hasn't said anything only because she worries how you'll react to the news.'

He said doubtfully, 'You think? Well, I'll give it some thought – later. Right now I'm more concerned about how she'll react to this. Maybe we can sit down and break it to her over a cuppa. She's bound to be curious about why you rang.' He looked suddenly nervous – or a like a farmer called upon to handle emotional issues rather than problems in the paddock, Kate thought. Almost as if he'd heard, he said, 'I'm glad you're here, Katie. Thanks for coming.'

'For Pete's sake, Ken, this is Heather! She'll handle it. She must've dealt with bushfires and snakebite and sunstroke over the course of her life with you. Yes, I'll boil the kettle. You just wade in there and tell her. Even this sort of news is better than what she's lived with for the last nineteen years.'

They were running along Mooky Lane to The Narrows gate. Kate opened and closed it, and on returning to the cab found Ken frowning at the dirt where a fresh vehicle track overlaid his own earlier one. 'Visitors,' he said. 'Who in God's name could that be?' When the house came in sight he gave an exasperated groan at the sight of the copper-coloured Mazda pulled up in the shade there.

'Who is it?' Kate could see a child running under the trees, and Fly making a prudent retreat, tail down, to the sheds.

'Ron Hall and family. Come for the afternoon and probably dinner as well, knowing Ron. Takes dynamite to shift him once he's settled in. And talk! That bloke could talk underwater. He took over the farm when old Adam had his stroke. Benny's still there but Ron's the boss.'

'Right. He can talk to me, then. You take Heather into another room and I'll entertain them. When you're ready just come back and say – oh, I don't know, that Heather's come down with a migraine? Or you could just tell them the truth – they're neighbours, after all, and everyone's going to know in a day or two.'

He said, 'It's really that simple, isn't it? Thanks, Kate.' Driving into the shed, he switched off and climbed out as Flash ran to his side. Taking a deep breath, Kate followed man and dog to the house.

Heather and her guests were on the wide latticed verandah, seated in cane chairs with the remnants of afternoon tea on a round, cloth-covered table between them. Sight of the large china teapot wrapped in a wool cosy reminded Kate of the possum kit, and she felt a pang of guilt at having forgotten it would need feeding again before dark. Well, perhaps Maxie would return – if he'd ever actually left. She still hadn't found wherever it was he hid out at the farm. Ron was rising from his chair and a short, sturdily built woman breastfeeding a young baby was eyeing her as Heather came forward.

'Kate, how lovely! This is a pleasant surprise. Of course, you remember Ron Hall, and this is Sarah, his wife, and baby Elaine. Jimmy's about somewhere too. He's five.'

'Yes, we saw him in the garden.' She kissed Heather, murmuring against her cheek, 'Ken wants to speak to you,' then turned to greet Ron. He had been a skinny boy but had matured into a heavy man with skin stretched tightly across sun-polished cheeks, and arms like hams. He had an expandable band on his watch with which he fiddled incessantly, clicking the parts against each other as he immediately launched into an account of his life over the past ten years, including how he and his wife had met.

'Oh, honey,' Sarah interjected, 'you'll bore her to pieces,' but it didn't stop Ron.

'I'll make fresh tea,' Heather said brightly, casting a puzzled look at Ken, who gave the briefest greeting to her guests and followed his wife out. Kate murmured appropriate responses to Ron's monologue and smoothed a finger over the baby's satiny foot.

'How old is she?'

'Born on the night of the Growers' Dinner,' Ron said proudly. 'I heard you went. Woulda seen you there only my little princess decided it was time. Well, there's some things you can't change – birth and death, to name a couple. Jimmy was the same, wasn't he?' He beamed fondly at his wife and Kate braced herself for a full account of the occasion, but Ron's mind had veered to another track. 'The old dad too, for that matter. He wasn't old, not really, and who'd of thought – but things can wear out or go wrong when you least expect it. A clot in the brain, the doc said, and bam! He's gone. Like your dad, come to think of it. Do you know,' he turned to Sarah, 'I was there when it happened? The last one, you might say, to hear Brian Doolin speak – that's something.'

'Ron!' Sarah frowned. 'You shouldn't. It must be painful for Kate —'

'It was years ago,' he protested. 'Gotta be eight or nine, at least.'

'Yes, it's okay.' Kate's pulse had quickened. She smiled at him. 'I never actually thanked you for what you did that day. You took the message, they said, called the ambulance. Even if it was too late, you did it, and I appreciate that.'

He beamed at her, saying deprecatingly, 'Yeah, well, I was fitter then. Marriage,' he patted his generous girth, 'agrees with me. But it's a fair distance from your hayshed to your house, and in work-boots . . . Well, I'm never gonna run a three-minute mile, am I? And I don't reckon they could of saved him if they'd been right there when it happened.'

'The hayshed? I thought Dad collapsed in his workshop?'

'No, no, Kate. That was me, I was in the old workshop – not collapsed, of course.' He smirked at the joke. 'I can see I'd best tell you how it was. See, I'd driven across in the old jeep we had back then, because I thought, well, I can stick the rocker in the back, 'cause it was never gonna fit in a car boot, on account of the high back, see, and the rockers. Brian made it for my gran, and he rang to say it was ready. Well, I got some old blankets . . . ' The tale wound on, tortuous in its detail, while Kate followed her own thoughts. All this time she had pictured Brian spending his last moments at the craft he'd loved. Where had that idea come from? Her mother, or Doug, or had she heard it at The Narrows? Did it really matter? Probably not – but any last words Ron may have heard certainly did. She waited impatiently for him to reach the crux of his tale.

'. . . so I'd just seen he wasn't there and reckoned I'd best go to the house when I heard him sing out.'

'Who?' Kate said. 'Who did you hear?'

'Well, Brian.' His mouth turned down, making his expression more dogged than certain. 'Leastways that's what I *thought*, though Doug said it was him I heard – but it sounded like Brian to me. He sounded – I dunno – angry, afraid even.'

'Go on.' Kate's hands were cold. 'What was it he shouted?'

Ron hunched his shoulders. 'I couldn't be sure, and later when Doug explained I thought, well, yeah, maybe he did, because it *seemed* likely, and it was a fair step from them to me and through the hay as well —'

Kate gritted her teeth. 'Ron, never mind all that. When you thought it was my dad, what did you think he shouted? Just tell me, please.'

He shrugged, turning up large muscular hands. 'It sounded like *What have you done?* But Doug said it was him. He reckoned Brian was already unconscious and he'd been yelling for five minutes for *someone to come.* All I know is they were in the hay shed. The tractor and forklift were there and the last of the old bales had been dragged out, and I think your dad had been sweeping the floor because there was a broom next to him. They were getting the place ready for the new hay.'

'But he wasn't conscious then?'

'Nah – he'd flaked out. So I took off for the house, and told your mum, only she was so rattled it ended up in me making the call. She didn't seem able to take it in – I'm like . . . *They're in the hayshed, Missus, and Brian's in a bad way* – but she just stared. *Oh, no*, she says, *he can't be.* So when I saw the phone sitting there I grabbed it and made the call. Then I legged it back and helped Doug carry him to the workshop.'

Kate frowned. 'Why?'

'Well, I dunno.' Ron looked perplexed as if the question had never occurred to him, then shrugged again. 'Closer to the road, I suppose. They'd have had to back the ambulance up else.'

'I suppose so. Anyway, I'm glad you were there, Ron. Nobody should die alone. I trust Mr Hall didn't either.'

'Oh, the old dad died in bed. He —' Ron seemed more than ready to regale her with the details, but she cut him off smoothly.

'And what about Benny? Is he married?' She gave Sarah an apologetic smile. 'I'm sorry, this must be so boring for you.'

'Oh no, Ron's always talking about the farming families round here so I'm really pleased to meet you at last.' She lowered her voice. 'He told me about the tragedy – the little girl who used to live here.' Looking down at her own daughter, who seemed to have fallen asleep at the breast, she reached one-handed to adjust her clothing. 'Dreadful. I can't begin to imagine how —'

'No,' Kate agreed. 'Could you excuse me just for a moment? And I wonder if Jimmy's all right? He's been very quiet for quite a while.'

Sarah craned for a look through the lattice. 'He has, hasn't he? Perhaps you'd better check on him, love.'

'He'll be all right,' Ron protested but he got to his feet and Kate slipped away to the kitchen. Heather looked up as she entered. She'd been crying and a photo of Megan, gap-toothed and freckled, her ginger mane in pigtails, lay on the table beside the abandoned teapot. Ken had been holding her, she saw, and awakened grief had crumpled both their faces.

'Are you all right?' Kate asked, hugging her. 'I don't know what it means, if it will help in any way, but once I saw it you had to know.' She stood back, still clasping her friend's arms. 'Only – please, Heather, don't think it has to mean she's still alive. I'm just so sorry for bringing it all back like this.'

'You didn't – it's never left. And it could turn out to be the key to finding her.' The smile that creased her wet cheeks was luminous with sudden hope. 'Even if she's dead. Thank you, Katie, for everything. Ron too. Has he gone?'

'That's what I came about. I've got him upright. Do you want me to get rid of him?'

Heather reached to squeeze her hand. 'Do you think you could? I should at least say goodbye, but I don't think I —'

'Leave it to me. You sit down. Come on. It was shock enough for me, so how you must feel —'

'Like a miracle's happened.' She was staring at the little carving cupped in her palm. 'It's perfect still after all these years. I don't know if I *can* give it up, Kate. Maybe the police can take photos and let me keep it?'

'We'll ask them, love, tomorrow,' Ken said. He looked at Kate. 'Shall I come with you?'

She shook her head. 'You're far too polite; you'd feel awkward and start talking and that'd be the end of it. What about a cuppa when I come back? Stay there, Heather. Ken can make it.'

The tawny hair bounced to her long stride as she left and Heather blinked as her tears fell again, thickening her voice. 'Our girl would've been like that, capable and caring. I know she would've. Ah, God! If we could just learn the truth, Ken, I honestly think I could leave. I know you've been wanting to; and I know you've stayed for me.'

'And I was wrong,' he said. 'We should have gone long ago and if they find her, we will.' His voice roughened. 'No more of this, Heather. No more dragging a corpse around with you.' She flinched from the image but he continued doggedly, 'You lose someone – it happens – but you grieve and you heal. That's natural. The life we've had since Megs was taken isn't. So tomorrow we go to the police and the media, and if need be, the Premier, but we'll have an answer, even if it's no different to the findings of the original inquest. And that's it. We accept it and sell up, and start living again.'

'This is very sudden.' Heather wiped a knuckle under her eyes and stared at him. 'I mean, why now? Because of this?'

He scrubbed a hand over his jaw, his face set. 'It's partly that. And partly what you just said – that Megs would have been like Kate. It made me remember when you were like her, and I want that Heather back. I've lost enough; I won't lose that woman too.' Slowly he added, 'I'd almost forgotten she ever existed.'

'Ken.' Heather rose and put her arms around him, resting her head on his hard shoulder. 'I'm sorry,' she sniffed. 'No woman could wish for a better man and you've had a shabby return for it all these years. All right, then. If that's what you want, we'll sell – after the new investigation. They will hold one, won't they? I mean, I couldn't bear it now if the authorities don't reinvestigate.'

'They will,' he said. 'They have to.' He kissed her forehead as Kate came back into the room, then let his arms drop. 'How did it go?'

She grimaced. 'Wordily. But they went. I don't know, it's like Ron talks for his whole family. I hardly remember Benny opening his mouth, and as for old Mr Hall —'

Ken smiled. 'I know. Only groom to ever make a one-word speech at his wedding because he'd already said, *I do* in church. Thanks for your help, Katie.'

'It's nothing – thank *you* for helping with Doug. Things were getting a bit tense there when you stepped in. Incidentally, you didn't buy that stuff about the diabetes, did you? It's all lies.'

'I suspected as much but he's so utterly convincing.'

'I know. That's his strength.' Heather, moving automatically to make the tea Ken had forgotten about, was looking bewildered. 'It's

Clover,' Kate explained. 'Doug knows so you may as well, too. She's left him. She asked me to help her get away. A friend picked her up from Harry's place and I drove her vehicle into town to throw him off the scent. That's why I needed Ken last night, to take me home. The tragedy is, she could only bring Andy with her, because Doug took Jeremy with him. She hadn't foreseen that, so the courts will have to sort it out now.'

'What a mess.' Heather shook her head. 'Is she somewhere safe? Because if he found her . . . ' Her gaze was troubled and she spoke apologetically as if excusing her thoughts. 'He was such a *horrible* boy.'

'He's a horrible man too. But Clove's in a women's refuge by now,' Kate smiled faintly, 'and she's got a tigress of a lawyer. Even Harry was impressed. Apparently she drives an eight-cylinder car, for whatever that's worth.'

'Ron could tell you,' Ken quipped.

'Then thank God I didn't mention it. But speaking of him, there was something I wanted to ask you about. According to Ron, Dad died in the hayshed and not his workshop, which was what I've always believed. Somebody told me that and I'd never doubted it. But Ron's version is that he helped Doug carry his body across to the workshop before the ambulance arrived. I've been wondering why.'

'For easier access?' Ken hazarded. 'Or he thought it was, I dunno – more fitting?'

'Then why not take him to the house? And as for access, as I understand it he was already dead. The doctor said the heart attack was so massive it must have killed him instantly. So it wasn't like stretchering the body an extra hundred metres was going to matter.'

Ken shrugged. 'Is it important? Perhaps he thought Brian could still be saved? He mightn't have known he was dead, Katie.'

'Oh, come on,' she said, 'Doug had no feelings for Dad. And he's a farmer! Are you telling me you wouldn't know the difference between a live body and a dead one?'

Heather put her hand on the girl's wrist. 'What are you thinking, lamb?'

'I don't know,' Kate confessed. 'Only, Ron thought Dad was alive when he got there, that it was Dad shouting, not Doug. If he'd already collapsed, you'd think he wouldn't have the strength to shout, so . . . I don't know. You can't make somebody have a heart attack – can you?'

'No,' Ken said sternly. 'Put that out of your head, Kate. His heart was bad, he told me so himself, and the doctor said it could've happened at any time. Brian's death might've been sudden but it wasn't unexpected.'

She met his gaze and he read the hurt there. 'Except by me. He didn't breathe a word about his heart to me.'

'Because he loved you. If it had been me in his shoes and Megs in yours, I would probably have done the same. Fathers want to protect their little girls, whatever age they are. It's how we show we love them.'

Heather waited a moment, then cleared her throat. 'On another subject . . . I don't know if you've seen him yet, Kate, but Doreen Pringle told me that your husband's in town.'

She blinked the sadness away and grimaced. 'I know, courtesy of Doug. The affair's over, it seems.'

'And he expected you to go back to him?'

Kate's lip curled. 'In his dreams. I told him I want a divorce.' She glanced at the carriage clock and pushed her teacup aside. 'Look, if you're not going into town today, Ken, could you run me back?' To Heather she added, 'Dinner apart, Maxie found a possum kit I'm caring for, and it's past time it was fed. I suppose you wouldn't have a spare eye-dropper?'

'I'll see.' She went out of the room just as Ken tilted his head to listen.

'Vehicle out front,' he said with mild irritation. 'Don't people stop home any more?' He sighed and left, leaving Kate to reflect that whoever it was would get short shrift for once from a place known for its hospitality, but a few minutes later he was back, with a visitor in tow.

'Max! What on earth are you doing here?' Her smile left no doubt that she was glad to see him and he grinned back.

'Happy new year, Kate.' Before she could guess his intention, he kissed her cheek, and then Heather's as she bustled back, saying, 'I do have a spare – Why, Max!'

'Happy new year, Aunty. May it be the one to bring you closure. Forgive the intrusion, today of all days. I've just come for Kate.'

'You timed it well, then,' Ken said, 'thanks. I was about to run her back. But what are you doing here? I thought you'd gone to visit your folks?'

'I did, and now I'm back.' He exchanged a few more words while Kate hugged Heather, murmuring, 'If you need company at any time, just ring me.'

'I know. Bless you, Lamb.'

Kate glanced back as they drove off and saw them both standing beneath the arch with the last of the sun's rays on their faces. She said, 'Poor souls. But thanks for coming, Max. I'm sure Heather would manage but it's best she's not alone right now. And incidentally, why are you back so soon? It feels like a week's gone by but it's still New Year's Day.'

'A pretty busy one too, it seems, and the few preceding it.' His hazel eyes glinted. 'Let's see: your brother, your husband, your sister-in-law-and-toddler, some skinny female in a man-sized car (I'm quoting Harry, you understand), Ken, your brother again, Maxie coming and going, and Ken once more – did I miss anyone?'

She laughed. 'Put like that it sounds like half the country. Harry's been a saint about it. And if you'd heard the way he handled Doug!' He was slowing for the gate into Mooky Lane. Grasping the door handle in readiness, she asked, 'So why are you back, Max?'

They stopped and the indignant chatter of a willie wagtail sounded clearly over the idling engine. 'For you, of course.' Her eyes leapt in a startled fashion to his face and he saw the satiny skin of her throat pinken as the blood rose to her head. 'Harry called me the day after your husband arrived. He was concerned for you – that you'd gone and got yourself mixed up in your brother's marital problems, I mean.'

'I like that,' Kate said indignantly. 'It was Clover who came to me. It was *her* plan; she asked if she could meet her lawyer at Rosebud so she wouldn't be seen in town. How was I supposed to refuse? And I did ask Harry's permission.'

'He said.' Max reached a hand across and ran his knuckles along her jaw. 'You can't help yourself, can you? Everybody's your business – lonely old men, misfit kids, unhappy wives. You even took pity on me when you thought I was in danger of being jawed to death.'

Kate wished for something witty to say but instead blurted out, 'But I *like* people.' She felt as gauche as a teenager, and foolish because of it, but it was a long time since a man had come on to her. Guy had been her first experience of love (if you didn't count a childish crush on Martin) and there had been nobody since. Not that there hadn't been opportunities but she had stuck rigidly by her vows. To prove, she thought now, that they meant something – to her, if not to Guy.

As if aware of her dilemma, Max said, 'Leave it. I'll get it,' and that propelled her out of the cab to fumble with the gate chain. When she climbed in again he turned the vehicle towards the pine plantation.

'Where are we going?'

'I'm taking you out.' He lifted a hand to still the protest that had risen to her lips. 'Don't worry. Harry's organised; Maxie'll feed the possum; and your clothes are fine. You'd be beautiful anyway, clothed or naked, like some trees I know.'

'Max!' she protested, half-entertained, half-shocked. He'd switched on the headlights and the backwash from the dashboard threw into relief the curve of his jaw and the strong masculine column of his neck. Her pulse leapt; she felt giddy and young all at once and awash with anticipation for whatever the evening would bring.

26

Kate had assumed they were heading for Laradale and possibly The Chef's Place or the dining room at The Railway Arms, but they ran through town without stopping. When the lights atop the railway silos were behind them she said, 'So where . . . ?'

'You'll see. You said you liked the skies here, didn't you? I'm going to show them to you.'

She said apologetically, 'Will it take long? I *am* a bit peckish. I missed most of my lunch.'

'All in hand,' Max replied, somewhat smugly, she thought. They must be going to a farm, then, very likely some property he contracted for, though in the middle of a holiday dinner was surely not the best time for unexpected guests to arrive – but a man mightn't think of that.

However, having negotiated another couple of paddocks and opened a gate, when they finally stopped the only visible lights were their own. Max switched off lights and motor and rolled his window down to let the night in. On her side Kate did the same, searching the blackness for a clue to their whereabouts. The scent of dry paddocks came to her, and the smell of the hot engine; a hesitant breeze carried a whiff of something sweet and she sniffed at it.

'Wattle,' Max said. 'There's a bit still out, here and there. Wait – let your eyes adjust. Tell me when you can make out the line of scrub to your left.'

'Got it,' she said after a moment.

'Good. Slide out your side and wait till I come round.' When he had done so he guided her to the front of the vehicle and to the centre of something he'd spread on the ground. 'Swag cover.' He tugged at her hand. 'It's clean. Lie down. Don't worry, I haven't any carnal ideas – well, that's not true but I don't intend to ravish you at present. Here, put this under your head.'

Kate took what felt remarkably like a pillow and arranged it as Max settled beside her. Then, pushing the hair back from her brow, she looked upwards with a gasp of awe at the star-spangled glory of the sky.

Max said, 'We're in the middle of a wheat paddock. You need space to really see the sky. It's something, eh?'

'It's beautiful.' She rolled her head to take in the full splendour of the Milky Way. 'When I was little Dad used to tell me stories about the stars. He'd spent time out in Central Australia and learned some Aboriginal legends – how the Seven Sisters came to be up there, and why the fisherman made the Fish Trap; that's it there.' She pointed to the Big Dipper. 'We'd lie on the grass and find patterns and pictures, then make up tales to explain them, which I expect is what the Aboriginals did anyway. Oh, look – there's a shooting star.'

'Or a bit of space junk.' Max raised himself on one elbow but it was too dark to see more than her blurred outline. 'Tell me about your dad.'

Kate was silent for a moment, then said slowly, 'He was my world. Mild-mannered, gentle, clever – he was a wonderful man. Of course, he must've had faults but I never saw them, though my mother did. When you're little you never think about your parents' marriage but when I grew up I came to see he was intensely unhappy in it. I'm sure he'd loved my mother once, but she didn't understand a thing about him. Perhaps because she was always focused on the farm. He was an artist but she never recognised that. She can be very . . . ' Kate searched for a word, 'cutting, my mother, when she doesn't approve of something. Anyway I interrupted them rowing once when I was, oh, possibly eleven, and she said in this truly *horrible* way, "*Oh, go and whittle something. It's all you're good for.*" I've never forgotten the look in his eyes. I cried afterwards, because she'd hurt him so much.'

Max said gently, 'I'm sorry.'

'People are strange,' Kate replied, 'and my family's stranger than most. I left home after Dad died. I mean, I'd already left for study purposes, but I've only been back once since and that was last October.

'Not even when you were married?'

'No. The ceremony was in town – a park wedding and a break-fast at the Railway Arms. Heather made my dress and Ken gave me away. Mum and Doug weren't on the invitation list but they came anyway, to stop talk. She's very proper, Mum, cares about gos-sip – or at least that she and the family are not the subject of it. She was furious about the whole thing, of course; and as it all turned out to be a hideous mistake, she can now say she told me so.'

He said, 'Surely not. She's your mother.'

'No,' Kate corrected, 'she's Doug's mother. I'm a sort of irritat-ing accident she had to raise because that's what people expect biological mothers to do. Why are we talking about her anyway? Tell me about the stars – or yourself.'

'Well.' He lay back down, moving his head closer to hers. 'The stars are up there. Regard them as a gift from me. Pretend they're diamonds and choose as many as you wish and I'll string them together for you.'

'Very pretty,' she said approvingly. 'That's quite a flight of fancy for a farmer. So what about your parents? I know your mother's still living, and your father was hurt in a farm accident.

What about your siblings? Heather said you had brothers. Are they married? And you – have you a wife somewhere?'

'Well, let's see, in order from the top.' There was laughter in his voice. 'Dad's got a gammy leg, walks with a crutch; Mum's fine, they're still on the farm. I don't know what's going to happen there, whether they've done any succession planning. I have three brothers who all have their own careers – and wives. Pete's an agronomist, Geoff's a marine biologist, and Kev's a diesel fitter. As for me – farm contractor, but no wife. Why not?' he mused and Kate found herself holding her breath, which was absurd. 'Are broken hearts a valid reason?'

'Could be,' she replied offhandedly.

'Ah, then I expect that's it. Michelle Creeley was the cause of mine. She was smart, and cute with it, and had the most gorgeous black curls, but maybe we were too young for it to last.'

'Really?' Kate's head turned towards him. She said suspiciously, 'How young exactly?'

'Grade Three. What's that – about seve— Oof!' He doubled up as she thumped him, then scrambled to her feet.

He shot up after her, catching her by the arms. Up close like that, the scent of her hair, her clothes and skin was intoxicating. He could see the merest glint of her eyes as he bent his head and kissed her, tasting the faint honey of her mouth before letting her go.

'You're an unusual man, Max Shephard.' Kate's breathing had quickened but she seemed in no hurry to get away. 'Do you bring all your dates to the middle of a wheat paddock? Did I mention I'm famished?'

'Ah, I knew I'd forgotten something important.' He went to switch on the parking lights, then rummaged in the large toolbox to produce a hamper and a thermos. 'You see? All contingencies covered. And I even have here,' he dived across the seats to open the glove box and extract something, 'a packet of baby wipes, in case milady wishes to clean her hands.'

She eyed him in amazement. 'You regularly carry those around?'

He laughed. 'Kate, have you ever stripped machinery in the field? One part stubborn nuts and the rest is grease. Make yourself comfortable and I'll see what we've got.'

It was a lovely meal. Kate wondered whether Max had ordered it, or left it to the restaurant chef's imagination. There were feather-light pastry cases, a mouthful each, filled with crab-meat; asparagus spears; ribbon sandwiches; an apple, walnut and celery salad in lettuce cups; sausage rolls; devilled eggs; and something spicy and cheesey they ate with slices of crusty bread. There was fruit to follow, purple grapes, lucent with bloom in the orange glow of the lights, and peaches of perfect ripeness.

Kate did it all full justice, licking cheese and later juice from her fingers, allowing Max to dab her chin with his paper napkin, and refusing more salad with a sigh of regret.

'It's heavenly but I'd better not; not if I'm going to have that peach – which I am.'

They talked as they ate, exploring each other's lives, comparing tastes, remembering the past. Max, watching the effortless way Kate sat on her heels, legs doubled beneath her, said, 'I don't know how you do that. Doesn't it hurt?'

'Teaching. First-graders spend more time on the floor than at desks.' She talked about her work, and about losing her job and returning home, which led to the Wantages and inevitably to Megan and the pendant Maxie had brought her.

'A dog your dad carved, Harry said.'

She remembered he hadn't seen it. 'Companion to this. He made us one each.' She pulled Blackie from her blouse and leaned forward to show him, liking the solemn way he turned it in his big fingers, smoothing the satiny wood. His knuckles brushed the skin over her clavicle, sending a slight frisson through her. Their heads bumped and she breathed in the scent of man and peaches, and the faint smell of his sweat.

'So,' he frowned slightly, 'you're thinking that her body was hidden somewhere in or around the quarry?'

'It's where Tam was found, so she had to have been there.'

'Even so, it must have been searched. I mean, an abandoned quarry? First place the cops would look.'

'Yes, but perhaps they didn't because they couldn't figure out how she got there? There was the same problem with Gypsy Pete. It was easy to blame him because he did hang around the school, but nobody saw his van on Mooky Lane and as you know there's no way off it, unless you're going to a farm, and that increases the risk about forty-fold, I should think. In fact,' she added slowly, 'it's so impossible, one would suppose that she was never on the bus. Only I saw her climb aboard myself, and the bus driver let her off.'

'There has to be a perfectly rational explanation. That's what my father used to say. Changing the subject, would you like coffee? And there seem to be chocolates.'

'Yes, please,' Kate said. 'Thank you, Max. It was a lovely meal.'

He smiled over the thermos top. 'I had lovely company.' He freed his hands to draw her closer, sliding them round her jaw to tilt her face before he kissed her again. Kate felt her pulse leap as she responded, then his arm shifted to encircle her back and she wriggled closer, revelling in the feel and smell of a man's nearness again. It had been two years or more since she and Guy had shared anything besides a bed. The coffee stayed undrunk and Max was working steadily at the buttons on her blouse when something caught his attention and his hands suddenly stilled.

'What?' She turned her head and saw it too, a burst of yellow light streaming up to the stars. 'Something's on fire!' Her stomach clenched in sudden fear. 'Dear God! That's not Rosebud way, is it?'

'No.' He got to his feet. 'Too far east. One of the Brathway farms is my guess, but their crops are harvested – anyway, it's not spreading . . . Could be the woolshed or a homestead, I suppose, but it seems a bit close for that.'

'Hard to tell at night.' Kate's fingers fumbled with the buttons he'd undone. The mood was definitely broken; without even thinking about it she bundled the pillows into the swag cover and dumped it on the Toyota tray. Max swept the hamper into the toolbox and had the engine firing before he'd slammed the door. The thermos, forgotten in the rush, was nudged aside by the wheels as he spun the vehicle in a tight turn.

'Hang on,' he said grimly and she nodded, unspeaking. Words were unnecessary. Both knew the awful cost of bushfires. A woolshed was bad enough but nothing compared to the loss of crops and stock if the flames reached the highly combustible mallee and the farmland it bordered. Not to mention any farmstead in its path . . .

Kate kept her eyes on the glow that had begun to shrink into itself, though the sky was still painted in fiery colours. Thankfully there was little wind. She said as much, adding, 'It's not spreading.'

Max grunted, jammed on the brakes and was out sprinting for the gate before she'd even realised it was there. Kate slid across and drove through, and was back on her side of the cab when he flung himself behind the wheel and sped on. The road was bending away, leaving the fire to the left. Kate said, 'We're heading away —'

'I see.' He stopped, slammed the gear stick into reverse and made a tight turn. The tailgate scraped on a tree, then they were round and speeding back, Max with his head out the window searching for a side track. He found it, saying, 'There's a stock gate. I'll get it.' Once through, he took off across the paddock, the headlights startling woolly rumps into bobbing flight. Kate sat silent; they were bouncing along a route parallel to the fire, but she assumed that Max was making for another gate that would put them back onto a road and would correct their position when he could. His face was grim in the wash of the dash light. The vehicle's front wheel fell into a hole, rattling her teeth. She braced a hand on the grab bar as he flashed her a look. 'Sorry. You okay?'

'Yes. Where are we now?'

'Bottom end of Rosebud. Those are Hollens' sheep. The fire's at their place. From the way it started, I'd say there's been an explosion. Fuel maybe. Unless they've shedded green hay.'

That could combust, Kate knew. 'Doesn't seem to have spread.' A metal gate loomed and she yanked her seatbelt free. 'I'll get it.' The road was just beyond. Max slewed onto it and they tore along it through a tunnel of scrub, wattle and mallee stems leaping briefly out of the gloom as the lights caught them, then vanishing again into the darkness behind them. Kate sniffed, smelling smoke, then ducked as a nighthawk flew up from the track and smacked against the windows in a handful of feathers the wind whipped away. Then the trees fell back and the flames, much diminished now, their gold laced with roiling black smoke, were before them. Max slowed and drove closer, staring at the two figures silhouetted against the fire, at the twisted steel skeleton set in a wide area of blackened grass.

'Dear Christ! It's Connie!' Numbly he switched off, unbuckled and got out, and all at once began to run. Coldness enveloped Kate. Her head spun as the blood drained from it and she gripped the door to keep from falling. Her mind screamed, *Maxie!* but her throat was locked shut as she stared at all that was left of Connie Hardy's caravan, while inhaling the dreadful smell of charred bone and burnt meat.

They must've been in it, she thought numbly, *or the uncles* – that was how she had come to think of the Hollen brothers because Maxie always referred to them that way – would not still be standing there, poking at the edges of the blaze. Whatever their feelings about her son, they must have loved their niece a great deal, for the shorter brother had a badly burned face and arm, and tears had cleaned a track down the soot-blackened cheeks of the other.

* * *

It was a long few hours attending to the aftermath of the disaster. Kate got through it with the mournful threnody of the child's name running constantly through her head. The fire was no longer a threat; the police and ambulance service had been called and were on their way. 'I dunno why we got them,' Jack said almost angrily. 'What's a bloody ambo gonna do for our Connie now?' Jack was the short one, the one who had tried to reach the caravan. Kate had looked helplessly at his injuries and, discarding the iodine and ancient bandages – which was all that their medical kit contained – soaked a pillowslip in tank water and gingerly covered the burned arm.

'They'll be able to help you,' she said gently. The side of his face was blistered and weeping, the eyelid fused to his cheek, most of his hair gone. She'd made tea in their grubby kitchen and ladled plenty of sugar into it, saw that he drank it, then fetched a blanket from one of the tumbled bedrooms in case he went into shock. The smell of fire hung over the place like a greasy pall, not the clean scent of smouldering wood but the stink of burning plastics and rubber, underlain by the awful smell of burnt flesh. Thinking of the origin of the latter made her want to retch.

It was the gas bottles that started it, Alan, the other brother, said. 'We heard this bloody great bang and something crashed into the roof. Time we run out, the whole van was just a ball of flame. Burning like a bastard. I swear I heard her scream – poor little Connie.' His eyes filled and he bit savagely at his lip, bringing blood. Neither of them mentioned the child.

'He might not have been here,' Max comforted, but his voice was strained. 'He was with Harry when I left Rosebud. He *does* stay over sometimes and there was the possum – I did say you mightn't be back till late, so . . . ' It was hope to cling to, to balance the fear she felt for Maxie.

The ambulance arrived then, followed shortly by a police cruiser with a sergeant and constable. Max and Alan spoke with them while Kate explained to the paramedics about Jack's arm and what she'd done.

The constable, gaping at the site, had summed it up with more truth than tact. 'Shit, Sarge! She was in there, she's cinders now – and the kid with her.' Nothing was left of the van save the twisted frame and the collapsed tyres from which tendrils of stinking smoke still rose. After Jack's heroic attempt at rescue, the Hollen brothers had worked frantically to prevent the fire spreading outwards through the short grass, and now the fruit of their effort shone black in the lights of the police cruiser.

'Bloody gas bottles,' Alan Hollen said. 'She had two house-sized ones, for fridge and stove. I reckon it was one of them hit our roof. Couldn't of been nothing else. But she was a careful lass. It'll have been that kid – little bastard was always interfering.'

'He might not have been here,' Max said coldly. 'He was over at Rosebud earlier and he may have stayed the night. I'll check and let you know,' he told the sergeant, whose gaze had gone to the business name on the Toyota door.

'Shephard – that's you?'

'Yes. I'm a distant cousin of the deceased and her son. We saw the fireball from about twenty k away and came to investigate.'

'We being you and the young lady? Who's she?'

'Mrs Doo— Gilmore,' he corrected. 'Kate Gilmore; she was a Doolin. Currently housekeeper at Rosebud. I'm taking her home now. If the boy is there, I'll ring through to the station.'

'Right, thanks. We'll be back in town soon enough. Nothing more we can do here tonight. When it's cooled a bit . . . ' His voice trailed off. They would rake through the ashes, Max surmised as he collected Kate, gather up whatever bones were left, examine them and the remains of the gas bottles, and eventually an inquest would be held into the cause and result of the fire. He said as much as they drove away, stomach cramped with dread, knowing she wasn't taking it in.

'How can we even tell if he's not there? He's got some possy in the sheds. He could be curled up in it and we won't know until the morning.'

'We can look for his bike,' Max said practically.

'Of course. Poor Connie. I'm so sorry, Max. She obviously meant something to you.'

'She was a sweet kid – even those two old blokes thought so, and they've got no time for most people. But Connie had that effect, because she was so full of . . . I dunno . . . trust and hope, I suppose. Like a child. And that poor bloody kid – if he's alive, he's got no one now.' He sighed heavily. 'God, what a turn-up! Believe me, I'd planned a rather different evening.'

'There was nothing wrong with the earlier part,' Kate said as one stating a fact; she had no heart just then for flirting. Maxie's thin face with its blazing intelligence and hopeful eyes filled her thoughts. They spoke little for the rest of the short trip and when they coasted quietly up to the gate at Rosebud both stepped quickly out and started up the path.

'It was somewhere here.' Kate's strained voice broke the silence. Their own shadows were blocking the fall of the headlights. She stepped aside and gave a little cry. 'There it is. He stayed! Oh, Max! He's safe.'

'Thank Christ! I'll ring the cops when I get to town and I'll be back in the morning.' He hesitated. 'Will you tell him or should I?'

She sighed. 'I'd better – well, Harry and I together would be best. You don't want to stay?'

'It's late.' It hadn't sounded like an invitation but he wasn't dismayed. The evening's grim events had put paid to the promise the early night had held. There would be other opportunities. 'Another time.' He kissed her gently and she slid her arms around his neck. He smelled of smoke, and she supposed she did too. 'We've plenty of that, after all,' he said.

When she stepped away to enter the house he stood watching, tall in the starlight, a dark figure beside the miracle of Maxie's rusty old bike.

27

Maxie turned up for breakfast carrying Vegemite in his box and followed by Flip. Kate watched their approach through the kitchen window, recalling that the dog hadn't barked last night. Which meant he'd been roaming about out of hearing, not a good practice for farm dogs. She met them at the door and, as if sensing her disapproval, Flip flattened his ears and sat with a deprecating wag of his tail.

'Bad dog,' she said sternly. 'Where have you been?'

'He ain't done nothing, Miss,' Maxie protested.

'He wasn't tied up,' she explained, 'and you can't have dogs running loose at night in sheep country.' She sighed, searching for words. 'You'd best wash before you come to the table. You were here all night?' The pointless question alarmed the boy. Perhaps he thought she would demand to know his hiding place, for he bristled instantly.

'You said you'd look after Vegemite, Miss, but you weren't here so I had to stay. He mighta died else. I give him three feeds while you were gorn. I reckon I'm gonna take him home if you ain't looking after him.' His pale eyes blazed accusingly at her, but there was disappointment there too. He had trusted her word and she'd let him down. Kate was drenched with remorse.

'I'm sorry,' she said. 'I had to help a friend. I meant to be back earlier but then something dreadful happened. Maxie . . . ' She had meant to wait until Harry was present, until after they'd eaten, but the words came then while he stood white-faced, clutching the shoebox to his narrow chest as he learned the truth. He didn't cry; Kate could see the effort it took for him not to lose control, but when he finally spoke the words took her breath.

'It's my fault, in't it? Because I found that rotten little dog. But why?' It was a cry of pain and she swooped to smother it in a tight hug.

'Of course it's not your fault! It was an accident, Maxie. She must've forgotten to turn the gas off, that's all.'

'She never!' Glaring, he thrust her aside, eyes blazing contempt for her stupidity. 'My mum *knew* about gas. She knew it were dangerous; just because she was different don't mean she were stupid! *Boom! Gas kills.* Every time she used it that's what she says. *Boom! Gas kills.* She never once left it on. It was somebody else. If I'd gone home, I would've seen him – or smelt it, maybe.' He thrust the shoebox at her. 'I gotta go.'

'Maxie, no!' She grabbed him, holding his yelling, flailing body until his struggles ceased and he went limp in her arms. 'You can't,' she said gently. 'There's nothing left, Maxie. Everything . . . burned up. One of the uncles tried to reach your mum but he couldn't, even though he got burnt. Nobody could've. I was there, with Max. I saw the ashes; that's all it is now, just ashes.'

'And my mum?'

Kate shut her eyes and rocked him. 'Ashes,' she repeated softly. His control broke then and he cried, awful wailing sobs that tore at her own composure. When he had calmed again she took him to the bathroom and by the time they re-emerged both Harry and Max were in the kitchen. She left him to their care while she scrambled eggs and fed the possum kit. Harry was visibly shocked but Max's thoughts had moved on to practical matters.

'There's a fire investigation team on the way,' he told her as she cleared and scraped plates, tipping Maxie's scarcely touched serving into Flip's dish. 'Standard procedure, apparently. And the problem of Maxie's future care has been passed on to Children's Services. It'll take a few days for them to work out his closest relatives and see if any are prepared to take him in. I told them he was okay where he was for the present. You don't mind? Only the woman I spoke to was all for dumping him in temporary foster care today.'

'Of course not! What does Harry say?'

'He's okay with it.' He rubbed his face and smothered a yawn. He looked tired, Kate thought, and resisted a sudden maternal urge to smooth his wiry hair.

'What about Connie's people? Are they still around?'

'Her parents? Both dead. She was a late baby – her mother was forty-five or something ridiculous when she got pregnant; probably the reason Connie had Down syndrome. And no siblings, so it's down to the Quickly side of the family.'

'Poor kid.' Kate had known what it was to be unwanted by one parent. She couldn't imagine what it would be like to have no one. 'Pity there's no record of his father. He could at least be made to contribute to his upkeep.' She remembered then. 'When I told him he said the strangest thing; that Connie had been killed because he found Tam. He blamed himself for her death.'

Max shook his head. 'Poor little bugger. He probably felt guilty about not going home. I think it's fairly usual for kids to blame disasters on themselves. I mean, it's one way of controlling events, isn't it? If you find a cause for it, some reason for what's happened, then you don't have to face the knowledge that nobody's in charge. That basically we have no control over life.'

'Even if it means believing you've caused your mother's death?'

'Safer than the alternative, perhaps? That life's an ant's nest that can be destroyed at any time just because it's there.'

'But why single out finding the pendant?'

Max shrugged. 'He doesn't do much, go anywhere. Could be the only different thing to happen lately? Who knows?'

'Well, I certainly won't be asking him,' Kate said. 'I'd best go see how he's doing. What're your plans?'

'I'll be about,' he said vaguely. 'I expect Ken'll be on his way to the cops now and who knows what activity that'll start? I told Harry I'd fix his gutters. Now's as good a time as any.' He didn't add that he had hurt his parents by returning early from his visit because Harry feared for her safety. 'That brother's as nasty a piece of work as I've seen. He's already threatened her. If she means anything to you, boy, you ought to be here,' the old man had said when he'd rung. Well, she meant a great deal, and he intended to hang around and ensure that no harm came to his difficult, independent love.

Kate had completely forgotten the Wantages. Her hand flew to her lips. 'Damn! And I told Heather to call me any time – but I can't leave Harry to cope with Maxie alone.'

'He won't be,' he said. 'You have to go, go. We'll manage.'

'Bless you, Max,' she smiled gratefully.

She smiled at him and as absurd as it seemed to his practical mind, he felt it pierce through to his heart. He opened his mouth to stop her but she was already whisking away on what he thought of as her make-and-mend missions. He had never met anyone like this slender, grey-eyed woman, and he wouldn't rest until he'd made her his. For a moment he visualised her shapely legs and the body above them, then levered himself off the counter with a silent groan, abandoning daydreams to make a start on the farmhouse gutters instead.

Heather didn't call that day, but the midday news mentioned 'a new potential lead for police in the case of young Megan Wantage, the nine-year-old schoolgirl who vanished on an October afternoon nearly twenty years ago.' That night the television news carried the story with footage of Laradale's police station and inspector of police; a shot of the current school bus; and details of the discovery of the carved pendant, which would become important evidence in any new investigation.

'There will be a new investigation, Inspector?' the reporter asked earnestly. 'Surely this new find, establishing as it does a solid base for Megan's whereabouts after her abduction, and which the previous search team didn't have, means a new investigation is imperative?'

Greg Simpson, who had a sharp nose and a receding hairline, tried to conceal his irritation at being put on the spot. He cleared his throat. 'New evidence in any murder case is always most carefully evaluated. We are still in the process of doing this in the case in point, as the pendant was only brought to our attention today. This was a very complex case. There are many aspects to consider —'

'So you think she was murdered, Inspector? Are you saying you *won't* be re-opening it, even though the nature of the old quarry, next to which the carving was found, contains, I understand, many places ideal for the concealment of a body?'

'I said we will eval—' The microphone was snatched back before he finished.

The girl continued with raised brows, 'And despite the mysterious fire that followed hard on the heels of the discovery of this clue – practically on the spot, in fact – where the necklace was lost, or possibly even torn, from little Megan's neck all those years ago? Do the police think that the two events could be linked? That some connection may have existed between the missing child and the woman who perished in the flames?'

'That's arrant nonsense,' Simpson snapped, then continued more cautiously. 'There's no reason, at this stage, to think that the fire was anything more than an accident, one that is, unfortunately, all too common with both caravan and boat owners. Of course if the evidence warrants it, we'll investigate. We always do.'

'Are you aware, Inspector, that Mr Wantage, the father of the missing child, has said he will go to the Premier if necessary, to have the case reopened?'

'That's his privilege. Let's wait and see, shall we? Good day to you.' He withdrew and Kate, who'd kept an anxious eye on the kitchen where Maxie was feeding Vegemite, switched off, then recollected herself.

'Sorry, Harry. Did you want to hear the rest?'

'Advertising,' he snorted, 'and bombings. I can live without it. Better the boy doesn't have to listen to that stuff.'

But Maxie had heard, anyway. 'They were talking about my mum and the little dog. So it's true – somebody did turn the gas on?'

'No.' Kate shook her head. 'The reporter was trying to make the policeman say more than he wanted to, that's all. She doesn't know anything about your mum, and she's never been near the quarry. It's just her job to say those things. Now,' she lifted the tiny kit, whose eyes seemed the biggest part of him, 'did Vegemite take all his feed?'

* * *

The phone rang after the seven o'clock news. Max had left by then and Kate wondered whether it was him. Harry had asked him to pick up a few essentials in town, like a toothbrush and comb and some pyjamas for Maxie. He'd protested his ignorance of sizes and general unfitness for the task until Kate had said impatiently, 'For goodness sake! A pair of shorts will do for now. I'll get something when I go for the groceries.' *He probably wanted measurements*, she thought, picking up the phone, but it was Clover's voice that answered.

'Oh, Kate, thank heavens! Have you seen him? Is he all right?'

'Clove, calm down. What's the problem? Who am I supposed to have seen?'

'Jeremy, of course! You said you'd call me when Doug got back. He must be home by now. Your bat of a mother would've phoned him the moment she realised I'd gone.'

Realisation flooded Kate. 'I'm sorry, Clove. I forgot. There's been rather a lot happening here. Connie Hardy's dead and I'm looking after her —'

Clover cut across her words, voice high with strain. 'But is Jeremy all right? It's driving me mad not knowing. Will you go across to the farm tomorrow and check on him for me? Please, Kate, I have to —'

'No,' Kate said definitely, 'I won't. I can't. Doug's already been here; I told him I knew nothing. I don't know if he believes me but he certainly won't if I turn up at the farm. Jeremy's perfectly safe. The last thing Doug is going to do is harm his son. You have to pull yourself together, Clove.' She softened her tone. 'I know it's hard but if you give up now, it'll all have been for nothing. If you doubt it, ring Bea and ask her. She'll tell you.'

The thin sound of Clover's weeping came to her. She waited and eventually her sister-in-law sniffled and spoke again. 'He'll forget me.'

'It's been four days,' Kate said patiently. 'A frog's got a longer attention span that that. He won't forget you. Tell me about Andy – how's he doing?' Speaking of her youngest son calmed the other woman; when she'd talked herself out she rang off. Kate blew out a long breath and Harry, on his way to his chair in the sitting room, quirked an eyebrow at her.

'More problems, Missy? You seem to attract 'em, the way jam does ants.'

Remorse stabbed Kate. 'And they all wind up on your doorstep – Clover, Maxie, Ken. I'm sorry, Harry; you're not getting much writing done, and now there's a possum in the house as well. We never even asked you how you felt about that.'

'Probably a good thing.' His tone was fierce but she wasn't fooled.

'It's a godsend for the boy – something to love, something that *needs* him now his mother doesn't.'

He nodded approvingly. 'For someone without kids you understand them pretty well, girl.'

'I'm a teacher,' Kate said dryly. 'It goes with the job.'

28

Heather rang the next morning. 'Did you hear?' she asked without preamble. 'It was on the six o'clock news. The police are reopening the case.'

'That's good,' Kate said cautiously. 'How are you coping? How's Ken? Have you told Martin yet?'

'He rang last night. He already knew, of course. I think the whole country must by now. He asked should he come home but I told him not to.'

'Wise of you, I think. You realise another search mightn't turn up any more than the first did? It's bound to be a long shot after all this time. I'll keep my fingers crossed, but —'

'I know, Katie.' Heather's voice was calm. 'I've faced a few things since Tam turned up. Win or lose this time, when it's over we're putting the place on the market. I've promised Ken.'

The news was so unexpected Kate was silenced. After a little she said, 'Are you okay? Should I come over?'

'It's all right,' Heather said firmly, 'I'm fine. Really, Katie, I am.'

* * *

The following day two police officers arrived at Rosebud to talk to Maxie. One was the sergeant who had attended the fire, the other a female officer, a stranger, one of the many drafted in, together with the local emergency workers, mostly volunteer firefighters, to help in the search. This, according to the television news, had assumed gigantic proportions. If the pictures could be believed, there were upwards of forty people combing the country about Macquarrie, without much success, it seemed.

'Early days yet,' the sergeant said dismissively in answer to Kate's question. He took a restive step down the hallway. 'Perhaps if we could see the boy now?'

'I'll try to find him, but chances are he's gone,' she said frankly. 'He usually does when strangers come.'

'Why's that, then? What's he afraid of?'

'I don't know. He doesn't like people much. He's dyslexic so he's had a hard time at school and been tormented a great deal, about that and about his mother.'

The sergeant nodded. 'Mental case, I believe.'

Kate glared at him. 'It's that attitude, Sergeant, that makes him bolt. His mother had Down syndrome, which did not make her a mental case.'

The policewoman, who had introduced herself as Linda, and was young with sharp eyes and a prominent chin, said, 'Why don't you wait in the vehicle, Sarge? He'll probably respond better to me than to a man. Less scary, you know?'

Giving her a sharp look the sergeant left, but Maxie was nowhere to be found. 'He can't tell you any more than I can, anyway,' Kate said. 'He seldom wears shoes and he found Tam by treading on him. I'd given him a Christmas gift and he wanted to reciprocate, so he cleaned it up and brought it to me.'

'Tam?' Linda looked up from her note taking. 'Why Tam?'

'He – it, the carving – was named for a dog we had. Megan Wantage was my friend. We grew up together on adjacent properties. My father carved the pendant and she called it after his dog.

Look, what else could Maxie tell you, really?'

'He could show us exactly where he found it.' Linda snapped her notebook shut.

'No,' Kate said baldly. 'You can't. His mother burnt to death there a few days ago.'

'Oh, yes. I heard something about that. Look, we'd really like to talk to him. Children are very observant but not at all good at recounting the whole experience. They tend to just focus on what concerns them.' Kate eyed her sharply, knowing how true this was – the woman must have worked with children, or perhaps had some of her own. 'So if you could bring him in to the station – perhaps tomorrow?' Linda suggested. 'In the meantime, where can we find your father?'

'You can't. He died years ago,' Kate said blankly. 'Why would you want to talk to him?'

'Oh, that's too bad. Still, he was there at the time, wasn't he – when the child vanished?'

Kate stared at her with mounting incredulity as the meaning sank in. 'Are you suggesting —?'

'We have to check everything,' Linda said imperturbably. 'After all, he made a trinket for her. Did he often give her things? Sometimes these are the little giveaways that can point to —'

'He'd made one for me too.' Enraged, Kate yanked Blackie into view. 'Megan was my best friend. That's why he carved Tam for her, so she wouldn't feel left out.'

'That could be so, but if there had been anything to notice at the time, you'd have been too young to see it,' the woman observed prosaically. 'Paedophiles' families are usually the ones most surprised when they're finally caught.'

'This one never will be, then, if you're going to suspect my father,' Kate snapped furiously. She slammed the screen door behind the woman and went off seething to fill the birdbaths before starting on lunch.

Later when Max turned up, she told him about it. He was, she realised, a comfortable presence to have around. He sprawled on a kitchen chair, looking very much at home as he watched her talk, studying the way her smooth brows knitted, and her pale eyes (so distinctive he could have recognised her by them alone) flashed with indignation. When she finished speaking he said, 'All hooey, my dear. She just hasn't read the original file. Only stands to reason that every man within a hundred-kilometre radius that day must've been checked out by the cops. A bow at a venture, that's all. Where's the boy?'

'With Harry,' she answered. His matter-of-fact assessment made good sense and her indignation eased. 'Why?'

'Because a copper visited me too. He wanted to rehash the night of the fire – when I first noticed it, what exactly I saw, if I could put a precise time on it. Of course, I couldn't tell them any more than I already had. They'll probably want to talk to you too.'

Puzzled, she knitted her brows again. 'But why? It was an accident, wasn't it?'

'Apparently not. Maxie was right – half-right, anyway. Some expert's looked at the bits of the gas bottles and decided that the explosion was caused by a rifle bullet. They think that somebody started a small fire under, or near, the caravan, then shot into the bottles and the gas did the rest.' He glanced at the door as if he could see through to the office at the far end of the house, and lowered his voice. 'It means that Connie was murdered.'

'But why?' Kate's hands had gone to her face. 'God! I sound like a parrot, but I have to ask. Of all the people in the world, why kill her? She harmed no one, she lived on a pension, you said, so she surely had nothing anybody wanted. So why? Which of course leads to the next question – who?'

'Ah,' Max drummed his fingers on the scrubbed pine. 'They were a bit cagey about that part, but I shouldn't be surprised if they're thinking the same as young Maxie did. What was it he said? Something about his mum dying because he found the dog? Perhaps it's true. If it is, then Megan's abductor killed Connie too.'

'But it doesn't make any sense! Why wouldn't Connie have spoken out long ago if she knew anything about it? Besides, would she have even been at Macquarrie nineteen years back? How old was she?'

He pondered. 'A few years older than you, maybe. And you're right. She got pregnant in her teens but only moved into the van after the boy was born.'

Kate sat opposite him, frowning at the clock on the wall. 'Then if that's so – about her killer and the abductor being the same person, I mean – it certainly wasn't Gypsy Pete. And,' she added, eyes kindling afresh, 'I'll make that snippy damn cop eat her words about Dad.'

He slid his hand across to cover hers. 'I love it when your eyes get all steely, like sword points. They're just doing their job, Kate.'

'Huh!' she snorted, recognising his effort to divert her thoughts. 'And how many swords have you seen, Mr Shephard? As a farmer, shouldn't you be looking for sharp, pointy comparisons among your machinery?'

He grinned. 'Like: *Your eyes sparkle like harrow blades*? Doesn't have the same ring somehow, Ms Doolin. Speaking of machinery, though, I've got to shift my plant across the Wolly tomorrow for my next job. Harvesting starts down there Monday. So I was wondering if you could get away Wednesday evening? We could have dinner somewhere and take it from there.'

He was smiling at her and the lazy warmth behind it as he turned her hand and fitted his own large fingers between hers turned her insides liquid. His touch was an electric jolt sparking desire like a fire inside her. She tilted her head, sternly repressing an answering smile, but aware that the little tremors of her lips were making it plain to him that she was.

'Where did you imagine we might take it to?'

'Anywhere you want, my dear.' But his eyes bore a wicked invitation as he leaned forward across the lazy Susan with its sugar bowl and collection of condiments to kiss the tip of her nose. 'You're a distracting influence but I have to go. Shall we say half seven Wednesday?'

She assented and walked him out and was rewarded with a proper kiss that left her shaken. Standing hugging herself in the shade, she wondered when she had last felt this way about any man – the sense of wholeness that his presence brought, and the immediacy of the loss that bloomed within her at his departure. She was not some infatuated teenager, she scolded herself, to swoon at a boy's noticing her, but she had not missed the *Ms Doolin* either. As if Max himself thought of her that way; not, as she knew herself to be, the product of a failed marriage and emotional mistakes.

* * *

The nine o'clock news that evening carried the story of Connie's murder. It was announced in the headlines, then the studio picture switched to Laradale and the same girl reporter, flanked by a small audience of locals, among whom Kate recognised Bert and Doreen Pringle. Greg Simpson did his best to parry her questions and insinuations that the investigation, *unwillingly undertaken*, was dragging its feet and achieving little more than the last one had, despite the vast amount of manpower put at his disposal. It was almost two decades since the original crime, he pointed out. In the interim people had died or moved away. It was always difficult investigating cold cases but his staff were dedicated and hard working.

'And possibly neglecting newer leads? Isn't it true, Inspector, that in the latest shocking murder case – that of Connie Hardy, the woman whose caravan was made into a bomb – you haven't yet even interviewed her son? The boy who allegedly found the clue responsible for reopening the Megan Wantage case.' The girl thrust the microphone forward aggressively. 'Do you deny it?'

'I don't have to confirm or deny anything.' He glared at her. 'How the police perform their enquiries is not the business of the press. The boy has just lost his mother. I daresay you'd be accusing us of insensitivity if we *had* interviewed him. Rest assured we'll speak to him when the time is right. That will be all, thank you.'

'A pack of dogs, the press,' Harry grunted. 'And about as many manners. I'm only surprised they haven't been out here to interview the lad themselves.'

He switched channels and Kate got up. 'I'll just check on Maxie and type up your stuff, then I'm off to bed.'

He grunted again, flipping through the channels. 'Nothing worth risking your brains on here.' Something rattled outside and he cocked his head. 'Wind's getting up. Don't knock yourself out, Missy. I only wrote a couple of pages today. It can always wait.'

'Best to keep on top of it. I've got a Tartar of a boss, you know.' She winked at him and vanished into the room that had become Maxie's; presently the old man heard the office door open and the muted wakening sound of the computer.

He considered taking himself to bed but it was comfortable on the couch with the fan blowing on him, and the familiar night sounds coming through the open window. A mopoke called – *the wind would interfere with its hunting*, he thought, *and that damn mill head needed greasing*. It squealed like a stuck pig when the blast hit it and the vane turned. Perhaps Max could do it next time he came.

His eyes closed momentarily, but the weight of his head slipping forward as his neck muscles relaxed roused him enough to think that it would be a proper scorcher tomorrow. One of those days with howling, furnace-hot winds. A summer rarely passed without this reminder of nature's mastery over man's puny efforts on the land. It should never have been cleared . . . The old man thought with satisfaction of his own life's work in revegetation, then nodded off again to dream of a pristine mallee forest in which the whirr of the mill blades became the soughing of wind through its tough leaves, and the feel of the fan-induced draft the touch of it upon his face.

29

Kate, going out next morning to let Flip off the chain and open the henhouse door before she prepared Vegemite's first feed, felt the hot, dry air rasp against her skin. Even though the sun lay barely above the horizon, the pale summer sky was smudged with blowing dust, and the pepperina branches thrashed in the gale. She could feel grit in the wind and her hair was electric with static. Latching the hen coop open, she turned back indoors, glad to retreat from the day. As she went in, the wind, as if to emphasise its dominance over frail humanity, shouldered the door roughly shut behind her, while from a shed roof somewhere a sheet of tin began a monotonous flapping.

The house was a haven of peace, its stone walls smothering the sounds of the gale. Maxie was up, wearing yesterday's grubby shorts and a T-shirt to which Vegemite clung, surveying the world through huge dark eyes. The little kit was thriving on milk and snacks of apple and carrot, and spent most of its time now either clinging to its owner's shirt, or curled up asleep inside it.

'It's a horrid day to be out,' Kate said, handing Maxie the vanilla bottle to which she'd fitted the eye-dropper teat, 'but I think we really have to go to town and get you some more clothes.'

Maxie looked doubtful. 'Do I gotta go, Miss?'

'You mean, *do I have to?*' she corrected. 'And yes, I'm afraid you do. We want them to fit you, after all. Perhaps we'll have an ice-cream after.' She wouldn't mention dropping in at the police station as well, she decided. Not until they were in the car – which brought another worry to mind: whether it would start. The battery was definitely on the way out. She should give Gleeson's a ring, she supposed, and see if they could change it; it'd be expensive, but better that than getting stranded halfway home.

Over breakfast she informed Harry of her plans. 'Do you want to come too? I'll be grocery shopping as well but I could drop you off at the library. Plenty of comfy chairs there. It's too hot to wait in the car. Is there anything you want me to get you?'

'I'll stop home, Missy,' he growled, 'but you can get me more paper. And I expect I'd better find the cheque book. You'll be wanting to spend more of my money, most likely.'

'Yes,' she said serenely. 'Make it two cheques, if you please. My wages are due, and I'll need another for household expenditure. Groceries, that is.'

'All right, girl.' The bristly white brows flagged his displeasure. 'I ran a business for longer than you've lived. I know what expenditure means.'

She grinned at him. 'You're such an old fraud but you don't fool me, Harry Quickly. I bet you just don't trust my driving. Did Edie drive? From all you've told me of her, she sounded a very capable woman.'

'Aye, Missy, she was that.' He nodded. 'Wasn't much my Edie couldn't do, but that said, it was a damn fool that let her behind the wheel. Only knew one pace and that was flat out. She hit more fence posts round here than most fencers ever handled.'

'So it's definitely my driving. Well, your loss.' She glanced at the clock. 'We'll leave about nine. That'll give us plenty of time to be home before lunch. You sure you'll be all right by yourself?'

'Course I will,' he said testily. 'Don't hurry back on my account. I'll enjoy the peace and quiet. Man doesn't get much of it round here.'

Kate's plans, though, suffered a setback, for when she went to start the car the battery was completely dead. 'Damn!' She tried the key again but the starter didn't even click. Her own fault, of course. She'd only turned the engine over twice in the last fortnight, and both times she'd driven just a few hundred metres; she should have run the engine regularly instead of letting it sit. She wondered if Harry owned a charger but a glance around the shed, where empty oil drums clattered and rolled in the wind scouring the open-fronted building, made it seem unlikely. Harry had quit driving ten years before, so the only farm vehicle was up on blocks and the battery in it would be deader than hers. Annoyed, but chiefly with herself, Kate slammed the Commodore's door and headed back out into the gale. She'd ring old Jack. Surely Gleeson's could spare a mechanic to run a charged battery out to the farm?

The phone, however, was dead. Kate replaced the handpiece and went to stand near the water tank where the line entered the house and squinted her eyes into the gale tracing the wires. As far as she could see they looked sound enough, swooping away down the sheep paddock fence line between the poles. But the poles were old – one of them could have blown over, or a tree might have come down across the wire. It happened all the time. Vexed, she bit her lip. It was annoying, but with no way to get a message out she'd just have to wait for Max or somebody else to come. Or for someone to try to ring through – any of the locals would immediately suspect the weather and report a line fault for her. Perhaps if she didn't turn up with Maxie, the police might even call back? It didn't really matter if she was alone, she told herself, only Harry's age meant she really *ought* to have a constant means of contact with the outside world.

Flip bounded up to her, his black and white coat blown ragged, Maxie following in his disgraceful shorts, a hand cupping his midriff where Vegemite slept. 'Miss,' he called.

'Tom Sawyer.' She smiled at him. 'Minus straw hat and fishing pole.' The reference went over his head. 'You can relax, young man. We're not going anywhere today. Dud battery.'

He wasn't listening. 'Miss,' he said again, but with more urgency, 'I can smell smoke.'

Instantly she breathed in and there it was, just the faintest trace, almost lost in the raging wind – the scent of burning eucalyptus. She turned her head, icy needles of dread in the pit of her stomach, and breathed in again, and this time it was stronger, the unmistakable smell of fire. Her gaze rose above the thrashing tops of the pepper trees but the wind would shred the smoke, drive it low, she thought, and there was so much flying dust you'd never tell the two apart.

For a long moment she stood there, mind whirling, seeking to conquer fear and think constructively, and to forget the images of the aftermath of a fire she had seen as a child. The blackened paddocks and skeletal scrub, the charred bodies of sheep, stiff legs spread like table supports and the crows pecking . . . The farm complex at Stones Place had been spared but they'd lost a crop and a paddock of wethers. She'd found a bird, a parrot, lying dead in drifting ash by the poor stripped creek bank, and cried, because parrots were strong, fast flyers, and if *they* could fall, then all the little birds, like the wrens and flycatchers, were certainly dead also . . .

'What are we gonna do, Miss?' Maxie's voice recalled her to the present. His young brow was creased but the blue-grey eyes radiated perfect trust in her ability to deal with whatever might befall them.

'We'll think of something,' she said steadily, but an inner voice yelled, '*What?*' Dear God, the phone was out and she had an old man, a young boy and assorted animals to protect, with no way of getting them out. Wasn't that what the authorities advised with bushfires? Prepare. Evaluate. Leave. She had little enough time for preparation, no way to evaluate anything, and it was impossible for them to leave.

Maxie clutched her hand. 'The gas, Miss! We gotta stop it blowing us up!'

'You're dead right,' she declared, released from indecision. That was something she could do. 'Tell you what – I'll disconnect the bottle while you roll the spare one away. Are you strong enough?'

'Course I am!' He seemed wounded she could even ask.

There was no time to salve his feelings. Max had left the spanner handy. She seized it, muttering, '*Left*-hand thread,' and five minutes later the cylinder joined its mate in the barren waste of the old garden. She ran inside, shouting at Maxie to bring the hose. If she could wet the verandahs – they were so dry they'd go up with the first spark. What could she put drinking water in? They'd need that if the tanks went. And blankets – fill the laundry tubs, soak as many blankets as she could. Was it her imagination or had the noise of the wind deepened in the last few minutes? The smoke had certainly thickened. She could taste it now in her throat.

'Harry!' she yelled on the run. 'Fire! Heading this way. You got any ideas?'

Then Maxie was yelling too from the verandah, where a stream of water was now spreading over the splintered boards. The pressure had seemed adequate for hosing her garden bed, and showering, but Kate, dismayed, saw now how slowly the water ran. It would take twenty minutes to wet the boards in front, which still left the side verandah dry. She needed a fire hose to make any difference. Maxie yelled again, leaping through the door space with Flip at his heels (ears flattened and tail low), and when she looked away from the slow spread of the puddle she saw why. Beyond the bright-green circle of pepperinas the mallee was alight, fire riding the tossing heads of the trees like demon jockeys dressed in flame.

Harry said, 'Waste of time. It'll burn. We've got to get out, girl.'

'Where?' Water spilled in the laundry, where a tub was over-flowing. She darted past him to jam a cooler into the sink and start the tap.

'Underground. The old tank. Maxie knows. Out the back way. Quick now, Missy. It'll be on us in a minute.'

'Won't the house be safe?' She jammed the lid down, wrestled the cooler free and gave it to him to carry, then bundled out of the tub the only blanket she'd managed to soak. The cold shock of the wet wool was delicious against her heated body. Food! She should've thought of that but there was no time now. On an impulse she ran back, dripping water, to slam the wooden front door.

'Might not if it gets into the roof. Heat melts the zinc, curls the iron. Time to go. Come on, Maxie.'

The screen door banged open as they left. 'Miss!' the boy, cradling Vegemite, called urgently to her as she hesitated, then turned back inside.

'I'm coming.' She ran into the office and back through the house, almost slipping on the trail of water, then she was outside, buffeted by the force and heat of the wind. She saw Harry's spare form huffing along, pitifully slow for all his effort, white hair streaming, beard blown awry, making for the sheds with Maxie. Flip trotted behind, the boy turning worriedly to look for her; Kate flapped a hand to urge them on.

Kate had been unaware of the tank's existence, although it turned out her car was parked on one end of it. Decades of dirt and accumulated junk covered the rest – in places you couldn't tell that the floor of the shed wasn't dirt. Timber was stacked in one corner, the walls were hung with dust-coated, spider-webbed harnesses – old collars, chain sets, winkers turned black and cracked with age. An early model tractor supported the rotted frame of a cart, and wooden packing cases shared the space with rusty old drums of every shape and size. Some she recognised from childhood as having held sheep dip or engine oil. The larger ones were probably fuel. Kerosene, perhaps, from the days when fridges ran on it? Kate just hoped they were empty. There were tyres stacked almost to the roof, rolls of rotting canvas, and enough old rope piled about to run Nelson's navy.

'It's a fire trap,' she blurted. 'Everything here will burn.'

'Won't matter,' Harry puffed. 'Concrete'll protect us. At the back here, girl. Come on, damn it!' for she had stopped in indecision. 'Lead the way, lad.'

Maxie sprang nimbly between the piled rubbish and vanished into darkness. Kate stumbled after him, battling her instinct to flee for the open country where the fire would be confined to stubble, or at the worst, a few inches of dry grass. But Harry would never make it. Hidden by deep shadow, the opening lay before her: a concrete lid, about a metre square, had been wrestled aside to disclose a man-sized hole, from the mouth of which a broad-stepped builder's ladder emerged. The boy was already at the bottom peering up at them, Flip clamped in his arms. It wasn't very far, perhaps two metres, she saw, grabbing the cooler from Harry's trembling hands as she snatched a look behind her. The fire roared, the sound drowning the wind; it was in the old shearers' quarters, the red and gold of the flames sucked higher and higher by the heat created as the fire fed. The closest shed was also burning. She could feel the radiant heat on her skin and suddenly it was there behind her, like some ravening hunter that had spotted its prey.

'Down you go. Mind your step.' Kate tried to keep her voice calm. She leaned sideways to drop the blanket to Maxie. 'Help him down,' she called. Her hair was starting to singe and she squinted her eyes against the searing heat. Smoke, like a stinking black fog, uncoiled towards her as the flames found the tyres and suddenly she could wait no longer. She flung herself at the ladder, coughing as her feet fumbled on the steps. She was blind, eyes tearing, head filled with a roar like a jet's take-off as the flames found the roof and the shed burst alight as if suddenly drenched in petrol.

Harry, coughing and shaking, was bent over catching his breath, but looked up at her arrival.

'All right, Missy?'

'Yes.' Kate checked on Maxie, looking for the bulge in his shirt before asking, 'How's Vegemite doing?'

'Okay, Miss.'

'Good. And Flip's fine.' She remembered the hens then. 'I'm sorry about your chooks, Harry. Here, sit down and rest.' The tank was cool and dim, save for the hellish glow cast by the fire. By its light she made out the shape of an old coir mattress in the corner. It was covered by a blanket. She helped him onto it, saying, 'Make yourself comfortable and I'll get you a drink.' To Maxie she said brightly, 'So this is your possie?'

'Yes, Miss.'

'Candles too. Well, we might be glad of those when the roof goes.' As if on cue something fiery fell with a clang, showering sparks through the hole. Kate stepped back. 'Not to worry. Bricks won't burn.' The tank, she saw, had been dug and lined with bricks before being plastered to render it waterproof. Only the top two courses were visible. She couldn't see how big the space was, for no light penetrated to the far end. 'It's not as deep as I would've expected,' she murmured, handing Harry the cooler top to drink from.

'Tanks need volume not depth, girl.' His breathing was ragged, she noticed worriedly. A racking cough took him and she steadied the cap in his hand. 'Any road, couldn't – go deeper – rock underneath.'

'Don't talk. We're safe. That's all that matters.'

They all had a drink, including Flip, who lapped from the water she poured into Maxie's cupped hands, then they settled down to wait out the fire. Smoke fed into the hole but it lay like a cloud under their concrete roof and didn't bother them. Harry made room on the mattress and Maxie sat cross-legged on the end, stroking the possum that had woken, fooled by the gloom into thinking night had come.

'He's hungry, Miss.' Maxie looked hopefully at Kate, sitting on a box that he'd previously brought down for storage. It contained many of his sketches, along with a bird's egg, bits of coloured rock, and a shanghai with a supply of lethal-looking ball bearings for ammunition.

'Well, I'm sorry, Maxie, but he'll have to wait till we get out.' Though if the farmhouse burned, there'd be nothing for any of them to eat. And all she'd have left in the world was what she stood up in. The Commodore would be a smoking ruin by now, so it was a good thing she hadn't been able to order the battery. Kate pulled herself away from her thoughts; they could be dead, and they weren't. Surely nothing else mattered beside that? Unless you were very old with limited time left. She fished the memory stick she'd gone back for from the pocket of her jeans and held it out to show Harry.

'Do you know what's on this?'

'Stop waving it around so a man can see the damn thing,' he said crossly. 'Of course I don't. You going to tell me?'

'Yes, you old grump,' she said affectionately. 'It's your book. I've been saving your words onto this. So even if the computer and all your papers have burned, every word of it is quite safe.'

'Is that right? On that bitty little thing?' He shook his white head. 'If my Edie could've lived to see that. Thank you, girl.' His eyes had moistened; they glittered in the gloom, and for a moment Kate was horribly afraid that he would cry. Her heart ached with pity for his age and helplessness, and for the first time she wondered how she was ever going to get him up the ladder again once it became safe to do so. Or alternatively, summon the help she would certainly need when the fire was over.

30

They waited for hours. The roof fell in quite early in the piece, and with that the noise diminished, for the fire had passed on by then, leaving desolation, red-hot and still blazing, behind. A section of roof iron half-covered the manhole, so a sepulchral darkness filled their sanctuary. Every so often as they waited in the safe, underground chamber, some hanging beam or partially burned post would be eaten through and collapse into the flames below, which they could hear but not see.

Occasionally bits fell directly into the tank to smoulder to death on the floor. Harry dozed and after a while Maxie did too, slumping into sleep in the way of young animals. Kate was relieved; he seemed not to have connected the flames they'd escaped from with the fire that had killed his mother. Because he hadn't seen the burnt-out caravan, she wondered? Or because bushfires were a part of the Mallee, like drought and salinity? Farm kids could sometimes surprise one with their hardy acceptance of facts. It was something the country bred in those who made their home in it.

Left alone, she paced about for a while, then seated herself again and looked through Maxie's stash of drawings, while her free hand unconsciously fiddled with the little horse figurine at her throat. She wore it always now – *something to be thankful for*, she thought wryly. The rest of her jewellery was probably toast. She thought about the bore at Stones Place, and wondered when the tank that presently sheltered them had ceased to be used for water, and how the town had managed in the early days, for the Wolly River was seasonal at best.

The drawings were really good. It would be a shame – no, a *crime* – if the boy never received training to hone this precious talent; but that would depend entirely on where he ended up. Some foster families made wonderful surrogate parents, others – well, others did not. *Parenting*, Kate thought, *entailed more than the provision of food and a place to sleep.* One needed to nurture talent, to give the young licence to follow their dreams, and the support to achieve them – and that took love.

She sighed, wondering if it would happen. Surely, as a twig of the mighty Quickly tree, there must be somebody willing to take him on? She had grown fond of the boy and couldn't bear the thought of him living in a spare room somewhere, on sufferance, inevitably dropping out of school because of his disability. No artistic career, but a life spent on the dole, or in a succession of dead-end jobs, where muscles rather than skill predominated. It wasn't going to happen, Kate told herself fiercely – then wondered how she could prevent it. Looked at dispassionately, she was no better off than Maxie, and less likely to obtain assistance. Sighing again, she got up to climb the ladder once more and stick her head out for a cautious look around.

Individual fires still burned in a landscape painted in black and grey and denuded of recognisable features. From her low elevation the engine block and frame of both her car and the old tractor obscured any view of the house, but the sheds and all she could see of the trees had vanished. Only blackened trunks and branches remained. Something about the mill looked odd and it took her a moment to see that the timber rods and half the platform had gone. The metal of the water tank was blackened but intact. She was climbing higher to check if the house still stood when her gaze fell on embers glowing in the drifts of ash that covered the sheet of iron half blocking the hole. It was still too hot to push aside. She retreated slowly, noting that the wind had dropped and the sun shone almost overhead. They'd just have to wait a bit longer.

It didn't matter; they were cool underground, and safe. They had water, and feeling a bit hollow wasn't the same as being hungry. Kate re-seated herself and Flip came to lean against her leg and yawned widely before licking her hand. She fondled his ears and stared around at the tank, wondering where, in the gloom, were the inlet pipes that must once have carried the rainfall from the farm roofs. Flip whined restively and she patted him.

'Patience, my friend.'

Harry woke then with a start and Kate got up and poured him a drink. Instead of taking it, he stared blankly at her. 'Do I know you? Where's this?' He looked around with mounting agitation and her heart sank.

'It's all right, Harry. The fire, remember? We sheltered here in the underground tank – you and me and Maxie. You'll remember in a minute. Are you thirsty? Would you like some water?'

'Water – yes.' He drank it, blinked at her, and recognition dawned slowly. 'Missy?' he said, his voice querulous and old.

'Yes, it's me. You were just a little confused.'

'How long?'

She intuited the question. 'Oh, hours. I've been up for a look. Not much left, I'm afraid, but we have to stay here until the ash cools. It's ankle-deep up there. Are you hungry?'

'A bit. What did Jackson say?'

'Who?'

'Jackson. Did he tell you about the sheep?' He didn't wait for an answer but stared agitatedly at the dog. 'That's not Franko.

What have you done with him?' He put two fingers in his mouth but on the point of whistling suddenly faltered. 'Missy?' he said uncertainly. 'Kate?'

She went to him. 'Well, after all this time you've finally got my name right! It's okay, Harry. You're just a bit wanderey today. What about having a walk around, get the blood moving?'

He struggled up but his step was uncertain and after a very short time she urged him to sit down on the box. 'I think we might make a move.' She needed his co-operation to get him out and there was no saying how long his current lucid spell would last. Bending above Maxie, who was still sprawled in sleep, she shook him gently, and then again. 'Maxie, come on, wake up.'

His eyes, fogged with sleep, opened reluctantly, then closed again. 'Mamma,' he murmured. His hand reached for her dangling necklace, 'Mamma's puppy.'

'Maxie!' He blinked, instantly awake, his softened features sharpening as memory returned with consciousness and whatever dream he'd been having faded. Sitting up, he looked around, his hands moving automatically to the warmth of the possum kit snuggled into his neck.

'Has the fire gone, Miss?'

'Yes. Do you know, I think you might start calling me Kate – if you want to. Maxie,' she knelt and held his gaze, lifting Blackie on his chain, 'just now when you were waking up, you saw this and said, *Mamma's puppy*. What did you mean?'

He looked confused. 'I dunno, Miss – Kate. I think I remember, but it mighta been a dream.'

'What dream? Tell me. Something that happened when you were very young that got mixed up with other things? Try to remember, Maxie.'

He frowned tremendously and rubbed his head. 'I can't. Maybe it was a real puppy the pretty man gave her?' His gaze sharpened.

'Is it about her getting killed? I heard what they said on the news, that somebody done it.'

'I don't know. What did you mean, *the pretty man*? Who is that?'

'My dad,' he said simply. 'Mamma told me that: *your dad's a pretty man*. She never said what his name was, but.' He scrambled up. 'Shall I have a look outside?'

'Yes.' Frustrated, Kate sat back on her heels. It was no use pushing him. Either the fragment of memory (if it was that) would be lost, or he'd make up something in an effort to help. 'Be careful,' she said, eyeing his bare feet. 'Very careful – don't get burnt.'

* * *

Afterwards, Kate preferred not to remember the struggle it was to get Harry out of the tank. Had he been a child, she could have climbed behind him with his body held within the cage of her arms, but his form was too big so she had to follow behind, trying to steady his limbs, praying he would remain aware of what he was doing. His legs were trembling and weak, and she feared that at any moment he would collapse. Once his chest and shoulders were through the hole he sagged on the ladder, increasing her fears. Quickly she called, 'Lie forward, Harry. That's it – get your body as flat as you can. Maxie'll pull you and I'll push. Can you do that, Maxie?'

'Yeah, course, Mi— Kate,' the boy piped.

'Then he'll be out in no time,' she said cheerfully, taking a grip on the old man's quivering thighs.

It was a desperate struggle. Harry might be frail but he was a big-boned man. By the time Kate sat panting on the ashy concrete, supporting his head as he lay recovering his breath, all three were filthy – clothes and skin, and in Harry's case beard and hair, smeared with ash and soot.

'C'mon,' she said at last, pushing herself up wearily, 'let's get you to the house.' At least it still stood, she noted thankfully, if not without damage. The stone walls had turned the fire but both verandahs had gone and smoke still rose from the back, most likely from the timber laundry, but she'd worry about that later. She tracked a path with her eye to the edge of the shed, avoiding the deepest sections of ash where heat would still linger. The stink of burning rubber was very strong and a fitful breeze lifted the blackened, tissue-thin remnants of burnt matter so that they drifted about before descending in a continual rain of soot.

Harry, his mind focused again, struggled up gamely. 'I expect you'll be claiming danger money now, girl,' he grunted.

'Bet your life on it.' She grinned at him. 'Best foot forward, soldier, and there'll be a cuppa and a sandwich at the end of it. Your house survived. That's something.'

'Built to last,' he grunted, edging slowly along, supported by them both. 'You've lost your vehicle. Was it insured?'

'That old heap? Not likely.' The fact that he had remembered she'd even had one cheered her, until, arriving finally at the front door, another difficulty presented itself. 'Right – so how do we get up there?' With no steps or verandah, the distance from ground to floor looked insurmountable. She stared at it dismayed.

'Easy . . . Hey! Car coming,' Maxie cried, just as Flip began to bark.

The white Toyota slewed to a stop, raising such a storm of black that Max didn't see the three of them, or they him, until he'd jumped the fallen gate and was running up the path. His pace slackened only slightly until he reached them.

'Jesus! What —? Are you all right?' His eyes were on Kate. 'Somebody reported a fire. I heard it on the CB . . . Holy Christ!' he added, turning in a slow circle to view the devastation about them, 'It's burned flat! How in God's name did you survive that?'

'The old underground tank,' Kate said succinctly. 'Look, Max, Harry's not the best. We need to get him inside out of the heat.'

'Yes, of course. You're not hurt? None of you?'

'Me bike's burned.' Maxie was staring at the buckled, blackened frame he'd just discovered, his dirty face struggling against tears.

'It doesn't matter.' Kate gave him a quick hug. 'You live here now, anyway. Getting into the house – you said it was easy, Maxie. Can you show me?'

'Course.' He sniffed, wiping his nose on his wrist. 'Just sit in the doorway, see?' He demonstrated, swinging his legs up and round. 'Easy-peasy.'

'Clever kid! Think you can manage, Harry?'

With Max's help he did. They got him onto his bed but the rest of Kate's program wasn't so easy to follow. There was no water or power, and though the gas cylinders had survived the flames, the pipes and fittings had not. Fire had cracked all the windows and burnt some of the frames; the kitchen steps and screen door had gone, but the laundry, which also housed the toilet, had suffered most. Using the pry bar from his vehicle, Max pulled the still-smouldering timbers apart, and shook his head over the gas fittings.

'Can't fix that.' He looked at his watch. 'I called for an ambulance the moment I realised the fire had hit the place. It should be here any time soon. Best thing you can do is let them take the old boy into the hospital for the night. And you and Maxie come to town with me.'

'I suppose.' Kate let her shoulders droop wearily as her reaction to the morning's terror caught up with her, and she leaned against the bench where she was making sandwiches. She'd washed her hands but there'd been no water to spare for her face. Max stepped closer and, tilting her chin, licked his thumb and gently wiped a smudge from her upper lip.

'Jesus, Kate.' His voice was husky. 'Driving here I had you dead a dozen ways. I've never been so goddamned terrified in my life.' He kissed her lingeringly and when he let her go she sighed and laid her head against his shoulder.

'Now you'll smell of smoke, like the rest of us.' Everything did – her clothes and hair, the house, the curtains, which by some miracle hadn't caught alight when the window frames burned. 'I was so worried about Harry. He lost it completely there in the tank for a bit, forgot where he was and who I was. And I didn't know how I was going to get help until you came. The phone went out before the fire got here, you see. The flames went past in a flash, but it took hours for the sheds to finish burning. And all Harry's trees have gone . . . Where's it got to, the fire?'

'They think the Wolly'll hold it now the wind's dropped. The riverbed makes a good firebreak. The brigade's out, of course, and the police. They're already saying it's arson. As for the trees, they'll come again. Mallee's tough.'

'But he mightn't live to see it. Today's been a great strain on him. It's a wonder his heart didn't give out just getting him up that ladder . . . Anyway.' She straightened. 'If I haven't said so, thanks for coming.'

'I'd come a great deal further for you, sweet Kate.'

In answer she proffered the plate. 'Have a sandwich, then. After all,' her smile was tired, 'you never know when you might need your strength.'

The ambulance arrived and Harry was taken out, sooty and dishevelled against the pristine cover on the stretcher. 'I'll be in to visit tonight,' Kate promised. 'There's a bit of work needed here before we can come back, but we can talk about that later.'

'Orright.' The word was slurred, unlike his normal crisp delivery. He caught her hand, eyes suddenly anxious. 'The boy, Missy . . .'

'Maxie'll be with me,' she said cheerfully. 'Don't *worry*, Harry. I'll take care of things.' He smiled wearily at that, then the doors shut and the ambulance drove off as the first crows came winging down into the sheep paddock, where the carcasses were already beginning to bloat in the heat. Kate turned away. 'I'll throw some things in a bag. Get your toothbrush, Maxie, and pyjamas. It seems we'll be shopping today after all.'

31

They dropped Flip off at The Narrows. Heather, horror-struck by their brush with death, was desperate for Kate to stay also but she declined. 'Thanks, Heather. Maybe later. I actually need to be in town, though, to keep an eye on Harry. It's been an awful shock for him. I have to do a bit of shopping, too.' And put everything she owned through the laundromat. 'And see about some transport. The car's gone, of course. I've been asked to drop in to the police station, too. Maybe in a couple of days – depending how things go – then I'd love to, if that's okay?'

'Of course it is, Lamb. And Maxie; that goes without saying.' She studied Vegemite's nose, visible above the neckline of the boy's filthy T-shirt. 'You wouldn't like to leave the possum too?'

'I'd love to,' Kate said frankly, 'but I don't think it's possible.' Maxie was already backing away. 'It's okay; you can bring him. Just be discreet when we get to the hotel.'

'What's *dis-creet*, Kate?'

'Pretend he's not there. In fact, if Mrs Wantage has a shoebox to spare, you can make out he's your luggage.'

The ploy worked admirably. Max carried her bag upstairs to the twin room Kate had booked. They'd both showered at The Narrows but Maxie was forbidden to sit on anything until new clothes could be arranged.

'We'll do that first,' she decided.

'I'll drive you,' Max said. 'And I heard what you said about transport. Don't hire or buy anything, Kate. Not for the moment, anyway. I'm free to chauffeur you about.'

'But your work?'

'I've got a good team. They can handle it for a day or two.'

She bought two complete sets of clothes for Maxie, and had him change in the shop. The dirty ones went into a plastic bag, which she sealed to keep in the smell of smoke, then added to the others in the nylon carry bag she let him choose. She bought socks and a pair of trainers, and a baseball cap with a flat peak, which he stuck on his head and then grinned at her, obviously pleased with the purchase. After that, all three of them had ice-cream. When they'd finished she said, 'Now we're going to see the police, Maxie. They want to talk to you. You're not in trouble. They just want you to tell them about finding Tam. It might help them work out who killed your mum. Can you do that for her?'

He looked scared; his hands tensed and Kate wondered if the uncles had ever threatened him with the police over some childish misdemeanor. 'Will you be there?'

'Yes.'

'Orright, then.'

They gave their names at the front desk and after the shortest wait the policewoman, Linda, came out and ushered the two of them into a plain room containing three easy chairs, a table and some filing cabinets. A noisy air conditioner blocked the window and there was a cold-water dispenser and plastic cups in one corner.

Linda was patient and skilled at her task, talking all around the subject to put the boy at ease. She asked him about the quarry, wondering if he'd ever climbed down into it, asking were there rabbits, and what sort of birds he'd seen there. Wasn't it lonely living so far from town? Did people ever come out that way, just to look?

Maxie laughed at that. 'The uncles wouldn'ta let 'em.'

She asked about the Hollens then, probing questions, to most of which the boy simply shrugged and repeated, 'Dunno.' He had as little to do with them as possible; the uncles didn't like kids – didn't like anyone much, really – but they were dead soppy on his mum.

That was when Linda, listening sympathetically, held out the carving. 'Tell me about finding this, Maxie. How do you think it got there?'

'Dunno. Somebody lost it?' It was just lying there, he said, and he trod on it, then squatted down to see what had pricked him. There'd been a camp at the quarry in the olden days, and you could find all sorts of stuff scattered about – shiny buttons made of shell stuff, and nails, and real old pen nibs. He'd found a penny once and even a fuel tank cap off a Harley-Davidson bike – well, that's what old Harry said it was.

'Did you show anyone the little dog? Your mum, perhaps?'

'No.' He looked aside.

'Why not? Wouldn't she have been interested? It's a lovely little carving.'

'I was gonna give it to her – to Kate, cause she give me a paintbox.'

'But your mum wouldn't have minded, would she?' Linda persisted.

'I dunno. She might've,' he muttered.

'Maxie,' Kate leaned forward, 'tell Linda about waking up suddenly and seeing Blackie hanging above you. You reached for it and said, *Mamma's puppy*, remember? Was that because she used to wear Tam? Is that why you didn't show her?'

He flushed and sprang up, eyes hunting about the room for an escape. 'I dunno,' he shouted. 'Maybe she did. Maybe there was a real puppy. I was only little and he never came any more, anyway, she said. Besides, if it was hers, she musta slung it or how come it was out there?'

He was trembling with anger or some other emotion. Kate rose and went to him. 'It's all right, nobody's blaming you. If the pretty man gave it to her and she lost it, that's not your fault. And I'm so glad you thought of giving it to me. It means we're friends, right?'

He eyed her carefully and nodded. 'Yes, Mi— Kate.'

'Good.' She hugged him and a brief pale smile flickered on his face and was gone.

Linda, waiting patiently, said, 'So who's this pretty man?'

'Mum said he was my dad. When I was little she used to sing about him, *Pretty man comin' to see his little babee,*' he mimicked. 'But he never.' He shrugged and Kate read the hurt in his eyes and abruptly rose, an unpleasant thought niggling at her.

'I think that's enough for now.' With a hand on his shoulder, she turned Maxie towards the door and gave him a little push. 'Go out and find Max. He's waiting for us.' As he obeyed she spoke without apology to Linda. 'He's been through rather a lot already today.'

'Yes, I heard about the bushfire.' Linda had risen too. 'Seems you're lucky to be here at all. Thanks for bringing him in.'

'Yes, about that fire. They're saying you suspect arson? Does that mean the two fires could be connected?'

'Why should they be? Plenty of bushfires are deliberately lit.' Linda shrugged. 'There's no shortage of pyromaniacs, or it could've been plain carelessness by someone – a dropped match, say.'

'It couldn't – not unless a camp fire got away, and as you know, they're banned through summer. If you'd dropped a match in that gale, it would've been out before it hit the ground,' Kate said positively. 'Besides, don't pyromaniacs usually steer clear of killing people? But it's stretching coincidence, don't you think, that both the recent fires could have claimed Maxie's life? Maybe you should tell the press you've spoken to him, just so nobody torches the Railway Arms tonight, thinking to prevent you doing so?'

'Do you really believe —?' Linda studied her and nodded. 'You think he's Megan's killer, don't you, this "pretty man" of Maxie's? He might have made him up, you know. Fatherless kids tell the weirdest lies to themselves, and others, about their non-existent dads.'

'I know. But whoever took Megan was local, so he's probably still here. And if he also killed Connie Hardy, then it can only have been because he was afraid she knew something that'd give him away. Like where the carving came from. So it makes sense to me that he might try to harm Maxie too. But there'd be no point if, for instance, it was on the news tonight that you'd already interviewed him. Besides,' she added with a flash of humour, 'it might keep the inspector from another savaging by that blonde Rottweiler of a reporter.'

Linda laughed. 'You've got a point there. Leave it with me, then.'

* * *

Harry was dozing when they reached his room in the hospital. 'We're just keeping an eye on him,' the nurse murmured. 'His BP's down a bit and he's a little confused when he first wakes, but he's fine really, for his age. Don't worry if he doesn't know you at first. It's just age, and shock, of course.'

Kate's heart sank. 'He was fine this morning. Sharp as a tack. He might be frail but there's nothing wrong with his head.'

'Still, by all accounts he's been through a terrifying ordeal. That'd shake anyone. You can't expect a ninety-year-old to bounce back like a teenager.' She rattled the screen back along its runner and went away.

Harry's white hair was spread over the pillow and his hands lay loose on the sheet, knuckles and veins prominent. His fingernails were thick and yellow and Kate saw that the tip of the little finger on his left hand was missing. She'd never noticed that before. His mouth was open to display bare lower gums, and she spied the dentures sitting in a glass on the bedside cabinet. Kate's heart smote her. He looked so vulnerable lying there, his washed beard like hanks of white silk, that she whispered in pity, 'Oh, Harry.'

Pulling the visitor's chair to the bedside, she sat, waiting for him to wake up. Maxie folded himself down on the floor while Max went to find another chair.

They stayed on until the sound of the bell signalled the end of visiting hours. Harry had woken clear-headed, giving Kate the confidence to broach the question of his immediate future. 'They'll probably want you to stay in for another day at least, maybe two,' she explained, 'but that's good because honestly, Harry, you couldn't go home now, anyway. There's no power or water. The tank's okay but empty, because the fire melted the polythene water line, and the rods have gone on the mill. Even the stove doesn't work because the couplings were burnt. And Max had to pull down most of the laundry, but the rest of the house needs very little work, considering – a new door or two, some window frames. We can organise that for you.' Unconsciously she included Max in the offer.

'I believe you could, Missy.' He sounded tired.

'Well, there's no need for you to think about it now,' she comforted. 'You'll feel stronger in a day or two and things will seem clearer then. And you could always rent something in town for a while – a month, say? Maybe that would suit you better.' She smiled at him. 'I can manage bread puddings pretty well anywhere.'

'So you'd stick around and cook for me, girl?'

'Well, of course. A bit of a bushfire doesn't mean you're not still my boss.'

They left it at that. Outside in the dull glow of the car park lights with the warm night air wrapped like a shawl about them, Max stood for a moment staring south, but no glow lit up the horizon. 'Looks like they got it out. Dinner at the hotel, or would you rather go out somewhere, Kate?'

'No, the hotel's fine, thanks. Are you hungry, Maxie?'

'Yeah.' The boy hesitated. 'Is Harry gonna be okay?'

'I hope so.' He had voiced her own fear. 'He is very old, though, and nobody lives forever, Maxie.'

'I know. You're not gonna die, but?'

'Of course not. And you mean *going to*, not *gonna*.' Reading his fear of abandonment, she pulled him close in the dark. 'Don't worry. I'll be here correcting your speech for simply ages yet, young man. Now, we'd better get back and feed Vegemite.'

At the hotel Kate and the boy headed upstairs. She'd boil the jug to warm the baby possum's milk, and take a shower. The knock came just as she turned from the sink, but before she could answer it the door had opened and Guy entered. Holding a bunch of flowers, he stepped in, looked around, and dropped his bag while she simply stared, too flabbergasted by his sudden appearance to respond, save with a question.

'How did you get in?'

He smiled and raised a placatory hand. 'It's okay, all kosher. I told them I was your husband. I heard about the fire – thought you'd need a bit of cosseting, so I brought you these.' He held out the flowers. 'How are you, babe?'

'I don't believe this. They just handed you a key?' Her eyes flashed furiously. 'We'll see about that.'

'No, wait!' He grabbed the phone she was reaching for. 'Calm down, Kate. I was worried about you, for God's sake! Can't we just talk? That's all I want to do. I'll stay the night and we'll talk, sort all this nonsense out. Where's the harm, eh? It's twin beds and we are married, for God's sake! Look, I've been staying down in the cabins on the riverbank and when I heard about the fire I knew I just had to see you. We need time, babe, that's all. So it made sense I be here with you. I mean, why not? You could've died – they're saying the whole farm was burnt! I really miss you, babe. You know I've never stopped loving you. I just want us to begin again, and I thought this'd be a good place to start.'

'And more comfortable than the cabins? You,' Kate declared, 'have a bloody nerve!' She glared at the drooping petals of the zinnias within their cellophane wrapping. 'So, what – you got the rejects from the supermarket and came to try it on? Give me that key and then get out before I call downstairs and have you thrown out.'

'I haven't got one,' he admitted. 'I gave the kid on the desk a twenty to come up with me and let me in. And I had to show him my licence first —' He broke off to stare at Maxie as he stepped from the bathroom. 'Who's this?'

'He's the one sleeping in the other bed.' She plugged in the jug and took the milk from the fridge. 'You're wasting your time, Guy. I told you, I want a divorce. There is nothing I'm interested in talking over, and as we have no assets to divide, it should be straightforward enough. If you want a shoulder to cry on, try my brother. I believe he's being divorced too. By the same lawyer. Isn't *that* a coincidence?' Tomorrow, she thought, she really must ring Bea and make her words an actuality. 'Now, you're holding me up. I have a dinner date. Are you going to leave or do I have to ring somebody?'

Maxie eyed Guy balefully. 'Want me to get Max, Kate? I know where his room's at.'

'*Where his room is*,' she corrected and smiled at him. 'Thank you, but I don't think it'll be necessary. Well, Guy?'

'All right,' he said sulkily, then with sudden belligerence, 'Where's the car? I paid for that, so it's legally mine.'

She crossed to open the door. 'A pity you didn't also pay the insurance, then. It was burnt up in the bushfire today. And you can tell your friend on the desk I'll be speaking to the manager about him. Here, don't forget these.' She picked up the flowers he'd dropped on the nearest bed and hurled them after him.

'You really gonna – going to do that?' Maxie asked, as she slammed the door shut. 'Dob that bloke in?'

'Yes,' Kate said firmly. 'He broke the rules, so dobbing is necessary.' She popped the bottle into a cup of hot water. 'Feed your pet while I take a shower. Poor Max will be starved.'

Dinner, however, was to be further delayed, for when they got downstairs a policeman was with Max. Both men turned at Kate's approach and took in her appearance in the blue dress that, she knew quite well, suited her colouring to perfection. She hid the smile the knowledge brought but found no humour in Len, the policeman. According to their arson expert, the fire had not only been deliberately lit but aimed at Rosebud Farm.

'Question is, why?' His hard official eyes inspected Kate. 'You worked there, Miss – uh, Mrs Gilmore. Do you know if the old man had any enemies?'

'No. The idea's ridiculous. Though the shock and excitement could easily have killed him.' She glanced down at Maxie, ears twitching beside her. 'You see that man over there near the door, the one with the white shirt? He looks after the dining room. You go and ask him to show you the table for Shephard, okay?'

'Table for Shephard,' Maxie repeated. 'What then?'

'You sit there.' She winked at him. 'Keep it for us. We'll be along shortly.'

When he'd gone, she said crisply, 'I've already spoken to a female officer about this, and she agrees that the two events could be connected. If the fire was meant to kill, then I think it was aimed at the boy. Somebody blew up his mother, after all. I asked that the media be told, but we missed hearing the early news. Can you tell me if it was on?'

The constable stopped his scribbling to nod. 'Yes, it was the main story: *Ten-year-old provides valuable clue in mother's murder*. Can't say if it's true or just what the journos made out of what the inspector said.'

'The main thing is, it's out there.' Kate was relieved.

'Incidentally,' Max spoke for the first time, 'just so you know, the losses from the bushfire – dead sheep, burnt crops – won't affect Harry Quickly. The property is sharefarmed by the Hollens brothers. So only the land is effectively his, and the improvements on it, so yes, he's lost a bit of fencing as well as his outbuildings. The Hollens have probably come off worse, though. Stock's expensive these days.'

'Noted, thanks.' The officer dotted a sentence, closed the notebook and shook hands with them. 'Thank you both. If there's anything else, we'll be in touch.'

They ate their long-delayed dinner in an almost empty dining room. *It had been an incredibly full day*, Kate thought. The waiter came to clear their plates and inquire if they wanted coffee, but she shook her head. Maxie was almost asleep.

'Let's just go,' she said to Max. 'We can have some instant stuff upstairs.' He held her chair and touched her shoulder.

'Did I tell you you look incredible? Can I see you later?'

She hesitated, looking at the boy. 'I don't know. It'd be leaving him alone in a strange room.'

He chuckled, breath warm against her hair as he guided her towards the lift. 'Kate!' His murmur was like a caress. 'This is the kid that chose to spend his nights alone in an underground tank. You think an empty hotel room will worry him?'

She smiled. 'When you put it that way . . . ' She found his hand and squeezed it. 'Okay, then. Once he's asleep we have an assignation.'

'Good.' He kissed her ear. 'In that case, I'll pass on the coffee.'

32

Kate woke with a smile next morning, and lay thinking about the man still sprawled in sleep beside her. It was a long time since she had been made to feel so special. She studied his angular face, tracing a finger down his long nose and across the sunburned ridges of his cheekbones. He mumbled something and moved his head. Catching sight of the time on the digital clock, Kate reared above him to plant a kiss on his lips. His eyes opened as he felt the pressure and he reached for her, but she laughed and sprang from the bed.

'Don't go,' he pleaded.

'I have to. Look at the time. I really don't want to explain myself to a ten-year-old, Max.' Quickly she bundled her clothes together and slipped the unused robe from its hanger in the wardrobe. 'Remind me to bring this back. I'll see you at breakfast.' She blew a kiss from the door and was gone.

Maxie was up warming milk for Vegemite. He looked guiltily at her. 'He made a mess on the rug.'

'We'd best clean it up, then.' There were tissues in the bathroom; she gave him a handful, saying casually, 'I had to see Max about something. Perhaps you should shut him in his box for now. I'll have to sponge that stain.' They couldn't, she realised, continue to stay here even if she could afford it. It seemed unfair to impose on the Wantages, when they were already caring for Flip; besides, doing so would leave her isolated without transport of her own, and cut off from her job.

Dressing after her shower, she decided that first thing she'd better go round the rental properties. Harry would need somewhere to live, possibly as soon as tomorrow. Finding accommodation for him would solve her own problem as well.

Max's offer to take Maxie off her hands for the day smoothed her way to doing so.

'I need to check in with the boys,' he explained, running a hand through his hair. He sighed. 'There's a problem with one of the machines. I don't know how long it'll take to fix. Could be a while if it's the hydraulics again. Where will I find you?'

'Here, or at the hospital if it's late. Take Vegemite with you, Maxie. I'll ask the desk if the kitchen staff can provide a small snack box for him.'

The boy looked alarmed. 'You aren't gonna – going to – tell them about him?'

'Probably not. So do your best to look like a kid with a dire need for apple and carrot.' Kate smiled at him and he grinned back, his normally wary face alight.

There was no sign of the desk clerk so Kate made her request to a waiter, who presently returned with a plastic takeaway tub of cubed fruit. 'Thank you,' she said. 'Is the desk not staffed yet?'

'I think the management's working on that, madam. Was there something I can help you with?'

'No, thank you,' she smiled, and he cleared their plates away.

'He probably got the bullet,' Max said. 'The clerk, I mean. He was having a brawl with a male guest last night, before you came down. That copper who spoke to us separated them just before the manager came out. From the look on his face I think the kid would've been out the door about five minutes behind the guest. Something about the man wanting his money back.'

'That'd be Guy,' she said unhappily. Dissatisfied with the results of his ploy to spend the night in her room, it would be just like him to look for someone to blame. 'He came to see me. Bribed the clerk to let him in, can you believe? When it did him no good I expect he wanted a refund. Particularly when I told him the car'd been torched. He wanted that back too.'

Max shook his head. 'You're smarter than that. How did you ever come to marry him?'

'How did you ever get to be christened Maximilian?' It was a fact she had learned in the night.

He grinned. 'You have a point. A momentary lapse of female judgement?'

'Exactly.' She rose, wrinkling her nose at him. 'C'mon, kid. We won't be long, Max.'

* * *

Doug Doolin had also experienced a lapse of judgement. Catching Greg Simpson between the police station and car park, he had hurried his approach, asking too soon for the favour he needed, apologising even as he asked. He was forced to continue walking as he talked when the policeman failed to even stop and listen to him.

'It's driving me crazy, Greg. She's alone somewhere with little Andy, and God knows if she's in any state to care for him. The doc says it's a form of hysteria – well, there's got to be some reason for her going, and as God's my witness I can't find another! I mean, it'd take a minute at most to check the public transport computers,' he pleaded. 'Just a destination. That's all I need.'

'Sorry.' Greg Simpson was brusque. He had his keys out; he clicked the thumb pad and headlights flashed from the reserved parking space. 'Bad timing, Doug. Besides, it's not really police business. You need a marriage counsellor. What is it with your family, anyway? That brother-in-law you wanted found – one of my men had to haul him off the desk clerk at the Arms last night. Trying to force himself where he wasn't wanted, apparently. Your sister seems happy to be rid of him.' He opened the door, slid behind the wheel. 'You think you've got problems? I've got the media on my back, a twenty-year-old case to solve, and now some frigging maniac's setting fire to everything in sight. About the only comfort is that we've got the bastard rattled, which means we're getting close.'

Doug realised he'd get no help and breathed in to control the spurt of fury he felt. 'Yeah, tough all right. A regular attack dog, that reporter. But there's always nutters setting fires.'

Greg's lips curled into a wolfish smile. 'Nutters is right. But this time it's all the one package. Murderers always overreach themselves – the ones that get caught, anyway.' Then the engine turned over and he was gone, and along with him any help Doug was likely to get. He swore and kicked the Reserved Parking sign, which hurt his foot and made him swear again. Of course he'd found the vehicle Clover had taken, but she hadn't caught the bus, or the evening train, which meant that somebody here in town had driven her to the next station or bus stop. The thought that she'd escaped him, was even now laughing at him, made him so angry his head threatened to burst from the sheer pressure of rage it contained.

When he found her . . . His hands clenched as he strode away from the place, ignoring the television crew piling out into the car park . . . He'd make her wish she'd never been born. By God he would!

* * *

It was after midday before Kate, hot and tired from a busy morning doing the rounds of the realtors in Laradale, reached the hospital. She stopped in the cafeteria to buy a sandwich and a carton of iced coffee, then continued up to visit Harry.

The same nurse from her last visit smiled a greeting and cast an understanding look at the lunch she carried. 'Good idea. It's quiet and cool here. Hot out?'

'Bake an egg,' Kate said. 'I'll be glad to sit down for a bit. How is he?'

'Resting now. His morning visitors tired him a bit, but he seemed to enjoy his lunch.'

'Somebody's been in, then? That's good. Stop him getting bored. I'd have come sooner if I could. He's not still confused?'

'Not a bit,' she said, 'If you were any sharper, I told him, you'd cut yourself. He laughed at that, said I reminded him of you – if you're Kate, that is?'

'I am.' Kate smiled. 'That's a relief. I'll stay for a bit.' She smothered a yawn. 'In fact, I could do with a bed too.'

She'd finished her lunch when Harry woke. He looked better today, relaxed in sleep rather than exhausted, the wrinkled lines of his face more dignified than vulnerable. Watching him, she saw his eyes flicker open and fix on her face. 'Edie?' The voice was tentative but before her dismay could register, the cloudiness cleared from his gaze. 'Oh, it's you, Missy. What time is it?'

'A bit after two in the afternoon. How are you feeling?'

'Fair to middlin', girl. One more day here, then the quack says I can go home.'

'Well, not home perhaps. It needs work, remember, after the fire? But I've found a couple of places here in town where we can stay until Rosebud is ready for you.' Kate fished her notes from her bag. 'You feel up to hearing the details? Or we could do it tomorrow.'

He harrumphed, shot her a look under his white brows. 'Might as well be now. You'll be on my back till I do. Where's the boy?'

'With Max – he's fine. If you make a decision and sign today, I can get the key and start getting the place ready tomorrow. I'll bring linen and so on from Rosebud and stock the fridge. Your computer too, of course, and if you want your favourite chair, I can get that. Both the places I looked at are furnished, but it's fairly basic, so it's up to you.'

'That's fine,' he said vaguely. 'Settle on whatever you think's best – with room for the boy, of course. Just show me where to sign.' He scrawled a shaky signature. 'I want you to find a builder – or a carpenter – and send him out to look over the farmhouse and figure out what's needed to fix it. He can drop it off at Forsyths and Grainer, the solicitors. Young Alec Forsyth'll okay it and see to payment. Wel—' His eyebrows shot up. 'What's the problem? Don't tell me there's something you can't do, Missy?'

'Of course I can. But – hiring builders? Wouldn't you rather trust that sort of thing to Max? I'm sure he'd be happy to help.'

He scowled at her. 'You mean you're not?'

'I didn't say that, but if you're going to be cranky, the visit's over.' Kate gathered her stuff and rose. 'I've still got lots to do. I'll secure the lease this arvo, which means I'll be flat out tomorrow, so you won't see me till the evening. And don't worry, I'll find a carpenter for you.'

'No need to make a song and dance about it, girl. Hand me that paper if you're going; and ask the nurse why I haven't had my tea yet, will you?'

'I will,' she said sweetly. 'Just don't be surprised if she throws it at you.'

She was smiling as she left. Despite the fright he'd given her, there plainly wasn't much wrong with the old boy now.

Almost the first person Kate saw as she left the hospital was Heather, who stood on the edge of the car park, hunting in her open bag for her keys.

'I just left some flowers for old Mr Quickly,' she explained. 'They told me he already had a visitor; I'd have gone in if I'd known it was you. How is he?'

'He's good,' Kate said. 'He'll be out tomorrow; I'm just off to rent a place in town for us, then he wants me to find someone to start work on the farmhouse. He's reading the paper. He's much brighter today – and thank goodness for that! I'll have to get out to the farm tomorrow.'

'We went across this morning, Ken and I.' Heather shook her head. 'It must've been a terrifying experience. It's a miracle any of you survived. Incidentally, Ken's boarded up the house; after what you said about the doors and windows, he reckoned he'd better take his battery drill and some sheets of plywood over. There wasn't much he could do about the laundry but he's going back this afternoon with some weld mesh; he said that'd make it as secure as any door.'

'Dear old Ken. Thank him for us, Heather. That was so good of him. I'll be sure to tell Harry.'

'Nonsense. What are neighbours for? It would've been safe enough once, but these days . . . There's some quite valuable stuff in that house, you know. The dining room's furnished with antiques, for starters.' She cocked her head suddenly. 'Anyway, you look very blooming for somebody who's just escaped a bushfire.'

'Do I?' Kate laughed, then blushed under her friend's shrewd gaze.

'Oooh,' Heather exclaimed. 'It's Max, isn't it? I thought he looked a bit – possessive, when he came out yesterday.'

'He's not like that,' Kate defended instantly, then blushed again. 'All right, so it *is* Max.' She looked away, smiling dreamily at the mixture of oleander and bougainvillea blooming against the car park fence. 'I'd forgotten what it was like, loving someone – the breathlessness when you hear his voice, the way your skin knows when he enters the room. Whoever first said that about your blood leaping . . . ' She laughed shakily. 'I'm talking like a fool, aren't I?'

'Like a woman in love,' Heather corrected, amused. 'Come, the car's just here. Let's go for a coffee. Have you much else to do?'

'Well, I have to confirm the lease and pick up the key,' Kate said. 'Could we do that before we get the coffee? The boys have gone off for the day. Some machine's broken down somewhere. Max said that repairing it wouldn't be quick, so I'll be at a loose end for the rest of the day.'

'Then come home with me,' Heather said at once. 'Leave a message for him and they can join us for dinner. Really, Kate. Flip's missing you and I'd love the company.'

She remembered then. 'I'm sorry,' she said remorsefully. 'Because I'm happy, I forgot. Have you heard from the police – if they've made any progress?'

'In a way. Greg Simpson thinks that poor Connie Hardy's death is definitely linked to the case, and it proves, he said, that a local man took Megan. It's funny,' she added absently, negotiating the main street with an eye out for a park, 'but he always seemed a superficial sort of a person, a time-server, if you like. Of course, I didn't really know him. Ah! That'll do.' She slid the car into a vacant park and switched off.

'But now?' prompted Kate, lifting her bag and opening the door to the enervating heat.

'On the job he's like a terrier after a rat, just won't let go. It's almost impossible to catch him at the station. He's been to every farm in the district since Tam was found. I think —' Her voice trembled a little. 'If he'd been in charge when it happened, they might even have found her.'

'He'd probably only just have joined up,' Kate said gently.

'I know.' Heather cleared her throat. 'Come on, write your note while you're in there and we'll drop it off at the hotel on our way through town.'

* * *

Flip gave Kate an enthusiastic greeting, overjoyed to be reunited with his mistress. Fly was more restrained but wagged her tail in civil greeting before turning back to the sheds. Sight of the garden reminded Kate of the loss of her own flowerbed and pot plants, but she declined Heather's immediate offer of cuttings.

'Not yet anyway,' she said. 'Once we're back at Rosebud, though . . . ' They were drinking their coffee in the garden, seated at the wrought-iron table under the willow shade. She said regretfully, 'I had such a nice lot of snapdragons, too, and the petunias were doing really well. Those multicoloured frilly ones, you know?'

Heather nodded. 'Tough as old boots – grow anywhere. I saw Edna in town shopping. She had Jeremy with her and I stopped to say hello. She'd heard about the fire. I told her where you were staying. Did she call?'

Kate shook her head. 'Not before I left the hotel, anyway. The police think that fire's linked to the case too. I've been expecting an ambush by the press all day. They came to the hotel this morning but Max got the waiter to tell them we'd already left.' It had happened while she was upstairs with Maxie – another reason to be grateful he was safely absent with Max, for it was the boy they'd want to interview.

'So,' Heather set her cup aside, 'what's he like – Max?'

'He's a good lover,' Kate said, then blushed. 'Ah, I forget you're of my mother's generation.'

Heather blinked and then laughed. 'I'm flattered. So – a fling? Or is it the real thing?'

'Maybe it's a fling for him.' Even the thought hurt and she closed her mind to the possibility. 'But not for me. Time will tell. He's a kind man; I'm sure you've seen that in him. What Ken would describe as a decent bloke. He's funny and gentle, and he's interesting. Of course, a common background helps. We know where each other's coming from, and that's a good thing. On reflection I think that was half the problem with Guy. It was his being different, as much as the man himself, that dazzled me. He had a city sophistication I'd never met with before.' She gazed at the white-painted table with its patterns of frozen iron, tracing them with her finger, then glanced up at Heather. 'I'm divorcing him. I rang a lawyer this morning, told her to start proceedings. You know he came to the hotel and bribed the desk clerk to let him into my room?'

'Don't tell me the clerk agreed? It'd be worth his job!'

'It was,' Kate said. 'I had every intention of reporting him, only he and Guy got into a shouting match first – with a bit of pushing and shoving, I think – and the manager fired him.' Her eyes smouldered, 'But it was so typically Guy. *Sorry* was the magic word for him. He thought you just said it and it made everything right. He arrived with a bunch of drooping flowers and the idea I'd just fall into his arms. Plus I think he fancied upgrading from the caravan park. He said he was short of cash. He's as self-centered as Doug in a different way – not that I ever remember *him* apologising for a single thing. I doubt sorry was a word he even learned.'

'It probably wouldn't have helped much if he had,' Heather observed. 'He was such a pretty child – beauty has its own burden, don't you think? You must have found it with teaching. The little princess type with the curls gets her own way more often than plain Jane in the corner.'

'Lucy Mainford,' Kate said involuntarily and laughed. Something in what Heather had said pricked at her, but she couldn't isolate it. 'God, I haven't thought of her for years! The dentist's daughter. Do you remember? Golden curls and blue eyes. And a will like steel. Always got to be the angel with the good news in the Christmas play. I wonder what happened to her?'

'No idea.' Heather got up. 'What do you fancy for dinner? I've got some nice cutlets. I'd settle for a salad but the men will probably want something more substantial.'

'We could do both,' Kate suggested, stretching. 'Here, let me take those cups. I can see to the clearing up.'

33

It turned into a good evening. Max's shout of 'Anybody home?' came as Kate was setting the table for dinner.

'I'll get it.' Heather, hiding a smile, watched Kate whip off the apron she'd worn to prepare the vegetables, and run her fingers through her hair before heading to the door. She heard Max say, 'Well, hello, gorgeous,' then the door closed, cutting off the rest, and they made their way outside.

'Hello yourself.' Kate returned his kiss. 'What have you done with your offsider?'

'He ran off with the dog. How was your day?'

'Busy, but I've got most of it sorted. What about you? Is the machine working again?'

He grimaced. 'No. Maybe tomorrow if the parts get in overnight. They're coming up express, so they should. Did you see Harry?'

'He's fine.' They had wandered deeper into the garden. His hands slid up her arms, goosepimpling the flesh, then they cupped her face and he bent to her lips. A buzzing, like a hive of bees, invaded her stomach as she twined her hands in his hair and kissed him back, tasting his salty maleness and feeling his stubble against her skin.

'You need a shave.'

'Sorry.' He rasped a hand across his jaw. 'Didn't have time this morning. Is that Ken coming?'

'Sounds like it.' The white glare of a headlight vanished as the motorbike poppled its way into the shed and was switched off, and a few moments later Maxie appeared silently out of the gloom, Vegemite riding his shoulder, and Flip padding behind. 'We'd best go in. How was your day, Maxie? Enjoy yourself?'

'Yeah. Veggie et – ate – all his snacks. And guess what, Kate? I drove one of them big tractors.'

'*Those*,' she corrected automatically. 'I hope Max wasn't too far away?'

'Yeah, those. He was there but it was me driving it.'

'You did a good job, too, mate.' Max ruffled his hair. 'Even if your damn pet did wee on me. Come on, time to say hello to our hostess.'

They'd no sooner sat down at the table than the sound of a vehicle had Ken cocking his head. 'Now what?' He rose wearily and looked regretfully at his dinner.

'I'll put it in the oven.' Heather got up and carried it out, while Kate and Max exchanged glances.

'It wouldn't be – Max, you don't think they've found her?'

It was the media, however, not the police.

'I sent them packing,' Ken said, reseating himself before his plate. 'Told them I'd talk to them at a civilised hour, not when I was in the middle of dinner. Turned out it was the boy they were after anyway.'

'Thank you, Ken. Was it that blonde girl?' Kate asked.

He grunted. 'Girl, was she? Human succubus if you ask me. And about as easy to shake off. She'll be waiting for you at the hotel,' he predicted.

Kate looked distressed and Maxie frightened. He pushed his dinner away, looking about him as if for an exit. 'I don't want to talk to nobody. I don't have to, do I, Kate?'

'No.' She put an arm around him. 'Max won't let them bother you, will you, Max?'

'Not me.' He puffed out his chest. 'I'm three times bigger than that skinny reporter.'

'There, you see,' Kate soothed. 'He doesn't know the names of all the stars in the sky, and you couldn't call him pretty, but he's big —' Her voice died, but nobody noticed for Heather spoke over her words of reassurance.

'I've a better idea. Maxie can stay here overnight and you can collect him tomorrow on your way to Rosebud. The reporters won't return tonight and they won't know where to find you tomorrow.'

'And the hotel won't have the possum.' Kate nodded. 'You truly don't mind, Heather?'

'Don't be silly, Katie. Of course, the pair of you will be all alone but I expect you'll think of some way to fill the time.' Her eyes twinkled. 'The only thing is, Maxie, I heard about how you all escaped the fire at Rosebud, but you mustn't try anything like that with our tank. It's full of water.'

'What? The underground one?' Kate said. 'Is it? I never knew that.'

Ken looked at her. 'How do you think she keeps this damn great garden going, Kate? Not just from the dam, surely?' Ken's father had sunk a borehole at The Narrows but it was dry, so he'd built a dam instead, below the house, and the farm existed on catchment water.

'I never thought about it,' she confessed. 'We had a bore at home. I guess I just thought everybody did.'

Max's expression of disbelief mirrored Ken's. 'And when the pump was running, what did you think then?'

She smacked his hand. 'All right, smartypants. There're always engine noises on a farm. Tell me something, Ken, honestly. Did Martin know there was water in it?'

'Yep. Whenever the pump broke down he used to help me fix it.'

'There you are, then,' she said triumphantly. 'What?' she

demanded, catching the look Max gave her.

He was too wise to answer and just shook his head. 'Forget it. Women!'

* * *

Maxie was in bed asleep before they left The Narrows. Kate trod softly into the darkened bluebell room to check on the slight, sprawled figure. He'd wanted to keep Vegemite with him but Ken had found an old birdcage and the possum was currently sharing the dog's space in the shed, made roomier by Ken's last-minute insistence on Kate taking the ute back to town.

'You'll need wheels to get out to Rosebud and it sounds like Max'll be busy. I won't be needing it for a day or two so drop it back when you've got the old fella settled in. There's tools in the back, including the drill. You think you can get into the place, now I've boarded it up?'

'I can undo a few screws, Ken.'

'That's okay then.' He kissed her goodnight and stood watching with Heather as the two sets of headlights vanished down the entrance lane. 'She looks different,' he observed. 'Something going on there, do you think?'

'Well done.' Heather patted his arm fondly. 'Not bad for a man, and a farmer at that. Yes, she positively glows, doesn't she? So different to when she arrived. Max too.'

'So it's sex.' Ken nodded as one enlightened. 'Thought so.'

'Love,' his wife corrected. 'They'll wind up marrying, you'll see. She's divorcing Guy. It's got to be love or she wouldn't bother.'

Ken yawned widely and turned to go indoors. 'I'm not surprised. I never liked him, and not because he was a city bloke. Martin,' he added irrelevantly, 'could be called that too, now. Nah. He was always a smart mouth, young Guy. No substance to him.' It was a damning description, she knew. Farmers applied the term reluctantly to crops, and soil and rain where it meant the certainty of a poor harvest; a gutless growth medium; or insufficient moisture, respectively. *Not fit to plant on.* The thought made Heather wonder – as so many things did since Kate's return – whom Megan might have married, and what Ken would have made of him. She stopped herself speaking of it and went instead to listen to the gentle, almost soundless breathing in the bluebell room, and was oddly comforted.

The reporter and her cameraman were waiting in their car and converged upon Max as he stepped out of his vehicle under the streetlight, the camera already rolling. The girl peered into the darkened interior. 'Mr Shephard, we'd like to speak to your companion and the boy about their ordeal in the bushfire. Aren't they with you?'

'No, sorry.' Kate passed them in the ute, heading for the private parking behind the hotel. 'I just gave them a lift to the farm, that's all. The lady's car was lost in the fire.' He shrugged, slowing his speech, 'You need wheels to get around out here. Know what I mean?'

The reporter's irritation was plain. 'So where is she now? We really need to speak to the child.'

'Oh, I wouldn't like to say.' He rubbed his jaw. 'Ken was gonna take them – that's Ken Wantage from out The Narrows, little place fronts onto Mooky Lane. His dad had it before him, and he had it from one of the Quicklys. I just disremember which one. There's dozens of Quicklys round here —'

'Mr Shephard,' the girl broke in, 'never mind that. Can you just tell us where they are?'

'I'm trying to, aren't I?' He let a little irritation show. The hotel door would be locked and would take a few moments to open. Max shifted his feet, forcing the reporter to turn with him. Now her back was to the door, but he could see it shadowed by the overhang and Kate approaching along the footpath, searching her bag for the key. 'It's because the lad's a Quickly – well, in a second-hand sort of a way, but family connections are strong out here. Know what I mean? That's why the lady was taking him – well, Ken was, seeing as how, like I said, she's got no wheels . . . ' He kept it up until Kate had vanished inside and then for another five minutes, finishing with a hopeful question. 'Does this mean I'll be on the telly?'

'You never know your luck, Mr Shephard,' the reporter said grimly, not quite drowning her cameraman's less complimentary remark. The light on the camera had gone off a while back. He bade them goodnight, found his own key and went in.

'What kept you?' Kate asked. She had filled the time by packing. 'Where've they gone?'

He grinned. 'To bed, if they've any sense. Otherwise they're going to get lost. I gave them some very complicated directions to a place I've never been to. Never mind them. I've been wanting to kiss your mouth all night, and several other places too.'

'Talk,' she scoffed. 'I know you farmer types; things are always going to happen next time – bigger crops, better seasons, actual rain.' His mouth silenced her and she melted into his embrace.

'Let's go to my room,' he said when they paused.

'Yes.' Her voice was husky and her body fizzed as though electrically charged.

'Incidentally, what was that about farmers?' he growled, nibbling her ear, then kissing the little hollow above her clavicle.

'Ha.' She grabbed her key, then slid a hand under his shirt to hug his waist as they made their entwined way towards the door. 'You've got the night to disprove it.'

***

Kate blinked awake and stretched luxuriously, eyeing the empty space beside her with a smile. Max had kissed her awake when dawn was a grey light at the curtain's edge, not willing to leave without telling her. His whispered 'I love you' became part of the dream she had slipped back into as the door closed. The sooner he left, he'd said, the sooner he could return. 'I'll come to Pierce Street.' She had given him the address of the new accommodation and the thought of it now made her fling the sheet off and head for the shower.

She had a full day ahead of her too. She'd check out after breakfast, call and see the builder Max had recommended, then take the baggage to the new place, where she'd have to ensure the utilities had been switched on before heading out to The Narrows. Perhaps she should take a cut lunch along? The packing up would take time; she'd better try and scrounge a few cartons, and some old newspapers for the crockery, before she left town. She could ask at the supermarket, then ring the hospital to let Harry know she'd collect him that evening. There was no way, she decided, she'd be ready any sooner.

Maxie was watching out for her when she drove up to the farm, his new trainers knotted together by the laces and hanging about his neck. He liked going barefoot better, he said.

'Well, you'll have to wear them in town,' Kate replied, 'so you may as well get used to them.'

'Do I gotta, Kate?' His pale eyes searched her face.

'You mean: *Must I?* Oh, I think so, Maxie. They'll soon feel normal.'

'Okay.' Slowly, looking sideways at her, he began to unknot the laces and she waited, knowing there was more. At last, still watching her, he blurted, 'Am I gonna – going to – stay with you, Kate?'

'I don't know, sweetie,' she said. His face closed up, hope fading from it as she floundered, unwilling to make a promise that might be broken. 'We shall have to see. I wish you could, but it's not my place to decide.'

'Who does, then?'

'Well,' she said helplessly, 'your relatives, I suppose. You're related to Harry somehow, so you must have heaps of them. Perhaps you'll just stay with him for the present, so we'll be together anyway. Now, are you ready? We've got plenty of jobs to get through today, so I'm relying on your help.'

Later, drawing up to the gate at Rosebud, Kate was stunned afresh by the destruction. She got out and leaned against the ute, surveying the scene. The house stood like something shipwrecked amid the desolation of blackened tree trunks and crumbled fences. The fire's passage had been too swift to burn the split timber posts, but the edges had caught in the inferno, leaving them to smoulder on once the raging flames had blown past. There was a smell of death from the paddock where she had taken her morning walks, with sated crows cawing from the blackened limbs of the mallee. *The trees would recover after the next rain*, she thought, but the shearing quarters and sheds had been reduced to twisted iron sheeting and the metal remains of machines.

'Well.' Kate looked at her small helper. 'Do you think we can get that gate moved? If not, we'll have to knock down a bit more fence.'

They chose the fence in the end, to get the vehicle close to the house. The panel of plywood closing the front entrance took ages to unscrew, and by the time the empty cartons were unpacked it was almost noon. 'We'll get the kitchen stuff first,' Kate decided. 'That'll wash the easiest. Dear me,' she regarded their filthy hands. 'I should have brought more water.'

They saved what little they had to wash before eating their lunch, then packed the linen while their hands were relatively clean. Vegemite slept in the cage Ken had donated while the panel was replaced, then Kate checked that the blanket-wrapped computer (packed about with pillows) couldn't move, wedged her own bag more securely under Harry's swivel chair, and rubbed her back, transferring a sooty patch to her blouse. 'That's about it.'

'You're all dirty, Kate. Here, and here.' Maxie touched his face to demonstrate.

She wrinkled her nose at him. 'I wouldn't call you squeaky clean either, young man.' She stooped to grimace at her reflection in the side window. 'Let's just hope we don't meet anyone.'

'I got some water left.' He offered it but she shook her head.

'Save it for drinking. Come on. Let's go.'

'Are we coming back for some more stuff?' Maxie asked as they drove off.

'Probably. We'll be in the new place a while.' On Harry's instructions she had paid two months' rent, so they'd need to move in some of the heavier furniture to see them through. The washing machine, for starters, and the television. There was little besides kitchen essentials, beds, a table and chairs, and one long sofa in the rental house. The bedrooms had curtains, but she'd needed to bring pegs, broom and mop – and there would be a dozen more things she *hadn't* thought of . . . Perhaps she and Max could come back tomorrow while she still had the use of the ute, and load up both vehicles. Meanwhile, she'd had enough; she could *feel* the dirt on her face and the sweat in her hair. Pierce Street could wait, she decided. She'd stop off at The Narrows to shower and change first.

34

As Kate was slowing in readiness for the Wantage's gate, Doug barrelled past in a cloud of dust, the white Toyota doing a good sixty, which meant he must've come from town rather than home. She had the briefest glimpse of his dark head above the wheel, and of a child in the passenger seat. Jeremy was with him. Both ignored the ute; her nephew was looking down, while Doug, she thought, would do so because he'd know it for his neighbour's vehicle.

Maxie had twisted about to stare after them. 'Who's that?'

'Somebody you want to keep away from. He's a bad man – he might hurt you.' She swung into the turning and pulled up, surreptitiously studying his hair and eyes and the shape of his face. The idea had come to her last night at dinner but she'd had no time to think it through just then, and later, she'd been with Max. But Doug's sudden appearance had brought it back. Heather had started it, though Kate had at first missed the significance of what she'd said. *He was such a pretty child*, was how Megan's mother had described Doug. And Connie, according to Maxie, had called his unknown father a *pretty man*. Had she been speaking of Doug? He was, she thought, perfectly capable of seducing a girl whose condition made her defenceless against the type of predator Doug was. Which would mean that the boy beside her was her nephew, even if she could see no family likeness in him – unless you counted his blondness. But thousands of kids had light hair, Kate told herself. She'd had classes where seventy per cent of them were fair-headed.

She watched the boy struggle with the chain then swing the gate wide, her mind shying from the rest of his disclosure. It couldn't be right, because it would mean . . . Her mind refused to go there. Not even Doug would do that; besides, he'd been only a boy at the time. She forced the thought away, slamming a door on it, but the wood was flawed and it gibbered at her still through the cracks.

Heather was at her sewing machine. She took one look at Kate and said, 'Chimney sweeps have nothing on you. I'll find a towel.'

'I packed some,' she protested.

'Well, you certainly can't unpack them in that state. And the boy's as bad. Tea when you're ready?'

'That would be lovely, thank you. The place is just covered with soot, and every footfall raises clouds of ash. We need another good gale to shift it down the paddock.'

Later Kate drank her tea abstractedly, her glance straying frequently to Maxie, who fidgeted nervously under it, leaving his last mouthful of scone uneaten.

'Give it to Vegemite,' Kate suggested. 'And make sure his cage is in the shade.'

'What's to become of him?' Heather asked as the boy dodged from the room. 'He's getting very attached to you, my dear.'

'I know.' Kate debated with herself but knew there was no way she could tell Heather of her suspicions about Maxie's parentage. It wasn't the knowledge that mattered but the reasoning that made it seem possible and led, inexorably it now seemed, to her darker suspicions. She wished Max was here, for there was literally no one else she could speak to about it, unless . . . Setting her cup down, she turned to her hostess.

'Is Mum likely to be home, do you think?'

Heather shrugged. 'Probably. But you could give her a ring, find out.'

'No-o. I'll just slip over there. Doug's away. We passed him and Jeremy on the road.' She rose, standing irresolute for a moment, then drew a quick breath. 'I won't be long. Tell Maxie, if he asks. Something I have to check, that's all.'

She looked a little pale, but determined.

With a faint misgiving Heather asked, 'Is something wrong, Lamb?'

'I don't know.' Kate said. 'That's why I'm going.'

* * *

It was years since she had been across the paddocks – not since Megan was taken. The way seemed longer than she remembered, the going harder, though it was no distance, really – a little more than half a kilometre. The fence she had once slipped through with ease now took concentration and a careful placement of limbs to avoid snagging her clothes on the barbs. The coarse stubble scraped at her shins, and the rough ground was unsuited to town shoes. After Megan's disappearance she'd always come round by the road through the gates, theirs first, then the Wantages, as if the shortcut was meant to be taken only by two pairs of running feet. It was hard, looking back, to decipher the arcane rituals and beliefs of childhood, Kate thought, struggling now to remember why she had always chosen the road. Would the other way have hurt too much, made her friend's absence bite more sharply?

She stood catching her breath on the final gentle slope, gazing at the farmstead set in its thicket of mallee below her. A fragment of memory came to her, muzzy as a dream – *in fact, it had been a dream*, she thought – something about poppies in the wheat. She held a picture for an instant in her mind, ginger curls and a freckled face, spiky plaits and tomblike teeth, squatting amid silvered stalks, heads together, carelessly rich in the promise of time that lay before them. Only somebody had stolen Megan's, she thought, and then Connie's. And had tried very hard to take Maxie's, and, whether incidentally or by design, her own as well. She refused to let herself think that Brian Doolin's remaining days might also have been thieved away. The vagrant suspicion was one she couldn't bear to contemplate at present.

The farm complex was quiet, only the occasional turn of the mill blades and the long draw of the rods in the light shifting airs broke the silence. Closer in, hens clucked about, then a rooster flapped his wings and crowed. As she passed by, the remembered odour of greasy wool drifted to her from the shearing shed where the yards lay wide and empty, drowsing in the sun. It was joined by the scent of hay from the nearer shed, and the scratchy feel of it; the smell of dust and cold steel in the storage shed; and spilled diesel impregnating the ground near the fuel tanks. The long-forgotten scents of summer, familiar to her from childhood, mixed now with fear and sorrow and the quickened beat of her heart.

The plastic trucks and trike had been tidied into the old wood box on the verandah. Her mother's doing, she guessed. Andy's toys; they would be too young to interest Jeremy. Hands clenched, Kate crossed the boards, banged once on the screen door and let herself in, calling, 'Mum?'

She found Edna in the kitchen, where a pile of vegetables – carrots, parsnips, potatoes and a wedge of pumpkin – sat waiting next to a chopping board and a casserole dish. Edna was engaged at the stove, browning meat in a pan, and started at her daughter's entrance, spectacles flashing as she lifted her head.

'Kathryn! What are you doing here?'

'I've come for some answers.' Kate pulled a chair out from the table and sat, unasked. 'Heather mentioned she'd seen you and that you knew about the fire at Rosebud. The place I worked at, remember? I was wondering when you were going to get around to ringing to check I was okay?'

Edna Doolin flushed. 'And you'd have been pleasant if I had? Anyway, the wireless said there were no fatalities.'

'And that's it?' Kate said incredulously. 'It doesn't matter to my own mother that it was a murder attempt? He tried to kill me, Mum! Me, and a child, and a helpless old man. We were all in his sights.'

Edna glared at her over the tops of her glasses. 'Now you're dramatising again – anything to get attention. *He* indeed! The bogeyman, I suppose? It was an accident of nature; most fires are.' But her gaze had flickered and Kate pounced.

'It was arson. The police said so and you know – or suspect you do – who's responsible. He was out that day, wasn't he? *And* the night Connie Hardy's van blew up. He must've thought it bad luck when he realised he'd missed out with Maxie – that the boy was spending the night at Rosebud. But not to worry,' she said acerbically, 'our summers are conducive to fire. That's certainly true. Ripe crops, dry scrub galore. People get killed in bushfires, and the gale must've seemed a godsend. You do know that Maxie Hardy is your grandson?'

Edna blinked before the hail of words. She'd abandoned the pan of meat and one hand had crept to her throat. Now her features twisted with fury as she spat, 'That's a damn lie!'

'It isn't, Mum, and a DNA test will prove it. Connie had Megan's necklace. And the only way that could have happened was if Megan's killer gave it to her. There was no other possible solution. The one Dad made her, remember?' Kate said remorselessly. 'And the only person who could tell the police that was her son. But the joke is that he wasn't even certain, not enough for a court to convict on, because he was simply too young to know. It didn't stop Doug trying to kill him, though. Because he gave it to her, didn't he? He was Connie's *pretty man* – wasn't he? Wasn't he?' she yelled, the words echoing off the walls.

When Edna simply stared she continued more quietly. 'You used to call him that too. *My pretty little man*, you'd say. And it didn't matter how many ribbons I put on,' she added dispassionately but with a flicker of pain for that wistful child of memory, 'or how good I was, you never looked at me.'

'You're jealous.' Her mother sounded relieved. 'That's what this is all about. Simple, nasty jealousy.'

'No,' she said. 'It's about Doug from the time he could walk, seeing something he wanted and taking it, as if it was his God-given right to do so. Or – because there was always something black and twisted inside him – seeing something and destroying it, because he could. The nests of bird's eggs he smashed, the day-old chicks that kept getting drowned – did you never wonder about them? The cat in the trap. He was responsible for them all. Dad knew. I'd catch him looking at Doug sometimes like he didn't want to be in the same room with him, but something – love or duty – wouldn't let him leave. It's harder to fool kids, though. Megan and I always knew what he did. But he couldn't get at me, could he, not with Dad around, so he took Megan instead.'

'You're lying!' Edna shouted. 'You dare to stand there and blacken your brother's name. Everybody knows it was the gypsy tinker who took that girl.'

'No,' Kate repeated. 'That's just the fiction you hide behind. Just like you pretend he didn't abuse his wife. Clover'll divorce him and fight him through the courts to get Jeremy back, and the farm will pay, you know, because these days the wife gets half of whatever a man owns when it comes to divorce. Something he didn't think of! Only he never reckoned on her defying him, did he? She could even cost him the farm. What about that?'

Edna sank into a chair, her mouth working as if she were trying out various ways to refute these statements. 'Why are you saying these things?' For the first time she sounded lost, no longer in charge, the way she always had been.

'Somebody needs to. He's got to be stopped, Mum. Can't you see that? Murder is not something you just overlook.'

Face strained, she pressed her lips together, looking suddenly old and defeated. 'It's jealousy, that's all,' she repeated mechanically. 'You don't *know* anything.'

'Is that how you managed? Told yourself you didn't really know? But you only have to remember, Mum. Gypsy Pete's horse, for instance. The one *somebody* was supposed to have hit with a vehicle. Only no one knew who exactly had done it – and it wasn't like there were that many contenders on a quiet afternoon along Mooky Lane, were there? If you asked me, I'd say about the only way it could have happened – barring a collision – was if someone used a horse bolt on him. It's funny the farm should just happen to have one in Grandfather's old veterinarian gear, isn't it? It's still there. I checked just now. They're designed to kill horses humanely – any large animal, I suppose – but I'll bet you could break a bone with it too. Even a large leg bone. What do you think, Mum?'

'I think you're talking rubbish,' Edna said contemptuously. 'You were never interested in the family. What would you know about your grandfather's tools, anyway?'

'Quite a lot.' Kate lifted her elbows onto the table and stared dispassionately at the woman she'd never been able to love. Edna Doolin's once black hair was streaked with grey and her face had soured as she aged, as if a lifetime of picking fault had dragged the lines on it into an expression of permanent disapproval. 'There was a time I thought I wanted to be a vet. I read all Grandfather Stone's books and used to amuse myself identifying his tools and their uses.

There are pictures of them in the books, you know. I just never put it together before. You think, *He's cruel* and that's it. You just don't go that extra step and think, *He's a monster*, even when it's staring you in the face.'

'He's nothing of the sort,' Edna flashed angrily. 'Farmers have to be tough. There are always animals that have to be put down. It doesn't mean —'

'Something else I remembered.' Kate's voice rode remorselessly over her mother's. 'The day Megan disappeared I was never on the bus with her. I didn't even have to lie about it because nobody asked me. You yelled, *Where have you been?* and I told you I was playing by the creek, and that was it. Megan had been missed by then so everybody had more to think about than me. Only when all the men had come to start the search I was in my tree and I overheard them arguing about where to begin. It's strange it didn't strike me then, but I guess I felt so guilty about the row we'd had I didn't work it out; and then I forgot it. Until today. I don't even know who Mr Hall was talking to, but I remember very well what he said because I'd never heard him talk so much before. He said: *Brian's boy saw the two little lasses leave the bus, so it happened after she started up the track home.* But Doug couldn't have seen me, Mum, because I wasn't there.'

'He was mistaken, then; he thought he saw you.' Edna propped an elbow on the table and let her head sink onto her hand. 'It doesn't mean anything,' she said weakly.

'It means he lied, that he wasn't where he said he was. When I finally got home I saw his bike tracks where he'd come through the gate. And I saw that he'd dropped the bike where both roads meet the fence and run along the boundary.' She waited a moment, heart hammering, hands gripping the table's edge. 'Did he – I don't know – hit her, smash her head in with a rock, then put her in the underground tank, Mum? I never knew we had one until today, but that's it under the feed shed, isn't it? I always thought it was just a concrete floor, raised up a bit against heavy rain so the hay would stay dry. Only sheltering in the one at Rosebud made me wonder what the farm did for water before Great-Grandfather put the bore down. You see, Harry told me that the Stones did the first drilling in the district, and grew a market garden here because of it, but they must have had a water supply before that. I found the manhole but I couldn't get a look at the tank because the shed's still half-full of hay, but the police will move it when I tell them.'

For the first time Edna's face registered panic. Her hand shot out to grip Kate's arm.

'You mustn't! All right, yes, you guessed right. He didn't mean any harm. He was just teasing her and went too far. It was an accident. She was only a slip of a thing and he was always a big, strong lad, but he never meant to kill her! For God's sake! He wasn't quite fifteen – just a boy. I couldn't turn him in for an accident; I'm his mother.' Her grip loosened as Kate jerked herself free.

'You're mine too, but it doesn't seem to carry the same weight. You couldn't turn him in because you needed him for the farm, to have Stone blood to carry on here. You're as sick as he is! All these years and Megan was right here! Did you never think what the Wantages were going through? I wonder how you can sleep at night with her poor bones in the tank.'

'I don't know they are,' Edna muttered defensively. 'He never said where . . . ' She trailed into silence. Her fingers trembled and she picked at her hands, her voice pleading, 'He's your brother, Kathryn. What are you going to do?'

'Report it, of course; but you'll tell me something first. When Dad died, was that Doug's doing too?'

'What do you mean?' Edna looked genuinely perplexed. 'Are you mad, Kathryn? Your father had a heart attack in his workshop. He was lying there in the sawdust when I saw him. But don't take my word for it, Miss! Ron Hall was there too, come to collect something your father had made, and the doctor said —'

'I know what the doctor said.' Kate silently absolved the woman from complicity in that death, at least. Her voice thinned and she glared at her parent. 'Only that wasn't how it was. I spoke to Ron Hall. He's quite the gasbag, isn't he? Dad actually collapsed sweeping out the hayshed. He shouted something Ron thought was *What have you done?* before his heart gave out. He was alone at the time save for Doug, and it was Doug who had him carried to the workshop. I think Dad opened the tank – who knows? Maybe he was going to sweep into it, and that's how he found her. He died knowing his son was a murderer, and he had to have guessed that you were complicit in it.'

There was a moment's silence, then boots scraped on the floor behind her and a sudden hand gripped Kate's shoulder.

'Well, little sister,' Doug smiled down at her, his brilliant eyes fathomless as a midnight sky, 'you have been busy. Always with the imagination, eh, Katie? And now you're going to wish you'd had a little less.'

35

Kate's breath caught in her throat. She hadn't heard the vehicle return or Doug's silent approach, then she realised he'd come from the laundry where the slip-proof mat covered the slate. Mastering her voice she said loudly, 'Where's Jeremy?'

'No need to shout. He can't hear you. I dropped him off at one of his mates' places. Quite a little history you've concocted there.' The dimple showed as he produced a rueful smile. 'Yes, not polite, but I was eavesdropping. Well, you've never really talked to me, have you? So I had to settle for hearing you talk about me and I must say the old saw is true – about what one overhears.'

Edna's voice was strained. 'She knows, son. It's all going to come out.'

'Because you couldn't tell a halfway decent lie,' he snapped. 'She didn't know, Mum, she made a few half-arsed guesses that you obligingly confirmed for her. Well, that's too bad, because there's no way she's going to the cops with this.'

'No!' Edna's chair screeched as she thrust it back to stand and face him. 'She's your sister, your blood. You said the other one was an accident. You promised —'

'Oh, for Christ's sake!' he snapped disgustedly. His expression was frightening, the blue eyes like pitiless wells of ice, all that was wrong and missing from his nature plain to read in the deadly twist of his thinned lips as he turned on his mother. 'You never believed that. Don't pretend you did. She laughed at me, the little bitch, and I killed her. Snapped her neck just like that. You can't imagine the thrill it gave me. She was in her tomb before she was even missed and if it hadn't been for Miss Clever Clogs here, that'd still be the case. At least the old man had the decency to take one look and keel over, but I'm afraid nobody's going to believe it a second time.'

'The Wantages know I'm here.' Kate's heart was thumping so hard she felt light-headed, her mouth was dry and every nerve in her body screamed at her to run.

'Doesn't mean they know where you went when you left,' Doug said, 'which you're about to do. People have road accidents all the time, even on quiet country back roads. Probably more so there because empty roads make you careless.'

Edna said hopelessly, 'Don't do this, son. You won't get away with it.'

'Yes, we will.' His confidence was frightening and Kate saw the older woman's resistance crumble as he continued, 'You can kiss Stones Place goodbye if we don't. If they lock me up, that bitch Clover will get her hands on Jeremy, and knowing her you'll never see my boys again.'

Watching for her chance, Kate eyed the door to the hall. Steeling herself, she swallowed, then said provocatively, 'You'll get a life sentence, Doug, and where will your precious farm be then?'

'If I do it'll be down to you,' he said conversationally and hit her just as she made up her mind to run. The force of the blow across her cheek snapped her head about; it drove her against the table's edge, knocking the breath from her. Kate fell across the scrubbed pine top almost senseless from pain, nose dripping blood and her ear ringing strangely. She heard her mother's sharp cry and then a shrill scream of rage.

'You leave her alone, you barssard!'

It was Maxie's voice, larded with fury and fear for her. The knowledge got her upright in time to see a small whirlwind whaling into Doug with what looked like the old copper stick that had lain unused along the back of the laundry tubs since Kate was a child. Doug, swearing furiously, wrenched it off him, cuffing him heavily enough to drive the boy to his knees, then raised his fist. Ignoring the pain in her ribs, Kate flew across the room to shield the child with her body.

'Don't you dare touch him!' And to Edna, putting all the scorn she could muster into the words, 'I hope you're proud of what you've made.'

Doug chose to be amused. 'The little bastard's bonded with his aunty, eh? Well, it'll just give a more tragic flavour to the reporting, won't it? Right, we're taking the car, Mum. Your daughter came to visit and borrowed the car for a bit, owing to hers being burnt in the fire at Rosebud. That's all you need to know. The brat wasn't here. She must've picked him up after she left.' He went to the back door and plucked a set of keys from the hooks there. Edna, catching her daughter's eye while his back was turned, gestured with her head at the hall doorway but Kate ignored it. If she'd had a moment in which to persuade Maxie to run, he might've been quick enough, but not the two of them. She couldn't leave without him, and given his impulsive defence of her she doubted she could make him go alone. He stood silently beside her now, tense as a coiled spring, trying not to cry, but she could feel his fear and the hand that crept into hers was trembling.

'It's all right.' She wondered if she'd ever said anything sillier.

'He hurt you.' He gulped the words, blind anger in his pale eyes, and she squeezed his hand urgently, fearful for him.

'I'm okay, sweetie. It was just a slap.' Her face was on fire and blood from her nose had dripped onto her shirt. She sniffed it back and ran her tongue over aching teeth. 'Listen, if there's a chance to get away, I'll yell. When I do you must run for it, okay?'

'Stop the whispering.' Before she could react or even guess what he was after, Doug had seized the child's thin neck. His large hand almost met around it and when he applied pressure Maxie began to squirm and gasp for breath, his face slowly purpling. By the time the pressure eased he was clawing frantically at the hand, the air whooping from his thin chest. Doug smiled at the terror on his sister's face. 'See? One good squeeze and that's it. We're going to the vehicle shed.' He turned the boy towards the door and she followed, dumb as a cowed dog, behind him.

It was like a nightmare from which you struggled but couldn't awake. Despite the blast of the sun, Kate's hands were icy, her movements stiff with dread. She saw the garden spade leaning against the laundry wall and her muscles tensed in readiness, but her feet carried her by without pausing. She thought of the slender stalks of the wild poppies and how easy they were to snap. Maxie's neck, ringed by Doug's brutal grip, looked as fragile as any flower's stem. She daren't risk it, not while another chance might still present itself. Maybe in the car. If she could get the door open, perhaps – or crash the vehicle. It was risky but so was driving tamely off with a madman, and Kate cherished no doubts now on that score. Her brother was mad – a full-blown psychopath.

The car was a silver Pulsar in good condition and well maintained, like everything else on the farm. It gleamed softly in the tidy shed alongside the white Toyota and a couple of mustering bikes. A truck filled the last bay, the whole as neat as a motor showroom with adequate room to open the doors. Kate's heart sank; she had hoped for less space. The locks made the squelch sound as they opened and she stepped as naturally as possible to the rear door. Doug grinned, his bright, dead eyes glinting in the subdued light. The shed smelt of petrol and degreasing oil, and the polish used on the car seats. 'You must think I'm stupid, Katie. Get in the front.'

She obeyed, fighting down panic. 'Sit there.' He pushed Maxie up against the door and tightened his hand just enough to make the boy gag. 'No tricks. We won't be long.' Dragging the silently crying child with him, he went to the bench at the back, took down the jerry can of fuel there and loaded it behind the driver's seat. The heady smell of petrol intensified in the car's interior as he thrust the boy across the front seat. The child fell against her and in the split second while the man lifted his leg in and only the lower half of his torso was visible, Kate whispered her urgent message.

'When I nudge you, grab the wheel. Pull it my way.' There was no time for more, to check if he'd understood, but Maxie was bright. She folded her arm around him, saying gently, 'It's all right, sweetie, I promise. Everything will be all right.'

He lifted his gaze to her face. 'Are you really my aunty?'

Kate swallowed sudden tears. 'I am. Brand-new, but yours.'

'Good.' His tear-stained face was pale but he forced a smile as Doug slammed the car into reverse and they tore backwards out of the shed.

'Where are we going?' Kate demanded, fighting to keep her voice steady as they spun in a tight circle to face away from the building.

'Why? You got a preference as to where you die?' Doug actually sounded interested. He was insane, she reminded herself as he turned to grin at her, his handsome face alight, the dimple in evidence. He'd belted up automatically – she supposed it was too much to hope he wouldn't, but if it saved him in a crash it would also slow his movements afterwards and that might be to their advantage. Except that she and Maxie had no such protection; she would have to try to brace for them both. Without waiting for her answer he said agreeably, 'Tell you what, we'll go up Mooky Lane past The Narrows. You can wave goodbye to your pretend family then. How 'bout that, Katie?'

She said, 'You're mad. You can't kill us and get away with it, you know. Nobody will believe I borrowed your car when I already had the loan of Ken's. It's too many deaths, Doug, all of them violent. Blind Freddy could work it out.' He'd have to get out at the gate. She tensed as it approached, but it stood wide open and they sailed through without stopping.

'Won't help you, though.' He sounded, of all things, cheerful.

'And how do you think it helps you?' She persisted watching the road, counting the bends in her head, waiting for the one where the big old red gums grew at the side of the track. 'The police will keep digging. Your mate Greg is re-interviewing everyone from Megan's case, you know. He'll turn something up.' She dug her elbow sharply into Maxie's ribs, then whipped her arm about his narrow shoulders, bracing her legs. 'He can't be stupid, Doug. The clues are there —'

Nothing was happening. He hadn't understood, she thought despairingly, watching the scaly trunks of the big gums hurtle towards them at seventy kilometres an hour. Then Doug swore furiously as the released seatbelt flew across his body and Maxie got both hands on the wheel and pulled with all his young strength.

There was too much happening at once to process. She thought: *Clever kid!* He'd noticed the seatbelt and taken that extra fraction of time to hit the release before going for the wheel. The Pulsar tore off the road, somebody screamed as bushes and fence posts hurtled past with a shattering bang; it was her, she realised, as her arm slammed painfully against the window. A flash of metal spun towards her; Doug was swearing and Maxie cried out as he was punched, left-handed, then there was a terrific *crash*! and the car hit. She was flung forward and the engine raced and died as the airbag exploded out of the steering wheel and everything went black.

Through the whistle of steam, of falling glass and crunched metal, Kate slowly raised her head and blinked at what she could see of the wreckage. The horn blared unremittingly, the noise abrading her nerves. Her feet were free so there was room to move. She saw that she had her arms about the boy and by some miracle had managed to keep his head from the windscreen. Doug was buried somewhere under his airbag but her own had not inflated. A strong smell of petrol permeated her senses, jolting her fully awake. *Get out*, her mind screamed, before he wakes up or the car explodes. In the panic of the moment she didn't know which to dread most.

The door was jammed. The lock wouldn't move; she hammered at it and thrust against it while the horn blared on and the panic built behind her gritted teeth. If she gave in to it, they were lost, but for all her efforts the door refused to budge. Maxie roused, calling her name in a blurred voice. 'Kate?'

'Are you okay?' she asked urgently. 'Can you move your legs?'

He tried. 'Yes. There's petrol, Kate. Quick, open the door.'

'I can't. Look, sweetie, if I help you, can you climb out through the windscreen?' The glass had crumbled in crystalline heaps across the seats and dashboard, and the smell of petrol was making her dizzy. 'Doesn't matter if you fall. It's not far. Get out and then run for Mrs Wantage. That's it. Stand on the seat. Up you go.' She pushed and he wriggled, scattering pebbles of glass as he went. Beside her Doug sighed and his arm made a tentative movement. With a convulsive thrust she launched herself after the boy, prodding behind her at the seat for purchase. She'd lost her shoes and her knees banged painfully on the dash as she struggled. Maxie was calling but the words were lost in the pounding of blood in her ears, then something grabbed her foot and she screamed, kicking out at the hands holding her, struggling to be free of the vice-like grip that was dragging her back into Doug's clutches.

'Kate! Listen to me, Kate!' The voice was beside her, not behind her, and deeper than the boy's. She drew a trembling breath and reason replaced panic. Max said firmly, 'That's better. All right, I can smell the fuel. Let's get you out. Your foot's caught in the seat. If I can't get the door open, I'll break the window and get to it that way. Just hold still.'

He vanished for a moment, leaving her to wonder if he'd ever been there. 'I'm not dreaming?' her trembling voice asked the space where he'd stood. 'You're really here? How – why?'

'Large as life and twice as useful. As to why, it can wait.' He smashed a rock against the glass, swiping the bits away like a bully killing ants, and manipulated the seat hinge with one hand while the other held and guided her ankle. 'There.' Behind the calmness he was breathless from effort, and his eyes were wild. He half drew, half supported her through the buckled opening, cradling her carefully as they retreated, 'God Almighty, Kate! Twice in two days. What in hell happened? Never mind, later. I've got to get him out, whoever he is.'

'It's Doug.' She shuddered. 'Let him stay there. He was trying to kill us.' Her teeth were chattering and her legs seemed suddenly boneless. She thought Max called her name but there was a strange whooping in her ears that seemed only to grow louder and was, she saw, by the time the momentary weakness had passed, attached to the two police cars that had suddenly appeared from the direction of town.

They roared up Mooky Lane and Max said, 'Thank God! Here, my dear, sit down. Maxie, stay with her, son. I'll be right back.'

Kate sat in the grass at a safe distance, nursing her various hurts, while the rescue work went on. The car had impacted against the gum she'd picked out. The driver's door had taken the brunt of it when Doug had wrestled the wheel from Maxie's clutch, and she guessed that the spilled fuel was from the jerry can rather than the car's tank, which was on the opposite side of the vehicle. Max had taken the fire extinguisher from his Toyota to spray the interior before the police began removing Doug's unconscious body. He couldn't have moved, or grabbed her – that had been her fevered imagination driven by panic. *The police seem very efficient and brave*, she thought, and wished Max would come away; despite the foam it could still catch alight. An ambulance arrived then, followed belatedly by the fire truck from Laradale and another police vehicle, this one carrying Linda the female officer.

The policewoman perched on a log, taking notes while Kate and Maxie sat together on the blanket the ambos had insisted on wrapping her in. Once her shivering stopped it had become unbearably hot, so she'd spread it beneath them instead. She was thinking clearly again by then, but it still took time to explain everything. Maxie was silent throughout; he'd picked a handful of wild barley and sat close beside her, his head bent, dissecting the grain heads with his thumbnail as she talked, telling Linda how she had worked it out. It was a complicated story built from fragments of memory, deduction and scraps of gossip and took the best part of an hour to recount.

'It wouldn't have come together for me without the fire,' she explained. 'Doug lit that and it was while we were waiting in the tank that I worked out what he must have done to Megan.'

'But it could have been anyone,' Linda objected. 'Why choose him?'

'Because he's never had a conscience, and only somebody without one could do it, could cause so much pain. He admitted it; my mother was there and heard it, but I doubt she'll say so again.' She stopped, flooded by the guilt that assailed her every time she thought of the Wantages.

The policewoman tapped a thoughtful fingernail on the many pages she'd filled, and put the book away. 'Thank you. Well, he's certainly got a case to answer. If he survives. We'll need to speak to his wife too.'

'She left him just after Christmas,' Kate said. It seemed months ago now.

'Do you have an address?'

'Only her lawyer's number.' She had a question of her own. 'How did you know to come?'

'Your mother rang us, said you were in danger.'

'I see.' She had tried to help them, after all. It counted for something. Kate listened to the cicadas drill the heat-laden air and for the first time in her life felt sorrow for her mother. 'He's quite mad, you know.'

'That'll be for the court to decide.' Linda stood up as the stretcher was lifted into the ambulance. 'Are you coming to the hospital? Probably wise to be checked over. We can give you a ride, you and the boy.'

'No,' Kate stood, 'but thanks. We're all right, aren't we, Maxie?'

'Yeah.' He brushed the barley grains away and got up, taking her hand. 'We're fine.'

36

The police left a lone patrol car guarding the wreck until it was collected, then one of the other cars followed the ambulance while the third preceded them up Mooky Lane and turned in through the open gate of Stones Place, leaving Max and his two companions to make their way to The Narrows. He parked in front of the garden and looked at his shell-shocked passengers.

'You need hot, sweet tea and plenty of it.' Taking Kate's chin in his hand, he turned her bruised face to look at it. 'You're sure you're okay?'

'I'm fine. At least, I think I am. Bruises heal. What about you, Tiger?' The boy's ribs were darkly bruised where Doug's fist had caught him in the car; careful not to jostle them, she squeezed his shoulder gently until he smiled. 'When Doug knocked me down in the kitchen he came tearing in out of nowhere and laid into him with the copper stick.' She touched her swollen cheek. 'Don't you think that was brave of him, Max?'

'Very,' he agreed, 'but I haven't got it all straight yet.' He turned to the boy. 'How did you know where she was?'

'Followed her.' Maxie shot a quick look at Kate. 'Just to see where you was going, like. Then I seen *him* coming back and I was gonna warn her because she said I shouldn't have nothing to do with him, so maybe she shouldn't neither? Only he got there first. And I wasn't gonna – going to – let him hurt her,' he finished indignantly. 'She's my aunty.'

'You did the right thing, mate.' Max rumpled this hair. 'Thanks for taking care of my girl.'

'So I'm officially yours now, am I?' Kate touched her aching face again. 'I still don't know why you turned up, but I'm glad you did.' She shivered, 'If you hadn't come . . . '

'The cops would've got you out. Enough, anyway. Don't think of it now, love. Here's Heather. Let's see about that tea.'

'Oh God!' Incredible as it seemed, Kate had momentarily forgotten about Megan. The memory of Doug's deed was a weight on her heart; she felt she could never frame the words to tell her friend the terrible truth, and panic weakened her legs. Then Max's arm was round her and Heather, looking aghast at her pallor and the blood on her blouse, was a bustle of solicitous questions as she was taken straight to the kitchen and settled in a chair, Maxie hovering at her side.

'Your cheek! What happened?' She snatched a tea towel from its drawer and ran cold water over it. 'Here, hold this to the bruise while I get some ice.' Her eyes narrowed. 'Did your brother do that?'

'Yes,' Kate said painfully. 'Before he tried to kill us. Where's Ken?'

'I just heard him come in. *Kill* you? How? Was that *sirens* in Mooky Lane a little while ago?'

'Yes,' Max said. 'The car they were in crashed so they're a bit shaken up.'

'I'll make some tea,' Heather said instantly and moved to the kettle, then stopped. 'What car? She left here on foot —'

Max, moving familiarly between dresser, table and fridge, getting out the cups and adding the milk and sugar, gave a brief version, while Kate listened with closed eyes, holding the soothing pad to her face. The carriage clock chimed five, then the back door slammed and a tap ran in the laundry. A muffled 'Damn!' sounded as the soap banged against the steel tubs, then after a pause footsteps carried Ken into the room. He said cheerfully, 'Max. Saw your vehicle out – Good God, Kate! What's happened?'

It had seemed best to wait until he was there too. Kate straightened and opened her eyes. She said. 'It was Doug, Ken. He did it. He killed Megan, and now she's been found.'

Afterwards she couldn't remember all that was said but she never forgot Heather's strangled cry, or the way the teapot fell from her suddenly nerveless hands to shatter on the slate floor. When the worst of their shock had passed she told the story again, her tired brain laboriously fitting it together like a jigsaw puzzle. She couldn't, if she'd wanted to, hide her mother's complicity, but in any case she felt no desire to do so. There was no excuse for the two decades of pain that, by keeping silent, Edna Doolin had inflicted on these two people. 'It was for the farm,' she said tiredly. 'That's why she didn't turn him in. He killed Dad too.' Her voice shook with grief. 'Or as good as, although she didn't know about that. And today it was very nearly us.' Hugging Maxie, still beside her, she said starkly, 'He intended to burn the car with us in it.'

'I made it crash, but,' the boy said proudly, and Kate hugged him again.

'You were brilliant.' She looked at Heather's silent, stricken countenance and touched her hand. 'Can you ever forgive me?'

'It wasn't your fault, Lamb. Don't ever think that,' the older woman responded quickly. 'If it hadn't been for you, my poor little girl would never have been found. After all these years . . . She was so close and we never once thought . . . '

'I daresay the police will be calling on you,' Max said, rising. 'We should be going. Is there anything at all we can do for you?'

'Yes, should I ring Martin, Ken? There must be something.'

Kate felt a desperate need to help, as much for her own sake as theirs.

'No, you get off, Katie. Lord knows you've had a tough enough time yourself,' Ken said judiciously. 'Look after them, Max. We'll wait, I think, to hear from the police before we contact Martin. They'll probably want a DNA test of the remains, before it becomes official.' He kissed her, careful of her bruised face. 'I wish I'd been there when he tried that.'

'Don't blame yourself, Lamb,' Heather whispered as they hugged. 'We don't.'

Outside Maxie suddenly remembered Vegemite. There was no room on the crowded ute for his cage so boy, possum and dog travelled with Max, following Kate into town and then to the Pierce Street address. Max hadn't wanted her to drive.

'You're sure? I could do two trips, or leave my vehicle here for now.'

'Don't be silly. I can manage.' She'd made it in a haze of tiredness, backing the ute into the short drive beside her new home, and was looking distractedly at her watch when Max, who'd parked in the street, came to her side.

'It's late, my dear, and you're worn out. Why don't I just chuck the gear inside for now and we can spend another night at the hotel? Hot shower, room service and bed.'

'Sounds wonderful,' Kate said wistfully, 'but I really can't. I'm supposed to have all this ready, including dinner, for Harry – whom I ought've picked up ages ago. I completely forgot —' She bit her lip, 'He's probably been dressed and sitting up there for hours, waiting for me.'

Max shook his head. 'He hasn't. That's what I was on my way to tell you,' he said gently, 'when I came onto the crash. Harry's gone, love. He passed away earlier today. That's why I was on Mooky Lane. I was coming to tell you. Don't cry, my dear.' He held her against him as her body shook with sobs. 'He had a good life, particularly these last few months. He was happier than at any time since his wife died. He told me so. Don't be sad for him.'

'I'm sad for myself.' Her sense of loss was overwhelming. 'He was such a dear. I promised him bread pudding for dinner tonight and I've got his favourite ch-chair on the ute . . . '

'I know.' He held her, rubbing her back comfortingly. 'But he wouldn't want you to grieve. He had great faith in you, Kate. You know he wanted you to take on Maxie? He saw the boy was getting fond of you and said you were the ideal solution. He —'

'Wait a minute. You saw him?' Kate blinked. 'I thought you meant he'd gone when you got there.'

'No. I finished early. The repairs went better than I'd hoped so I dropped in to see him. He was up and dressed, sitting in a chair. He wanted to talk about the farm, said he'd always meant for me to have it. I didn't think anything of it – the timing, I mean – then he spoke about you and the boy. He was quite clear in his head, maybe a little tired. He didn't say anything to make me think . . . It was more like I was there, and we had time, and he was just telling me what was on his mind. Not that he was expecting to die today.'

'And then?'

'In the end he nodded off in his chair and I went down to the cafeteria and had a bite to eat. When I came back he was gone. The woman who brought his lunch tray found him.'

Kate wiped her eyes. 'I'll have to tell Maxie. Poor child. First his mother, now Harry. He'll have nobody left to him that matters.'

'He's got you. And something tells me you plan to make that permanent, don't you?'

Kate had not consciously pondered the matter but her answer came immediately from a level of conviction that required no thought. 'It seems that I'm his closest relative, Max. I can't abandon him.'

'He loves you too.' There was a little smile in his eyes. 'And you need each other. That's fine. I just wish the old bloke knew you've turned out to be Maxie's aunt.'

His name brought her back to the present – to the buzz of mosquitoes rising from the grass and the dull glow of the street-lights coming on as evening fell. Maxie, the day's terrors temporarily forgotten, came tearing back from exploring the house and she directed him to take Vegemite's cage in and feed the kit. She'd tell him about Harry later, she decided – after they'd unpacked.

When the last of the stuff was in, it was easier to make a meal from the food in the house than to think of dressing up and going out. She took it for granted that Max would stay.

'A bit of a squash. It'll be hot,' she said, eyeing the single bed she'd made up in the room that was to have been Harry's.

'There's a fan,' he replied, pulling the curtains across. 'You go to bed. You're worn out. Leave the locking up. I'll do it. I'll bring my vehicle in off the street first.'

There was just room to squeeze it in behind the ute. The gate had a cranky hinge; he wrestled with it before getting it closed and then had to fiddle with the bolt, which was also stuck in position. The possum's eyes shone yellow from the cage in the corner of the tiny verandah as he switched off the light and, locking the door, made his way to the bedroom.

Kate was already asleep, the bedside light she'd left on for him casting dark shadows across her bruised face. There was a frown between her brows and she muttered something as he undressed and slipped in beside her, shaken by the sudden strength of his feelings for this woman with the narrow waist and the spill of tawny golden hair. He heard her murmur *Harry*, then her body suddenly tensed and she thrashed about, panting, making little incoherent sounds. He could feel her heart racing inside her rib cage.

'Kate, Kate, my dear.' He stroked her shoulder until she woke with a little cry, then gentled her with voice and hands. 'Shhh, my love, just a dream. It's all right. Go to sleep.'

She murmured, 'Car . . . fire . . . Doug . . . ' and slept again. He lay holding her, their bodies spooned together under the sheet and the turning fan, thinking of the future – one, he conceded wryly, likely to include every stray that crossed their path, but still desirable nonetheless. Tomorrow there would be plans to make. About Harry's funeral, and the repairs the builder had been contracted to carry out at Rosebud. He would have to see the old man's solicitor, find out who his executor was. Then there was the lease of this house, which Harry no longer required but Kate and the boy did. And the mess that Kate's mother now found herself in. Max wondered if the police would hold her. If not directly involved in it, she was at least an accessory to murder. Even if Doug Doolin survived – and Max didn't give a toss if he didn't – a manager would have to be found for Stones Place. Very likely there would be nobody but Kate left to make that decision.

He yawned and kissed the back of the sleeping head beside him. None of it mattered compared to the miracle of this woman nested in his arms and the fact that he'd found her. For a moment he envied old Harry, who'd had sixty years with his Edie. Starting late as they were, he might get fifty, at best. Well, it would have to do.

37

The following morning Kate had slept well enough to be the first out of bed. She showered, adapting herself to the new bathroom with its lack of places to hang or put things. Birds carolled as she dressed while the first fingers of sunlight poked in through the window. She tapped lightly on Maxie's door, then pushed it open to reveal him still sleeping, clad only in the soft shorts she'd got him for pyjamas. She hesitated, about to leave, when his eyes opened on a yawn and found her standing there.

'Hello.' He yawned again. 'Is it time to get up?'

'In a little bit, Maxie.' She sat on the side of his bed. 'Did you have a good sleep? I wanted to talk to you about something. There wasn't time last night and anyway we were all too tired.'

He bolted up, sleepiness vanishing, his gaze suddenly apprehensive. 'You aren't gonna – going to – send me away?'

'No!' Kate was startled. 'Of course not, Maxie. You'll be staying with me. Is that what you want?'

'Course!' The relief on his face made her eyes prick. 'You're my aunty.' His brow knotted over a sudden thought. 'Is she my grandmother, that old woman you don't like?'

'Yes, but don't worry,' Kate said hastily, 'you don't have to see her. No, I wanted to talk to you about Harry. You know how very old he was, don't you? I think he loved you, Maxie. He told

Max he wanted me to look after you . . . because he trusted me. He said —'

'You said *was*. Did he – is he – dead?' the child asked. He'd paled a little and his air was solemn, somewhere between awe and sadness. 'Did he get sick?'

'No, sweetie; he was just very old and tired and he went to sleep for good. Max was there. He was talking about you and me to Max and then he nodded off, the way he did when he napped, and just didn't wake up again. It didn't hurt him at all – he just fell asleep. We're going to miss him dreadfully but as long as we remember him he won't be entirely gone.' She waited to see if he needed the comfort of a hug but he sat on, silently. After a moment she said, 'I thought you might want to get dressed and take Flip for a walk – only on his new lead, please – and just think about things. Or if you want to stay here with me, that's okay too.'

Maxie nodded and rose. She left the room to let him dress and presently heard him go out. Crossing to the front window, she watched boy and dog moving slowly away down the street.

Max came up behind her and snaked his arms around her waist. 'Did you tell him? How is he?'

'All right, I think. Shocked, of course, coming as it does on top of Connie's death, but he'll weather it with our help.'

'Do you want me to say something to him?'

'Not unless he asks for details. Children process stuff at their own pace.' Kate turned in to his embrace to kiss him. 'Just your being here will help. What do you fancy for breakfast?'

***

There was a big turnout for Harry's funeral. Most of the farming community made the trip into Laradale and followed the cortege from the Anglican church to the Garden of Rest cemetery on the northern side of town, where two columns of mallee divided the older section of burials from that begun since the end of the First World War. A good third of the mourners were related in some fashion to the deceased, Max estimated, exchanging greetings and handshakes as they made their way back to the cars after Harry's coffin had joined Edie's in the twin plot that already bore his name. Only the date needed to be added. Maxie, wearing his first long pants and proper lace-up shoes, walked soberly beside Kate. He'd shut himself in his room the day after Kate had broken the news, and when he emerged again he'd done a drawing of the old man, the pencilled lines and shadows capturing the narrow face with its high-bridged nose, bristling brows and luxuriant beard to perfection.

'For Harry. Instead of flowers,' he'd said, giving it to her.

Kate wondered where he'd learned that blossoms accompanied death. 'It's wonderfully lifelike,' she said. 'What if we get him some flowers anyway, and you keep this to remember him by? It's very good, Maxie – honestly. It's so like him I almost expect to hear it say, *Missy.*'

He'd nodded silently, then asked another question. 'Will my mum have a funeral?'

'Yes; probably quite soon now that the police know who killed her. We'll get flowers for her too.' Two days before she wouldn't have felt comfortable making such promises; she was out of a job and had rent to pay and Maxie to keep. But that was all doable now because of the letter that had arrived from Harry's solicitor.

* * *

'I can't believe it,' she told Max, sitting across from him at the table, with the typed sheet between them. 'He left me something. I only knew him for, what, three months? There's a cheque for my pay here, and an appointment to *finalise the details of the late Mr*

Quickly's bequest to you. Bless his old heart. He's probably left a sum to see his book published.'

'That's like him,' Max said. 'I told you he left me the farm, didn't I?'

'Yes, but I'm not surprised. He seemed to have outlived all the family members he cared about. What will you do with it?'

'Depends. The existing arrangement can stand until the Hollens' contract runs out, then we'll see. Do you fancy being a Mallee farmer's wife?'

For a moment her breath went. It was, from the very ordinariness of the tone in which it was asked, the last question she had expected. Her eyes searched his, then she nodded, heart fluttering, and placed her hand over his, her wrist nudging the sugar bowl aside. 'Why not? Though not right away, Max. I need to finalise my divorce first.'

'You couldn't be one right away – a farmer's wife, that is.' His grin was lopsided with relief. She saw with some amazement that he'd feared she'd refuse. 'The will's got to be probated.' He leaned towards her, his lips nibbling at her face, at her nose and chin and finally her lips. 'I love you, Katie Doolin.'

'I love you too, you know,' she said, and in a little while, 'You don't mind that there's Maxie?' Her mouth made a little moue of despair then. 'I'm married, with another woman's child. You're sure it's not too much baggage, Max?'

'I was married once myself,' he said. 'It seems like a lifetime ago now. I thought I'd never feel this way again, so bugger the baggage. In the long run it's only history.'

Kate was astonished. She pulled back to stare. 'Married? Since when? You didn't tell me – and I do remember asking.'

'I told you I didn't have a wife, and that was true. But I was married, if only briefly.'

'What happened?'

'She died of a brain aneurysm six months after the wedding. She was nineteen, a child. We both were, really. I was only twenty.'

'That's dreadful!' Kate was shocked. 'Poor girl – and you. What did you do?'

He shrugged, playing with her fingers, the rasp of his callused skin sending little electric tingles through her. 'What everybody does. I got through it. The pain becomes baggage you lump with you, then the baggage turns into history. We all have it, Kate. I loved Celia with all the passion a boy could muster but she's long gone, and now I love you. Our lives are our baggage; I wouldn't want to share my life with someone who had none. It would mean they hadn't lived at all. What about you?'

'You're right. The only sort you don't need is the like of Doug's.'

She thought of her brother, who'd regained consciousness and was now listed as serious but stable. He probably had a police guard at the door of the city hospital room he now occupied. Her mother had been detained by the police in Laradale, and Clover, now in her seventh month of pregnancy, had returned to be reunited with her eldest son and take charge of the farmhouse at Stones Place.

The media was all over the story of the Megan Wantage case, the blonde reporter in her element. She had interviewed Ron and Benny Hall for background on Doug – what he was like as a child; as a teenager; how his mates had regarded him. Ron had told her, a lifetime's reticence swept away by the knowledge that caution was no longer called for. He'd painted a picture of a cruel and conscienceless individual but had confessed that even with his knowledge of Doolin's capabilities, he'd still been shocked to learn he was a killer.

'An *alleged* killer,' the reporter had corrected before wrapping up. Even Doreen Pringle had scored a few minutes' air time. Ken

Wantage had made a short statement thanking the police for their perseverance. They would be holding a private funeral for Megan once her remains were released from police custody, he'd said, and no, he had no opinion on what Doolin's fate should be – that was up to the court to decide, and he was thankful to have it so. Forensic examination of her body had confirmed Doug's callous boast; as it would subsequently emerge at the trial, Megan had died of a broken neck, some twenty minutes before Heather and Martin turned up at Stones Place in search of her.

Megan's funeral would be many months, perhaps even years, in the future. It was unlikely to take place before the court case was heard, so a memorial service was to be held instead to help the family, and the community, draw a line under the tragic events begun almost twenty years before.

EPILOGUE

The service took place a week after Harry was laid to rest. It was another hot day edged with exhaust fumes and dust as the community gathered, in cars and four-wheel drives, at the local church. No invitations had been issued but a general announcement was made on the local radio station and printed in the weekly paper.

'Do you think there'll be a big turnout?' Max asked, knotting his tie in the house at Pierce Street. Kate was already dressed and similarly occupied with Maxie's. Max had driven in from his latest job to attend the service, and she feared they were running late.

'Half the town, at least. Hold still, Maxie,' she admonished. 'The Pringles have been spreading the word. Did you see the flowers coming through town? Doreen's behind that too, bless her.'

Laradale's P&C had placed a wreath spelling Megan's name on the school gates, Pringles' cafe carried another, there were balloons and a teddy bear in the window of the farmers' bank, and even Gleeson's Autos had a bouquet tied to a corner post on the forecourt. Satisfied, Kate rose from her task and glanced between her two companions. 'You look very smart, both of you. Got the key? Let's go, then.'

There was no parking left. They found a spot a street away and walked. Judging by the vehicles alone, every farming family in the district seemed to be there, and half the town as well. The church was packed, many of the latecomers standing in the vestibule and along the side walls. Martin Wantage, sitting beside his parents, had been keeping an eye out for them. Kate spotted his tall form beckoning them up front to the seats Heather had saved them; they slipped in beside her as the pastor rose to speak of the child Megan, whom he'd known, of a life cut short and the suffering and grief caused by her disappearance. Kate let her eyes wander, picking out faces in the crowd – the Pringles, Bert half-hidden behind Doreen's enormous hat, the wrinkled map of Jack Gleeson's face, the absorbed attention on Sarah Hall's . . .

The church was full of flowers, and Ken, unfamiliar in a grey suit as he made his way to the lectern, brought tears to Kate's eyes when he likened his daughter's short life to those of the wild poppies that bloomed amid the crops. The day before the service she'd asked Max to bring her a handful of ripened wheat, the ears full and whiskered, which earlier that morning she'd arranged in a fluted vase, mixing the wheat with crimson celosia and stalks of scarlet salvia from Heather's garden. It stood beside Ken as he spoke, like an offering, the glowing colours a reminder of the vibrant child they all mourned.

Kate dabbed at her cheeks and Heather squeezed her hand. 'Sorry,' she whispered. It was she who should be giving comfort. Heather had lost the most, after all. But it was a loss, she realised, that the community shared, for somebody was sniffing behind her and when the service concluded, the people who came to press the Wantages' hands were visibly burdened with a share of their grief.

Clover had attended the memorial but refused the invitation to refreshments at The Narrows afterwards. 'I couldn't,' she told Kate wretchedly. 'I can barely look them in the face when I think . . . Perhaps later, when I've had more time to come to terms with what Doug did. Can you explain for me, Kate? Tell her how sorry I am?'

'Yes, of course. How's Jeremy?'

Clover grimaced. 'He worshipped Doug. Right now he's blaming me but he'll come round, given time.'

Kate sighed. There were no easy solutions to human emotions. She said as much to Heather later that day as they stood in the garden of The Narrows watching the last of the invited guests leave. Her friend's face was sad but composed. 'It can't be easy for Clover. It was kind of her to attend the service – but people are kind. It's been nineteen years and more, and yet everybody still came today. It's good to know Megan's never been forgotten. I've lived with grief so long that you begin to think it's only you who cares, who remembers. But since she was found we've had hundreds of cards, some from people I don't even know. And the flowers!'

'Well, you're the queen of them,' Kate said. She had taken a car load up to the hospital and some to Harry's grave, but pots of them still filled the main rooms of The Narrows' farmhouse, their combined scents cloying in the warm air. It was good to be outside for a while, where the fresh smells of humus and damp earth reigned instead. She caught a glimpse of Maxie, still in his good clothes, hurtling past with Flip at his heels, and thought that she might as well resign herself to the dog becoming his. At least it took his mind off Harry. 'What are your plans now? Are you really moving?'

'Oh, yes.' Heather looked about at her plants as if preparing, there and then, to bid them farewell. 'Of course, it could be another year or two yet. Properties don't sell overnight. It'll give me time to strike cuttings from my best roses.' She smiled faintly. 'I'll not leave it all behind. What about you? Another job search?'

Kate shook her head. 'I intend to homeschool Maxie.' She laughed, a happy, bubbling sound giving vent to the joy in her heart. 'We're getting married, Heather – as soon as I'm divorced, that is. Max and I,' she added to make it perfectly plain.

This time Heather's smile stretched her face. 'I'm so pleased! Good for Max! So, will you keep on renting, or move into the van with him? Though with three of you in it . . . '

'Neither.' Kate sobered. 'Harry left me the Rosebud farmhouse. No strings, no explanations. I've never been so surprised – that he'd do it, or even that it was possible, excising a building out of a lease – but he probably thought it didn't matter because he left Max the farm.'

'He must've felt very sure about the way things were going between you,' Heather said, half entertained, half shocked. 'When did this happen? It must've been quite recent.'

'It was a new will, drawn up while he was in hospital. He didn't say a word to me about it, and it all happened the first morning he was in there. He got a nurse to ring Forsyth and Grainers and it was Alec Forsyth – he handled Dad's will too – who set it all up; the new will, and arrangements for repairing the house. I don't know if he had a presentiment of his death or – but it was like him to make up his mind then act on it immediately. Apparently Harry told him he wanted the work paid for even if he died before it was done, so he had him draw a cheque for it there and then. He still had the cheque book in his pocket when he got into the ambulance, because he was just about to pay my wages —' Kate's voice wobbled, and she paused to get it under control, 'when the fire hit us. Anyway,' she sniffed, 'the repairs are all finished now; we went out for a look this morning. Our first job, Maxie's and mine, will be to replant the trees that died. Then I'll start a garden.'

Heather hesitated a moment. 'And Stones Place?'

'That's for Clover to decide. I can't imagine she'll stay but if she does I expect Maxie should get to know his half-brothers.'

'Well.' Heather drew a long breath, like one finally laying down a burden, and gazed around at the garden filled with the familiar shapes and colours of her creation. 'It's like everything has changed for Ken and me, and yet nothing really has – except I've found a sort of peace. My worst fears have come true but somehow I feel a sense of quietude.' She hesitated, searching for words. 'It's like the struggle's finally over, and even though I lost, there's a release in knowing it. Does that sound mad?'

Kate shook her head sympathetically. 'Not in the least. Come on, let's go in and shake up the teapot. Martin's seeing to dinner, he said, and Max will give him a hand. He's quite useful in the kitchen, you know,' she added proudly.

As they turned to leave, a wind sighed through the mallees, its hot breath cooling as it went, and the sprinklers came on, their arcing sprays touched with the rays of the westering sun. The patter of the drops falling on the broad leaves of the elephant ears was like the run of childish feet, and Kate's head turned sharply. Then she froze in place because for a nanosecond she could have sworn she glimpsed a little girl's freckled face and flying ginger pigtails racing through the spray. *You can't catch me, Katie!* The gleeful, childish cry echoed, dreamlike, in her head. Then the shadows shifted and the image vanished.

An extraordinary feeling of contentment suffused her. It washed over her like a wave, carrying away the grief and lingering sense of loss that had followed her since childhood. Was this, she wondered, what Heather had meant when she spoke of everything having changed? Closure, perhaps? That overused word that simply described the process of turning baggage into history. She hoped so, for it would mean that Megan's ghost had finally been laid to rest.

Quickening her pace, Kate quitted the garden, following Heather in to where Max and a cuppa waited, and the company of friends.

Acknowledgements

My thanks to Don and Rae Kube
for friendship and the inspiration for
this work. And for the many splendid
people at Penguin and their skill and
dedication to their job – thank you
for making it happen.